AMBA

ANDREW HALLMAN

ROUGH
EDGES
PRESS

Amba
Paperback Edition
© Copyright 2022 Andrew Hallman

Rough Edges Press
An Imprint of Wolfpack Publishing
5130 S. Fort Apache Rd. 215-380
Las Vegas, NV 89148

roughedgespress.com

This book is a work of fiction. Any references to historical events, real people or real places are used fictitiously. Other names, characters, places and events are products of the author's imagination, and any resemblance to actual events, places or persons, living or dead, is entirely coincidental.

All rights reserved. No part of this book may be reproduced by any means without the prior written consent of the publisher, other than brief quotes for reviews.

Paperback ISBN 978-1-68549-109-3
LCCN 2022931205

*To James Rahn,
mentor and friend*

AMBA

ONE

November 30, 2000

The tiger's body sprawled like a landscape. Undulating black ridges and orange valleys stretched away from the dorsal ridge, the thick fur dotted with white flecks of snow. Near the hindquarters the orange and black squeezed and narrowed, fell away into the long tail. The white fur that grew from the underside there turned dark. Crimson. Matted.

The tail and hindquarters fronted a pool of blood. A dark lake, the waves congealed, evidence of a volcanic struggle that had long ceased. A jaw of steel held both of the tiger's rear legs in its impassive maw. A length of chain rose taut from the trap to its anchor at the base of a nearby tree. The teeth had flayed the fur and flesh and muscle from one leg, exposing the bone to the cold air. The other leg's tibia had clearly been snapped by the force of the impact when the trap clamped shut.

This was the first live tiger Yuri Kaskilev had ever seen in the wild. He crouched behind the bole of a tall Korean pine, five meters from where the tiger lay in a small clearing. His breath steamed in the air between him and the tiger, the snow beneath him crunched as he sank to his knees.

This was his fifth winter with the Anti-Poaching Brigade in the Sikhote-Alin mountains, in Primorsky Krai, the Russian Far East. He'd seen stills of tigers caught midstride in camera traps. And he'd seen carcasses, confiscated contraband stretched out lifeless on the ground, or in the backs of trucks. But out here, in the taiga, they were elusive creatures. Since taking the job he'd wanted nothing more than to see one. Not like this, though. Not like this.

The tip of the tail, black hairs caked to a paint-brush point, lifted free of the red snow, then collapsed. The central valleys and ridges expanded briefly, then sank. A rasped flutter escaped from the end furthest from the wreckage. A sigh of resignation.

"A hell of a thing." His partner's voice broke his focus.

Yuri glanced over his shoulder. He'd forgotten Evgeny was back there, kneeling in the snow, several paces behind. Evgeny had been the one to find the tiger. When Yuri caught up to him, he'd moved past him for a better look through the tree trunks.

Evgeny took off his glove, wiped his hand over his face, over his reddened nose, down over his thick black beard. As though the blood were on his fur. He'd been on the Brigade for nearly fifteen years, the senior man except for their boss, Vassily.

"You were right," Evgeny said, his voice uncharacteristically soft, little more than a whisper, but it carried in the frigid silence. "Should've known better than to doubt *Serzhant Ser'yeznyy*."

Sergeant Serious, that was the nickname the other men in the Brigade had given Yuri. Only Evgeny ever used it in his presence.

He wasn't actually a sergeant—not anymore. There were only a dozen men in the Anti-Poaching Brigade at any given time, no need for any rank other than seniority. And while he'd held that rank in the army, in *spetsnaz*—elite Russian special forces—he was pretty sure that the other men weren't aware of that when they hit on his nickname shortly after his arrival.

"Vassily's not going to like us proving him wrong," Evgeny said.

Yuri spat into the snow. *Fuck Vassily*, he thought. Did not need to say.

One of the tiger's triangular black ears stood free, the white dot in the center of that triangle poised, like an eye, watching. The ear twitched in their direction, the head began to roll on its shoulders but then the entire body tensed as this merest motion dug steel teeth deeper into flesh, scraped exposed bone. A groan escaped the tiger.

Yuri backed away slowly until he hunched next to his partner.

"What are we going to do?" he asked.

"*We*," Evgeny said, "aren't going to do anything. *You're* going back to the vehicle to get the shotgun, so we can put her down. I'm not going anywhere with these goddamn traps lying around."

They had left the Land Cruiser back in the village, maybe half an hour, forty-five minutes away. A villager had heard the yowling, called the Sikhote-Alin Biosphere Reserve, who'd called the Brigade. Once in the woods, they'd split up; Evgeny had been the one to hear the cries of pain, track them to their source. He'd brought Yuri running with the walkie-talkie, the only piece of military-grade gear that they carried. They did not typically carry guns—poachers were about as elusive in the wild as tigers. They each carried a couple of flares, in case they were to cross paths with a tiger, the idea being that the bright, hissing flame would be enough to scare it away. Yuri had never needed to put this theory to the proof.

"I'll get the gun," he said. "I don't know if I can pull the trigger."

"I'll be surprised if it's even necessary," Evgeny said. "She doesn't have long."

"She?"

Evgeny glanced off into the trees. Heaved a sigh that puffed a cloud of vapor into the air.

"Her name is Tatiana." At Yuri's puzzled frown he

explained. "She's got an old radio collar with her name inked on it."

Yuri glanced back toward the clearing. He hadn't noticed the collar.

"Besides, she's not big enough to be a male."

She seemed pretty big to Yuri. He retraced his steps back toward the clearing.

"Where are you going?" Evgeny whispered.

Yuri turned and held up his finger. He wanted one last look. He didn't want her to suffer any more than necessary, but he wanted to remember this moment. Wanted to remember her. Tatiana. He hadn't seen her collar. Hadn't even seen her face. He moved off to his right, from tree trunk to tree trunk. These were tall Korean pines, wooden columns that rose straight from the earth, suspending green crowns many meters above the forest floor. A few short, needle-less branches stuck out, grasped at Yuri's parka, at his gloves, as he moved from one to the next, working his way around to the tiger's head. He spotted the collar Evgeny had mentioned, a break in the valleys and ridges where the fur surged over the loop of nylon. Her left ear swiveled toward him as he moved.

Breath snorted from her nostrils, a ghost of steam escaped into the frigid air. One eye opened in his direction, the other held closed by the snow. Yuri held his position. The eye seemed glazed, milky, unfocused. Every move he made elicited a subtle response from her, and every move she made intensified the pain that she had been living with for who knew how long. Possibly days. Now he could see down the length of her body, past the white fur of her belly also marred with spatter of her own blood, down to where the merciless trap had pinioned her hindquarters.

Her distended midsection reminded him of the bellies of malnourished children that he had seen in refugee camps, children displaced by war, in Afghanistan, in Chechnya. Children that were starving, their bellies appearing to be glutted with food, their sallow cheeks and hollowed eyes belying the appearance.

He ran back to Evgeny. A howl of pain followed him, likely caused by his sudden movement, the fact that he was no longer taking care to move quietly.

He fell to his knees at Evgeny's side. "She's pregnant."

"No shit."

"Why didn't you say?"

"It makes no difference," Evgeny said.

Yuri turned back toward Tatiana. Because tigers are solitary creatures, even pregnant females need to hunt right until the very end of term. They only begin to show in the final two weeks. Her swollen belly had worked its way down into the thick snow cover, so her pregnant state was not apparent from this dorsal angle.

"If she dies, do the cubs die right away?"

"Of course," Evgeny said. "Their oxygen comes from her blood, so once that stops pumping, they will die."

"But how long will that take?"

"Go get the gun," Evgeny said. "Stop dragging out her torture."

"How long?"

"Do I look like a biologist?"

"I'm guessing a minute," Yuri said. "Maybe two."

Evgeny grunted.

Yuri moved back toward Tatiana, head down, doubled over at the waist, knees bent, as though snipers had zeroed in on their position. He removed his gloves, dropped them into the snow. He fished in his side pouch, pushed past the two flares there, wrapped his fingers around the burled wooden handle of his Yakut knife. Removed the short, stout blade from its leather sheath. He clenched the blade in his teeth and shrugged out of his parka. The thin bubble of warmth around his flannel work shirt soon collapsed under the shock of cold. His breath steamed past the knife. At the edge of the clearing, two meters from the pulped wreckage of her hindquarters, he stopped, and wrapped the parka's bulk around his left forearm, tucked one sleeve under the thick fabric at his bicep, held the other sleeve firm in his left fist, secured a knot. He retrieved the knife from his mouth. The wooden handle quickly warmed in his grip.

The tiger's head rolled up, and the chain anchoring the trap pulled taut. Her head fell back heavy into the snow with a huff.

"Easy, *mamulya*," he whispered. "We want your cubs to have a chance, don't we?"

He held the knife in the familiar saber grip, his thumb extended along the flat, sturdy spine. The edge was keen, the blade stout. It had been his father's knife, two decades ago. Here was a chance, after all these years, to use it to rescue rather than to destroy. A chance to bring life into this world, instead of cutting yet another life short.

A chance to be the "good guy." That was why he had left the army and joined the Anti-Poaching Brigade in the first place.

A large, meaty hand gripped his shoulder.

"What the hell—" Evgeny began, his voice a hoarse whisper. He leaned down over Yuri. Spittle flecked his bushy black beard. He remained at the perimeter of the clearing—half in, half out—as though Tatiana might break free of the trap and leap to the attack. A healthy respect born out of his decade and a half on the job, in the unforgiving taiga. "What the hell do you think you're doing?"

"What has to be done," Yuri said.

He looked at his partner and smiled. Evgeny frowned, and in that moment of hesitation, Yuri broke free from his partner's grip, and ran into the clearing, toward Tatiana.

TWO

Thought banished, his body guided him. Thumb along the spine, he followed his knife's edge.

With each crunching step through the snow, time slowed to the measure of the tiger's shallow breaths. The entire forest, deathly silent, breathed in tune with her. She stirred, turned toward him, slowly, almost languorously. She uttered a yowl as the steel teeth dug further into her hindquarters. He was one with the pines, with the frigid air, with the snow. One with his knife, the blade an extension of his fist. The spirit of the forest entered him, possessed him, flowed through him.

He lunged. Threw his left leg over her left foreshoulder to keep her from turning on him, to keep her from reaching him with her claws. His *spetsnaz* training emphasized the legs as the soldier's base of strength, speed, and stamina. Tatiana's initial yowl of pain became a battle roar that nearly deafened him as he wrapped his left arm around her head to pull her chin up. Despite her weakened state, despite having her rear legs pinned in place, she wrenched around beneath him—she was fast and strong, but he hung on, pulled her on top of him, desperate to keep her spine pressed against his belly. He was aware of her forepaw swatting at his head; he tucked his own chin to his chest to minimize the blows. He tried to get his right leg up to block her arm, but her body weight and the snow kept it pinned under her. The hand that held the knife, the entire arm, also dug into the snow beneath her.

She wrenched her head free of his lock and closed her jaws around his arm, the arm he'd wrapped in his parka. Her teeth clamped down. The thick winter parka suddenly nothing more than a thin covering of tissue paper. *You will know my pain*, she seemed to say, *you will know what it is to have your limb caught in an unrelenting steel trap.* He pulled his arm, used her grip to pull her entire body on top of him. Her teeth broke skin, bore down further.

Then his right leg was free. He swung his knee over her upper shoulder, clamped her right forearm to her body with his thigh. Her writhing weight pressed him down into the snow, the overripe tang of her blood and scat and pinebark fur flooded his nostrils. He wrenched one more time until she faced back toward the place where he and Evgeny had been watching her, and his right arm came free. He raised his left arm as best he could, lifting her chin, extending her neck. He plunged the knife in the white fur, until he felt it soft and warm against his knuckles. He sought for her jugular. Prayed for her jugular.

A yell beyond his control erupted from his throat, filled his ears, shook his body.

Then the pressure on his arm relented. Slackened. Gave way altogether.

Release. He pulled the knife free, then prized his arm from her jaws, disentangled the parka from her fangs. Distantly aware of pain, but more like a bad bone bruise. Had she been stronger, she would have snapped the radius and ulna like twigs. Even in her severely weakened state, it had been close. He found he could move his fingers.

He closed his eyes. Inhaled the earthy, resinous scent of her fur, her last breath, her last scat, her musk, her pain and rage and desperation.

Now for the hard part. He placed his right fist, still wrapped around the knife, the blade and his thumb and forefinger stained red with her blood, against the black and orange fur of her shoulders and pulled his left leg from beneath her. He stepped over her lifeless body, fell to his knees in the snow near the pure white fur of her distended belly. He reached his left hand to the warm fur, felt for hard outlines beneath the layer of winter fat. The bulky parka still clung to his forearm, a sleeve or a shred of fabric dangled into the snow, but there was no time to unravel it. With his right he placed the red blade against the white. His hand trembled.

He inhaled deeply and began to cut. Sharp as his knife was, he still had to hack through the tough skin, the layer of fat. He worked his way toward the bulge deep in the belly, down by the wreckage of her rear limbs.

The blood that poured from the flesh in this area made it impossible to know what he was cutting into. He tried to clear it with his left—now an ache as he moved his arm and applied pressure with his left hand—but the blood kept coming. Great gouts of blood.

"Evgeny!"

"What?"

The voice at his ear startled him. He hadn't been aware of the other man's approach.

"Water." He indicated with the knife. "Go easy. Just so I can see what I'm doing."

Evgeny washed away some of the red, which allowed Yuri to make another deep incision, peel away more flesh and intestine and organs. Yuri had skinned, field dressed, and butchered many deer in his life. Chickens and goats back on the family farm, when he was a boy. He knew these animals' parts, where they belonged in the body. He didn't know tiger parts. Especially not those of pregnant tigers. His cursory anatomy studies hadn't prepared him for this.

Steam rose from the snow. Yuri cut by feel now. He exposed a bulging red-gray sack. He pushed in with his left hand, soaked in red, steeped in red. Pushed hard. Something pushed back. Movement. The womb.

He gathered up the membranous tissue in his left hand.

Pain lanced from his wrist into his shoulder and back to his fingertips, but still he kept that grip, fighting against the greasy slipperiness, fighting against the nausea. As he cut, the weight of the insides pulled the tissue open ahead of the cut he was making, and the hole opened wide.

A bloody sack slopped out into the matted snow between Yuri's knees, trailing a length of mottled cord. Yuri put the knife in his teeth—sudden rank, vomitous taste of viscera—and tore open the amniotic sac with his two blood-soaked hands. Within was a drowned cub the size of a full-grown housecat, only with a much larger head. He picked up the bedraggled bundle of stripes and fur and transferred it to the crook of his left arm, wiped the caul away from its mouth and nose and still-closed eyes. It quivered at the touch, weakly waved a paw. It was alive. Yuri took up the umbilical cord in his left, swiped his right palm dry on his pant leg as best he could and with the knife severed the cub's last connection to its mother. His mother, Yuri could see that now.

"Evgeny!" Yuri lifted the cub toward the other man. "Cradle him, dammit!"

"My parka—"

Yuri forced the cub into Evgeny's hands.

He returned to the womb, forced his left hand into the gaping hole, deep into the slippery warmth. This pungency was nothing he had ever smelled before, the tiger's death scat and her urine and the stench of digested matter making its way through her intestines, torn open by Yuri's knife, decomposing matter in her stomach that Yuri had inadvertently opened up as he hacked though the belly fur and fat reserves.

His hand found what it sought. Another sac. Just one—one more to go. He cupped his hand around it and pulled. It wouldn't budge. He shifted the knife to his teeth—again that queasy tang—and with both hands buried in the tiger's belly up to his forearms, straining against the parka still balled around his left, he managed to pry the second sac free. This one he did not let spill, quickly transferred the bundle into the parka-cushioned cradle, stripped away the amniotic sac, which released a sudden dampness into his ribs, down onto his left leg. He ran his knife through the umbilical and then stabbed the blade into the snow so he could swipe the slimy caul away from this cub's scrunched face as well.

The rounded ears popped erect. This one turned its nose into Yuri's shirt and began nuzzling, looking for mother's milk, for comfort. He rose to his feet.

The tiger splayed at his feet was a ruin of her former, noble self: legs shredded, guts spilled, blood seeping into the snow from her gaping wounds, dark smears marring the white belly fur, blurring her stripes. The blood bright red and shiny slick in some places, black and encrusted in others.

He bent to retrieve his knife from the snow. He brought his head close to hers. "Forgive me, Tatiana," he said.

He stood and turned to Evgeny. The other man cradled the squirming cub in both arms, against his belly. His black eyes flashed.

"What the fuck, Yuri," he shouted. He raised his hand as though to strike Yuri, but then had to return it to contain the wriggling bundle of striped fur in his arms. "You should have — you could have—" He spluttered, trailed off.

"Should have what?"

"I could have helped you. We could have come up with a plan—"

"There was no time," Yuri said. "Besides, you would've talked me out of it."

"She could've killed you!" Evgeny said.

"No sense in both of us risking our lives."

"I'm your partner," Evgeny said. "You need to trust me."

"Next time," Yuri said.

He exited the clearing, left the bloody wreck of the tiger named Tatiana behind. He turned when he heard only his own boots crunching through the snow. Evgeny stood immobile, looking down at the tiger. His breath escaped his body in great clouds that drifted upward toward the boughs above.

"Our day isn't done yet," Yuri called to him.

Evgeny shivered, lifted his head, began to move.

THREE

He led the way back through the forest, following Evgeny's trail through the snow. Moving as fast as possible while aware that he could trip over a hidden root or rock and spill his precious cargo. As the adrenaline wore off, as the sweat evaporated, he began to shiver without his parka, still wound around his aching forearm.

They reached the access road, deep ruts in the snow carved by winter tires, and now they could jog.

Soon Evgeny was panting. "Not so fast," he called out.

Yuri slowed his pace to check on the other man, encourage him, and make sure he wasn't crushing his cub. As the two entered the village square at a trot, the elderly residents emerged from the café and a few younger ones from the bar. They gathered around as they reached the Land Cruiser, clamoring, wanting to see.

Evgeny began to show off his cub—proud, now, of the blood. Basking in the attention and accolades, even beginning to tell of how Yuri had extracted the cubs from a tiger that he had been forced to kill with his bare hands. Meanwhile, with his free hand Yuri unlocked the rear hatch and grabbed the spare blankets. He threw these into the back seat, made a little nest, and placed his cub down gently. He took the second cub from Evgeny.

"Drive," he said.

Evgeny lifted his slick muddy hands. Yuri tossed him one of the blankets. "We have to get them to Samuel. To the scientists."

Yuri got in the back seat with the cubs. They couldn't raise their heads. Their paws pushed feebly at the blankets, eyelids still sealed shut.

He wanted nothing more than a long, cool draft of water. With ice in it. With a slice of lemon. Or a sprig of mint, like they served it in Afghanistan. Or nothing at all, just something to wash the fetid taste of tiger guts from his tongue.

He sank back into the seat as Evgeny reversed, slowly, pushing his way through a crowd of twelve, fifteen, maybe even twenty, that had gathered around the vehicle, pressing close to get a glimpse of the cubs, their smiles of delight changing to something else when their eyes landed on Yuri. He supposed he must be quite a sight, covered in blood and gore. His right cheek burned. He touched his fingers to it, found strange shreds hanging in place of the skin that he had shaved smooth that morning. His fingertips came away daubed in fresh red. His own blood.

"Water," he croaked.

Evgeny shook his head. He beeped his horn and nudged the vehicle forward, despite the press of people, who scurried back, then pressed forward again. Finally he was clear of them and able to run through the gears. They bounced and slid over the narrow snow-covered road.

"Coffee from this morning," he said. "That's all we have left."

Yuri patted the man's shoulder, hand outstretched. Evgeny handed him the cup.

He sloshed that in his mouth while he lowered the window. The coffee was partly frozen and sickly sweet, heavily sugared and loaded with cream that had begun to clot while they had been away. Still it was better than what he had been tasting. He spat the liquid out the window. Brilliant waves of color washed across his vision, then vanished.

His arm ached. His cheek and jaw burned. The right

breast of his work shirt was bright red with blood—his own blood. As he examined it, another drop fell. Then another.

Evgeny glanced at Yuri in the rear-view mirror, then stared, jaw slack. Returned his eyes to the road, his knuckles tight on the wheel.

He figured it was probably best to leave the balled-up parka, still wrapped around his forearm, to stanch the blood. The knot holding the coat in place had loosened. Trying to tighten it made him dizzy.

"Well, well," Evgeny said. "What do we have here?"

Ahead, on the side of the road, a pickup truck had pulled over into the deeper snow. Three men dressed in heavy fur-lined winter gear stood close to the truck, two at the rear, one near the driver's door. As Evgeny approached and slowed, they begrudgingly moved to the side to allow him to pass. Something about the men's movements, their bearings, their expensive-looking parkas and boots, told Yuri and Evgeny that they were not locals.

As they drew near, the three men turned toward them. Their faces hardened as their eyes settled on the Anti-Poaching Brigade shield painted on the Land Cruiser's doors, the black-and-white tiger face in a circle of green with white Cyrillic lettering. One man at the rear called out something to the third, who had moved off the road in front of the cab, and this man pushed his way through the snow until he reached the other two. All three leaned casually over the flatbed, their hands out of sight.

"Bet I know where you bastards are going," Evgeny said. He removed his foot from the gas and reached forward under the dash, brought up the shotgun.

"Keep driving," Yuri said.

"Not often we get to see such assholes in their natural habitat," Evgeny said.

"No evidence."

"Tatiana might disagree with you, partner."

"And her cubs are back here with me, don't forget."

Evgeny kept his left on the steering wheel, while he laid

the muzzle of the shotgun on the passenger door armrest. He clicked the safety off with his thumb.

With his left hand Yuri reached a loose corner of the blankets to cover up the cubs. He picked up his knife in his right, rested his fingertips on the door handle, braced his left foot against the hump in the floor that made room for the drive shaft.

As they came level, Evgeny lifted the first two fingers of his left hand from the steering wheel in a greeting. He smiled broadly, nodded vigorously. He murmured in a sing-song, "Big surprise waiting for you fuckers out there."

The three men returned his nod, but slowly, unsmiling. The two at the rear—one tall and broad, the other small and hunched—looked toward the one who had been at the front of the truck. At a word from him these two stared at Evgeny, watching for any sign of hitting the brakes or sudden movement. This third man, however, stared at Yuri. And Yuri, recognizing that he was the leader, kept his eyes on him. The tires ground slowly over the packed snow, a steady crunch.

Yuri recognized this man. The shock of red hair, the bristly red goatee. The dark, close-set eyes. He knew him from Chechnya. From Iliakov's Wolfpack. What the hell was he doing here, of all places?

The man's mouth opened slightly as Yuri came level with him. Did he also recognize Yuri? Or was it surprise at the unexpected sight of his mangled face, bright red with gore?

What was his nickname? The Weasel? No, that wasn't right. Something like that, though.

The dark eyes shifted away from Yuri's, peered past him, deeper into the vehicle. Focused for a moment on the seat beside him. And then they were past. Yuri turned away from the men, back to the cubs. They had wriggled free of the blanket.

Evgeny craned his neck to keep an eye on the men as they receded in the rear-view mirror. "Must be your lucky day," he whispered. Then, louder, "Everybody's lucky day today, eh, Yuri?"

He grunted. The Land Cruiser slalomed through the

snow as Evgeny returned his heavy foot to the gas pedal. The cubs squirmed and whimpered. Yuri leaned over them, pushed them together for warmth. For companionship.

Maybe not so lucky. The man had been in his *spetsnaz* unit. Like Yuri, a highly trained *saboteur*. A killer. He'd been one of the new recruits when they redeployed from Afghanistan to Chechnya in '91. They styled themselves as "Iliakov's Wolfpack," taking the name of their C.O., Major Ivan Iliakov. As *starshina*—Senior Sergeant—Yuri had kept himself apart from the new generation as he trained them. They seemed savage to him. They reveled in the chaos, exulted in the bloodshed. They thought killing made them men. Maybe he, too, had been like that in his early years, when he was a raw recruit in the terraced hills of Afghanistan, but he didn't think so. Iliakov had trained him to be a professional at all times.

He considered telling Evgeny, but the thought of moving his jaw, flexing his cheek, to speak and answer the inevitable questions made him hold his tongue.

Evgeny radioed dispatch, told the operator to alert the scientists at the Biosphere Reserve that they were coming, what it was they were bringing. He had to repeat himself three times.

They didn't say anything for a while. They had a two-hour drive ahead of them, to the scientists' compound.

He remembered coming in from a mission in Chechnya. Not just any mission. The mission that had turned him against the war. Against the army. Against Iliakov. The mission that had caused him to quit. And that man—Oleg, that was his name, Oleg Chernichev—had been standing at the side of the trail then, too, on guard duty. "Welcome home, *starshina*," he'd said. No matter what he said, it always came out with a sarcastic tone, spoken out of the side of his mouth. Yuri didn't have any words for him, back then. Didn't have any words for anyone, for a long time.

With a start, he remembered. He wiped his right hand against his pant leg, trying to clean it, though the blood was now dry and encrusted. He reached into the parka bundled around his left forearm, trying not to yank it free from the puncture wounds hidden underneath. He gasped with pain as he fumbled through the heavy folds until he found the interior pocket he searched for. From this pocket he tugged free a small square of paper, folded once, slightly yellowed. A fresh hole the size of a bullet had been punched into the center by one of Tatiana's fangs, sharply crinkling the thick photographic paper.

He unfolded the photograph carefully. Over the years the paper had grown fuzzy at the edges, the crease down the middle had nearly worn through. The smiling face of Kamal, his former comrade, with his arm around Vida, his dour wife, stared back at him. The hole, duplicated, ran through each person's belly, sparing their faces. He felt something like relief, tinged with regret.

The tigers kept mewling, nuzzling into the nearby blankets, but finding no solace. Yuri wiped and then licked his pinky finger clean as best he could and let one suckle on it. This seemed to occupy the little one for a while, even though of course he could get no sustenance from it. At least it busied him, allowing him to follow his instincts. He didn't have teeth yet, but his gums pressed down hard. His tongue gripped and scraped. Yuri didn't know how the mother tiger would be able to stand it. It made him intensely happy, to watch the little cub. Fighting, from birth, from its first second of life. Fighting for more life. It distracted him from his own pain, and from his thoughts of poor Tatiana. There had been no other choice, he told himself. Right? Should they have summoned the scientists, the veterinarians? Could they have saved her? He didn't think so, not with her legs mangled in that way. Not as far gone as she was. He didn't know. He just didn't know.

"What do we have back there?" Evgeny asked over his shoulder. He guided them surely through the monotonous tunnel of trees and snow.

"A boy and a girl," he said. "Kamal. And Vida."

"Too foreign," Evgeny said. He repeated the names as

though the words curdled on his tongue. "What's wrong with good old-fashioned Russian names?"

Kamal had been in his unit, too, but in Afghanistan. From Yuri's earliest days. A Chechen and a Muslim, he'd taught Yuri enough of Islam and Arabic to pass for a foreign *jihadi*. A skill that had saved his life behind enemy lines in both Afghanistan and Chechnya. Vida was Kamal's Afghani bride.

When the unit redeployed to Chechnya, Kamal was gone. He'd gone home, to fight for the rebels. A deserter, Major Iliakov had called him. A traitor. Yuri had still thought of him as a friend. Even though they weren't supposed to have friends. *No trust. No fear. No surrender.* All the Wolfpack had the unit's motto tattooed on their left shoulder, with the leering wolf's head on the right.

Yuri didn't have any tattoos, other than his scars. He'd just picked up a few new ones, he supposed. He held these words sacred all the same. Iliakov had drilled them into him while the so-called Wolfpack were still in grammar school. Those words might as well be tattooed on his heart.

He shifted his finger to the other cub, and she sucked at it just as strongly, just as painfully, just as futilely. He felt a smile growing but instantly suppressed it as he could feel his stretching lips beginning to tear at the crust of blood that had formed on his cheek, his chin.

Kamal would have done the same, had he been faced with Tatiana. He was sure of it.

"Another hour," he cooed into their tufted ears. They wrinkled their faces in the wind from his breath. "Almost there."

"You realize," Evgeny broke the silence that had settled over the vehicle, apart from the drone of the engine, the steady crunch of tires in the snow. "You might be in line for a medal."

Yuri grunted.

"I'm serious. If word of this gets to the right people..." Evgeny's voice trailed off.

He turned back to the cubs. He had his share of medals.

FOUR

The senior scientist at the Sikhote-Alin Biosphere Reserve was an Australian named Samuel Carrington. He and another man met the Land Cruiser in the parking lot, waved them in as close to the entrance as possible, opened the vehicle's rear doors. The frigid blast quickly penetrated the cabin.

Samuel's thick gray beard sprouted from the wrinkles surrounding his watery gray eyes and flowed down over his chest. He smiled at Yuri as he reached for one of the cubs—the slightly smaller one, the female, Vida. Yuri gathered Kamal into his arms, grimacing with pain at having to move his left. The other man stood at his open door, held his hands outstretched to receive the cub. As Yuri turned toward him he said "Holy Christ" and staggered back a step. Yuri slid down from the seat.

The man composed himself, stepped toward Yuri, reached for the cub. "I'll take that."

Yuri shook his head, brushed past the man to meet Samuel at the building entrance.

Evgeny tossed his keys to the man. They bounced off his still-outstretched hands into the snow. "You can park the jeep."

Evgeny opened the door for them. "Quite the day you've had," Samuel said, as they quick-stepped down the hall.

They reached the lab, brightly lit with fluorescents. White cotton blankets covered a lab bench, a black concrete slab. Two men in denim overalls squatted on top of a second lab bench, a box constructed of plexiglass panels between them. They wrestled with a metal armature that held a red lamp centered over the box. A third man in a white lab coat set down a metal tray laden with syringes and white boxes with tiny black lettering near the cotton blankets.

Samuel stopped at the threshold, turned toward Yuri. "You're hurt," he said.

Yuri shrugged. The burning tension in his cheek warned him not to speak.

The man from the parking lot came clomping down the hallway. He was pudgy, with rounded shoulders, dark hair slicked back over his head, dark eyes, a closely trimmed beard that only accented his jowls. When he caught up to them, Samuel introduced him as Anatoly, the felid veterinarian. Samuel passed Vida into Anatoly's arms, then reached toward Yuri, for Kamal. Anatoly shambled toward the lab bench, and the heads of the two workmen and the third scientist turned to follow him, watched while he placed the tiger cub down among the blankets.

"Let us take it from here," Samuel urged. "Go clean yourself up."

Yuri stepped forward, but the older man swung into his path, placed his palms on his shoulders, brought him to a halt with surprising strength.

"We can't have your germs contaminating the lab," the scientist said. "Go get yourself a drink."

"Come on, partner." Yuri felt Evgeny's hand on his shoulder. "Don't know about you, but I'm parched."

Yuri peered past Samuel. The clean whiteness of the lab soothed him. He had learned the basics of tiger anatomy, biology, and behavior from the Australian when he first arrived in the Sikhote-Alin. He'd watched him work enough times in the past five years to know that this was not just a job to him. It was his vocation. His calling. He relinquished Kamal into Samuel's large leathery hands.

He winked at Yuri. "Thank you," he said. Then, to Evgeny, "We'll be down to look at him as soon as we can."

Yuri turned away from the cubs, toward his friend. Evgeny pointed. "Mess hall, this way," he said. At the far end of the dark corridor the two windows set into the double doors glowed with pale light from the waning day. The glimmer seemed to recede even as he took steps toward it.

"Hey," he heard Evgeny say, then felt the man's arm wrap around his back, holding him up. Evgeny stooped, and pulled Yuri's good arm over his shoulders.

"My legs are fine," Yuri said. "I don't need—"

"Shut up," Evgeny said. "Unless you want me to carry you there."

They shuffled down the hallway, pushed through the double doors, into a courtyard surrounded by several other concrete buildings.

They were in the scientists' Polygon, so named for the multi-sided shape the several buildings formed when drawn on a map. The various structures, built by the Soviet government in the '60s and '70s, included the laboratory facility they had just left, holding pens, an education center for school groups and visitors, a mess hall that doubled as a recreation room, a warehouse, a garage joined to a repair workshop, an administrative building, and the scientists' offices.

Concrete pathways, sheltered by rounded plexiglass roofs to keep the paths free of snow in the winter, lined the perimeter of the courtyard, connecting all the buildings. The snow that filled the courtyard glowed a dim purple, a pale reflection of the still-bright evening sky above. A family of snow people, with coal for eyes and smiling mouths, turnips for noses, and pine branches for hands, saluted them as they walked through the chill air to the mess hall. The largest, presumably the father, wore a jaunty red scarf that fluttered in a gust of wind that Yuri scarcely noticed, even though he still wore his parka in a knotted ball around his forearm.

When they pushed through the door into the mess hall, the chatter of voices and clacking of metal utensils on plastic plates suddenly ceased. The clip-clop of a table tennis match at the rear of the hall continued for another couple of hits, then fell silent. Only a call from within the kitchen for more bread, and then the slam of the door behind them broke the silence. A dozen, maybe fifteen bearded heads turned to face them, some with their knit caps still on, despite the steamy warmth of the hall.

The chatter began again, more urgent now, the cadences rising. The nearest men stood to their feet, came toward Yuri, but Evgeny put his right arm out and pushed them back, bulled through the men toward the ping-pong table, calling out "Make way, make way!" He led Yuri behind the table, to the low-slung, well-worn leather couch along the rear wall. He crouched, eased Yuri off his shoulders and down onto the cushions, pulled his feet up. He reached for Yuri's left arm, wrapped in the parka, but Yuri batted his hand away with his right. Inhaled sharply as he pulled his own arm up onto the couch next to him, laid it gingerly across his belly. He knew he needed to remove the parka at some point. He could feel the fabric stuck to his skin, anchored to his hairs. He didn't have the strength to face that yet.

Exhaustion surged through him. Exhaustion, and relief. He'd done what he had set out to do. The cubs were in Samuel's and Anatoly's expert hands.

Evgeny stood and turned to face the gathered, murmuring crowd. Some of the men wore the white coats and thick glasses of biologists and ecologists, but others were burly machinists, foresters, hearty lumberjacks in the off-season, and still Evgeny towered over all of them. He raised his blood-stained hands.

"Nothing to see here, folks," he said. "It's been a long day—"

"He's the one that rescued the cubs?" one of the men asked. Apparently word had spread. Another voice added, "The one that killed their mother to get them?"

Yuri looked for the man who had said this, to address him. But he couldn't pick him out in the swirling sea of dark beards and colorful caps. Even if he could have, he was not sure what he would have said. How could he explain what he had done?

And, in the end, what had he done? Had he rescued these cubs, only to doom them to a life in captivity? A mere shadow of the life that ought to have been theirs, in the wild?

"Bring us a drink," Evgeny boomed. "For all that is holy! Would you look at this man?" He swept his arm down toward Yuri. "It's not every day you get to toast a hero!"

Instantly a bottle of vodka and two glasses appeared on the ping-pong table. Evgeny filled them, stooped to hand one to Yuri.

He reached for it with his right, his good arm. His hand was trembling. His fingers were stiff—not from soreness or tiredness, but from the blood caked in the joints that made it hard to flex his knuckles. He waved the glass away and shook his head.

"Water," he said.

"To the Amba Patrol." Evgeny lifted his glass.

Sometimes—on good days—Evgeny called the Anti-Poaching Brigade the Amba Patrol. *Amba*, the Udege word for tiger. The native Udege people had co-existed with tigers for millennia, and were now almost as close to extinction as the great beasts they revered. *Amba*, literally translated, meant "spirit of the forest." After a successful interdiction or apprehension, when they were feeling fine about their job and about the world, they would raise glasses with their comrades in the pub, "to the Amba Patrol!" On the good days. Such days were few and far between.

Evgeny knocked his drink back, then lifted the one he had poured for Yuri.

"And to heroes." He winced as he swallowed.

He called for water as he turned to the table to pour two more.

A bottle of water was handed down toward Yuri. He forced his right hand to wrap around it, crinkling the plastic, and lifted his head from the armrest so he could spill the cool liquid into his mouth, and down his chin, and along his neck. He drank in long greedy gulps until the bottle was empty.

"Something for the pain?" Evgeny asked. Maybe for the second time. Yuri opened his eyes to see the man leaning over him.

"No." He closed his eyes again.

When he next opened them, Samuel's gray eyes stared down into his, concern evident. He winked. "Your turn," he said.

"The cubs?" Yuri asked.

Samuel smiled.

"Doing just fine. Thanks to you."

Anatoly, the veterinarian, stood next to Samuel. He peered down at Yuri, scrutinizing his face. Yuri moved his right hand toward his cheek, but Samuel stopped it with his hand before he could touch anything. His left arm tingled as though he had slept on it. Somehow, even though he'd only closed his eyes for a moment, there were no longer any men in the mess hall. Only Samuel, Anatoly, and Evgeny remained. The ping-pong paddles and the bottle of vodka had been replaced with a small heap of gauze, bandages, sutures, syringes, pill bottles, white boxes with large red and fine black lettering. The net had been removed. The green table covered in white cotton blankets.

The veterinarian stepped forward. He, Samuel, and Evgeny lifted Yuri to the table. Anatoly offered him medicine for the pain, but Yuri shook his head.

"This will hurt," Anatoly said.

"You'll move and make things difficult," Samuel said.

"No."

There was a part of him that welcomed the pain. In exchange for what he had done to Tatiana. A penance of sorts.

With his right hand, his good hand, he grabbed at Samuel's wrist before he could move away.

"What will happen to them?"

"They will live happily ever after, of course," Samuel said. He looked down at his blood-encrusted hand on his sleeve. Yuri did not relent.

"No, I mean—what will become of them?"

"They're in a very delicate state," the scientist said. "We'll take it one day at a time—"

"I shouldn't have killed their mother," Yuri said. "I should've brought her here."

"Impossible."

"Brought you to her then."

"She would've died long before I could reach her side," Samuel said.

"I should've let her die, then," Yuri said. "The law of the taiga. It was stupid of me—"

"They're alive right now," Samuel said. "That's all that matters."

"But where will they wind up?" Yuri asked. "In a zoo? In a cage?"

"There is hope," Samuel said. He winked at Yuri. With his other hand he pulled Yuri's fingers back from his wrist. "I have hope."

"Hope for what?"

"For something much better than a zoo. Quite the opposite, in fact. I don't want to give anything away too soon," he said. "But I've placed some phone calls. With a little good fortune..."

"Dr. Carrington," Anatoly said.

Samuel nodded, raised his index finger and placed it across his closed lips. He stepped aside.

Anatoly set to his task. He worked quickly, with a steady hand. First he flushed and sterilized Yuri's cheek. Smoldering acid seared his jawbone. Then he injected several shots of benzocaine.

Yuri forced himself not to flinch, and only to close his eyes when instructed by the vet. He watched as the hooked needle stitching the sutures through his flesh lifted and lowered, lifted and lowered. Twice Anatoly cursed softly and shook his head. After the second he looked into Yuri's eyes and said, "you're going to need to go to Vladivostok. To see a plastic surgeon. You've lost too much skin here. You'll probably lose some muscle control on this side."

"So he's going to have a crooked smile?" Samuel called from the other side of the table.

"The bastard never smiled anyway," Evgeny said. They clinked their vodka glasses together, drained them.

At that Yuri almost did smile—until the pain halted him. Anatoly cast a dirty look toward the other men.

"You're going to need a proper doctor," he said to Yuri. He turned back to his work. "Whether you go or not, that's up to you."

After Anatoly finished the cheek the three men shifted Yuri over to the other side of the table, so the vet could work on his left arm. Yuri's parka was still wrapped around it. As they worked on cutting it away, each cut seemed to carve into his own flesh, so fused with his wound had the fabric become.

Clammy sweat chilled his forehead, his armpits, his groin.

"Hey."

His mouth was dry. His tongue, stuck. Samuel and Anatoly peered down at him.

"I'll take a pill."

Anatoly gave him three.

He swallowed them.

FIVE

December 1, 2000—Cubs one day old

Miko Katanabe held a cigarette in her left hand, the filter poised between her index and middle fingers, between the middle phalanges, the knuckles gently curved. The tips of the fingers trembled. In her right, she held a metal lighter, hood flipped back, her thumb on the flint wheel. The bit of flesh pinched between the wheel and her thumbnail whitened from the pressure.

She raised the cigarette, and her mouth opened, though she did not bring it all the way to her lips; the lighter naturally followed in tandem, a path ordained by long habit.

But she did not strike a spark. Instead she lowered her forearms back to her knees. Closed her eyes. Breathed in. Exhaled. Opened her eyes.

She averted her gaze from the cigarette to the light rain that pattered steadily on the elephant ear that fringed the small yard. She sat cross-legged on a batik-covered wicker couch on the dormitory's screened-in porch. Beyond towered the broad-leafed kempas trees, in Way Kambas National Park, Sumatra.

Her home for the last five years. She would miss this place. She would miss her tigers. In that time, she had come to see them as hers. As her family. Both those in captivity—the ones she saw every day, as her team nurtured them back to health, or simply fed and cared for them, if they were too old or too damaged to return to the jungle—and the wild ones, the ones that she and her team tracked and studied as best they could, glimpsing them via remote camera traps and the occasional pugmark or scratched tree. Color-coded pushpins on a map marked sightings, strings connected the pins, penciled hatches shaded territories. These were the ones she would miss the most. The elusive ones. The ones she never saw, except in grainy, fragmentary photographs.

She would miss it, yes—but she was leaving. She had never felt more certain about any decision in her life. The time had come. The opportunity that Dr. Carrington had presented to her was singular. Incredible.

Two infants, scarcely a day old. A male and a female. Born even as their mother perished, apparently. And, somehow, they survived. They continued to survive. She feared the jangle of the telephone, sure it would be Dr. Carrington calling to tell her, no, sorry, they didn't make it. We did all we could...

Again, she found the cigarette at her lips, the tension on her thumb unbearable.

She just needed a moment, to clear her head. She could do that by breathing, though. She didn't need to contaminate her lungs to organize her thoughts. She knew that.

The air so humid. Her shirt plastered against her back, her armpits. She'd been sweating during the phone call, and now couldn't seem to stop. Unable to believe what Dr. Carrington was telling her. That the "project" they had fervently discussed in previous years at conventions in San Diego and in Singapore might now become a reality, after years of dreaming. And some preparation as well: she had studied Russian, he had set out to secure funding. For their hypothetical, capital-P "Project." The funding not yet "secured," he told her, but "assured." He had wrangled temporary facilities for their exclusive use in the meantime.

"Come," he had said. "Come quickly. Come tomorrow, if you can."

She would, she told him. She would leave tonight. She said good-bye, disconnected, and immediately dialed to book her flight.

There would be no time for goodbyes and farewells. Probably for the best. She wouldn't miss the people nearly as much as she would the tigers. And she knew better than to flatter herself to believe that they would miss her, either. She could be demanding, she knew. Blunt. Bossy. A bitch. She had overheard some of the men—and they were all men—call her that. She didn't mind. So long as they did what she told them to. Not Janpur, of course. He wouldn't say that. But even he probably thought it, at times.

Then, after another call to arrange for a driver to take her to the airport, she had dug to the back of her lower desk drawer: the emergency pack. The cigarette she presently held, poised.

Probably stale, she told herself. Almost certainly it would not satisfy, would not live up to the craving. Definitely would make her feel miserable afterward. She'd made it for six months. Six months of daily battles. She hadn't bothered with patches or gums, hadn't tapered. Cold turkey. Because she had willpower. She had determination. Because she was a woman, not a weak-willed little girl. She had shown that, amply, in those one hundred and eighty days. In that half of a year. Did she really want to throw that away now?

For the Project to work, isolation was required. The tigers needed to be kept away from human contact until they were mature enough to survive on their own. Two years, give or take. One hundred and eighty days, times four. Seven hundred and twenty days in the Russian Far East. In Primorsky Krai. The last refuge of the Siberian tiger. It would be her job to train these two cubs. To teach them, somehow, how to survive in the wild. How to hunt. How to socialize. The sorts of things they would normally learn from their mother, now dead.

If they could introduce cubs raised in captivity into the

wild, and prove that they were viable, that they could not only survive, but thrive—that would be revolutionary. This had never been done before. Had never even been attempted. Assumed an impossibility. But if she were successful, and if her methods could be replicated elsewhere with other tigers born in captivity, then scientists would be able to prop up the numbers of Siberian tigers in the wild. Presently hovering at a dangerously low figure, an estimated population of three hundred and fifty, maybe four hundred. Total. In all the vast wilderness of Primorsky Krai. In the *taiga*, that was the word. Reintroduction would also allow scientists to diversify the tigers' genetic pool, which, with such low numbers of tigers breeding, had become dangerously homogeneous. Too much interbreeding weakened the stock, made them susceptible to diseases and defects. To potentially damaging traits.

Two years. She was used to working on her own. In remote corners of the world. Surrounded by men. But she had never been to Russia. She knew she would get there someday. She just hadn't imagined that it would be this soon. She had learned the language to read the papers published by the Severetsov Institute and by the scientists at the Sikhote-Alin Biosphere Reserve. Dr. Carrington among them. An Australian who had lived in Primorsky Krai for decades now, who had devoted his life to studying *panthera tigris altaica*.

She wanted to do the same.

If she guided the Project to success, she would be able to do just that. Wherever she wanted. Any university or institute involved with felid conservation would open their doors to her. She might even be able to steer tiger management policy around the world. A post with the WWF. The United Nations, even. Certainly she would have a say.

Two years of isolation. Two years of sacrifice. Two years of deprivation.

Another two years of those things, rather. Intensified. Compounded. In a harsh country, a harsh culture, a harsh language.

Another two years, to carry her out of her mid-thirties. Two years *minimum*. Even after release—if they managed to get to that point—there would be further months of monitoring the tigers' progress.

But what was she going to do, have children? Start a family? Here, in Sumatra?

And who would be the father? Janpur? He had made clear that he had no interest. Not that he wouldn't mind her having children, of course—always complaining about the condoms she insisted on. No, he wouldn't mind, and why should he? He wouldn't be the one stepping away from his career for a few years to raise the child. Or children. He had made that very clear. So progressive and egalitarian—unlike most of the men she had worked with over the years—until it came to the question of who would care for the children. Who would sacrifice their career?

She flipped the lighter closed. Tucked the cigarette behind her ear. Stood up. Stretched her arms overhead.

He was the one who had placed the cigarette in her hand, who brought it waveringly close to her lips.

No, don't blame it on him.

It was her decision whether to smoke or not.

Just as it was her decision whether to end this or not.

It had been over for a long time, now. Two, three, maybe even four months. This would just confirm it. Make it real. Possibly painful. She wasn't sure about that. About whether there would be pain. She had done her best not to think about it during that time. Not to think about him. He'd been gone for much of that time. Off in Java, then on the mainland, making his pitches at fundraising dinners, in corporate boardrooms, at sparsely attended lectures, doing his best to get people with power and people with money, with their ever-diminishing attention spans, to designate ever-diminishing tracts of land as sanctuaries, reserves, refuges, parks.

She entered the old plantation house. The telephone was in the lobby, empty at this morning hour. Normally she, too, would be at work. But today was not a normal day.

She picked up the telephone. Dialed Janpur's number.

He had a cellular telephone now. And not just one suit, but several. And matching ties. A leather briefcase with brass fittings.

The phone rang and rang. As it so often did, when she called.

She hadn't asked *Why me?* She knew her worth. So did Dr. Carrington. It was beneath her to ask whether he had tried to reach Janpur first. Or whether, perhaps, Janpur had refused. He would consider this a folly. A sideshow in the larger war.

A pipe dream.

Impossible.

She wanted to hear him say it. So that when she did succeed, she could remind him of his words, when she next saw him. In Hong Kong, Kuala Lumpur, or wherever the felid scientists of the world gathered.

Ring. Ring.

That would be two years from now, three years, maybe four. To truly know that the Project had been a success. She would be famous. She would be at the top of her profession. She would be 40. It would be worth it.

Ring. Ring.

It would have to be. She replaced the receiver in the cradle. Time to start packing.

She pulled the cigarette from behind her ear. Snapped it in half. Tossed the two pieces into the rubbish bin behind the counter.

She wasn't going to start smoking again for some man.

SIX

December 3, 2000—Cubs three days old

A doctor from Melnichnoye came to check on Yuri the next day. The doctor added a few stitches, redressed the wounds, but pronounced the work done by Anatoly as "sound." Gauzy bandages covered his right cheek; medical tape wrapped up over his head and under his chin, met behind his left ear to hold the bandages in place. His left forearm was also swaddled in bandages that covered the four puncture wounds left by Tatiana's fangs: two from above, two from below, on the outside of his radius. A splint on his wrist kept him from flexing the forearm muscles, and a sling around his neck held the arm immobile.

Samuel arranged with Vassily and the Anti-Poaching Brigade for Yuri to stay at the Polygon to recuperate. Samuel insisted. Yuri needed rest, and a full course of antibiotics. His bandages needed to be changed every day. The pain meds would make him sleepy.

He spent the next three days following Samuel around not unlike a stray that had been taken in by a kindly stranger. Samuel let him feed the cubs their carefully concocted formula of goat's milk and water, laced with a protein supplement, antibiotics, taurine, and a touch of mineral oil to encourage them to vacate their bowels. Three times a day. Yuri never missed the opportunity to hold them, though he had to scrub carefully and wear protective gloves, a mask, and a sterile apron. He would sit first, and hold his left out to cradle the cub, despite the pain provoked by the cub wriggling against his forearm, and then give it the bottle with his right.

The other men at the Polygon largely avoided him. If it wasn't for Samuel's company, he would have taken his meals in the mess hall alone. He could sense that the other men were both drawn to him and repelled by him. When he entered a room, the voices ceased, but there were nudges, whispers, and eyes that watched his every move. When he turned, the eyes glanced away. As he walked through, the men parted, moved to the edges, or even stopped whatever they were doing and left. As though he might gut one of them just as he had gutted Tatiana.

The first night he slept in Samuel's office, on a convertible sofa that could swing out into a bed when Samuel needed to stay overnight. When Yuri asked him if he didn't want to use it to monitor the cubs, the older man shook his head and said that normally he would feel obligated, but with Yuri present, he could go home and rest easy. "My wife thanks you," he said with a chuckle. "She doesn't know you, but she thanks you." Besides, Anatoly was the one chiefly involved with caring for the cubs.

On the wall above Samuel's sofa-bed clustered a kaleidoscopic collage of photographs, some within narrow plastic frames, most with no frames at all. Photographs of Samuel and his Russian wife Klara, their two children at various stages of life, babies to toddlers to children to young adults. Then the children with children of their own, new infants in the laps of their grandparents, sitting back from the table, crowded with the cheery remains of a meal, smiling. In and among the pictures of family, glimpses of tigers snapped from hidden camera mounts, snowy taiga as the stark backdrop. At the center, faded photos of dusty foothills and gnarled trees unlike any Yuri had ever seen. Australia, he supposed. The first pictures Samuel had hung on his arrival, decades ago.

Despite the drowsiness of the pain meds, he slept uneasily. He had to keep his right cheek off the pillow, and he couldn't put any weight on his left forearm either.

The second night he dreamed of Tatiana approaching him, slowly, her shredded belly trailing blood in the snow. He couldn't tell from her implacable facial stripes if she meant to thank him or to take her revenge. He found himself powerless to move until she stood right in front of him. He could feel her hot breath on his face. Her whiskers tickled his nose. As her lips began to curl back from her yellowed teeth, he snapped awake, drenched in sweat.

He wrapped Samuel's flannel robe over his pajamas, stabbed his feet into Samuel's shearling-lined slippers. Along the dimly lit hallway, each office door was festooned with photographs, welcome signs in various languages, schedules, whiteboards for leaving messages.

In the lavatory he stepped to the sink and opened the tap, let the cool water run over his right hand. Stooped to the water bubbling and pooling in his palm. He closed his eyes as he did so, ignored the twinge of pain in his cheek as he pursed his lips together to suck the water into his mouth. Thirst slaked, he straightened, and caught sight of his partially covered face in the mirror. He reached his right hand to the bandages, dug at the tape along his nose with his fingernails, peeled back the edge. Lifting the bandage felt like lifting the skin from his cheek. Probably what he was doing, quite literally. A slick redness welled up in the fluorescent glare, and he lowered the bandage back into place, smoothed the tape down against his skin, though it seemed to have lost some of its tack.

He crossed quickly through the frozen December night into the mess hall. Empty at this late hour. Dim lights over the doors provided scant illumination. The net stretched across the ping-pong table again, as though nothing had happened there.

From the mess hall it was back out into the subzero cold

and then into the laboratory building. The hallway here was dark, but he knew the cubs were in the lab three doors down to the left, in the darkest center of the building.

The red glow of the makeshift incubator warmly welcomed him. The lamp hanging above them was nothing more than a heating lamp taken from the mess hall buffet line and repurposed.

Within the cubs squirmed and pawed and rolled, mewling weakly all the while. They were always more active at night. They were the size of full-grown tomcats, only with outsized heads and paws, and rounded ears rather than pointed. Their eyes were shut tight, as though the eyelids were glued together. Their eyes would remain sealed for a few more days, but even after the lids opened their vision would be blurred. The enforced blindness of the first three weeks or so, Samuel had explained, would keep them in the den while their mother hunted. Only their mother would hunt no more.

They seemed to be in a half sleep, where one would wake the other in the process of getting comfortable enough to fall fast asleep, only for the other, now wakened, to return the favor while seeking a comfortable position. Each growing annoyed all the while requiring the warmth and closeness of the other. It was quite comical. Yuri had to remind himself not to smile, as any tensing of his jaw agonizingly stretched the raw tissue there, the many small muscles and tendons.

A memory from his childhood, long submerged.

His dog, Ruka. A Yakutian Laika—similar in appearance and willing temperament to a Siberian Husky. Snow-white face and legs, black hood and cape, the two colors swirled together in the bushy vortex of the upward curl of his tail. His pale blue eyes glowed with light, with life. His quick smile, and the sharp bark that had earned him his name.

He and Ruka had used to spend hours running in the woods together, leaping and bounding through the snow, tackling each other, then up and running again. From the time Yuri could run, until... until he was taken away. Seeing the cubs squirming, their striped flanks pulsing with breath, brought rushing back the memory of sleeping in the barn with Ruka—even sometimes in the dead of winter—the two cuddled together in a tight little cave Yuri had constructed of straw bales and lined with heavy blankets. Especially when his father was on the drink and didn't bother enforcing Yuri's bedtime, or even his whereabouts. He basked again in the warmth of it, smelled again Ruka's hot breath, stroked the bristles of his fur, fought the cinder block solidity of the dog's head as it pushed into his ribs, the occasional stretch digging his paws into Yuri's thighs or belly.

How had he forgotten? He supposed the Home for Boys, and then the Army, had drilled all that foolishness out of him. But the sight of these helpless little balls of fur curling into each other brought it all back.

He absently bumped his forehead against the plexiglass barrier and he straightened sharply, afraid that he would collapse the entire thing. But the walls held. It was sturdy enough. Indeed, the plexiglass walls were dotted with oily prints left by the fingers and foreheads of all those who had come through the lab to see the new arrivals.

The warmth brought on the drowsiness again. He walked around the lab bench, sat cross-legged on the linoleum floor, leaned his back against the stainless steel refrigerator door. He couldn't quite see the cubs from this angle, but the red light warmed his face, and when he closed his eyes the lamp's baleful afterimage glared in the darkness.

He woke with his hand wrapped around the burled wooden handle of his Yakut knife. The short, stout and sharp blade gleamed redly in the dim glow.

What had wakened him? There it was: a sound, from the hallway. Now at the door. The knob turning, slowly; the bolt grinding free from the catch; the faint squeal of hinges opening. He uncrossed his stiff legs, crouched behind the lab bench. Lifted himself so he could peer through the incubator. The cubs lay still, flanks pulsing. The dark silhouette of a man propped the door open behind him, began to stalk toward Yuri, toward the cubs. As the man's legs entered the cone of red light, Yuri stood. He laid his thumb along the spine of the blade. The man took one more step, bringing the gray of his military fatigues into the light, then halted. His face remained in shadow, but Yuri recognized him from his stride, from his barrel chest, his ramrod bearing. His unmistakable aura of command.

Could it be? he wondered. *Or am I still dreaming?*

"There you are." The calm, steady timbre of the man's voice erased the sliver of doubt, dispelled the last cobwebs of sleep. "Should've known I would find you here."

Upturned, empty palms lifted into the light. Another stride forward brought his face into the incubator's glow. A wolfish smile of red teeth. A bristly mane of close-cropped gray hair. The sclera of his eyes reflected the red light as well.

Major Ivan Petrovich Iliakov. Yuri's C.O. No, he corrected himself—his *former* commanding officer.

SEVEN

"You watch them as though you were their mother," Major Iliakov said.

First Chernichev, now the Major, Yuri thought. *Not a coincidence.*

"Why are *spetsnaz* here?" he asked.

"Ah, yes—the Ferret." *Yes, that was his nickname*, Yuri thought. *Not the Weasel.* "I came as soon as he told me he'd seen you."

"He was behaving very suspiciously. Like a poacher."

The Major heaved an exaggerated sigh. "Unlike you, our former comrade Oleg Chernichev is not covering himself in glory out here."

Yuri slowly walked around the lab bench, the knife handle warm in his tight grip. As he approached, the Major lifted his hands, opened his arms and strode toward him. He enfolded Yuri in his embrace, pulled him into his chest. The cloying reek of the sweet Cuban cigars that the Major preferred filled Yuri's nostrils. He kept his arms at his side, tucked the knife blade behind his leg.

The Major stepped back, held Yuri's stiff shoulders in his hands. He glanced down at Yuri's clenched right hand. He smiled, and his teeth reflected the heating lamp's glow.

"A little jumpy, are we?"

"I don't understand why you are here."

"Fate," Iliakov said, lingering over that word, "seems to have brought us back together."

"You always said we make our own fate."

The Major chuckled. "You remember."

"Why now?" Yuri asked. "Why here?"

"I've been in Primorye for almost a year," the Major said. "It wasn't long after I arrived that I learned you were here, too. I kept telling myself that I would contact you. Always next week, when work slowed. But then this—these..." He nodded his chin toward the incubator. "If not now—when?"

Yuri glanced toward the stirring, wriggling cubs. Their hushed whispers seemed to have disturbed them.

"I know we didn't end on the best of terms," Iliakov said. "But I think you know you were always my favorite. That's why you were my *starshina*. My right hand."

Suddenly he felt like a kid all over again, a scrawny seventeen-year-old kid, facing this same man—only then he'd been Comrade Captain Ivan Iliakov, and his hair had been shaved tight along the sides of his scalp into a razor-sharp flattop. They faced each other in the entry hall of the Yakutsk Home for Boys, and the Comrade Captain extended his hand to Yuri, extending with it an offer to leave that godforsaken place and join the saboteurs.

You're a born hunter, Iliakov had said to him, after seeing him shoot, in a frozen field across the highway from the Home. He hadn't held a rifle for years and shooting one again had felt like going home. *I'm looking for hunters.*

"How long has it been?" Yuri asked.

"Five years."

Five years since they had seen each other last, in Grozny. But Yuri knew the answer to the underlying question. Twenty years since they met at the Home for Boys, give or take.

"You would be very welcome back in the unit, *starshina*," Iliakov said. "The men need a leader like you. I need a leader like you. You always were my favorite, you know."

"What unit?"

"The Wolfpack, of course."

"A military op?"

"No," the Major shook his head. "Mother Russia no longer had use for me in her army, so I came here, to the land of opportunity. Beautiful, sunny Primorsky Krai."

Yuri had come here to put as much distance between himself and the war as possible. To leave the army behind. "What could possibly have brought you here?"

"I've accepted reality, my friend. The capitalists have won. Despite all our years of fighting them, shoulder to shoulder, they have won. Greed and corruption have infiltrated our defenses and sabotaged our resolve more effectively than any *spetsnaz* op could ever hope for."

"What's your angle, Comrade Major?" There was always an angle. Always a gambit.

"There is a buyer who is very much interested in these cubs," the Major said. "Alive, not dead."

"That's not an option," Yuri said.

Iliakov raised his hands in mock surrender.

"Obviously, your presence has changed the calculus. If you come back—if you agree to be my *starshina* again—then Chernichev and our buyer would be made to understand that the cubs are off limits. He's obsessed with these cubs right now. He feels that you stole something that belonged to him."

"The cubs belong to no one," Yuri said. "But there is no way I will allow him to take them. Not him, not you, not anyone."

Iliakov rubbed his stubbled cheek. "I understand you were the one to name them."

Yuri nodded.

The Major smirked. "A tad sentimental, wouldn't you say?"

"Kamal was my friend," Yuri said.

"He was a Chechen rebel, and a traitor." Iliakov exhaled. "He was directly responsible for at least three deaths in our unit alone."

"I know," Yuri said. "I was there."

"Believe me, if there was anybody else I could have given that assignment to..." Iliakov's low voice became even quieter. "But you were the one."

Yuri didn't say anything. What was there to say? This was ancient history. This was the war he had left behind. This was why he had come to Primorsky Krai.

"You were always the one," the Major said, his voice hoarse. "It took its toll on you."

Yuri waved this away. "What does the Wolfpack do these days?"

"The project I'm currently the most enthusiastic about," the Major said, "also happens to match your area of expertise. There is that word again: fate. We're establishing our own version of your quaint Anti-Poaching Brigade. Only ours isn't about to be shut down by the accountants and bureaucrats back in Moscow."

"What are you talking about?"

"I'm sorry to say it, but your state-sponsored Brigade is about to run out of funding. Our brigade, however, is an independent, for-profit venture."

"Who pays you to stop poachers, if not the state?"

"The poachers themselves."

Yuri frowned.

"The poachers pay for our permission to hunt, in a tract of our choosing. A license, if you will. If we catch men hunting without making said arrangement with us, then they pay a very different kind of price. It's all about resource management. Imagine what a team of dedicated, highly trained men could do. Men whose hands aren't tied behind their backs, the way yours are. Men who do not have to abide by any rules of engagement. We make examples of a poacher or two, and word will quickly spread among both the hunters and the buyers. They'll fall in line. We'll control the tiger population. We'll shepherd them into the twenty-first century."

Yuri stared at his former C.O. "You haven't changed."

The Major grinned, and his teeth glowed red in the incubator lamplight. "I certainly hope not."

"You know I can't—"

The Major waved him quiet with one hand, while he pressed an earpiece further into his ear.

"Yes, I know," the Major murmured. He tucked his chin to his collar where, Yuri presumed, a microphone would pick up his voice. "He's standing in front of me. With the cubs, yes." A pause, a brief exhale, almost a sigh. "We are having a civilized conversation about how best to preserve the world's remaining Amur tigers."

The Major glanced up at Yuri, smiled. "That won't be necessary," he murmured to his collar. "I said no."

"The Ferret?" Yuri asked.

"Your partner would be welcome as well." Iliakov said to Yuri, ignoring his question. "His experience would be a great asset. We could name him Vice President or Chief of Operations or some such. We don't all have to be miserable ex-*spetsnaz* sons of bitches."

He reached into his left breast pocket, pulled out a business card. It bore nothing more than his name, Ivan Petrovich Iliakov, and a telephone number. He extended it toward Yuri.

"I will have to consider it," Yuri said.

Iliakov pursed his lips together, narrowed his eyes.

"The tigers are already extinct, my friend," he said. "What are their numbers—three hundred? Four hundred? Say it's even as high as five hundred—so what? The Sikhote-Alin is nothing more than a glorified zoo. The mining companies and the logging companies are subdividing their territory into smaller and smaller parcels every year. Do you want to help manage the population? Or do you want to wear a badge and bury your head in the sand? Or, I suppose I should say, in the snow?"

"I said I'll think about it."

The Major tucked the card back into his pocket and buttoned it closed.

"Don't think too long," he said. He lifted his jaw and

raised his right elbow. Clipped his heels together and snapped his flattened hand to his forehead.

Yuri returned the salute, briefly. Iliakov held his for a moment after Yuri had raised and lowered his hand. For the Major, a highly unusual sign of respect. Of deference, even.

The Major pivoted on his heels, and walked to the door. He pulled the door open, then stopped at the threshold. He stood in darkness, beyond the small diameter of warm light emanating from the incubator. He cleared his throat.

"In Grozny you once said you wanted to be one of the good guys," he said.

Yuri nodded. "I remember."

"Congratulations, *starshina*."

The door closed behind him. Yuri turned back to the cubs, placed his hands on the bench. The incubator's red light bulb seemed to tremble, and flicker. The encroaching darkness solidified around him, threatened to swallow him.

He closed his eyes. He remembered the beacon on board a chopper in the Panjshir Valley—a nighttime extraction—glimmering red through the swirl of smoke and dust kicked up by the rotor wash, twisted by the spinning blades. A much younger Comrade Captain Iliakov urged Yuri on as he limped heavily, his right arm over his C.O.'s shoulders, until Iliakov picked him up and carried him the last several meters, shoved him through the open hatch. The helicopter should have been ordered into the air—they were taking small arms fire, somewhere in the foothills the *basmachi* were passing out RPGs, loading them with rockets. Yuri should have been left behind to fend for himself, but Iliakov had kept the bird grounded until they all were on board. He had left her and charged into the outskirts to bring him back, to get all of his team aboard. That, at the time, had been enough. Enough to earn Yuri's admiration. His adoration. He was so very green then.

After five years away from the army—five years free of Major Iliakov—he had begun to feel that he was putting the war behind him. But now, suddenly, the Major was here.

Chernichev was here. In an instant, it seemed, the war had caught up to him again.

A glimpse at the Major's phone number had been long enough to commit it to memory. He didn't need the card as a reminder. His *spetsnaz* training wouldn't allow him to forget it if he wanted to.

The war would never leave him alone, not completely.

EIGHT

December 4, 2000—Cubs four days old

He stayed in the lab, dozing fitfully, until light began to filter in through the hallway, and people began moving about. Anatoly entered for the morning feeding, and while he did not seem terribly surprised to see Yuri there before him, he did frown slightly, told Yuri he needed to sleep more and worry about the cubs less.

Yuri could only nod. He fed the cubs, and then retreated to Samuel's empty office. His left forearm and right cheek ached. Shoots of pain radiated into his elbow and shoulder, into his jaw and skull.

He sat on Samuel's sofa-bed. The pill bottle sat on the desk, next to a bottle of water and the strip of bedsheet knotted in a loop that he used as a sling.

He straightened his left elbow, slowly curled the fingers of his left hand into a fist. He couldn't quite make a ball, the splint around his thumb stopped him. As did the ache in his forearm. He attempted to roll his left hand around his wrist, but the splint prevented him from flexing too far in any direction. Sweat stood out cold on his forehead. He could do without the sling.

He picked up the plastic container of pain pills. He

didn't like the way they made him feel during the day: numb, fuzzy, like he was walking around in a fog. Like he was following himself, observing himself over his own shoulder as he moved through the day, walking and eating and feeding the cubs, at a remove.

He also didn't like the strangely vivid dreams that came with the pain meds. He remembered the heat of Tatiana's breath on his face. Even the Major's visit had a certain dream-like quality to it. Had Iliakov's visit been a dream as well?

No, the Major had been there. He was sure of it. If Iliakov was nearby, he needed to be sharp. He needed to be fit, both mentally and physically. Major Iliakov was the smartest man he knew. If he had come to the Polygon looking for Yuri, it wasn't for sentimental reasons. It wasn't to reminisce over the good-old bad-old days.

He contemplated the pill bottle. The pain would return, but so would his control over his body and his mind. Pain he could tolerate. Pain wouldn't last. This wasn't the first time he'd been stitched up. He tossed the bottle in the rubbish bin under Samuel's desk.

The only other item at the bottom of the bin drew his eye: a slip of paper, covered in numbers. With his foot he dragged the metal bucket toward him, scanned the sheet without removing it or disturbing it. Three columns of numbers with totals at the foot of each column, possibly in rubles; then several pairs of numbers being multiplied, possibly calculating area in square meters.

In the lower right corner, a single phrase in Russian, with a question mark: "Red Stag?"

He pushed the bin back into place.

He reclined back onto the sofa, swung his legs up, pushed off the shearling slippers. He wondered if the cubs would still be there if he hadn't happened to be in the lab watching over them at 0300. Or if they would have vanished. What was Iliakov's game?

Soft taps on the door opened Yuri's eyes. His right hand clenched around the handle of his knife, in the pocket of

Samuel's robe. The door opened, and Samuel's wizened eyes appeared in the gap.

"Great news," he said. "Our dreams have come true!"

"Dreams?"

"There's somebody here that you've got to see."

Yuri swallowed. "Is it the Major?"

"The who? What?" Samuel frowned. "No, it's—you'll see. Come on. It's about the cubs."

Yuri did not bother to dress, kept Samuel's long, heavy robe wrapped around him, pushed his feet back into the slippers. He followed the senior scientist from the office building, skipping to keep pace with the Australian's long strides. In the courtyard, the family of snowmen had begun to dwindle and sag, the mother's turnip nose had fallen from her face, as the snow evaporated in the dry air and strong breezes that swept through the complex.

"Remember how I said there was hope? That the cubs might not have to go to a zoo?"

He led Yuri into the lab building, down the hall, to the familiar third door on the left. The room where he had encountered Iliakov only a few hours before.

"Dr. Katanabe," Samuel called out as he entered the room.

Yuri hesitated on the threshold, scanning for signs of Major Iliakov. His right hand in the robe's front pocket, fingers loose around the knife handle. Three figures in white lab coats surrounded the incubator.

These three turned to face him and Samuel. One of the men was Anatoly. Yuri had seen the other man at feeding times. The third was a woman he hadn't seen before. The only woman he'd seen since he'd arrived at the Polygon, he realized.

She was Japanese, he guessed, from her name, with pale skin, wide eyes, raven black hair that shimmered midnight blue under the fluorescent lights. She separated herself from the other two, walked toward him, her right hand outstretched.

"You must be Yuri," she said, in stilted Russian.

Their eyes met, briefly, but then hers settled on his bandaged cheek, drifted down to his left arm.

"This is Doctor Miko Katanabe," Samuel said.

He took her hand into his. It was small, but her grip was firm.

"You had an adventure," she said.

"Doctor—" Yuri began.

"Miko," she said. She pulled her hand free. Then, in her stilted Russian, "Prefer to call me Miko, please."

"What's going on with the cubs?"

The woman stared at him, then looked questioningly at Samuel.

Samuel said something in English, then repeated it in Russian. "He feels responsible for them."

She turned and pointed to the incubator.

"They are safe," she said, her voice close to his ear. She stood on his right. He glanced away from the cubs. She was inspecting his bandaged cheek.

"Claws?" she asked Samuel, without looking away from Yuri's bandaged face.

"She got his arm in her jaws as well," Samuel said. "He's lucky she let him keep it."

"I would like to see the wounds," she said to Samuel.

"What for?" Yuri asked. Her eyes shifted briefly from the bandages to his eyes, then back to the dressing.

"Curiosity," she said. "If you don't mind."

"You could observe when Anatoly changes the dressings," Samuel said.

"Now?" she asked.

"I suppose we could—" Samuel began.

"What's going on?" Yuri asked. Who cared about his stitches? He stepped away from her, toward Samuel. "Why is she here? What's going on with the cubs?"

"I apologize." Samuel raised his hands. "Let's back up a moment. Dr. Katanabe has just arrived from Sumatra. She is going to train the cubs so they can survive on their own. In the wilderness."

Yuri snorted. Even he, with his limited training, knew that this was impossible.

"When I told you they might have a chance," Samuel said as he rested his palm on her shoulder, "Dr. Katanabe was the person I had in mind. She's been studying the process of rehabilitating tigers born in captivity to be reintroduced into the wild."

"You saw potential for these cubs to live, yes?" she asked. He nodded.

"We will realize that potential," she said. "We will give them that life."

"In the wild," Samuel urged. "As they ought to live."

"But that doesn't work," Yuri said. "Everybody knows that. Without their mother to teach them, they won't make it on their own."

"It can work, but their... exposure to people has to be minimized. We contaminate them." She was speaking faster now, and her Russian was not always able to keep up. She turned to Samuel. "Can you explain to him, please?"

Samuel said, "These cubs are a once-in-a-lifetime opportunity. They are *tabula rasa*. They don't have a mother to teach them, but if we can find a way to replace their mother's training with our own, then we will release them back into the wild. And they will survive. So Dr. Katanabe is going to take them to a secure, remote location and begin their training."

She held up her right hand, her first two fingers. "Two things are critical for them to learn, in the first eighteen months," she said. She folded down the first finger with her left hand. "To hunt on their own." She folded down the second finger. "To socialize with other tigers."

"You left out a third," Yuri said. "Maybe the most important." The two scientists looked at him expectantly. "To fear man. How will you teach them that, when you're their source of food?"

"They won't know we're the source," she said. "We'll be hiding."

"You're going to hide," Yuri said, with a smirk. "From a tiger."

"Dr. Katanabe is the leading expert in the world on this topic," Samuel said. "As soon as I saw these cubs I knew I was going to call her in. I didn't say anything at the time because I didn't want to get your hopes up, son. But she is that chance I was telling you about. She came sooner than I could possibly have hoped—because she realizes that this is our best opportunity to test our hypotheses in the real world."

He grabbed Yuri by the shoulders.

"They will have a chance to live a life in the wild!" he said. He lightened his grip on Yuri's left shoulder when he winced at the jostling of his left arm. "And it's all because of you."

"If you turn them loose in the taiga without their mother's training," Yuri said, "you're signing their death warrant. Poachers will get them. And if they don't, the wilderness will. Other tigers will. The cold will."

"Aren't those the risks that all tigers face, on a daily basis?" Samuel asked. "Besides, we have you and the Brigade out there to watch over them."

He recalled what Iliakov had told him about the Brigade's imminent demise. Was this true? How could the Major be so confident?

He turned toward Miko. "You've done this before?"

It was a guess, but he could tell from the way her shoulders stiffened that it was a good one. She stood in front of him, straightened her spine.

"Listen with care," she whispered, in stilted but correct Russian. "I know who you are. I know what you did. The risk that you took. You gave them their names. But I am here to give them a new life. These cubs are mine now."

NINE

"You're giving them to her?" Yuri demanded of Samuel.

Samuel crossed the room to the other two men in lab coats. They were studiously keeping their backs to Yuri and Miko, intently focused on the cubs. Or pretending to be, while the voices steadily rose in pitch and intensity behind them. Samuel patted their shoulders, whispered to them. They left the room, each with a quick glance toward Yuri and his bandaged face.

"They're not mine to give," Samuel said as he closed the door behind them, leaving the three of them alone with the cubs. "Any more than they're yours to keep, my friend. They don't belong to any of us. You know that."

"What did you think?" she asked Yuri. "Were you going to train them? As your personal pets?"

Now it was she who had scored a good guess. Not that he would admit it to her. He had known all along that it was nothing more than a foolish, childish fantasy. But still... something about Samuel's promise of hope and his knowing winks had made him think that he would at least be involved, somehow.

"Where are you taking them?" he asked.

"We can't tell you that," she said.

"Because we don't even know yet," Samuel quickly

added. "I'm still lining up the site and the funding. This is all happening quickly—for all of us. Hey—" He placed his right hand on Miko's shoulder, his left hand on Yuri's. Gave them little shakes, as though to wake them up. "We all have to pitch in together on this."

"I want to help," Yuri said.

Samuel glanced at Dr. Katanabe, then back at Yuri. He pushed his lower lip up over the lower fringe of his mustache and nodded, as though resolving an internal debate. "I'd like to propose that you bring Yuri with you as well," he said. "I'll vouch for his character."

"He is injured," she said.

"This is nothing," Yuri said. He lifted his left arm, rotated his hand around his wrist without grimacing. The talking was beginning to take its toll on his jaw, though he was now practiced at moving his tongue and making words without moving his lips. "I've stopped taking the pain meds."

"I could probably find some money in my budget for a small stipend," Samuel said.

She said something in urgent, guttural tones to Samuel, who replied in more English. They both refused to look at Yuri, speaking about him as though he weren't in the room. He stood with his hands clasped behind his back.

"I can talk to Vassily," Yuri said, interrupting them. "Arrange for an extended leave."

They continued talking in English. Arguing in English.

"Hell—if he gives me a hard time about it," he said, "I could even quit."

"Let's not be hasty," Samuel said.

"If it's about the pay—" Yuri began.

"It's about qualifications," she said, switching back to Russian now. She turned toward Yuri. "You have no training."

"It's a different sort of training," Samuel said. "But it could prove useful, out in the taiga."

"Let me guess," she said. "Army."

Yuri became aware of his "at-ease" stance, feet at shoulder width, hands behind his back, shoulders squared.

Stiff. He tried to slouch. Tried to relax. But it went against the grain of his body. His breathing had become shallow. He was doing his best not to overreact. She was testing him, he told himself. Just as Iliakov had done in the early days.

"I haven't had good experiences with soldiers in the past," she said. "The officers always want to be the boss. And the enlisted men never think for themselves. Which were you?"

He didn't take the bait. "I'm not a soldier anymore," he said.

"Once a soldier," she sighed, "always a soldier."

"I left that all behind," he insisted. "Years ago."

"For the past five years he's been on the Anti-Poaching Brigade," Samuel said. "One of their best men, one of the most dedicated."

"I have my team picked," she said. "There is no room for another. As you know, Dr. Carrington, we have to keep the number of humans involved to an absolute minimum."

"How many others are going to be there?" Yuri asked.

"Dr. Stasevich," she said, meaning the veterinarian Anatoly, who had just left the room. "And me."

Yuri stared at her. Thankful for the bandages keeping his jaw from falling open and betraying his disbelief.

"What?" He turned toward Samuel, then back toward her. "The two of you? In some remote corner of the taiga? With these two cubs?"

"Correct."

"That's crazy."

"The way it has to be."

"Do you have any idea what's waiting for you out there?" He turned toward Samuel.

"This isn't Sumatra," Samuel said, gently. "Winter in the Sikhote-Alin can be tough. As they say out here, *the nights are long, and the snow is deep.*"

"Dr. Carrington, I grant my career isn't as long or as distinguished as yours," she said. "Not yet. But in the fifteen years I've been doing this, everywhere I've gone has been just as remote, just as isolated."

"This isn't about the cold," Yuri said. "It's about greed."

He pointed toward the incubator, toward the two cubs curled up inside.

"Those two cubs would bring one hundred thousand dollars. *Amerikanskiye dollary*, not rubles. Fifty thousand each. No—the male would bring sixty, or more. A bonus for male genitalia. Men who are desperate to be able to get an erection or to cure their cancer are willing to pay a fortune for these folk medicines, and men who are desperate for money will do anything to meet that demand. This isn't a joke."

"And everywhere I've gone," Miko said with a sigh, "there have been men trying to kill tigers for money. And for fifteen years I've been surrounded by men who insist that I must need their help, because I'm a woman."

Samuel and Yuri exchanged glances, silenced for the moment.

"And every goddamn time, I've proved those men wrong," she said. "Which is why you called me, Dr. Carrington, and not somebody else."

She turned to Yuri. "To be clear, if I didn't have to take Dr. Stasevich to appease the Severtsov Institute and share the credit with the Russian Academy of Sciences, I would go by myself."

"Last night—" Yuri began. "There was a man here. I couldn't sleep, and happened to be in the lab, watching the cubs. If I hadn't been, we might have found the incubator empty this morning."

Samuel frowned. "What the hell are you talking about?"

Yuri told them about his late-night encounter with Major Iliakov. He did not mention that he knew the man's name, nor his connection with the man.

The two scientists exchanged glances. She said something to Samuel. Though she said it in English, she said it in low tones, as though she didn't want Yuri to hear the words at all, regardless of whether he could understand them.

"Are you sure?" Samuel asked. "The pain meds can sometimes—"

"He was standing right here," Yuri said. "He'd heard about the cubs. He came here looking for them."

"Lots of people have come to look at them," Samuel said.

"Which is why we need to move them," Dr. Katanabe said.

"You don't get it," Yuri said. "This man, he won't stop. He'll find out where you're taking them. He'll keep coming until he has them."

"It sounds like you know him," she said.

"We served together," he said.

"In the army," she said. It was not a question.

Yuri swallowed his protest. Her presumption was accurate.

"So you say there was a man here to take the cubs away," she said, "and you say you know this man. Even so, you expect us to trust you to accompany us and—I suppose—to protect us." She turned to Samuel. "Does that make sense to you, Dr. Carrington?"

"Maybe he followed you somehow," Samuel said to Yuri.

He considered this. If Chernichev hadn't recognized him and told the Major about him, would they have bothered pursuing these cubs? Or was Yuri's presence compelling the Major to get involved?

"This is what he does," Yuri said. "This is who he is."

Was she right? Were they better off without him involved? He could see now how she might think that he was trying to infiltrate their team in order to discover their destination. Perhaps he had even brought the cubs to the Polygon to ensure their survival, and then to learn how to feed them and handle them, for his own ulterior motives. She didn't know him. She didn't trust him. He respected her for that. Just mentioning his midnight meeting with the Major, he realized, had tainted himself with the stink of corruption.

Maybe she does have what it takes, he thought.

"In the spring," Samuel said. "Once they're bigger—"

Dr. Katanabe turned toward Samuel. "Don't get his hopes up," she said, in English. "He's clearly too emotionally involved as it is."

"Winter is poaching season," Yuri said.

She turned back to Yuri, switched back to Russian. "You'll be of much more use to your Poaching Patrol."

A knock at the door turned all their heads. Anatoly pushed it open, leaned his head into the lab.

"Supply truck is here," he said.

"We're finished, right?" Dr. Katanabe asked. She looked from Samuel, to Yuri, back to Samuel. After neither replied, she began to walk toward Anatoly.

Samuel sighed. He placed his left hand on Yuri's right shoulder, patted his good cheek gently with his other hand. "Look kid," he said, with a wan smile. "We tried."

"What the hell is she trying to prove?" Yuri asked.

"She's trying to prove all the experts wrong," he said. "She's trying to upend decades of received scholarship. So we've got to let her do it her way."

"Dr. Carrington?" Miko called from the doorway. "A word while we walk?"

"Uh-oh." His back to her, Samuel winked. "Gotta go."

TEN

Yuri shuffled over to the incubator, as though drawn by a magnet. Within the plexiglass box the cubs slept soundly, their striped flanks pulsing rapidly with their short breaths. The overhead heating lamp had been switched off.

From the door, Samuel said, "Turn the lights out when you leave, okay?"

Yuri nodded absently. A pushcart covered with more of the white cotton blankets waited next to the lab bench. On the cart were a couple of syringes, nylon straps, a small defibrillator with tiny paddles.

It was like he was in Afghanistan all over again. The PDPA troops were on the same side as the Soviets, fighting alongside them against the mujahideen. They had proven themselves over and over. And yet, he couldn't help but look at them with suspicion. He didn't like feeling that way back then, and he didn't like it any more now. They were on the same side. She had dedicated her career to learning about and helping tigers—much more than he could say.

Surely Samuel had good reasons for bringing her in. Surely her heart was in the right place.

Was it though? They were her cubs now, she'd said. *Her* cubs. She didn't want to share them. Because she didn't want to share the glory if she were successful. Not even with

Samuel and the other scientists at the Polygon, it seemed. Not if she could help it.

Who was she to think she could change the course of nature? Who was she to presume that she could challenge the law of the taiga?

But wasn't that exactly what he had done, when he cut the cubs free from their mother?

It was hard not to fear for the little cubs, knowing what he knew about Primorsky Krai. Having seen what he'd seen these past five years. The carcasses stretched out in barns and in sheds, hidden under tarps in pickup trucks and cargo vans. All it would take is one person to leak the cubs' location to the wrong person, and who would stop them from walking in and taking them? Soft, pudgy Anatoly? Hardly. This woman? Tough as she thought she was? He couldn't see it.

Then again, maybe he was wrong. Maybe she did have the strength and the smarts. People were the concern. More than the fragile cubs, more than the harsh elements. People. Including him. If he continued pushing, he would only look that much more suspicious in her eyes.

All it would take would be one person. One weak link. Like Vassily. He and Evgeny had found Tatiana in a sector that Yuri had been pushing to patrol. A sector that Vassily had insisted was secure, and too remote to waste their time on. A lot had happened since they found Tatiana, but he hadn't forgotten. There would be a reckoning.

Yuri shook his head at himself. The darkness, returning. He was angry at her, and displacing it onto Vassily.

No, that wasn't right. He was angry at himself. For not being properly trained. For not having the skills she was looking for. For not having spent his life more productively, for learning only how to destroy and maim and kill. Of course he was angry. He couldn't make the darkness go away. But he could control how he responded. He inhaled deeply.

He touched the bandage on his cheek, pressed the edges back against his cheekbone, his mandibular joint. The tape was beginning to work its way loose, as the gauze became weighted with his blood and pus, as fluid seeped between his flesh and the tape, loosening the tack. He needed Anatoly to change the bandages and apply fresh tape, as he'd been doing the past couple of days around this time. But Anatoly was busy, he supposed.

From the supply cabinets he gathered fresh gauze, medical tape, cotton swabs, a scissors, and bottles of antiseptic. As he'd seen Anatoly do previously. He arranged these things on the lab bench that did not hold the incubator. Took some of the cotton blankets from the pushcart and spread them out over the black concrete. He searched for a mirror, but finding none, removed the syringes from the polished metal tray on the pushcart. The silvery surface reflected back a distorted image of his face, compressed in places, elongated in others. It would have to do.

Who was he to involve himself in the affairs of scientists and conservationists, when it was clear that nobody really wanted him there? Not Vassily, not Samuel, not Anatoly—and certainly not Dr. Miko Katanabe.

With his good arm he hauled himself up onto the bench, stretched himself out on his back so his head lay back against the blankets. Makeshift mirror in his left, he used his right hand to peel the bandages from his cheek. The tape at the edges was now less sticky than it ought to be, so that went quickly. But the gauze had stuck fast in places. It lifted his skin, tugged at the stitches.

He'd left the Army because all he could ever be there was a tool. A useful weapon of the Soviet State, and then of the Russian Federation. Who was he to hope that this would change just because he was no longer in the army? Just because he no longer had to salute, and he no longer had to kill on command?

With his right hand he twisted open the bottle of antiseptic. The cap slipped through his fingers, fell to the floor and rolled under the bench opposite, under the incubator. He listened to it roll until it hit the large steel refrigerator door behind. Where he had dozed the previous night, before the Major's visit.

He closed his right eye, lifted the mirror in his left hand, trained it on the red wreckage of his cheek and jaw. He lifted the bottle in his right. Anatoly had always daubed this area with cotton swabs and gentle motions. But he was going to irrigate the wound. He was going to flush it clean. He began to pour. He could hear the bubbles foaming. He clamped his jaw shut to keep from stretching the stitches, to keep from cracking open the newly formed scabs, to keep from screaming.

He wasn't going to call the Major. Whatever his game was, he wasn't going to play it.

When the bubbles finally ceased fizzing, he lay there panting. Waiting for the wound to air dry. He dabbed at the edges with a fresh blanket. Then he cut strips of gauze and laid them over the wound, as he had seen Anatoly do. He needed both hands to apply the tape, and he had to stop and check his progress in the mirror. It didn't look as neat as the veterinarian's work, but it would do.

It was a good skill to learn. He would have to do this on his own soon enough anyway. Dr. Katanabe was right. He would do more good on the "Poaching Patrol," as she called it.

It was time he got back to work.

ELEVEN

December 5, 2000—Cubs five days old

The next morning Yuri woke early. He strapped on Samuel's snowshoes and hiked into the forested hills that surrounded the Polygon. He hiked through the powdery snow until his thighs and calves burned and he had to loosen his scarf and lower the zipper of his parka. His breath burst into clouds in the air in front of him, and when he removed his fur-lined hat as he returned to the compound, he could feel the steam lifting from his sweat-plastered hair as well.

He went immediately to the warehouse, stripped out of his winter gear, down to his cashmere base layer and wool socks. A barbell, a few plates, a bench with a cracked vinyl covering and a rack of hexagonal-headed dumbbells collected dust in a corner. He ran through as many exercises as he could remember, with as much weight as he could bear, four sets of each: squats, deadlifts, presses, curls, extensions. Until he was dripping sweat, and his bandages sloughed off on their own.

Spetsnaz training emphasized the legs above all. The legs provided the foundation. From the legs the soldier drew his strength and athleticism and endurance. So he finished with a series of step-ups on the bench while clutching a thirty kilogram dumbbell in each hand, until he could no longer lift his legs, and his thighs quivered and his knees buckled. His cramping hands dropped the dumbbells with a thud and he fell to the floor after them, lay in the thin coat of mud formed by his sweat mixing with the dust, and panted, watched the motes drift lazily in the air above him, stirred by his exhalations. He felt horribly out of shape. He didn't even have the breath to curse properly.

The lavatory in the scientists' office building had a shower stall, and when he could stand and walk he made his way there, aware of the other men's startled stares, as they glimpsed the ragged remnants of his cheek, his stockinged feet and long underwear peeking out from beneath his loosely wrapped parka. He didn't even acknowledge their stares, didn't look at them to see if they would look away. He was used to their reaction to him by now. He knew they saw him as some sort of monster. So be it.

He made a detour to the laboratory building, for fresh gauze and tape. But he didn't venture all the way down to the third door on the left. Light poured from the open door and the window into the dim hallway, along with the sounds of movement and chatter. He could not make out what was being said, or even identify any of the voices, but he assumed that she must be there, along with Samuel and Anatoly, making their plans for the cubs. The previous evening when he had gone to feed them, she had turned him away, saying they had to start limiting the cubs' interaction with humans now. There was too much of a risk that they would identify the human giving the bottle as a parental figure—imprinting, she called it—and that had to be avoided from now on. She was dismayed that he had been allowed to hold them and feed them as long as he had, but what was done, was done.

Instead he ducked into one of the dark labs, and hunted around in the cabinets until he found the white boxes with black lettering that he sought. When he stood and turned to leave, his arms full, head spinning and vision clouding from his exertions, from dehydration, Anatoly stood in the doorway.

"Would you like me to help you with that?"

"I can manage," he said as he brushed past the veterinarian.

In the lavatory, he stripped out of his underwear and immersed himself in the steaming water, let it wash over him. He peeled off the bandages on his forearm as well, let the water run over the crusted blood there, let it wash over his raw cheek. Not too much, as it burned, and he didn't want to soften and remove all of the scabbing that had set in. He sat on the floor of the small shower stall, elbows on knees, and let the warm water drum on his shoulders. After drying off, he reapplied the bandages, first to his forearm, the easy part. Then to his face.

To work on his cheek and jaw, he tilted his head back, so that gravity could lend a hand in holding the fresh gauze in place until he applied the tape. He did not look himself in the eyes. His eyes reminded him of his mother. They were small, almond-shaped, the irises large and light brown. His mother's people were Evenki, a Yakutian tribe of reindeer herders. Nomads. His three older sisters and he all had his mother's eyes. Only his younger sister Sveta had their father's steely blue Russian eyes. His mother died not long after giving birth to Sveta, when he was five. He had little more than blurred memories of his mother, vague sensations, fragments of speech. Faded photographs spilled from a box, into the mud.

Back in Samuel's office he lowered the blinds, locked the door. On the desk sat a short stack of file folders. He began to leaf through the papers within. Looking for anything that might relate to the tigers, anything that might give him some sort of clue as to their ultimate destination. But most of the folders contained drafts and proofs of scientific papers submitted to the Senior Scientist for review, and the one folder that contained administrative paperwork bore dates at least a week old, older than the cubs, and so of no use. He returned the papers and folders to the neat stack he had initially found.

A gentle knock at the door startled him.

"Yes?" he called out. "Who is it?"

"Wake up, you lazy bastard," Evgeny said. "It's almost noon."

He opened the door. Evgeny wore the fleece-lined flannel work shirt that he used as a coat on all but the coldest days. He never seemed to mind the cold. Yuri didn't mind it either—he'd grown up in Yakutia, in the heart of Siberia, where frost could settle on your eyelashes and the cold could burn your lungs—but Evgeny seemed to have a higher internal temperature than most men.

"Sleeping, eh? You're going to sleep through lunch."

At the mention of a meal, Yuri's stomach growled. He held up his bandaged, splinted arm. "The doctor told me to rest."

"Come on. There's something you'll want to see."

Yuri wrapped Samuel's robe around him, pushed his feet into his shearling slippers.

As they walked toward the mess hall, Evgeny told Yuri that he'd returned to the Polygon to check on his partner—it was his day off—only to find the parking lot full, the entrance swarming with activity. Hunger forgotten, they skirted the mess hall, and walked around the side of the lab building as well. His legs wobbled beneath him, and the cold gnawed at his fingers, his ear lobes, his nose. He jammed his gloveless hands into the pockets of Samuel's robe. He remembered his knife, tucked under a cushion in Samuel's office. Just as well that he had left it behind.

A large paneled Mitsubishi truck waited between graying mounds of snow that had been plowed to the sides. Samuel pointed and called directions as men in jeans and heavy jackets moved crates, containers, cases, shipping pads.

A simple logo was omnipresent, painted on the doors of the truck, sewn onto the breasts of the workers' uniforms, stenciled on their yellow hardhats: a green capital M on a field of brown, enclosed by a thick circle of white. He'd seen the logo before. On flatbed trucks, carrying pine boles, freshly cut timber.

A forklift, also bearing the M logo, carried an incubator,

but not the makeshift one from the lab. A new one, one that looked like it was designed for premature human babies. Or perhaps custom-built for tiger cubs, even. Yuri had no idea. It was empty.

"What's going on?" Evgeny asked.

"They're moving the cubs," Yuri said.

"What do you mean, moving them?" Evgeny asked. "Moving them where?"

Samuel looked up from his clipboard, waved them over.

"Today's the day," he said, with a cheery smile.

"Already?" Yuri asked.

Samuel nodded.

"Where are you taking them?" Evgeny asked.

Samuel explained the rehabilitation project. Said that the cubs were being taken to a facility outside of Melnichnoye so they could be monitored by Dr. Katanabe and Dr. Stasevich, until the main site could be finalized.

"Too many people here," he said. "Everybody wants to see the cubs. They've become a tourist attraction. People are coming from other reserves to see them. I should've been charging admission."

He laughed, but Evgeny and Yuri didn't join him.

"Where is the main site going to be?" Evgeny asked.

Samuel's lips pressed together in a tight smile, his gray eyes hardened.

"Even if I knew I wouldn't be authorized to tell you," he said. He glanced at Yuri. "But I don't know. Nobody does."

Evgeny turned to Yuri, dark eyebrows knit together over his reddening nose.

"They're the experts," Yuri said.

"Every day they spend here," Samuel said, "every hour, even, they become more likely to imprint on us, to learn that humans are the provider. Which will lead them to become reliant. Domesticated. There are simply too many people around. You can see that, right?"

"I get all that," Evgeny said. "But how are we going to protect them if we don't know where they are?"

"It's no longer our concern," Yuri said. "They've made that clear."

"It's winter," Evgeny said. "It's poaching season. Of course it's our concern."

Samuel leaned toward them. "Look, lads, even I'm out of the loop on this one. But as soon as I know something—"

One of the workers called out for Dr. Carrington. He straightened, glanced over his shoulder. "Here they come."

The entrance to the lab building opened, and Dr. Katanabe emerged, walking beside a pushcart covered in a bundle of thick woolen blankets. She lifted a corner and peered under, let the fabric drop. Anatoly pushed the cart. They moved briskly toward a cargo van.

"What does the 'M' stand for?" Yuri asked.

"Meyerhaeusen International," Evgeny said. "Loggers."

Samuel turned back toward Yuri. "They've generously agreed to underwrite the Project, for the time being," he said. "The foundations wouldn't touch it—too controversial. And procuring a grant from the Academy of Sciences could take months. You know how the accountants and the bureaucrats are."

"But," Yuri began, hesitated. "Loggers? Why—"

"They must stand to gain something," Evgeny said.

"Publicity, I suppose. A public relations bonanza if the Project is successful." Samuel began walking toward the cargo van, toward Miko and the cart bearing the cubs. He paused and turned back toward Yuri and Evgeny for a moment. "*When* the Project is successful."

Evgeny tapped Yuri's shoulder. "Come on," he urged.

They followed Samuel over to the cart. It stopped at the rear doors of the black van, each door decorated with one half of the green M on a brown field in a white circle.

Dr. Katanabe saw Yuri. She pressed her lips together in what he supposed was meant to convey a smile. She rubbed her bare hands together and then cupped them in front of her mouth, blew into them. A foreigner's response to the cold.

Samuel lifted the blankets.

Beneath, in a dim cave, the cubs were stretched out, one next to the other, held in place by nylon straps. The dull black and orange stripes did not move. Their ears did not twitch, their noses did not wrinkle. They looked dead.

A premonition, Yuri thought. He forced himself to breathe deeply, through his nose.

"They've been given a mild sedative for transport," Dr. Katanabe said.

Evgeny reached his hand toward the nearest cub. She slapped it away, quickly stepped between the men and the cart. "The oils from your hand will stay on their fur for days," she said.

"Let's load 'em up!" a worker inside the van said. More men came to lift the cart from the ground into the back. Anatoly climbed in after. The doors slammed shut.

Evgeny said to Dr. Katanabe, "You have proper paperwork to move them?"

Dr. Katanabe said something to Samuel in English.

"Come on, now," Samuel said to Evgeny. "You know there's no paperwork for this. I know this is happening quickly—but this is a once-in-a-lifetime chance. Either we do this now, or they wind up in a zoo."

"The sedative is already starting to wear off," Miko said. "We're off to a late start as it is, and the clock is ticking."

"Let it go," Yuri said to Evgeny. "Let them go."

Evgeny raised his hands in surrender. "If you say so, partner."

Miko stepped to Yuri. She extended her hand toward him.

He pulled his hand from his pocket, half expecting to see his knife clutched in his balled fist. He opened his hand, and she reached for it, gave it a brisk shake. "Thank you," she said. "For all you've done. I won't forget you."

Yuri returned his hand to the pocket. She walked around the side of the cargo van and hauled herself into the passenger seat. The van coughed into life.

What did she mean, she wouldn't forget him? Would she include his name in the acknowledgements at the end of some scientific paper that would appear in an obscure journal published to line the shelves of libraries and research institutes? Would she mention an anonymous "park ranger" at the end of a presentation to her colleagues at some academic conference? Did she really think he cared whether she might forget him, or not?

"Well, shit," Evgeny said. "I didn't even get to hold one."

TWELVE

December 6, 2000—Cubs six days old

Yuri hitched a ride with Evgeny to Terney, to the offices of the Anti-Poaching Brigade. Evgeny drove one of the Brigade's old Nissan Pathfinders, which carried them on a bouncy, jarring, mud-splashing ride along the pitted tracks and snow-buried roads, as though they were riding a bare-bones skeleton of a machine with no cushions.

As they drove they discussed the fate of the tigers, and the likelihood that Dr. Miko Katanabe's plan would work. Yuri supposed that it was possible—they were the scientists, after all. They were the specialists.

But Evgeny couldn't fathom it. "They need to learn how to hunt from their mother. The cubs stay by the mother's side for nearly two years before they're ready to set off on their own. Is she going to train them for that long?"

Yuri shrugged. "I'm not privy to their plan," he said.

"They'll be taken by poachers as soon as they're set free," Evgeny said. He banged the steering wheel with his hand, lurching the vehicle out of the tire ruts in the snow. "They won't know any better."

Yuri agreed with his partner, but he'd been through all this with the scientists. And he'd already explained to

Evgeny how he had offered to accompany the scientists, and that Dr. Katanabe had deemed his services unnecessary. "Surplus to requirements," as they liked to say in the army.

"There must be something we can do," Evgeny said.

"We have no idea where in the Sikhote-Alin mountains they'll take them," he said. "We don't even know for sure that they'll stay in Sikhote-Alin. They could take them down to the Zheludinsky Sanctuary, for all we know."

"Don't you want to do something?"

"Yes, of course," Yuri said. "That's why we're going to headquarters."

"You think Vassily might know something?"

"No—not yet, anyway," Yuri said. "But his maps might have something to tell us."

"Ah, yes," Evgeny raised his index finger. "His precious maps."

They drove along in silence, aside from the dull groan of the engine, the continual crunch of knobbed winter tires rolling over packed-down snow.

The Sikhote-Alin Biosphere Reserve—a United Nations-sanctioned nature reserve, or *zapovednik*—surrounded them. This was an immense territory of undulating hills and low mountain ridges, traced with an infinitude of rivers and creeks and streams but few lakes, almost all of the land densely forested with evergreens of various types—pines, larches, firs—but also birches and Mongolian oak at the lower altitudes. The central Core of the Reserve was strictly forbidden to humans—even the scientists and rangers required special permits—while certain areas within the surrounding Buffer zone were designated for use as parks, hiking trails, small villages, family farms, the occasional logging operation or mine.

The scientists like Samuel, the conservationists and the park rangers worked for the Biosphere, as overseen by the Russian Academy of Sciences and the Severtsov Institute of Ecology and Evolution. Their activities were limited to the *zapovednik*, that is, to the Core sanctuary and the Buffer zone surrounding it. They were responsible for managing and maintaining all of the flora and fauna within, not just the tigers. The Anti-Poaching Brigade, however, came under the command of the Department of the Interior, and ranged far beyond the Biosphere—throughout the entire expanse of the Sikhote-Alin mountain range, in all areas of Primorsky Krai where tigers roamed. Their sole concern was protecting the Amur tiger population. When convenient, the two groups cooperated, at times coordinating their efforts. Their missions certainly overlapped. But the Brigade did not have its headquarters in the Polygon, or even in the larger *zapovednik*, but rather in the small coastal town of Terney, where half of its dozen or so patrolmen lived for most of the year. The other half were based near Melnichnoye to the southwest of the vast Reserve.

Evgeny parked at the motor pool, then went to have dinner with his wife and daughters. Yuri trudged uphill to the Brigade's small suite of offices, only to find them empty. He checked the log, saw who had been assigned where, and saw that Vassily had signed in at 10:15. The clock on the wall read 16:45. Knocked off early, he supposed.

He went to his desk, but there was nothing there that he needed. He rarely spent time at his desk anyway. He rapped lightly on the glazed window set in the door to Vassily's office. No light emanated from within. The entire office was shrouded in shadow with the setting of the sun. He tried the doorknob. Locked.

He returned to his desk—it held something he needed after all. He kept a master key hidden at the rear of his drawer. Old habits. The *spetsnaz* specialty: *razvedka*. Infiltration. Reconnaissance. Information gathering. Assessment of the enemy's disposition, materiel, supply lines, morale.

He eased Vassily's office door open, thumbed on the light. A photograph on the wall above the switch caught his eye. It seemed to depict a football team sponsored by the local pub, posed before a match: five men squatting on their haunches in the front row, six men standing behind them, arms folded across their chests or clasped behind their backs. Except instead of wearing shorts and brightly colored jerseys, they all wore dark green fatigues. Black and white circular patches on their left shoulders.

He lifted the plastic frame from its nail. There he stood, in the upper right corner, at the far end of the rear row, slightly apart from the other men. His fatigues were sharply pressed, his one visible boot gleamed. A hint of a smile on his clean-shaven face. The new guy. His first week.

Evgeny stood in the center, arms outstretched over the men on either side, mouth open, saying something frank to the man behind the camera, something sure to break all the other men into laughter in the following frame. Yuri involuntarily started to smile, but the pain in his jaw halted him. His eye was drawn to the man crouched in the center of the front row, who peered up toward the camera from under the sweep of his dark hair as though a burden made it difficult for him to fully lift his head and shoulders. Vassily.

Yuri returned the photograph to its spot on the wall. On sagging shelves behind his boss's cluttered steel desk leaned volumes of detailed maps maintained by the Brigade. The maps showed the access roads and rivers of course, but also power lines, mining railroads, gas and oil pipelines, construction sites. They also marked what areas in the Buffer zone were licensed, by whom, and for what purpose. Perhaps he could find a clue within.

Dr. Katanabe and Samuel had said the site would be remote. Removed from human habitations. Out in the vastness of the Sikhote-Alin, that didn't exactly whittle down the possibilities.

The most likely area seemed to be somewhere west or north of the *zapovednik*. There were too many little towns and villages and podunk farmers along the eastern edges, near the Sea of Japan. Too much mining on the southern edge. Over on the west there were some logging operations, but north of Melnichnoye the people thinned out. Aside from the remnants of the Udege, an indigenous people native to the region from long before the arrival of the Russians. Hunters, gatherers of pine nuts and ginseng roots.

Too far north and the network of access roads tapered

away, became passable in the summertime only, and then outright disappeared.

Yuri opened the first volume of maps. Began paging through.

The cubs would need room to roam. Not immediately, but eventually. In a couple of months or so. They would need limits—a fence, a wall, a pen of some sort—to keep them from straying too far, and to keep them apart from predators such as bears, or even other tigers, that might scent these little ones. There would have to be a den for them, and a place where they could be fed. This was the part of the "training" that Yuri couldn't visualize—if they were to be fed, how were they to learn to hunt for themselves? If they were to be sheltered, how were they to learn to fend for themselves? He understood that this was the transition that every cub would have to make in the wild as well, from cub to juvenile to young adult. But how would this woman teach them this in the absence of their mother?

But there would still be at least two people living there. And humans required water, food, and shelter. In the harsh winter of Primorsky Krai, that meant buildings. Semi-permanent quonsets at a minimum. Electricity, plumbing, telephone wires—these weren't strictly necessary, but he considered them highly likely. An access road, to get them in and out, and for regular resupply.

One by one he pulled map books from the shelf behind Vassily's desk, spread them out over the clutter, leafed through them.

How would they remain a secret? The better question was probably for how long could they hope to remain a secret? They would produce food smells, and food waste. Their own bodily waste, and the accompanying stink. Lights. Music, radio, television—accompaniment for the long, dark nights. Generators, perhaps, for the electricity. Trucks, to bring them supplies. Machinery, at least at first, to excavate earth, build structures, dig fence posts. Diesel engines. Infrastructure. Always easier to use existing roads and power lines and rails than to build new ones.

Meyerhaeusen was underwriting this little experiment. Presumably their pockets were deep. Nonetheless, he had to assume they would be likely to keep the location close to one of their logging operations. To simplify logistics and minimize expenses. That might help narrow down his search.

Even so, he could spend every day for the rest of his life stalking through the woods, and still only cover one percent of the Sikhote-Alin.

It wasn't a needle in a haystack. He was confident he could systematically dismantle a haystack and find said needle in one day. Easily. With or even without a magnet. No—this was a specific pine nut, in a specific pine cone, in an entire hectare of Korean pine trees. And him with nothing more than spiked boots and a leather strap to shimmy up the boles.

In the middle of winter, no less.

THIRTEEN

The clock read 18:43 when he heard movement in the outer office. A door closed. The reflection of his bandages gleamed brightly in the window, turned into a dark mirror by the incandescent bulb overhead and the dark night beyond. Footsteps shuffled to the office door, a shadow stained the glazed glass. A key fumbled in the lock, even though it was not necessary.

Finally the door swung open. Vassily.

His mouth gaped as he took in the small mountain of maps and log books spread out over his desk, and Yuri sitting in his chair behind them. He reached his right hand into the pocket of his coat, and his frown relaxed, his mouth closed.

"*Serzhant Ser'yeznyy*," he said, with a wan smile. "You're back."

Yuri nodded. "I have a request."

Vassily came around to Yuri's side of the desk. He stood near Yuri, glanced at the maps spread out before him. Looked down his nose at Yuri. His eyes were bleary and bloodshot. Several strands of his thinning hair, normally swept sideways over the crown of his head, had freed themselves and dangled like yarn over the ear close to where they grew.

"What's going on here?" His speech was slow. Measured.

His right hand remained dug into his coat pocket. He turned this side away from Yuri, so that his back was to the desk.

"I'd like a new assignment."

"You're on medical leave."

"No longer necessary."

Vassily held out his empty left hand, lifted his fingers several times.

"Come on," he said. "Up. Up."

Yuri stood, but did not move. "Let me show you," he said.

"My desk," Vassily said. A warm blast of ethanol hit Yuri's nostrils. "My goddamn office. How did you—"

Yuri walked around to the other side of the desk, remained standing so he could point to the appropriate map. Vassily took the cover of the topmost volume in his left hand and began to close the book. As he did the maps within began to slide, and then avalanched over each other, until the cover hid them all from sight with a thump. The map books were too bulky and heavy for any man to move with only one hand, so he had to remove his right from the jacket pocket in order to heft the book back up onto its shelf.

As he did, the pocket sagged, revealed an angular bulge. Protection. Was he worried that Yuri might come for him? Or was somebody else making him anxious?

"Go home," Vassily said. He closed another map volume, shelved it. Then another. "Rest. Take more than a week."

"I don't need to rest," Yuri said. "I'm ready to get back to work."

"What we don't need," Vassily said while he continued reshelving the books Yuri had gotten out, "is a wounded man with one arm and one eye running around getting himself into trouble."

Yuri ignored this. He had full use of both eyes. His left arm was weakened, but not incapacitated.

"You heard about the tiger we found?"

"Of course," Vassily said. "Who hasn't?"

"Funny how we found her in an area you said we didn't have to cover."

"Funny how you went against a direct order not to waste your time there."

"Clearly it wasn't a waste of time."

"Even a blind squirrel finds a nut once in a while."

Vassily sat down heavily in his chair; the cushion hissed as his weight sank down into it. He motioned across his empty desk for Yuri to sit opposite him. Yuri remained standing. Vassily shrugged and fished out a pack of Marlboro Lights. He began to extend it across the desk, but before Yuri could decline the offer he retracted the pack. He pulled a cigarette free, rapped the end against the pack, and lit it. Exhaled a plume of gray smoke that filled the air between the two men, slowly rising toward Yuri's face.

"Listen, my friend. You are a hero."

He pulled open the shallow central drawer, removed a manila folder. He held it up.

"I filed my report, with the Home Office. I can't make any guarantees—you know how it is—but if there is any justice in the world you'll be in line for the Civilian Order of Freedom."

Yuri stared at Vassily through the drifting smoke. He let loose another plume with a faint hiss, knocked the growing ash into an overflowing ashtray. Vassily returned the folder to his desk drawer.

"Regardless of what the Home Office decides, you're a hero. Everybody in the Brigade is talking about you, and these cubs. Everybody in this goddamn town. So go home. Rest. Recuperate. Bask in it a while. I don't want to see you again until you no longer need those bandages. The poachers will still be here when you get back, don't you worry."

Vassily wasn't wrong. He knew that he was in a weakened state. Knew he needed rest.

Vassily cleared his throat. "I'll need your badge while you're on leave."

Yuri reached into his pants pocket, removed his wallet. The only thing it contained, aside from his identification card, was his badge. A circle of pressed tin, the painted-on silver-gilt well-rubbed, the black paint on the Cyrillic letters that spelled out "Sikhote-Alin Anti-Poaching Brigade" flaking.

"It's just protocol."

Yuri set it down on the desk, released it, lifted his hand.

Vassily wouldn't look at him, wouldn't lift his eyes from Yuri's badge. He didn't reach for it, though—his hand had lowered out of sight below the desk. Probably jammed into his coat pocket. In case of trouble.

"You're the only guy in the Brigade who makes taking leave feel like a fight." Vassily said. "Every guy in this sorry-ass outfit would kill to hear me tell them to take a holiday."

"I'm coming back for that," Yuri said.

Vassily stabbed the cigarette into the ashtray, blew a final cloud of smoke over the table.

"It'll be here."

Yuri turned on his heels and left Vassily's office. When he had rifled Vassily's desk looking for clues about the cubs' eventual destination, he'd found a manila folder in the central drawer. The same folder that Vassily had waved in the air, the one that he said contained the After Action Report detailing their encounter with Tatiana, typed up for the Home Office.

Only when Yuri had opened it, the folder had been empty.

As empty as the man's words.

"*Serzhant!*"

Vassily's shout brought him up short just as he reached the front door. His boss's voice boomed through the open door to his office, echoed through the lobby.

"Go somewhere warm. Find yourself a nice piece of ass."

Yuri shook his head as he pushed out into the night. He had what he needed. Three medium scale maps depicting Meyerhaeusen logging concessions in the Buffer Zone along the western edge of the *zapovednik*. One of which contained a cluster of rectangles and squares marked with the words *krasnyy olen'*. "Red Stag."

"Take a goddamn vacation for once in your life!"

FOURTEEN

December 21, 2000—Cubs three weeks old

Yuri stopped skiing for a moment to check his compass, to make sure they were still heading east by southeast. Since leaving their snowmobile along the maintenance road that followed the oil pipeline, they'd been skiing through old-growth Korean pines, tall, evenly spaced, crowns swaying high above. Now that he was stopped, now that his breathing had calmed, the columns and the stillness reminded him of the old mosque in Jalalabad, where Kamal had taken him to teach him the ways of Islam. Properly oriented, Yuri pocketed the compass. His sweat froze in the stillness.

He dug his poles into the snow, shrugged out of his T-frame backpack, rested it against a tree trunk. Strapped to the pack was a rifle: a Great Patriotic War-era five-shot bolt-action Mosin-Nagant 91/30 that Evgeny had smuggled out of the Brigade's temporary evidence warehouse in Terney. Before leaving, Yuri had disassembled the gun and given it a thorough cleaning, attached the PSO-1 scope that he'd used through most of Afghanistan and all of Chechnya, and zeroed it in. Now he raised the stock to his shoulder, brought his eye to the telescopic sight, and slowly pivoted, moving the crosshairs through the trees, searching the stillness for any movement, for any signs of life.

Soon the crisp *schuss* of Evgeny's skis broke the silence, followed by the wheezing huff of his breathing. Yuri had also stopped to wait for his friend. In addition to the T-frame backpacks that both men wore, Evgeny dragged a pulk behind him: a plastic sled loaded with two duffel bags full of supplies and tools. He had volunteered to pull it through the woods, and Yuri had gratefully accepted. He was recovering well from his injuries, but he was sore, and his exertions with the ski poles had caused a dark stain to blossom across the bandage around his forearm. The bandage covering his cheek had loosened. He lowered the rifle, returned it to its place on the pack, barrel pointing down so the stock wouldn't interfere with his ski poles as he drove them into the snow.

When Evgeny reached Yuri, he stabbed his poles into the snow and shrugged out of the pulk's nylon and aluminum harness. Sturdy aluminum braces kept the sled a constant distance behind him, prevented it from sliding forward and bumping into the puller on the downhills. There hadn't been many downhills since they'd left the snowmobile behind. If anything they'd been skiing up a gradual incline.

"Let's eat," Evgeny said. He reached for Yuri's backpack.

Yuri grabbed the pack before Evgeny could, and swung it up onto his shoulders. "Not yet," he said. "We're almost there."

"Bastard," Evgeny said. "Slave driver."

"Come on," Yuri said.

"Wait," Evgeny whispered.

He stared at something over Yuri's shoulder. Yuri didn't fall for it though, didn't turn and swing his backpack within his partner's reach.

Evgeny lifted his right hand, pointed into the trees. "Tiger sign."

Yuri turned. Off in the snow-flecked trees, some twenty meters from where they stood, long scars dug into the bark of a tall pine bole, from higher than a tall man could reach down to about the top of a man's head. The magnification of the scope had rendered the markings invisible to Yuri as he had searched the trees earlier. Evgeny loosed a low whistle.

The two men kicked out of their skis and trudged through the shin-deep snow to investigate, gathered around the tree. Strips of bark had been flayed away from the trunk, long gouges dug into the bole, a few curls of bark hung loosely suspended. Yuri knew that males scratched the trees to mark their territory, and to sharpen their claws.

"How old?" Yuri asked. There were no tracks in the snow, so the markings were more than a week old, at least. Some of the wood that had been revealed still looked bright, freshly exposed.

Evgeny lifted his nose toward the scratch marks, sniffed. Lowered his nose to the base of the tree, where the tiger would have sprayed a blast of his scent before walking away. He looked at Yuri.

"Not fresh," he said. "But definitely from this winter."

Yuri removed his glove, stretched up to touch the flayed bark, traced the gouges he could reach. He placed his naked palm against the trunk. In the winter the trees slowly hardened, to better withstand the cold. Everything had to adapt to the environment, in order to survive.

The sun was lowering in the sky when they reached the first buildings, distant gray silhouettes partially glimpsed through the trees. Concrete structures, with gentle curves that tapered into sharp points.

They reached a narrow, straight path through the trees, most likely marking an old road. This soon led them out of the forest, to an imposing concrete structure with a domed roof. A pair of large wooden doors at the base seemed small in the tall, window-less wall, even though once they reached the doors, they were easily twice as tall as Evgeny, and twice as wide as the two men standing together. Yuri pushed against one, but it resisted. He put his right shoulder against it, and slowly it groaned open.

The doors opened into a massive space. The floor fell away in terraces, as the ceiling soared high above into shadow. Old couches and stuffed arm chairs were scattered about, some arranged around low tables, some paired up, others overturned. Light filtered down into the dim space from a wall of curved windows on the far side of the hall.

They kicked out of their skis. Evgeny dragged the pulk through the doors, then shrugged out of the harness. They helped each other ease their packs down from weary, aching shoulders.

Evgeny put his back against the door, pushed it shut with a clang, and then slid down it until he was sitting, legs splayed. His head tilted back, thudded against the door.

"If you see the angel of death, kick me," he said. He winked. "Or when the vodka comes out."

Yuri grabbed his and Evgeny's packs and dragged them down the tiers to the center. An enormous chandelier of multi-colored globes hung down from the distant ceiling, suspended over what seemed to be a circular wading pool, now filled with debris and brightly colored yellow and orange and red shards of the globes that had broken.

His breath steamed in the air. They were sheltered from the wind, but the cavernous room was not heated.

The far end of the hall was dominated by an enormous fireplace, one of those that you might expect to see in a royal's winter retreat or a hunting lodge, large enough for a person to enter and walk around in. Flagstones spread out in front of the fire area, and reached up the wall to form the chimney. Along the base of that wall a tarp covered what seemed to be a secondary wall, varying from waist to chest high. Yuri pulled back a flap of the tarp, revealing neatly stacked firewood.

Convenient, he thought as he transferred some of the wood to the hearth, set about lighting a fire. The wood, like the tiger markings, didn't look or smell like it had been chopped yesterday—but it didn't look as old or abandoned as the rest of the furniture. The fireplace, too, had been swept free of ash. Somebody else had been using this place, and regularly enough to lay in a supply of firewood. He soon had a small pile of kindling burning, placed a few logs in the iron rack above the licking flames.

"What is this?" Yuri asked. His voice echoed in the dim emptiness, fell away. "Where are we?"

"A relic of the Soviet era." Evgeny said, his voice faint from across the hall. He stood near a low countertop that faced the doors. He leaned back, stared up at the wall behind the counter.

Yuri climbed the terraces to join his friend. A painted plaster bas-relief dominated the wall that faced the entrance. The sculpture started behind the low counter and then stretched up toward the ceiling. In the fading light from the windows, he could make out four youths, evenly spaced, facing out but looking up, rather than down on Yuri and Evgeny. They looked up at a circular window high above. They seemed to salute it, or reach for it, even. He craned his head back, but had a hard time making out the details far above in the shadows. He tried to imagine how on a summer's day light pouring in from the wall of windows opposite would brightly illuminate the frieze, and the window above would fill with radiance, representing the sun, perhaps. A stand-in for the glorious leader.

Evgeny spread his arms, and turned around in the empty space surrounding them. "An old sanitarium, I'm guessing, for Party families. A place to spend your state-mandated holiday. A place to refresh and rejuvenate after all the work and sacrifices you had made to further the work of the Party. Summer camp where proles can mix with Party members."

His voice echoed down the terraces. To the left and right of the counter small dark openings led deeper into the building. Yuri wanted to explore, but he knew that it would be pitch black within soon, and he was famished. He returned to the fireplace.

The blaze began to crackle, and Yuri shucked his overcoat. Evgeny appeared at the edge of the red firelight, stepped closer, took off his gloves, rubbed his hands together and laid his gloves near the blaze. He retrieved an overstuffed armchair and dragged it to the hearth, where he lifted the cushion, inspected it, turned it over, and sat down in a puff of dust. He sighed, then sneezed.

Yuri sat on the flagstones, close to the fire. From his pack he extracted two boxed meals. He tossed one to Evgeny, followed by a fork. They gulped down their first substantial food of the day.

After, Yuri took off his boots and his socks. He stretched the soles of his feet out toward the heat, wriggled his toes. Spread his wool socks out so they could dry. Soon a jumble of hats and gloves and scarves and socks and even underlayers festooned the broad black stones, like the tattered tents and banners of an occupying army laying siege to a castle that they had already set ablaze.

"This place was to remind everybody of the ideal world we were building," Evgeny said, his voice quieter as he chewed and mulled.

A simpler time, Yuri thought. It still struck Yuri as strange to consider the Soviet Union as being in the past, but that was reality.

What had happened to Communism? To the ideal of the commune, the community, the shared spirit, the shared goals? He had grown up relatively isolated, but after he was sent to the Yakutsk Home for Boys when he was twelve, the schooling had been full of Communist indoctrination and propaganda. As a young man in Afghanistan, he struggled to understand how it was that the Afghanis did not all embrace these same ideals, as he came to learn about the ideologies that competed with Communism in the world. It was only under the Major's tutelage that he began to understand the concepts of "indoctrination" and "propaganda."

Then, in a few short years, it was all washed away. Many of the monuments and most of the ideals. Why? Major Iliakov said that Capitalism had won. But what did he mean? How had Capitalism overthrown the old Soviet Union without firing a shot? Were all the lessons he had learned, all the values that had been instilled in him, were they all worthless? Were they inherently weaker than Capitalist values? Or was it simply that the temptation of money was so strong? He had never understood that temptation. But he had seen plenty of men—women as well—in its thrall. Why did the coming of Capitalism mean that places like this would be abandoned, to one day collapse into ruin and disappear from memory? He didn't understand.

"A simpler time," Evgeny echoed his thoughts. "Which isn't to say easier."

FIFTEEN

Gray light filtered into the room from the milky, mildewed windows, seeped through layers of grime, through the cloud of fine dust that hung in the air. Yuri felt as though he and his still-sleeping comrade were lying on the bottom of a lake, where the light could barely penetrate to their depth.

The cavernous hall was cold again. He climbed out of his sleeping bag, added kindling to the embers, blew gently until they caught, and then added more logs. Evgeny shifted and stirred, did not seem inclined to fully wake up.

He dressed and set out to explore the silent hulk of a building. He shivered as he moved from the hearth, into the early morning gloom of the cavernous space. It was cold, of course, his breath still steamed in the air, mingling with the ghosts of Soviet apparatchiks and their families.

He stopped in front of the low counter, stared up at the crumbling frieze. In the morning light he could see it more clearly: it didn't depict four young men, as it had seemed to him the night before. It depicted a family—father and daughter on the left, looking up and to the right; mother and son on the right, looking up and left. The window at the center of their attention was not the sun, but a ball of some sort. Their arms were upraised not in salute or worship, but in trying to keep the ball in the air. Each figure had a knee bent, a foot raised: was it a soccer ball? That seemed awfully European. A balloon? Too frivolous. He'd mistaken it for a sun the night before, a symbol of the glorious leader, and that was certainly still appropriate, especially in the way all of the family members were giving it their rapt attention.

Much of the plaster had crumbled away, but enough remained of the girl's pigtails, the boy's shorts, the father's broad shoulders and the mother's bright kerchief holding her hair. He stepped to the dust-covered counter. A mound of fallen plaster of various colors and shapes and sizes had built up on the floor and along the wall behind.

"Checking in?"

Evgeny stood beside him.

"You will enjoy yourself, comrade," he said, in mock-stentorian tone. "Recreation is required for the health of the Soviet state. You and your wife will procreate as well, for the People's future."

Yuri smiled. Even in Yakutsk, he, too, had seen his share of these Soviet-era installations.

"Get your coat on," Yuri said. He was already wearing his, unzipped. He had his cap and gloves in his hand. "Let's see if we're in the right place."

They skied past several low single-story buildings. Through darkened windows they could make out metal bedframes and slumping stacks of mattresses. Children's dormitories, they guessed. They moved past a larger, several-story monolithic building. A gymnasium. One wall consisted entirely of windows, and when they pressed their hands and faces against the plate glass they could make out an empty swimming pool, black lane lines painted on the sloping floor, two diving platforms towering above. They then passed a cluster of smaller separate wooden buildings with peaked roofs that looked like summer dachas.

Yuri stopped. He'd caught a faint scent of something burning. Not wood-smoke—or at least not purely.

"Do you smell that?" he asked.

"No—but I can see it."

Evgeny pointed beyond the buildings, toward a thin

column of black smoke streaming up into the gray morning sky. At least three or four kilometers distant, Yuri guessed.

The smoke led them from the sanitarium complex and across a flat, open space several square hectares broad and long, with a stand of low, bushy pine trees lining the far end. The smoke lifted from the other side of the trees. The two men skied through a single rectangular soccer goal that remained standing in the snow, somewhat camouflaged by what was left of the white paint curling away from the rusted metal posts beneath. They were crossing athletic fields. Soon they were both warm.

They kicked off their skis and entered the trees, pushed their way through the close branches. They came to a fence of slim vertical iron bars spaced maybe a hand's-width apart. Beyond the fence a gentle slope fell away into a basin full of fresh snow. On the far side of the basin, maybe a kilometer away, sprawled a stone-and-wood two-story hunting lodge and a sway-backed barn. Nearby squatted a pair of rounded quonset huts that seemed out of place.

Yuri knelt, and stretched himself out on his belly in the snow. Evgeny squatted beside him. Yuri pointed the rifle toward the buildings, sighted through the scope, slowly settled the crosshairs on the lodge.

"Looks like it dates from the time of the czars," Evgeny said.

Yuri believed he was probably right. Red Stag seemed an appropriate name for a royal's hunting cabin.

He made a broader scan of the far horizon, found the source of the smoke. Along a stretch of black fence, presumably the same fence they were lying behind, four workmen stood near a barrel-contained bonfire. The fence had collapsed. A snowcat was parked not far away, the telltale "M" logo painted on its door. A flatbed trailer hitched to the snowcat contained black metal poles and a tightly wound cylindrical coil of chain link fencing.

He handed the rifle to Evgeny.

"They're repairing the fence," Evgeny said, after

watching through the scope for a time. "The bonfire is to thaw the ground so they can drive in a new support post."

He handed the gun back to Yuri.

"Looks like you made a good guess," Evgeny said.

Yuri nodded. The tigers would eventually need some space to roam, but within limits. A fence to keep them from getting out into the taiga, and to keep other tigers from getting in. He shifted the sight back to the lodge and the barn, but could detect no movement or signs of life. Still, the activity at the fence was a positive sign.

"No fires in the daytime," Yuri said. He backed into the trees before standing up. "We don't want to give our presence away as easily as they have. We don't want to spook them."

"I need some coffee," Evgeny said. "Even if it is instant."

"We'll use the butane burner." He'd been hoping to conserve its precious fuel, but he knew how his friend relied as much on coffee in the morning as he did on vodka in the evening. They trudged back through the trees to collect their skis.

They'd found it. The Project. He hadn't seen the tigers, or any sign of Dr. Katanabe or Dr. Stasevich, but he was sure of it.

After a breakfast heated over a butane flame, they returned to the cluster of summer dachas. They found one whose windows and doors were still intact, whose roof hadn't collapsed, that wasn't water damaged or overrun by vermin.

None of the dachas were insulated or winterized. The sanitarium had been designed for summer use. Among their gear they had a collapsible saw, a hammer, a mallet, various screwdrivers, a manual drill driver, a heavy steel file, a box of nails and a box of wood screws. Lastly he pulled out his old entrenching tool: the *spetsnaz* spade. This appeared to be an ordinary military entrenching tool: short wooden handle, squat shovel blade. He'd used it to dig foxholes and shelters all through Afghanistan and Chechnya. However, all three sides of the shovel blade had been sharpened. *Spetsnaz* soldiers prided themselves on their ability to use the small shovel as a weapon, both in hand-to-hand combat and as a deadly hurled missile. They trained ceaselessly with the spade, more than with knives or any other hand-to-hand weapon. They staged competitions to see who could dig the fastest, who could throw the most accurately, who could split the thickest log. The spade became an extension of their bodies, a third hand.

Yuri hadn't hefted his spade since he'd arrived in the Sikhote-Alin. It felt natural in his hand.

Each dacha had two rooms downstairs—a living area and the kitchen—and two bedrooms upstairs. Yuri decided that they would seal off the kitchen from the rest of the house, so that he could use the brick and iron oven to heat the small space at night.

They salvaged what they could from the upstairs bedrooms and from nearby dachas. Several mattresses that hadn't been turned into nests or otherwise savaged by vermin they dragged into the living room and cut open, to use the stuffing to chink any gaps in the wooden walls. They tacked blankets and batting up against the walls, then stretched and hammered down strips of the cotton ticking to hold the insulating layers in place. One mattress they left intact for Yuri to sleep on. They took it outside and beat a decade or two of dust out of it.

The kitchen's two windows were still intact, and smaller than those in the larger rooms in the rest of the house. Even so, they filled one windowsill with more of the batting, held it in place with cotton ticking, and then nailed boards from a disassembled table across the opening. Daylight would only enter through one window—south-facing, fortunately—but that would give the cold only one entrance point as well. At night he could fit wadded up blankets into that window as well, if needed.

They found a stash of wool blankets in one closet, and they shook these out, and spread several layers down over the linoleum floor. From the main building's kitchen they retrieved four metal baking trays. Three they spread over the blankets around the base of the brick oven, to catch any stray sparks. The fourth they placed just inside the exterior door, to hold the supply of firewood they would transfer from the entrance hall to the dacha.

"Not bad," Yuri said. He stepped back into the center of the small room and turned about. At the outset they had lit a small fire to be sure the oven and the flue worked, but then they had let it die, so as not to give away their presence. Even so, by working steadily the men had warmed enough to strip down to their undershirts.

"A padded cell," Evgeny said. "For the resident lunatic."

Yuri laughed.

"Let's eat," Evgeny said. They had worked without a break for lunch. The day was drawing to a close.

"We still have work to do." He wanted to move as much firewood from the enormous stash they had found in the entrance hall over to the dacha as they could.

From his backpack Evgeny produced a bottle of vodka, a garish label depicting a pair of Russian knights riding horseback side-by-side, one on a white horse, the other on a red horse that had faded to orange. Russkaya.

"To ward away the cold," Evgeny said. He unscrewed the cap and took a slug, wiped his mouth and beard with the back of the hand that held the bottle. He handed it toward Yuri, who waved it away.

Evgeny shrugged. "Suit yourself." He took another quick pull before recapping the bottle.

They returned to the entrance hall, where they carried armfuls of chopped wood to the pulk waiting in the snow, returned twice for more, and then each took one of the lashes and threw it over his shoulder. The dark dormitory windows watched them blankly as they dragged their weighty burden through the snow.

SIXTEEN

"Let's think about this," Evgeny said when they reached the dacha that would be Yuri's home for the foreseeable future. "I mean, you know this is crazy—right?"

"And you realize how easy it would be for a couple of men to walk in there and take the cubs, right?" Yuri stood in the doorway and Evgeny straightened and handed an armload of split logs up to him. "It's just the woman and the veterinarian."

"Don't forget about the workmen, fixing the fence," Evgeny said.

"Unarmed."

"You don't know that."

"Untrained." Yuri stacked the logs. "They're not going to stick their necks out. And they'll be gone as soon as their work is done."

Evgeny handed him more wood.

"Why do you have to be the one to stick his neck out?"

"Because that's my job."

"Oh? And who's paying you?"

"Just because I'm not getting paid—"

Evgeny lifted the emptied canvas pulk and smacked loose fragments of bark onto the matted snow.

"For once we know where the tigers we're trying to

protect actually are," Yuri said, as he stacked the last load of logs. "That leaves a much smaller area to patrol."

"In the dead of winter."

"I'll be fine."

"Oh? You think it will be easy?"

"I didn't say that." He closed the door behind him. It closed silently, as they had lined the jamb with strips of wool. He stood on the top of the two steps, and still was only just taller than his friend.

"You're used to Mother Russia providing your food and drink, your shelter and medicine," Evgeny said. "Sure, it's often not enough, and it's never very good. But it's something. You run into trouble out here, there won't be anybody coming to the rescue. The taiga will swallow you."

"I can handle myself," Yuri said.

"You think you're just going to be skiing around? You're going to run through this firewood in no time. And then you're going to have to go out and chop more."

"So I'll do that."

"And when you run out of food?"

"I can hunt. I can trap."

"So now you're hunting, you're trapping, you're cutting firewood, melting drinking water. The days are short. You won't be keeping watch for poachers. You won't give a damn even about those cute little tiger cubs—if they ever even come here. You'll be shivering and thinking about your empty belly."

"Are you my partner?" Yuri asked. "Or my mother?"

Evgeny stabbed a piece of kindling toward Yuri. He blocked it aside with his right, but not before it had touched his coat, punched into his chest.

"You think you're going to save the day for this fancy doctor lady. Is that what you think?"

The larger man tossed the wood to Yuri. The piece was roughly sheared flat, a couple of hand lengths long, a few centimeters across. The size of a large knife.

Evgeny swung another, larger piece at Yuri's left cheek,

his good cheek. He raised up the piece of kindling to block, but not before Evgeny had tagged his cheek.

"Wha—"

"Not fast enough."

"I wasn't ready."

"Exactly. Because you're dreaming. 'Oh, Yuri, you're my hero. Come stay in my bed.'"

He swung again, this time at Yuri's left forearm. Yuri yanked his arm back, and the wooden sword whistled past. Yuri winced as his barely healed wounds strained to contain the blood and tissue beneath, disturbed by the sudden pendulum swing of his arm.

Evgeny pressed the attack. The wooden pieces clacked together when Yuri managed to block Evgeny's swing, though mostly he tried to dodge. On one parry, Evgeny's machete-sized piece of wood rapped Yuri hard across the knuckles wrapped around his own wooden blade.

He shifted the wood to his left to shake out his right hand, but Evgeny did not relent, forcing Yuri to defend with his left. This he found painful, each shock of wood coming together jarred the puncture wounds in his forearm.

He ducked one wild, heavy swing that would have knocked him cold had it landed, and moved into the larger man, kicked his legs apart, wrapped his arm around Evgeny to hip throw him. But he couldn't get the proper leverage in the snow or with his weakened left arm, and Evgeny stood stock still, then picked Yuri up by the trousers and dumped him down. Fortunately he did so in a fresh drift of snow that softened his landing.

Still, he struggled to catch the breath the impact forced from his lungs, and before he could get up Evgeny was pressing the attack, striking down hard with the piece of timber. Yuri struggled to shift to the side and get to his feet, but now the deep snow that had cushioned his landing obstructed his movement. Each blow that landed did so with force, on his gut, his thighs, his shins once he pulled his legs up, even painfully on the crown of his head, and with each blow Evgeny called out, "Dead! Dead! Dead!"

"Okay," Yuri said. "Okay! I get the point!"

Evgeny relented, but as soon as Yuri relaxed, the piece of wood was driven like a stake down onto his sternum. Evgeny leaned down on it with his full weight, driving Yuri down deeper into the snow. His attacker's black beard blotted out the sky, his reddened nose and bloodshot eyes filled Yuri's vision.

"Evgeny," Yuri gasped, both hands on the piece of wood, but unable to budge it. The weight was making breathing difficult.

"No time-outs in the taiga." Evgeny wagged his head side to side above Yuri, with a maniacal grin.

Yuri hooked his toe around Evgeny's heel, pulled his leg forward. He wrapped his other leg in front of the exposed knee and pushed. The uncomfortable hyperextension forced Evgeny awkwardly back, relieved the pressure from the wood. Now Yuri slammed his calf and heel across his friend's chest and sternum, knocking him back into the snow. Soon he had his hands around Evgeny's boot, wrenched him around until he was face down in the snow, with Yuri sitting on top of him, facing his friend's legs. He pulled the heel toward his friend's backside, with his own leg tucked behind Evgeny's knee, threatening to dislocate the joint.

Evgeny's panicked scream was muffled by the snow. His arm flailed behind him trying to tap Yuri, to get him to stop.

Yuri released him, stood to his feet. Rubbed his chest where the wood had borne down.

Evgeny slowly straightened his knee, made sure he still had use of it, massaged the joint.

"Point taken," Yuri said.

"Fuck off," Evgeny said. "I didn't even go after your face. Even though it's an obvious weak point."

"I know," Yuri said.

Evgeny rolled over onto his back, reached out his hand. Yuri helped him to his feet.

"Where's that Russkaya?" Yuri asked, as he massaged his own sternum.

"Now we're talking," Evgeny said.

In the morning, Evgeny and Yuri skied back to the power line maintenance road, to the place where they had left the snowmobile hidden beneath pine branches.

"Take care of yourself," Evgeny said. He rested his hand on Yuri's shoulder. "You're not as strong as you ought to be."

"Not yet." He knew his friend was right. "I'll be careful."

Yuri turned and skied back the way he had come, through the tall, silent Korean pines, back to the sanitarium complex. Back to the empty buildings, inhabited only by the mute, invisible ghosts of commissars and patriots past.

Snow began to fall. Soon their tracks would be filled in, erased. Soon Yuri, too, would be little more than a ghost.

SEVENTEEN

The tiger glided like a ghost through the trees, through the faint starlight. He patrolled languidly, trampling the fresh snow. He stopped at a tall pine, the lower trunk bare of branches. He used to be able to raise himself up on his rear legs to his full height all in one smooth motion, but not anymore. The ember that burned deep within his breast prevented that. Now he had to grab the tree with his claws and climb his way up to standing. A painful process, but necessary, to stake his claim, to ward away any younger males who might seek to challenge him. He didn't smell any, but that didn't mean he could lower his guard or cease his vigilance. He had to mark the trees on his route, had to place the claw marks high on the trunk, so any who might follow in his wake would see his magnitude, would grasp his full length, would understand immediately that this was a territory that was out of bounds, off limits. Beyond all pretenders.

He dug his claws into the bark, peeled back strips and shreds of tree. The claw marks not only needed to be high up the bole, they needed to be deep, they needed to prove the strength and length of his claws, their keen sharpness, the breadth of his grasp, the strength of his grip. He bore down with his weight through his forearms—a trick he had learned, over the years, to dig his marks even deeper—but leveraging his weight through his shoulders like this caused him to cough, a harsh bark, as the ember in his breast began to glow white hot. He dug through the pain. His mark the symbol of his strength. No—his mark *was* his strength. He had never left a shallow mark, and he wasn't going to start now.

Satisfied, he freed his claws and dropped his forepaws to the ground with a thud that jarred the burning within, caused him to cough again. He turned his hindquarters to the tree and lifted his tail clear, sprayed the trunk with his scent. A final warning to those so bold, or so foolish, as to have ventured this far within his woods.

His territory not so vast as it once was. When he roamed too far the ember burned brighter, hotter, impinged further on his lungs. Wormed its way closer to his heart. But because he did not range so far did not mean that he could be trifled with.

He demanded respect. He inspired fear. He was Khagan. The King of Kings.

He followed the smell of smoke through the trees. To the place where the two-legs used to live, before this territory was his. When he was younger he'd claimed these buildings as his own, even though their smells were so fresh, so powerful, so frightening. No other tiger would go near it. He conquered his fear, and made this man-haunted place his own.

A two-legs had returned. Trying to make his own claim. He was a clever one. Shy. Sly. Khagan knew well that the stick he carried over his shoulder shot lightning, brought death. His ember had come from such a stick. Two-legs used it to bring death to animals. Also carried it as a totem, to ward death away from the one who carried it.

He walked among the mazy walls. Came to stand next to the wall behind which this new man slept. He opened his nostrils. The mellow odor of wood burning low, covered in ash. The smell of this creature, this aberration, asleep, unsuspecting. And yet. Underneath that even. Another scent. Unrecognizable. Yet familiar.

He heard the man roll over, stand up. The smell of fresh

wood added to the fire, the sound of flames licking the bark, curling strands of pine. The limpid ring and the pallid tang of the man making his thin, weak water. How was it that Khagan had to fear—no, respect the better word, Khagan feared no animal, on four legs or two—how was it that he had to respect such a weakling?

It was the lightning stick. And the unforgiving snares. The fires. The metal machines. All his unholy tools.

The tiger moved on from the challenger's lair. Out in the open now, a dark shadow sliding over the gray snow that faintly reflected the stars crowding the sky above. He came to the fence that blocked his way and moved along it, staying wide of those places where the fires had raged, releasing their greasy black gouts into the sky, even though he knew these fires were the pets of men, hungry cubs with widening maws and grasping orange paws and flickering blue tongues.

So many fires lately. So many two-legs in his forest. Unusual behavior, even for these strange creatures.

EIGHTEEN

January 4, 2001—Cubs five weeks old

Two weeks had passed since Yuri's arrival in the sanitarium.

The business of survival and staying warm overwhelmed him. Evgeny had been right. It was not easy. There was always more to do, and it left him little time for patrolling the perimeter. Although he'd been hunting since he was old enough to hold and fire a gun—which his father had taught him how to do when he was six years old—he'd found precious few signs of game. The times when he had sat in a blind watching over days-old deer tracks had proved fruitless.

He knew that even though the sanitarium was abandoned, it was likely that the scent of man was still heavy in that place, scaring animals away. If he could venture further afield, perhaps he might be able to find a group of deer, a wild boar. But that would mean skipping some of his other daily duties, to ensure that he had enough firewood and water to last the night. Would mean forgoing the exercises that he needed to rebuild his strength. There were only so many hours available in these short winter days.

The cold was unrelenting. In the morning, his head often hurt, from shivering after the fire had gone out. He would throw more of his precious logs into the embers, wait anxiously for them to catch. His very bones ached from the cold.

Why could he not be more like a tiger? Able to cover kilometer after kilometer, tirelessly, effortlessly, big paws padding like snowshoes, aided by superior senses of smell and hearing and night vision.

Today, he was determined to find game. If that meant pushing beyond his usual patrol, so be it. He headed east through the forest until he reached a metal sign bolted to a tree with red letters marking the boundary of the Core, warning all to turn back before entering a prohibited zone. The bolts had rusted, the lettering faded. He turned and skirted along the edge of the Core. His legs were more powerful, his stamina much improved.

He was "reading the white book," as hunters in the Sikhote-Alin called it. Stalking through the snow-filled forest, carpeted and clothed in white, blank page after blank page, white ink invisible against the white paper. But there were ways to read this book, passages to decipher. Scat, spoor, hoof-prints or pugmarks in the snow, perhaps signs of tree scratching or rutting. Once the hunter found these signs, in sufficient abundance and of recent enough vintage for him to suppose that more creatures of this kind might pass through this area in the near future, only then would he construct his blind. Then the waiting game would begin.

He did find some tracks. But not animal tracks. Human bootprints.

He knelt, inspected. The ridges were sharp, clearly defined, rather than rounded, eroded by wind and evaporation—fresh tracks. A day old, maybe less. Three men. Pulling a sled behind, but the runners did not dig deep ruts into the snow—unladen.

A small hole in the snow off to the side of the tracks drew his attention. He unsheathed his knife, used the blade to slowly widen the hole, excavating down until he found what had been tossed aside: a cigarette butt. An American brand. Not much of a clue, except that the men had expensive tastes. He held the butt close, observed the beige residue of chemicals the filter had kept from the man's lungs. He put the butt to his nose: a faint but acrid tang of smoke. These footprints were barely more than a day old. Any longer in this cold and the cigarette smell would have vanished, at least to his nose.

These men were headed into the Core of the *zapovednik*. The heart of the nature preserve. Strictly forbidden to humans.

He remained crouched, slowly scanned through the forest around him. Larches and pines surrounded him, but not the tall Korean pines he'd grown accustomed to—these were the shorter, squat sort that branched out near the ground, that blocked visibility, made hiking difficult. A perfect place to build a blind and lie in wait for their return. Assuming they would return the way they came.

Or should he follow them into the Core? That would mean that he, too, would be trespassing, without a permit, without paperwork. With his rifle on his shoulder, he would look as suspicious as anybody else who might be found violating the Core. Not that he expected to be challenged in this remote place.

What if they were scientists on official business? Rather than poachers, as he was assuming? Either way, they had a day's lead on him. He wasn't going to catch them.

Perhaps he should follow against the trail, back to the snowmobiles or snowcat that he presumed had brought them here. Possibly waiting at the same power line access trail that had brought him and Evgeny to the sanitarium.

Hunters don't try to catch up to their prey. They lie in wait. And men typically leave the woods the same way they came in. Following their own footsteps like a trail of breadcrumbs leading them from the labyrinth. The danger is that others can find those crumbs as well.

Yuri broke a branch from a nearby fir, began sweeping snow over his own tracks. Erased the marks he'd left as he approached the trail. Then he walked parallel to the trail, up a small slope, until he had the high ground. He paused with every step to sweep the snow behind him with the branch. It wouldn't stand up to close scrutiny, but would deceive the casual glance.

He found what he was looking for a hundred meters on: a close stand of firs off to the side of the trail, but with a clear view down over it. The trees had forced the men to curve around them, in fact. Still sweeping with the branch to obscure his own tracks, he went around to the other side of the cluster of seven trees. He got down on his knees, and worked his way in and under the lowest branches. Some snow had managed to filter through, but there was only a thin layer of the white stuff on the ground. He brushed it away and set up his little pup tent, covered it with a dark green poncho, to match the trees and provide some insulation. He positioned the opening to face downhill, so he could keep an eye on the trail without leaving his shelter. The trees' branches sprouted from the trunks almost immediately after clearing the ground, and they inclined toward the ground as they stretched away from their boles. Vertically his view was very narrow, but horizontally he had a good field of vision. He would see them coming long before they saw him. And he ought to hear them as well, with the valley below serving as an echo chamber, bringing any noises they made up the hill.

He lit a candle, put it in his little metal stove to keep it from casting light, and used that to warm the small space inside the tent. Soon he was able to lower his hood, remove his heavy mittens—though not his gloves—and his knit hat. This was the sort of observation post he had often argued they should use along known poachers' trails. But Vassily and the other men had demurred. They didn't want to wait, for hours on end—for days, even—in the cold. They wanted to be closer to a campfire, to warm food, to drink.

It was the sort of suggestion that Yuri had always known would obtain better results. Also the sort of suggestion that had earned him his *Serzhant Ser'yeznyy* nickname.

He laid his Mosin-Nagant down alongside him. He got out his jerked venison, his crackers, his pine nuts. He set his canteen of beef broth on the butane stove, let it absorb the warmth. He kept the tent flaps closed, but unzipped them and peered down the hill on occasion, both with the scope and without.

He would lie in wait, for a time. It would be as difficult for these men to stay in the woods overnight as it would be for him.

He could feel that old sensation, that quickening of the pulse, the high alert of all senses. The war catching up to him again, in this remote place. They could just be hunters. They could be scientists. He could not be sure.

But he was sure. And while he was still technically on the Anti-Poaching Brigade, he was not here in an official capacity. Did not wear the parka with the bright cloth patch on the sleeve. No longer carried his badge. Did that mean that the rules had changed? That he no longer had to obey the rules?

He didn't want violence. He wanted to stay in control. He had the gun. He knew how the poachers worked—if carrying contraband, they would typically leave their weapons behind, so that they could not be blamed for having killed the animal themselves. If they were not carrying contraband, if they were not successful, then he would not have any evidence, any proof of their intentions. And they might well be carrying firearms.

He would have the advantage of surprise. But he would also be outnumbered.

He checked the chamber, the magazine. Checked to make sure the safety was on. Sighted through the scope down over the churned-up snow. Settled in for the long wait.

NINETEEN

January 4, 2001—Cubs five weeks old

Miko Katanabe skied along the matted tracks left by the snowcat the workers used on their daily commute out to the portion of the fence that they were repairing. Through the heavy iron fence on her left she could look down into a shallow, snow-filled basin, dotted with stands of pine trees—the enclosure that would soon be the tigers' territory for the next year and a half, until they reached maturity. To her right, pine trees began to crowd down toward the fence, toward her, slowly encroaching on the black iron. Ahead of her, a dense column of smoke lifted straight into the air. The workmen's bonfire, her destination. Somewhere high above a current caught that dark pillar and smeared and streaked it against the sky, feathered it into the pale blue. She was skiing up a gradual incline, and by the time she reached the plateau at the far end of the enclosure, her heart was thumping in her chest.

"I am—seeing benefits," she huffed. "Improved"—inhale—"lung capacity"—exhale. She wouldn't have been able to make it this far back when she was still smoking. She stopped, leaned forward on her ski poles. *Really ought to be doing this every morning*, she thought. Her evening yoga routine didn't seem to be doing much for her stamina.

Off to the side, a bright twist of red flapped in the wind: a candy bar wrapper. She shook her head, bent to collect this scrap. Who knew what else lay buried under the snow? Once the spring thaw came, the workmen's detritus would reveal itself. Each item's scent would remain. She pocketed the evidence.

Finally she reached the workmen and their bonfire. The foreman, Sergei, had spotted her, in her bright orange parka, as she approached, and trudged through the snow to meet her. To intercept her.

"What brings you out this way, *mèm?*" She hated the way he insisted on calling her ma'am. "It's dangerous."

Earlier that morning she had watched Kamal jumping at the tin-paneled wall of the much smaller paddock where the cubs were allowed out. Every day he came closer to reaching the top with his forepaws. When he finally succeeded he might be able to scramble himself over the top. Or hurt himself in the process. Vida seemed to accept the wall as the limit of her world. But Kamal refused to accept the boundary.

The goddamn workmen should've finished and gone home by now. The cubs should be able to roam in the larger enclosure. When she and Anatoly had arrived with the cubs three weeks ago, the foreman had told her they would be finished in two weeks—"three at the most." Yet here they still were. These cats needed more room. How was the larger fence not finished yet? Only one section—barely even ten meters—remained to be repaired.

"I need to allow the cubs out into the enclosure." She swung her arm out to her left, toward the fence. "And yet here we all are. Still unfinished."

He half turned toward his men. Each man was now a study in concentrated effort, head and shoulders bent to his task, only occasionally attempting to steal a glance at the woman they had nicknamed "tiger lady." She'd overheard the epithet once or twice. She didn't entirely mind it. Hell of a lot better than *mèm*.

"You can see we're all working hard." He waved his hand in their direction. "The ground is frozen solid—"

"How can we move things along?" she asked.

"Aside from bringing on the thaw—"

"It's early January," she said. "Waiting for spring is out of the question."

He glanced back over his shoulder. "Some of the men are spooked."

"By what?"

"Tiger tracks," the foreman said. He spread his hands apart in front of his face. Held them there, slightly wider than his face, even with his bushy beard. Miko felt her eyes widen. "Deep, too," he said. "A heavy one."

"When was this?"

"A little over a week ago," he said. Before she could demand why she had not been informed sooner—though she knew the answer, *we didn't want to alarm you, mèm*—he turned and pointed out beyond the fencing, past the bonfire, added, "And today."

"Show me," she said. She drove her poles into the snow, kicked out of her skis.

He led her past the smoke-spewing bonfire, past the workmen. "Keep at it!" he said as heads lifted. They didn't have far to go. The tracks were visible from the supply trailer. They traced a course parallel to the fence, just within cover of the first line of trees. The workmen had clearcut all trees that grew within five meters of either side of the fence, to keep the cubs from escaping the enclosure by climbing, which they would be able to do very soon, and to keep potential predators from getting into the enclosure by the same means.

She stooped to investigate, careful not to brush snow clinging to low branches into the pugmarks. These were easily the largest paw prints she had ever seen. Prints in fresh snow were less reliable than those in earth or mud, as the snow tended to slip and shift, exaggerating the size. But even so.

"Big, isn't he?" the foreman asked.

"Definitely a male, no question about that." A box that would fit around the prints formed a square, rather than the rectangle, slightly longer than wide, that a female's paws would leave. Some snow had begun to fill in the tracks before the flurries ceased mid-morning. So he had passed this way in the early morning hours, almost certainly while still dark. Less than twelve hours ago. Her heart, which had slowed after her hike, began to thump in her chest again.

"Do you have anything to measure with?"

The foreman pulled a tape measure from a pocket of his parka, handed it to her.

"How about something to write with?"

He had a grease pencil but no paper. She fished out the candy bar wrapper she'd found, carefully split the seams so the white interior could be used to write on. She handed this to the foreman.

"Take notes," she said. She began to measure, calling out names and numbers. The foreman flattened the wrapper against his palm and began to scratch words and numbers as she rattled them off.

"Left forepaw length: nineteen centimeters. Breadth: twenty centimeters. Print depth..." And so on for each paw. She measured the steps—the ground covered by the alternating left forepaw and right forepaw, as well as the left hind paw and right hind paw—and finally the strides, the distances covered by each paw, left forepaw to successive left forepaw, and so on. She noticed that two claws on the rear left paw seemed to be permanently extended, leaving marks in the snow. She noted the lengths of these as well.

The foreman handed her the wrapper, and she folded it carefully and tucked it inside her parka.

"He's a bold one," he said, "to be coming this close."

"It's highly unusual for one to come so near to where people are working," she said. She wondered if perhaps he had caught the scent of the cubs. A male would have no qualms about killing unattended cubs. Both for food, and, in the case of a younger male, to eliminate a potential rival.

They stood up, walked alongside the tracks for a few paces.

"I want to follow," she said.

"What if he's still out there?"

The trail swung away from the fence, headed deeper into the forest. The trees quickly became too dense to allow the snowcat to penetrate. She would have to follow on foot. Much as she wanted to see where the trail led, it would have to wait. She needed to get back to the lab, back to Anatoly.

"You're right," she said to Sergei. "I need to get back."

"I'll drive you." He gestured toward the snowcat.

The return on skis would be much faster, as it would be mostly downhill. But she had to admit that the sight of those tracks had spooked her as well. Had she known of this sighting that morning, she still would have come out—but she would have taken the snowmobile rather than skis.

"I don't want you to lose any more time."

"I'll make sure the lads keep working," he said. He walked among the four men, giving instructions, in his calm, steady voice. He returned to the vehicle, opened the passenger side door for her, then climbed into the driver's seat.

She got in beside him and he fired up the engine. She reviewed the figures he had scrawled on the candy bar wrapper, made sure they were legible.

"By the way, if I find another one of these"—she waved the wrapper—"whoever is responsible will be fired."

He shifted into gear, and the snowcat lurched forward, began to trundle alongside the fence.

"I'll be sure to tell the lads, *mèm*."

TWENTY

The sun arced slowly across the sky, toward a solid bank of clouds. When the clouds had fully swallowed the sun, the day grew darker, but also somewhat warmer, as the humidity rose. There would be snow before long. Heavy snow, it seemed. The sort that would obliterate these tracks. Time to pack it in, before the snow hit. A few large flakes were beginning to drift down lazily through the trees.

He'd made his decision, built his blind, staked out his zone, and it had not paid off. He felt fidgety. He had skipped his morning exercise to be able to cover as much ground as possible, and now the hours of immobility were getting to him. Deep breathing exercises were all well and good, but he needed to move, to sweat, to exhaust himself. So that he could sleep like a dead man at night instead of lying awake, remembering.

A scrape, then a pause.

Scrape, pause.

Scrape...

He slowly parted the tent flaps. Cold air rushed in. Movement, down the hill. He lowered the flap, stretched out on his belly. Lifted the rifle, checked the safety yet again. Steadied his breathing, slowed his pulse. He eased the barrel out through the flaps, until the scope also parted the curtains, fitted his eye to the viewfinder.

They were coming up the hill. Three men. One man leading. Two following, abreast. The men's heavy winter boots stabbed into the hillside, the sledge's metal runners ground through the snow.

He settled the crosshairs on the lead man. He wore a fur-lined hood and mirrored goggles, a scarf wrapped loosely around his chin. He walked with his head cast down, gently inclined toward the trail, placing his feet in the tracks that they had made much earlier in the day.

He shifted to the two behind. They were leaning further forward, almost doubled over, heads bowed toward the trail as they climbed. They strained against straps that stretched back over their shoulders. They pulled a sledge along behind. The source of the scraping, grinding sound. All he could really tell was that one man was larger than the other, and seemed to be having an easier time of it, while the other man's arms flailed and boots scrabbled for purchase in the snow. He could hear them huffing for breath.

The sledge was made of bright blue plastic, like a child's toy, on broad metal-lined runners. On top of the sledge, a bundle, wrapped in a green plastic tarp, held down by bungee cords.

Shhhff... Shhhff... Shhhff...

Poachers. They'd found their target.

In his years in the Sikhote-Alin he hadn't carried a gun, except for the few times in the summers that he and Evgeny had gone deer hunting. Never one to use against people. Not since Chechnya. He appreciated that about the job. That it didn't require him to kill.

But a part of him had always wanted to execute these criminal bastards. Shoot them on sight. Leave their corpses on display along the trails that they used with a sign hung around their necks, painted in their own blood with the single word, **Браконьер**.

Poacher.

That would put a stop to that man's poaching, at least, and strike fear in the hearts of his fellows.

Major Iliakov had mentioned what a team of dedicated, trained professionals, unrestricted by any rules of engagement, would be able to do to unsuspecting poachers. He'd often thought the same thing.

Yes, he'd fantasized about killing these men. Punishing these criminals. But he'd never killed except in war, with explicit or standing orders to do so.

These men were poachers. The bundle on the sledge a tiger's carcass. He knew it as sure as he knew he held a rifle in his hand. Knew it as sure as he knew that if he removed the safety and squeezed the trigger the top of the man's head, where the crosshairs had settled, would disappear.

He shook his head, tried to calm his breathing, to clear the boiling blood from his vision. He had no proof. Only his intuition.

And he was one against three. They were trespassing in his territory, though. Not only that, but they came from inside the Core. These men walked along, heads down, without a care. Accustomed to accessing this area. Probably along this same trail. Using the buildings of the sanitarium as a base from which to access the Core. So how long would it take them to discover the cubs in the enclosure just a couple of kilometers away? They wouldn't care why the cubs were there. They would see them as easy pickings—a gift wrapped in a small paddock of tin, guarded by no one.

Except for him. This was why he was here. He wasn't going to kill these men. He wasn't even going to confiscate their carcass. He would keep tensions low, though he would certainly let them see his gun. To see that he meant business. He would warn them away. Go, and don't come back. Or there will be consequences. The Sikhote-Alin was vast, they could find other places to ply their trade.

He gathered his knees under him. They were close enough now—any closer and they might see him emerge from his blind, might reach for weapons. He'd never attempted an interdiction on his own. Without backup.

Without Evgeny. That went against protocol. Even with the two of them, if they were outnumbered the policy was to make a note, get a license plate, get pictures, collect as much evidence as possible, maybe try to follow, but above all, safety first, interdict later, in force, with the provincial police if needed.

He crawled through the flaps, stood up slowly. His legs were stiff. He rolled his head around his neck to relieve the painful tightness between his vertebrae and his shoulders. He checked the safety again, made sure it was on. Held the rifle below his waist, right glove off but finger away from the trigger, the barrel pointing down and to the left. Ready to raise up at a moment's notice. But it would not come to that. He would be calm. He would project authority, the way Evgeny had taught him, simply inform them that this area was now off limits. Take whatever it is you have collected with you—as a sign of good faith—but don't come back.

They had stopped for a break maybe fifty meters from where he was hidden. They were out of breath. The smaller man with hands on knees, the larger man pulled his scarf down from his face and lit a cigarette. The lead man unscrewed the cap of his canteen. He wondered if it contained water, or alcohol. Or some even more toxic sort of stimulant. Many of the poachers used meth for endurance and to become practically impervious to cold.

Now. He stepped from behind the trees.

"Hello," he called out.

The three men straightened, stiffened. He began to walk down the trail toward them. The lead man looked over his shoulder at the other two, held up his hand toward them, urging them to stay, and to stay calm. He would be the one to address. They waited for him to come closer.

"What brings you into these woods today?" he asked. He stopped about ten meters away.

The lead man eyed the Mosin-Nagant.

"I might ask the same of you," he said. He lifted his goggled eyes from the gun to Yuri's face.

"I'm with the Anti-Poaching Brigade," Yuri said. "But—"

Before he could continue with his explanation, the lead man blurted, "It *is* you! The Monk! I fucking knew it!"

Yuri hadn't heard that nickname in a long time.

The man pointed at his face, at his bandage. "That was you the other day—with your face all torn to shreds! I knew I recognized you! They didn't want to believe me—"

"Do I—" Yuri began.

The man raised his goggles, revealing close-set black eyes. He pulled his scarf down, revealing a trimmed red mustache and goatee, and a broad grin.

Oleg Chernichev. The Ferret.

He looked beyond Chernichev, to the two men behind him. The larger man, with his wispy black beard, his high cheekbones, his narrow black eyes and bushy eyebrows, he recognized from the side of the road where he'd seen Chernichev, after Tatiana. The third man had stood up, but he wore a cashmere face mask and goggles, so Yuri couldn't make out his features. He remembered that the third man standing at the roadside had been shorter, had looked vaguely Korean. This could be that same man. Seemed likely.

How was it that the same three poachers he'd seen near Tatiana, five weeks prior, were now here in these woods?

He took a step back. Were they all *spetsnaz*? He suddenly felt acutely alone. He touched the safety catch with his thumb. His bare hand was beginning to feel the bite of the cold.

TWENTY-ONE

When she arrived back at Control, she found Anatoly reclined in the desk chair, feet up on the table next to the computer monitor, his heels shoving aside her carefully organized notes. Reading a comic book, of all things. A comic book!

As she entered, he lowered his feet. Folded the comic closed and slid it into the gap between his side paunch and the arm rest. She told him about the tiger tracks, and gave him the candy bar wrapper to plot the figures on the laptop.

While Anatoly tapped at the keyboard, she sat in front of the closed-circuit television monitors. "Control" was the name she and Anatoly had given to the portion of the barn's hayloft that the workmen had converted into an enclosed, insulated room. The ground floor of the barn they had divided into the lab and the garage. The lab contained a workbench—an old wooden table that the workmen had salvaged from the lodge—supply cabinets, and the main computer, where Anatoly reviewed and archived the footage recorded on the CCTVs onto DVDs. The garage contained two snowmobiles and the two snowcats the men used to get out to the fence and back.

They had installed darkly tinted windows along the wall that looked out over the paddock—with the larger enclosure spreading out toward the horizon beyond the paddock's low tin walls. A bank of fifteen CCTV monitors, three rows of five, lined another wall. These monitors were connected to cameras mounted on the roof of the barn, the roof of the lodge, and at various points along the iron fencing, facing inward, pointing into the larger enclosure. Most of them were presently dark. Three glowed green. These were connected to light amplification cameras stationed within the cubs' den, an earthwork that abutted the barn, so they would be visible at all times.

The cubs were sleeping in their den, and she watched them on one of the green-tinted light-enhancing cameras. Watched their pulsating flanks, their sleepy grins and grimaces. Her heart began to slow, her breathing became more regular. She felt calmer. This was always the effect of watching the cubs. To the point of feeling drowsy. Partly from her exertions, but also because she was becoming more nocturnal, syncing herself with the tigers' activity. This was partly intentional, partly inevitable. The cubs were snoozing less now, and if she wanted to observe them when they were active, then she had to be awake through much of the night.

Five weeks. Was that all it had been? On one hand, the time had flown by. She found the work entirely absorbing. So much new footage, so much raw data, so many notes to take, so many journal articles to read. Each day she and Anatoly had to calculate the cubs' nutrition and medicine plan, had to plan when to release them into the paddock for exercise and when to call them—with food—into the den to minimize their exposure to the workers' comings and goings, all while keeping it from falling into a steady rhythm, to mimic conditions in the wild. There were no predictable routines in the wild. The cubs' intake had to be steady, of course, to ensure growth and health, but now that they were past four weeks—now that it was clear that they were viable—it was imperative to begin introducing a sense of variety to their diet, and intermittence to their feeding patterns. Every day brought a steady stream of challenges and chores. She loved it. She was in her element.

But when it came to the workmen, time seemed to crawl. She needed them gone. Needed their trash gone. Needed their diesel engine rumblings gone, their chainsaw whines, the black smoke of their bonfires, their rowdy dinners and late-night bawling of drinking songs. Their stink and their noise didn't bother her so much—she was quite used to living and working with men—but she was seeing everything now from the perspective of her two beautiful cats. She was acutely aware of how much they were absorbing, how much they were learning, despite the tin panels lining the paddock fence, to keep them in but also to keep them from seeing out. Their senses of hearing and of smell were of course much more acute than hers. The cubs were well aware of all the nearby activity. They were curious. Well, Vida seemed curious. Agitated might more accurately describe Kamal.

Anatoly leaned back in the chair, scratched his bearded neck. He beckoned Miko over to the computer.

"According to my calculations, that tiger you were following is a very large, very mature male. He must weigh around three hundred fifty kilos, maybe more."

"Wow." Miko leaned forward to inspect his figures. "I knew he was big—"

"Look at this though." Anatoly had used her measurements to model the tiger's gait. "See here? How his left stride is shorter than his right? He's favoring that left front leg. He must have an injured paw."

"Hmm." She leaned back. "I don't think so."

"The computer model—" Anatoly began.

"The impression in the snow is as deep as the others," she said, "so the paw is fully weight-bearing. However, he can't reach it as far forward."

Anatoly frowned, tapped in some adjustments on the keyboard. "Okay, right. An old trauma of some sort?"

"Most likely. You saw that two rear claws are permanently extended?"

"An unrelated injury, I would say." Anatoly scrolled through the model, then leaned back in his chair, shook his head. "I've never seen a cat this big."

"Clearly not intimidated by humans."

"If you saw his tracks within meters of the fence," Anatoly looked up at Miko, "I'd describe him as downright curious."

"Potentially a conflict tiger?"

Amur tigers avoid humans and their habitations. Despite the easy pickings that livestock and domesticated animals—and people themselves, for that matter—might seem to present for a solitary, crafty, ravenously carnivorous predator. Only the very old, the infirm, the injured, unable to hunt game for themselves anymore, dare forsake the mountains and abandon the cover of the taiga in search of easy pickings. Those that do are labeled "conflict tigers."

"Let's just say it's probably a good thing you didn't encounter him on your way there," Anatoly said, with a shake of his head. "I told you to take the snowmobile."

She reserved the snowmobiles for emergency use only. The buzzsaw racket of their two-stroke engines would disturb Kamal and Vida.

"I'm more worried about the threat he might pose to the cubs," she said.

"With the fence in between," Anatoly said, "he might even help them socialize."

Part of her plan—in the summer months, once the snow had lifted and transport vehicles could move more freely—was to bring a captive tiger or two to the enclosure. To introduce the cubs to mature adults. They would keep them separated by fencing, of course, but the sights and smells and interactions would help the cubs learn how to behave when encountering a fellow tiger in the wild. The ability to socialize properly would play a huge part in their ability to survive. Socialization is such an important part of any creature's survivability.

"They're going to flip when they hear of this back at the Polygon," Anatoly said. "I'll send Dr. Carrington an email."

Miko nodded absently. Now, in addition to her pack of recalcitrant workers, it seemed she had a rogue male on her hands. How was she supposed to get any work done?

TWENTY-TWO

"Brother!" Chernichev said. "Surely you recognize me! It hasn't been that long!"

He stretched his grin even broader, into a smile that revealed tobacco-stained teeth.

"The Weasel," Yuri said.

"The Ferret," Chernichev corrected.

"Right. How could I forget."

The Ferret had been one of the new generation. One of the newer recruits added after Yuri's unit returned from Afghanistan. They hadn't fought in that war. Their baptism came in Chechnya. In Grozny. He had always called Yuri *starshina*—senior sergeant—not "Monk," his nickname from Afghanistan. Some of the younger men had tried to dislodge Yuri from that position—rank in a *spetsnaz* unit was a fluid thing, as much determined by toughness and respect earned by bravery in combat or by unarmed hand-to-hand battles when out of a combat zone, using *sambo*, the Russian mixed martial art that combined judo and karate and boxing. Though they had sparred, the Ferret had never been so bold as to challenge Yuri directly. But every unit needed men like the Ferret as well. Devious. Slippery. Quick. Slick. They couldn't all be Bear or Tank or Monster.

Chernichev opened his arms and took a few steps toward

Yuri, as though to embrace him. But above the smile Yuri could see the cold calculation in his eyes. He took another step back. Three against one.

But the one had his gun drawn. And now raised in their direction. Centered on the Ferret's chest.

Chernichev stopped. Raised his hands slightly.

"That's the Monk for you." He laughed, softly. "Always so fucking serious."

Chernichev turned his back on Yuri, said to the other two, "Don't worry guys, it's cool—I served with this guy in Chechnya! What a motherfucking coincidence." As he turned he lowered his hands, brought them together in front of his chest. Possibly—no, certainly—to use hand signals.

"Cut the shit," Yuri said. "What the hell are you doing out here?"

Chernichev turned back toward him. "I could ask you the same thing."

"I'm with the Anti-Poaching Brigade."

"That's what I heard." His head angled slightly. "But you're not supposed to be here."

"This is my territory. Just assigned to it."

"Assigned, eh?" Chernichev, still smiling, shook his head. "Oh, I get it. So the Major called you in, did he?"

Stalling, Yuri asked, "Major Iliakov?"

"No, Major Motherfuck." He spat into the snow. "Of course, Major Iliakov."

"Haven't seen him," Yuri said.

"Right, right. Sure." Chernichev shook his head. "Whatever he's paying you, I can double it. Easy."

The man looked into Yuri's eyes. The man's watery blue eyes widened, and he gave a low whistle.

"Oh, I see—he's not paying you at all, is he?" he asked. He chuckled. "Of course he isn't, the cheap bastard. You always were his right hand man. His loyal *starshina*. He's playing you for a fool, then."

"I'm not *spetsnaz* anymore," Yuri said.

Chernichev shook his head. "There's a saying out here—maybe you've heard it, comrade." A brief glance back toward the tarp-wrapped bundle on the sledge. "A tiger can't change his stripes."

"You don't seem to have changed," Yuri said.

He shrugged. "Still the same old Ferret. After our dear leaders caved in Chechnya, I came out here for the sport." He raised his arms toward the trees, slowly turned around. "I've been hunting deer in these hills for years now. This is my territory."

"You're telling me that's a deer," Yuri said.

The other two each took one sideways step out from behind their leader. Then another. Small, shuffling sidesteps in the snow. As though they were simply shifting their weight, tired of standing around in the snow while these two old friends got reacquainted.

"We haven't seen any poachers out here," Chernichev said. "I'd tell you if we had."

"Stop moving," Yuri said to the other two.

The Ferret made a signal with his hand, partly obscured behind his back, and they stopped. But in the meantime they had each put another couple of steps between themselves and their guide. They were trying to flank him. Trying to space out his potential targets. Yuri took another step back, but here the slope became steeper, the snow slippery.

The men were nervously touching their faces. Hand signals?

"Nice gun," Chernichev said. "Looks like a museum piece."

"What's in the tarp?" Yuri asked.

"A deer. Like I said."

The cold was beginning to stiffen his ungloved hand. Tingling his straightened, exposed trigger finger that he still hadn't inserted into the trigger guard.

"What'd you kill it with?"

"We wrapped our rifles up with the carcass. No one wants to shoulder a rifle as well as pull the sledge ropes."

"So you won't mind me taking a look."

"You know my word is good—right, brother?"

"It'll just take a moment," Yuri said. "Get one of your friends to unwrap it."

The other two glanced nervously at Chernichev. They were even further apart than before, and had stepped closer to Yuri. He was having a hard time keeping them all in his sight at once. He knew this was the idea.

"Hold on a minute," Chernichev said. "You say you're with the Brigade—but I don't see any insignia. Where's your badge?"

"I left it—" Yuri said. He didn't want to give away the fact that he had a base camp nearby. "Back in my truck."

"Well, then." The stained grin spread wide again. "Seems we're at an impasse."

The Korean took another nervous shuffling step to the side, off the trail, toward the trees. Yuri switched his aim from Chernichev to the Korean, but kept his eyes on Chernichev.

"Tell your friend to stop moving," Yuri said.

The larger man exhaled a cloud of smoke and vapor into the air. Yuri recognized him, too. A late replacement, near the end of his time. He didn't remember his nickname. It had something to do with the many tattoos that covered his torso. The vapor from the man's breath vanished, while the thin cigarette smoke continued to lift higher into the air.

Chernichev said something unintelligible, and the Korean said something back. Sharp, high-pitched. Yuri couldn't understand what the man was saying, but he could sense the nervousness. The fear.

"I don't want any trouble," Yuri said.

Chernichev's gloved hands had lowered to his waist, the palms still facing Yuri, a semblance of surrender and compliance.

"Nobody wants trouble," he said.

Now the larger man said something in a low voice. The Ferret shook his head. Kept his eyes trained on Yuri, the grin still there, but strained.

"Whatever it is you're dragging," Yuri said, "you can take it."

"Well, obviously," Chernichev said. "There are three of us, after all."

Yuri turned the gun back toward his former comrade. "There's only one of you."

The grin left the man's face. "That's right—you specialized in offing those who were once your brothers." The Korean continued talking, but Chernichev ignored him. "Is that why you followed me here?"

Yuri shook his head.

"Why not just snipe me from behind cover?"

Yuri swallowed. The Korean continued to fidget. The larger man raised the cigarette to his lips, sucked it down to the filter, down to the thick gloves protecting his fingers. Yuri could see burn marks on the leather from countless previous cigarettes. He tossed the smoking butt into the snow.

"You wanted to see my face first, is that it? I hear that's how you killed that towelhead. What was his name again? Oh, that's right: Traitor."

The Korean put his hand into his coat pocket. Yuri swiveled toward him now. With his gloved left hand he thumbed the safety off. "Stop moving!" he shouted.

The man kept speaking, gesticulated with the hand that was not in his pocket.

"Tell him to get his hand where I can see it!"

The larger man let another cloud of smoke escape into the frigid air with a hiss. Yuri glanced over his shoulder at Chernichev, who stood watching impassively.

"Brother," Chernichev said. He raised his hands slightly and took one step toward Yuri. "Let's not get carried away."

The Korean shouted, and Yuri glanced back toward him. The hand remained buried in his coat pocket, balled into a fist. Wrapped around something.

"Tell him!" Yuri raised the gun to his shoulder and stepped directly toward the man, the barrel centered on his face.

Chernichev said something, but Yuri could not understand it. The other two were out of his line of sight now. He had to keep them from getting any closer, until he had this one down and submissive.

"Get on the ground!" he yelled. He curled his finger, stiff with cold, around the trigger.

Fear and fury shone through the man's goggles. The man fought to pull his hand free, but the thing in his hand had snagged on the pocket opening.

Yuri didn't move his eyes from the man's hand, but he removed his left hand from the Mosin-Nagant's wooden barrel guard, pointed back over his shoulder toward Chernichev, to let the other two know he hadn't forgotten about them.

"You two—" he began to say, when the gun went off.

TWENTY-THREE

The kick staggered Yuri as the man lifted from his feet. He sprawled on his back in the snow and the report echoed among the trees, rippled throughout the valley.

Yuri spun on his heel and raised the gun, braced for an onslaught from behind. The larger man froze when Yuri centered the gun on his chest. The Ferret had disappeared.

Keeping the gun trained on the big man, he stepped quickly to where Chernichev had been standing, followed his prints, caught a glimpse of the man's back as he ran. The trees prevented a clear shot. He spun back toward the third man, who remained standing, staring down at his dead comrade. The ringing in Yuri's ears slowly dissipated, replaced by the receding churn of the fleeing man's footsteps crunching through the snow.

Keeping his eyes and the gun trained on the big man, Yuri backed toward the Korean, sprawled on his back in the snow, legs twisted. He glanced down. He didn't need to take a pulse. The bullet had shattered the left goggle, then tumbled, and as it exited took the back of the man's head off. Blood leaked steadily into the matted snow. The man's leg twitched, then ceased.

He looked back toward the larger man. Considered whether he should shoot him. As a potential future enemy.

There was a time when he would not have even hesitated. There was a time when the man would have been dead already. But that time had passed. He lowered the rifle.

"Zenit," he said. That was his nickname. He was from St. Petersburg. A diehard football ultra before joining *spetsnaz*. Tattooed with the faces and numbers of his favorite players, trophies the team had won. Scalps they had collected.

Zenit balled his gloved fists. He took one step toward Yuri, then another. Another. Another. Only when Yuri lifted the rifle did he stop.

"Big mistake," Zenit said.

"He should've listened," Yuri said.

Zenit raised his hand, pointed at Yuri with the gloved finger marred by cigarette burns. He stared at Yuri for a long time.

"Big mistake," he said again.

Then he turned and began to walk along the trail of bootprints, following the path that had brought them into the woods. Continuing on as though nothing had happened.

"Wait," Yuri called out. He had many questions for this man, but the main one was why were they here? How was it that he had seen these same men at the site of Tatiana's death, and again here?

But the man kept walking. Yuri's right hand shook. It burned with the cold. He watched the man's back until he reached the ridge and disappeared. Then he turned and began to jog after Chernichev, following the man's prints in the snow. This was his chance to get some answers.

As he ran, he familiarized himself with the size, the contours, the tread pattern of Chernichev's boots. A single four-letter word in Western letters within a rectangle between the heel and the toe box would make them very easy to identify.

He jogged along in the newly carved trail, down the hill. A quick glance at his compass told him the tracks led north. Away from the Sanitarium, roughly parallel with the Core boundary to the east and the power line access trail to the west, in his estimation.

He paused every so often to listen, and watch. Chernichev did not carry a rifle, but he might have a handgun, and would almost certainly carry a knife or even a spade for close combat. He couldn't sprint headlong after him, even though the spacing of the man's bootprints indicated he'd been running as fast as he could. Eventually the deep snow took its toll, and the space between the prints began to diminish. The trees also grew thicker here. The trail became harder to follow, as the snow the fleeing man brushed from pine boughs filled in the prints, but Yuri used the freshly bared evergreen branches as guideposts. He moved more cautiously, rifle at the ready, keenly aware of his limited visibility.

This had to be more than coincidence. In relative terms, in the vast Sikhote-Alin, they were not far from where they had found Tatiana. Chernichev had called this "his territory." One ex-*spetsnaz* soldier guarding the Project, protecting the tigers within. Two more ex-*spetsnaz* soldiers hunting the forest nearby, poaching tigers. There was a third party involved, of course. Also ex-*spetsnaz*. Their commanding officer. Major Iliakov. Had he wanted to bring them together in this way?

He had questions, and only Chernichev could answer them. He needed to capture him, interrogate him. A much tougher challenge than simply killing him, of course.

The trees suddenly ended. A broad basin spread out before him, filled with fog. Nearby stood a few tree trunks, but they were all dead, stripped of branches, gray crooked fingers that reached from the earth toward the sky, strangled by the fog.

The bootprints continued, clearly now, moving at a walk, into the fog, where they vanished.

He followed after. Slowly now. Rifle extended, finger on the trigger, warmed by the adrenaline and his exertions. He checked the safety, made sure it was off.

In the summer, he supposed, this must be some sort of swamp. A bog. Filled with standing water that killed the trees. But in the winter the water would freeze, support the snow. It was deep here, up to his knees, drifting higher in places. He wished he had his snowshoes. But he knew that Chernichev suffered a similar handicap.

The fog thickened the further he ventured into the bog. The vague outlines of twisted trees came to resemble men. Or men's souls. Angling for heaven, while rooted firmly in hell. The torture of the damned. Reaching for the overcast sky above, but anchored, unable to attain it. Barely able to glimpse it.

He stopped and listened. Heard the scrunching of the snow as it packed around his knees. It was working its way down into his boots, despite the sleeves and the drawstrings at the leg openings. His feet were beginning to numb. The adrenaline was wearing off. He was coming back to himself.

He reached a pair of gnarled tree trunks. One had fallen against the other, which also leaned, or perhaps they had both fallen into each other, their stunted branches tangled and twined. A desperate, clinging embrace, simultaneously holding each other up and dragging each other down. They formed an 'X' that reminded him of his father's blood-stained drying rack, where they field-dressed game. Chernichev's prints detoured around the 'X' and disappeared into the wispy tendrils.

He had the advantage in firepower, but the limited visibility had eliminated that advantage. And perhaps turning the advantage to the man he was pursuing, should he decide to stop and set an ambush. He could be looping around behind Yuri even now. Could be leading him in circles in the fog—the sky was invisible now, and he had no bearings aside from the solitary trail of footprints that he was following. Blindly following.

He raised the rifle to his shoulder, the scope to his eye, swept the crosshairs along the horizon. Nothing. No movement. No visibility at all, except for the occasional gnarled trunk. He couldn't even be sure that he was maintaining a view along the horizon, as gray snow blended with gray fog in gray light.

He turned back. The afternoon was wearing on. He would have time to return to his dacha, but only just.

He left the fog, began the gradual uphill climb, plowing through the snow, bulling his way through the grasping trees. He listened for sounds of Chernichev following, the ringing of the gunshot still faint in his ears.

Back at the site of the interdiction, there was no sign that Zenit or Chernichev had returned. He tugged the dead man's hand free from the pocket. A sheaf of thousand-kopek notes caught in the wind and burst into a green and yellow cloud that slowly fluttered and dispersed down the hillside. Not a gun. A bribe.

It wasn't the first man he'd killed, not by a long shot. Just the first he'd killed in the Sikhote-Alin. The first outside of the army. The war, it had caught up to him, even in this remote corner of the taiga. No matter what he did, where he went, he couldn't seem to leave the war behind.

He crunched through the snow to the sledge. He laid the Mosin-Nagant down alongside it. Released two of the bungee cords, peeled back a corner of the tarp. An orange stripe, and a black, and another orange. The thick neck, the flat head, the black triangle of the back of an ear, with the eye-shaped white spot of fur in the triangle's center. So that when a tiger sat with its back to another tiger, a pair of eyes would seem to be watching. He stroked that ear with his bare, cold, killer's hand. Soft and velvety between his trigger finger and thumb.

The snow began to fall. It would be dark soon. The snowfall should obscure his tracks, keep them from returning the next day and tracing him to his dacha. But that didn't mean he'd seen the last of them.

Eyes in the back of his head. That's what Yuri would need now.

TWENTY-FOUR

He sat down heavily in the snow, next to the sledge. He placed his hand on the tiger's pelt. Pushed his fingers deep into the thick fur. There was no inner warmth there, the body stiff and unyielding, but still the fur brought life back to his fingers, to his hand. Reminded him that the man he'd killed had taken the life of this creature. He pulled the tarp back so he could inspect the tiger's face, the convoluted curls and twists of black and orange, the background of white around the mouth and the eyes.

A young tiger. Inexperienced. Naive. Not unlike Kamal or Vida would be when turned loose.

Big mistake.

Zenit's simple statement echoed in his head. He knew there was no going back. Knew the finality of death.

He wasn't going to pity the man. The man was a criminal. A killer. Murdering a creature like this, when only three to four hundred remained alive in the wild in the entire world, seemed worse to Yuri than killing a man. And for what, a few thousand *Amerikanskiye dollary*? He'd known the risks he was running. He hadn't expected to die on this day, certainly. He hadn't had time to prepare himself. Then again, who ever does?

Snow was falling now, heavy flakes. Drifting down, but

every so often the wind picked up, swirled them more aggressively. Soon they would be driving down, pelting even. The sky was darkening, and not only because the cloud cover was now total, and thick. Behind them the sun was lowering toward the horizon.

They must have an extraction point nearby. A vehicle of some sort waiting for them, capable of carrying three men and a carcass. A snowcat, a pair of snowmobiles. Probably using that same access along the power line that Evgeny and he had used to reach the resort. The more he thought about the men's carelessness, their nonchalance, their lack of perimeter security, the more he became convinced that this was not their first time in this forest. Not their first time venturing into the Core from this point. Chernichev had even called this their territory. They'd had success here before, in seasons past.

They knew this area was not patrolled. They knew it wouldn't be patrolled.

Assurances had been made. By whom? Who else knew this area wouldn't be patrolled?

Vassily.

Yuri had specifically asked to patrol this sector. Had given good reasons. But had been dissuaded.

"I will make the assignments," Vassily had said. "I'm not in the business of playing favorites."

The word choice hadn't struck him at the time, but now he had to wonder: *what sort of business are you in? Eh, Vassily?*

The forest remained silent aside from the gentle hiss of snow falling on snow, the occasional flurry of wind. Chernichev and Zenit were not returning to the scene. True to his nickname, the Ferret had moved swiftly, decisively, and probably hadn't slowed down since.

That left him with two bodies. A corpse, and a carcass. A thin layer of snow already covered the man, still warm enough to melt the flakes that landed on the exposed skin of his face. But not for long. He couldn't bury the body—the ground was frozen solid. Besides, the incoming snow and encroaching night meant that he needed to get going.

He grabbed the lifeless man's arms and dragged him to a nearby tree, pulled him up to sitting. Leaned his ruined head back against the trunk.

He unsheathed his Yakut knife, and cut away a corner of the tarp that wrapped around the tiger, the size of an unfolded napkin or a small placemat. With the knife he punched two holes into the upper corners of the plastic. Then he loosened one of the bungee cords that held the bundle fast to the sledge, and passed the cord ends through the holes. He then wrapped the cord twice around the mans' chest and the tree trunk, lashing him tightly in this sitting position, the tarp covering his torso like a bib. He dipped his glove into the sticky red blood still leaking from the dead man's head, and roughly painted the single word:

Браконьер

He hadn't wanted to kill the man, even though he was a poacher. Seeing Chernichev again had thrown him off. The man had refused to remove his hand from his pocket. His trigger finger had been numb.

Big mistake.

It was the sort of slip he would have suspected Chernichev might make. Not himself. Not Iliakov's *starshina*.

And he had now invited Chernichev to return, probably with reinforcements. When they came in search of Yuri, they might well find the lodge. The barn. The paddock. The Project. Kamal and Vida. Miko and Anatoly. Easy pickings. He would have to be on high alert now.

Chernichev asking him about Iliakov had disturbed his concentration. *Whatever he's paying you, I can double it.* What was Iliakov paying him? How was Iliakov playing him?

The Ferret and Zenit and their comrades of that generation had struck Yuri as savages. The hellish months of training were designed to turn a man into a savage, howling beast, ready to kill. But there was something about the

Ferret's cadre that seemed to take a sadistic pleasure in destruction and death that he had never felt.

They were the ones who called themselves "Iliakov's Wolfpack." Iliakov had confided to his *starshina*, as they played chess during a lull, that he shared Yuri's low opinion of the new men. But Yuri could see the secret smile, the flash of pride in the Major's eyes, when the younger men bayed at the moon, or when they all went out on the town and got roaring drunk and returned with tattoos of wolves on their shoulders. One more symbol, lost among all their other ink.

The snow was falling steadily now. Daylight dimming.

That left the carcass. He didn't want to leave it here, for Chernichev and his comrade to collect, or for scavengers to pick apart. Something about leaving it where it lay felt indecent. From his own gear he tucked the butane burner in with the tiger, just in case. The tent he would return to collect another day. If he was caught out in this, it wouldn't help him anyway. He could not get caught out. He needed to travel as lightly as possible if he was going to make it back to his dacha with any daylight to spare.

He pulled the tattered tarp flap back into place and shifted the bungee cords a bit to compensate for the one he'd removed. He wasn't sure what he was going to do with the carcass, but he wasn't going to leave it to the elements. Perhaps Miko and Anatoly could make use of it, if he left it for them on their doorstep. Or they might at least have a proper way to dispose of it. Or he could even store it in the subzero conditions until the thaw came, and then bury it properly. Along with whatever was left of the Korean man.

He picked up one of the leashes attached to the sledge, and slung it over his right shoulder, hoisted the other over his left. The rifle he slung diagonally across his chest, in case the Ferret did decide to return and pick up his trail. The snow would soon make that difficult. But it would also make moving this burden even more of a challenge. His own footsteps were beginning to vanish under the snow. As he looked up the slope he regretted not letting them drag their burden the entire way to the crest of the ridge.

He'd spent the entire day prostrate, stationary, fidgeting for lack of activity. This would be his exercise for the day. He leaned forward into the leashes, dug his toes down into the snow. Strained against the straps with all he had, until the healing scars on his face felt as though they were about to burst open again. With a crack the sledge runners broke free of the snow's grip and sprung forward. He charged up the hill, desperate to keep the sledge's momentum going. By the time he reached the crest his thighs were burning, his calves cramping, his lungs on fire from deep inhales of the cold air, sweat pooling along his sides, down his back, in his groin.

And all the while he ran, that crooked finger pointed at him. The gloved finger, the leather scarred and mottled, pointed at his chest. That voice in his head continued to whisper:

Big mistake.

TWENTY-FIVE

He was in trouble. His trail through the trees had long since vanished, covered over by the fresh snow, which continued to fall steadily, piling up, making each step more difficult. He'd sighted with the compass along his last glimpse of the trail maybe half an hour before. Surely the sanitarium compound was large enough that even if he veered slightly to one side or the other he would still encounter the buildings, the clearings. But now the light was fading, and still no sign of familiar landmarks.

During a previous short break he'd removed his outer coat, rolled it up and laid it over his shoulders like a yoke, to better cushion and distribute the weight of the straps that were clawing into his shoulders. His body at that point was overheated anyway—he'd been running for a while, making good progress, determined to cover as much ground as possible while the trail was still clear. He'd also tucked the Mosin-Nagant in under the bungee cords—the strap had been chafing his neck and the bouncing of the gun was a distraction he didn't need. Chernichev wasn't following him.

But now that the way forward was no longer clear, he had slowed. His legs ached. His body was cooling rapidly in the cold, the snow building up on his heavy fleece-lined wool shirt. His extremities were numb. He was beginning to shiver.

He stopped in a small, flat clearing, and the sledge ground to a halt behind him. He hoped he would have the strength to get it started again. He lowered the straps from his shoulders. He groaned as he straightened and unlocked each of his soldered lower vertebrae one at a time. He unfurled his coat, shook it free of snow, forced his arms back through the frozen sleeves, fought with trembling hands and numb fingers to get the zipper to catch and rise. It was like donning a blanket of ice, but he knew he needed the extra insulation now. He found his last piece of jerked venison, sucked on the salty meat. His stomach turned in on itself. He needed more fuel. He'd been melting snow in his mouth occasionally, but he knew he was dehydrated as well.

He dug his compass out, took his bearings with the last of the light. The trees still stretched on endlessly ahead of him. They were short pines though, their low branches laden with snow. He'd been brushing up against these, pushing his way through these, for the last few minutes. They slowed his progress, and they forced him to change direction far too frequently. Because they limited his visibility so severely, he might also be only twenty meters from the clearing, from the compound. He had to keep pressing forward.

The falling snow hissed around him. He reached down for the straps. The bundle he was dragging was piled high with snow, gray and dingy in the dying light. He swept some of the snow free with the back of his hand, made sure the rifle was still secured.

He jumped back, startled. Had the bundle growled at him?

Impossible. The tiger was dead. He'd felt its cold flesh against his fingers.

Snow sloughed off the branches of a nearby tree, freeing the dark green tufts of needles to sway in the wind. Through the branches, had that been a shadow, a blur of movement?

Keeping his eye trained on that tree, he stepped sideways

toward the sledge. Reached down for the gun, tried to pull it free.

Then again, the low rumble. The echo of distant thunder.

He was being stalked. But not by a Ferret.

The cord would not surrender the gun. Of course not, he'd looped it through the gap between the scope and the barrel.

He slowly turned. There, across the clearing, maybe thirty meters away—movement, behind the tree. More snow shook from the branches as the enormous creature brushed against the other side. Circling him. The last of the light revealed an enormous bulk, too dark to make out the stripes, but he knew it was a tiger.

Had he continued bulling forward, had he not stopped to don his coat, the tiger would have ambushed him. He would be dead now, or dying.

The growl closer now. A diesel engine coughing to life.

His breath caught in his constricted throat, as the tiger's head emerged from low branches.

The creature's eyes were large, burning slits, hooded by thick white whiskers. His facial stripes were numerous, mottled, forming a samurai mask. The black stripes etched a fierce frown above his eyes, even while white patches below formed a broken line of tears that dripped from each eye, down toward the whiskers, broken and sparse: pain mixed with ferocity. Pride, too, in the milky beard that descended from his chin.

Yuri slowly reached into his parka pocket for his Yakut knife. His only weapon.

As he did, the tiger turned to the side and moved through the trees, revealing more of his enormous body. With each placement of his paws his head undulated side to side, beneath the slow roll of his sharply peaked shoulders. Traces and tracks marred the fur of his forequarters, long scars that stretched up from his paws and forearms like ivy tendrils, clustered into bare patches around his powerful shoulders, along his neck, and crossed the crown of his enormous head.

He stalked along the perimeter of the clearing, reluctant to part from the cover of the trees. His low-slung body seemed to stretch and stretch, his back swayed low to the ground. His long tail swished behind, hypnotically twitched one way, then back, in time with each deliberate step. The long white strands of his chin whiskers wisped over the snow, along with his white underbelly fur, and the white underside of his tail.

He circled Yuri, as though he wanted his prey to first appreciate his full majesty before he moved in for the kill. As the tiger stalked around the perimeter of the clearing, Yuri pivoted to keep facing him. The creature's yellow eyes remained locked on Yuri unwaveringly.

Tatiana had been the first tiger he had seen alive in the forest in his five years in Primorsky Krai, and the sight of her —stretched out in the snow and struggling to breathe her last breaths as she was—had filled him with awe, with a sense of wonder, with respect for the fragile beauty of these great cats.

This, however, was another feeling entirely. This was a feeling he hadn't experienced in quite some time. Not since his earliest days in Afghanistan.

This was fear.

TWENTY-SIX

His hand wrapped around a cylindrical object and he pulled it from the pocket: not his knife, but a signal flare. Of course. He carried one at all times. He removed the safety cap, struck it down against the primer. A bright red arrowhead of flame burst free, spewing smoke and a sulfurous reek of potassium perchlorate. He raised it up like a fiery sword and strode toward the tiger. The beast melted back into the trees, into the shadows, the *basso profundo* rumble partially drowned out by the spewing hiss of the flare. It trembled, in time with his shaking hand.

Tigers feared the flare. Evgeny said they would run away. But this one stayed close, as though determined not to lose sight of its prey. He sat and watched, waited patiently to see what Yuri would do.

He returned to the sledge. He considered freeing his rifle, but there was no time for that. He would have to leave it behind, along with the carcass and his cookstove. He could return for those later.

He took a sighting from his compass and began to move again, heart racing, his sympathetic nervous system kicking in to tell him first it was time to fight, now it was time for flight. The adrenaline coursing through his body warmed his extremities, gave him the surge of energy he needed to cross the clearing, the tiger on his right, just out of sight in the fading gloom. The red flare light revealed the solid wall of trees ahead of him. He plunged in among their branches.

He could only hope he was moving in the right direction.

He held the flare high in front of him. It spat at his face, left him with a large blind spot swimming in his retinas. He turned and thought he glimpsed movement back along the trail he was leaving.

The flare would give him fifteen minutes. Should give him fifteen minutes. He hoped that would be long enough to reach the compound. On he drove, brushing through the trees, snow up to his shins now, drifting up to his knees even in some places. Fresh and loose, so it wasn't grabbing his feet or slowing him down, but forcing him to lift his legs clear. Tiring him.

He had to be close to the compound. He had to be. This next tree, he would get around it and burst into the clearing, see the dark hulks of the dachas, the dormitories. Through these trees. On the far side of this tree. Or past this tree. The next tree. One more tree, and...

The flare shortened. Dripped spent fuel down along his glove. He couldn't feel it, but he could smell the leather burning. The flare began to sputter. The steady hiss now intermittent. The light winking.

And then, inevitably, blackness. He let the flare fall from his hand.

He kept moving forward. He stumbled blindly through the trees now, the branches pelted his face, his arms, his legs. His mind gone, given over entirely to directing his body with one simple instruction: forward. Onward. Move. Live.

Behind, the echo of thunder rolled toward him. He imagined he could hear the footpads crunching through the snow after him. He told himself he was imagining this to spur himself on. But he wasn't sure it was his imagination. A percussive backbeat echoed his own crunching footfalls, at the edge of perception, or the edge of madness.

An orange light, in the distance. The afterglow of the flare, burned into his retinas from holding it so close to his face. He could still smell the smoky reek of the spent fuel, clinging to his glove, to the fur lining of his hood.

Then the light was gone, winked out. He altered his course slightly, and the light reappeared as he moved round a tree that had come in between himself and the light. He held that as his beacon, steered toward that, leaned forward and drove his legs through the snow and into the earth with the last of his strength, feeding on his final adrenaline surge.

The light took on a shape: a square. The orange light had a pale quality, warm and inviting, but thin. Like glass. He was driving toward a window. A sudden gust of wind howled at him, drove against him, pushed him back, and he wasn't sure if the screaming in his ears was the roar of the tiger leaping at him from behind or his own yell of desperation as he fought through the gust.

He staggered the final steps to the window, to the small, dark hut that the window was set into. He banged on the wood next to the window. He couldn't tell if it was a door or a wall.

"Please," his voice cracked. "Open."

The wood he leaned against fell away from him, spilled him into the small room. Warm light enveloped him, a myriad of colors swirled around him—diagonally patterned rugs were strewn over the floor, festooned the walls. A lantern hung from the ceiling, the source of the light. His body too numb to feel the warmth.

"You," a voice said. A woman's voice. Unsurprised at the sudden presence of a visitor.

Hands under his arms helped him inside. He leaned forward, collapsed onto the floor.

The door did not close behind him, however. A diminutive figure stood at the threshold, looking out into the dark.

He rolled onto his back, chest heaving, eyes squinting against the sudden influx of light. Stomach heaving at the smell of whatever was cooking in the pot that sat on an iron cookstove in the corner.

"Close the door!" Yuri shouted hoarsely. "Tiger."

"Amba followed you?" a voice asked. A woman's voice.

He recognized the Udege word for tiger, *amba*. He nodded. "*Amba*," he said.

The woman laughed. She stepped out into the dark.

"Shoo, Amba!" he heard her calling out into the wind, waving her arms against the snow. "Leave us be!"

She stepped back inside, pushed the door closed. The wind ceased its howling. His legs had started cramping, and he fought to straighten them, pounded his gloved fists into his hamstrings and calves to keep the muscles from locking up painfully.

She turned toward him. Her eyes were small, her cheekbones high, crow's feet crinkled next to her eyes as she smiled down at him as he continued to knead at his legs.

"I wondered when you would come see Utiuki," she said.

TWENTY-SEVEN

January 5, 2001—Cubs five weeks old

A burst of cold air whipped around Yuri where he lay on the floor, under the hand-woven rugs she had laid over him as blankets. The woman entered the hut, carrying an armload of firewood. She closed the door, and the swirling cold stilled, settled back into the close warmth of the small hut. Tendrils of steam rose from a copper pot that sat atop the stove that occupied the center of the circular room.

Last night she'd helped him out of his coat, and gave him a wooden bowl full of a rich brown stew with chunks of soft potatoes, carrots, onions, and tender boar meat. He had scraped every last bit of gravy from the bowl with a hunk of black bread. They'd introduced themselves—Utiuki was her name—and not long after, the warmth from the fire and the contented feeling in his belly and the exhaustion in his limbs had caused him to drift off to sleep.

He'd startled awake once in the dark, with the feeling that a weight was pressing down on top of him. When he opened his eyes he realized it was only the heavy rugs she had draped over him for warmth. He soon fell back asleep.

In the pale morning light that filtered in through the solitary window—the beacon that had saved his life—he studied her. She squatted on the other side of the stove, added a couple of neatly split logs to the fire within. She straightened and stirred the contents of the pot with a wooden spoon, cooed a few words in a language he did not understand.

Suddenly he was back on his parents' bed, where his mother had been confined since the birth of his sister Sveta—it had been a difficult pregnancy, his older sisters told him, a difficult birth. He'd been expelled from the room, but could hear her moans and cries, could hear his father's low voice pleading with the midwife. Yuri had come to their still-warm bed after breakfast as he always did and he lay there in the hollow left by his father's body and watched his mother pull back the cloth that swaddled his newborn sister so she could gaze at her face. He watched his mother's eyes as she traced the contours of Sveta's face with her fingers. Watched his mother's mouth as she, too, spoke words softly, in a language that he didn't understand. His mother raised her gaze to Yuri, and smiled. Her eyes brimmed with tears.

"What do you see?" she whispered.

He was back in the cabin. The woman's hand had stopped moving, and her dark eyes had lifted from the pot to meet his.

"My mother," he said. He knew she wasn't talking merely about what he could see with his eyes, in front of him. "I haven't seen her since I was five."

"Amba gives you a gift," she said.

Yuri wiped the sleep from his eyes and sat up.

She stood up and walked around the sledge, came to stand in front of him. He had a hard time gauging her age, the skin that covered her high cheekbones was smooth, and yet pinched into shallow creases at her lips. She crouched in front of him, inspected him. She held her empty hand in the air, a surprisingly small hand, the fingers rounded and plump. She held it above his right cheek, unbandaged. Exposed. Raw.

"This from tiger," she said. A statement, not a question. Her eyes met his. "Can I touch?"

He reached his right hand up, touched the areas at the

edges of his wound, where the bandage would normally be anchored. He felt strangely naked without it, especially now that she was staring.

He lowered his hand and nodded, once, turned his face to the left. Toward the window, toward the rugs hanging on the wall.

Her touch jolted him. She pulled her hand back as though shocked, but then slowly reestablished contact. Traced the outlines of his ragged skin.

"Is it bleeding?" he asked.

She shook her head. She continued following his jawline with her fingers, gently, and then she moved her hand higher, along his cheekbone, and the sensation of her touch flickered in and out, between sensitive and numb. He had lost nerve endings through that area.

"Did you make these rugs?" he asked.

She nodded, thin lips pursed in concentration.

"Husband build the cabin," she said. "I make the rugs."

Yuri frowned. *Husband?* "Was he... is he... out in that storm?"

She removed her hand from his face, shook her head, a rueful smile.

"Five winters ago he came here to hunt, same as every year. But he never came home." She returned her gaze to his cheek. "Now that my daughters are married I come here to wait for him."

He returned his head to neutral. He needed to apply fresh bandages. Even though the wound seemed to be healing well, he could not afford an infection.

She remained squatting in front of him, sitting now on her heels, her knees jammed into her armpits, her chin on her forearms crossed in front of her.

"Are there any others?" he asked. "Any other people? Living around here?"

"For four summers and five winters, just me and the ghosts," she said, with a shake of her head. "Now, all of a sudden, Utiuki has neighbors on all sides. Like living in the village."

"Well, I'm glad you're here," he said. "If not, I don't think I would've made it. I don't know how I got so far off track."

"Hard to find your way in the dark," she said.

He nodded. He'd been lucky. Sometimes it was better to be lucky than good, but luck never lasted. Major Iliakov had drilled into him the certainty that luck would always, eventually, run out.

"I owe you," he said. "How can I repay you?"

"You help me dig out," she said. "The snow is very heavy for Utiuki."

TWENTY-EIGHT

January 5, 2001—Cubs five weeks old

Miko sat in Control monitoring the snoozing cubs and planning out the afternoon's activities when the thump-thump-thump of an approaching helicopter shattered the morning stillness.

"What the hell," she said. The racket woke the cubs, who yawned and stretched and now sat alert.

She went down to the lab. Anatoly already stood at the door, peered through the small window. The helicopter lowered to the snow in the space between the lodge and the stables. She pulled on her parka and opened the door, caught her breath in the blast of cold wind and the deafening roar of rotors. The black Kasatka's side door bore the familiar green 'M' on a field of brown, enclosed in a circle of white. The door slid open, and a man in a gray greatcoat and a matching gray *ushanka* hopped from the deck into the knee-deep snow. He raised his hand in acknowledgement and began striding toward them, lifting his knees to clear his boots with each step. Behind him another man stepped down into the snow, then another, then a third, larger than the first two. These men wore pale gray parkas, dark woolen caps, gray trousers that bloused over drab boots. They retrieved several black duffels from the guts of the helicopter and tossed them into the snow.

"Who is that?" she asked.

"We're about to find out," Anatoly said.

They stepped back to allow the man into the barn, closed the door behind him. He stamped snow from his shiny black leather boots. Smiled a bright white toothy grin.

"Major Ivan Petrovich Iliakov," he introduced himself. "Chief of Security at Meyerhaeusen International. I believe Dr. Carrington was going to call, to tell you to expect me?"

Miko turned toward Anatoly, but he lifted his shoulders and empty palms.

"Perhaps he did not expect me to visit quite so soon," the man said. He doffed his *ushanka*, revealing a close-cropped mane of gray hair only a shade paler and sparser than the cap's thick fur.

"Your pilot landed entirely too close," she said. "Against protocol."

He raised his hands, opened his mouth to explain.

"Aside from the biweekly supply drop," she interrupted, "there aren't supposed to be helicopters flying or landing anywhere near here, period."

"Ah, but I bring gifts," he said. From under his gray woolen greatcoat the visitor produced a bottle of red wine. He handed it to Miko. A pinot noir, from the Russian River Valley, in northern California. Not only her favorite type of wine, but from one of her favorite vineyards. And a reserve vintage older than any she had tasted. She held the chilly bottle in her hands for a few moments.

"How—" she began.

"*Razvedka*," he said, with a slight inclination of his head, the sketch of a bow. "Intel. A specialty of mine. I've also brought steak and lobster."

Anatoly cooed, but ceased at her glare. They had been hit with a lot of snow overnight, and they had a lot of work to do.

"We will eat well this afternoon," Iliakov said.

"What's the occasion?" she asked.

"Dr. Carrington alerted us to the presence of a conflict tiger in the vicinity," he said. "These men are here to resolve the conflict for you."

She was surprised to discover that the idea that these men had come to hunt a tiger did not immediately result in a decision to expel these men from the Project site. She would never request such a thing, of course. But would it be so awful to sacrifice one old, infirm male to ensure that these two young cubs would have a clearer chance at life in the wild?

Of course she was morally opposed to hunting tigers. For sport or profit. But this didn't quite fit in either category. The tiger was a male almost certainly past his prime, past his mating years. If he was sniffing around this close to human activity, he would almost certainly prove to be a "conflict tiger," who would have no qualms about killing and devouring Kamal and Vida. Whether during their training, if he managed to find a way into the enclosure, or immediately after their release, a year and a half or two years from now. Two years of work, two years of emotional investment, just to have the experiment wiped out by a tiger too ill to survive independently?

"Your timing is terrible," she said. "It's hard to go anywhere with all this snow—"

Iliakov smiled. "The snow will give them a chance to acclimate," he said. "You can go over all the rules and protocols with them, and the foreman can bring them up to speed. I'm sure there are tasks they can assist with. At the very least you'll have three more men to help dig yourselves out."

"I'm going to have to make sure Dr. Carrington authorized this."

"Of course."

"Well, you've woken the cubs," she said.

"Can I see them?"

She glanced at Anatoly.

"On the monitors," she said.

Anatoly led the way upstairs to Control. They showed Iliakov the bank of CCTV screens, the wall of tinted windows. He eagerly inspected everything, including the papers spread out over the long table pushed against the wall of windows. Feeding schedules, medicine schedules, nutrient formulas, length measurements taken from photos, weight estimates based on their lengths, data collected from urine and scat samples dug out of the snow once the cats were back in their den.

"Impressive," he said.

"Let's open the den," Anatoly said.

She could tell he wanted to give their guest a show. Wanted to please him.

Anatoly had set out food puzzles in the snow earlier that morning. These were wooden contraptions of sliding panels with knobs attached that hid morsels of raw deer meat. If the tiger managed to figure out how to manipulate the knob to move the slide, he or she would receive the reward within. Not mimicking anything in nature, but rewarding problem solving and persistence. The puzzles also gave them a challenge that occupied their minds as well as their bodies. The tigers quickly found them when they emerged from their den. Kamal raced back and forth between the two puzzles, trying to control both of them, but as soon as he took over one from Vida, she simply moved to the other.

This was the second time they had seen the puzzle. Vida quickly began moving the slides with her paws. Kamal would try to swoop in to take the meat, but she was too quick for him, the morsels too small. Frustrated, he returned to the other box. Grabbed it in his jaws and threw it around in the snow. It sank into a drift, and he plowed his way through to retrieve it. Meanwhile, Vida stretched out on her belly, the box between her forepaws, solving one slide after the other, sniffing, turning the box over.

"She's so smart," Anatoly said.

Kamal had taken to hurling his box against the tin wall of the paddock until the slides began opening from impact, releasing the meat within.

"Two equally valid ways of solving the problem," Iliakov said. "I must say, I admire the brute force solution."

"The military way," Miko said. She had guessed from his job title, his bearing, his posture, and his close-cropped mane of gray hair that he was ex-military.

"Regretfully," he said with a sigh, "more often than not."

They went back downstairs. The helicopter's rotors still swung, slowly and silently now. The three other men sat on their bags, smoking cigarettes. They quickly stood when Iliakov, Miko and Anatoly left the barn. Iliakov did not acknowledge them, but instead attempted to peer over the paddock wall to see if he could glimpse the cubs within, but the panels were too high. The new men tossed their cigarettes into the snow and bent for their duffels.

"Hey!" she called out. Only the larger man glanced up, slowly pivoted in her direction. The other two hefted bags to their shoulders.

She stepped toward them. "Hey! Assholes!" Now she had their attention. A bemused grin slowly spread across the larger man's face. The other two looked at her, then toward the man who had brought them. Their boss.

She still hadn't decided whether she was going to allow them to stay. If they were to stay, however, she needed to establish immediately who was in charge. She assumed that their sweet-talking boss was not going to stick around.

"Pick up those butts!" she said.

"You heard her," Iliakov said. "No traces."

The men slumped the gear bags back to the ground. Each stooped, searched and sifted through the snow until he had retrieved his spent cigarette.

She turned back to Iliakov, shook her head. "If they are going to stay," she said, "they are going to have to learn and follow the rules. We have to minimize any risk of contamination."

"As you wish," he said.

TWENTY-NINE

Yuri spent the morning shoveling paths from Utiuki's hut to her shed and her wood supply, and then he cleared snow from the roof of her hut. All under her supervision.

"Why does Amba bring you here?" she asked, when they broke for lunch, which was the stew from the previous evening warmed again over the fire. "Why do you watch the tiger cubs?"

Clearly, he hadn't been as stealthy and invisible as he had supposed. "Why do you watch me?"

"Because you're funny."

"No one's ever called me that before."

"You watch the cubs, but you also watch the one who thinks she's their mother."

He laughed at her description of Dr. Katanabe.

"I'm here to protect them," he said.

"Why are you outside?" she asked. "Why not inside with the others?"

"They don't know I'm here."

He tried to explain the Anti-Poaching Brigade to her. She understood that there were men who hunted tigers —*biryuk*, whereas she called the poachers wolves—but she seemed surprised to learn that there were other men who tried to stop them. He left out the fact that this was never technically a Brigade assignment, or that he was on medical leave. He might not be part of the Anti-Poaching Brigade any longer, but he was still on the Amba Patrol.

What she could not fathom was the plan to release the tiger cubs into the wild when old enough, without having learned from their mother. Trained only by their human mother.

"Impossible," she said with a sharp shake of her head.

"That's what I tried to tell them," he said. "But they are scientists. They want to prove they can do it."

"So—these two cubs are an experiment?"

He nodded, slowly. He hadn't really thought of it like that, but yes, that's what they were. An experiment. With the scientists determined to convince themselves that they were in control. But the laboratory was enormous. The laboratory was the entire Sikhote-Alin. Not nearly as under their control as they liked to imagine. Not under their control at all.

"How did she get these cubs?"

Yuri pointed to the scar on his cheek. Explained what had happened. He was beginning to tire from so much talking. His jaw stiffened. He'd spoken very few words these past weeks, he realized. He was out of practice.

She shook her head, staring at him all the while. At his eyes now, not his cheek.

"And last night Khagan follows you."

"Khagan?"

"Big tiger," she said. She lifted a hand, waved it above her head. "King of kings. These are his woods."

"I was lucky," he said. "I had a flare. And then I saw your window."

"Not luck," she said. "Amba brought you here. Amba walked at your side."

"He chased me here," Yuri said. He felt a smile tug against the stiff flesh of his wounded cheek. His face felt strangely naked without a bandage—another thing he needed from the supplies at his dacha. "He wanted to eat me."

She touched his arm and *tsked* dismissively. "No—Amba

revealed himself to you. Amba touched you—" She pointed to his face. "So you become like Amba."

He wasn't sure what to make of this 'Amba' talk. He knew that the Udege viewed tigers as a sort of deity. Knew that their word *amba* literally meant "spirit of the forest." But to hear somebody talk about a tiger as though it had special powers made him uncomfortable. He was not a religious man. He'd always found strange the fervor of the Muslims he had prayed among, alongside Kamal.

A tiger was nothing more than an animal, after all. Larger than most, of course. Arguably one of the more beautiful creatures in the world, certainly much more deadly than almost any other predator aside from man with his weapons and technology. But still an animal. Like man himself. And there was nothing divine in man, that he had ever found.

The wind picked up outside, though it was only noticeable in the soundness of the walls because he and Utiuki had fallen silent, and he wondered, jokingly, if that was Khagan answering to his thought of him. Reminding him of his desperate flight the night before.

After lunch, he and Utiuki plowed through the deep snow into the woods, trying to retrace his steps, to find the sledge and its burden. The heavy snow had erased his tracks. It took them most of the afternoon to find the sledge's telltale hump.

He cleared away the snow that covered the sledge, and with great effort pulled it clear. He found the straps and laid them over his aching, tender shoulders. It was nearly dark by the time they returned to her hut, and he was exhausted.

Utiuki insisted that he bring the sledge and its tarp-wrapped bundle into the hut with them, because she didn't like leaving the dead tiger out in the cold.

But it's dead, Yuri thought. He did as she asked, however.

All he wanted to do was eat and sleep. But first, he was determined to disassemble and clean his gun. As he worked, Zenit's face appeared to him. Intoned, yet again, *big mistake*. As he stood over the dead body of the man whose life he had taken.

"That *biryuk* was a bad man," she said.

"You saw?"

Her eyes sparkled, reflecting the last light of day in the window. "Utiuki watches you."

"It was a mistake," he said. "I didn't mean to—"

She pulled a flap of tarp back, revealing the tiger's face.

"Look how small this tiger is!" she said, her voice rising. "Too young to learn the way of the forest. Did he deserve to die?"

She was right, he was small for a male. Barely an adult, possibly even a juvenile, less than two years old. About the age that Kamal and Vida would be when they were scheduled to be released, he realized. How could they possibly stand any better of a chance than this one? How could they manage to avoid this fate?

"No," he said, hoarse. "I get it."

She nodded toward the sledge. "Tomorrow you help me take care of Amba. Send this one on his way."

He looked at the carcass, still wrapped in the tarp. At the black and orange and white stripes on its exposed face. Puddles of melted snow slowly darkened the rugs beneath the runners. He nodded.

"We take care of Amba," she said, "Amba take care of us."

THIRTY

Two of the men—the larger, silent one, with tattoos peeking out from under the high collar of his turtleneck sweater, who went by Zenit, and the smaller one, with the shock of black hair and enormous, hairy ears, who they called Abrek— dragged a crate of supplies from the helicopter into the kitchen. Iliakov began to oversee the cooking of the midday meal, and soon the fragrances of warm oil and melting butter began to fill the room.

Abrek and Zenit disappeared with the duffel bags into the depths of the lodge, while the third man, slim, with broad shoulders and narrow hips, bright red hair spilling out from under a skull cap and a red goatee showing a few strands of white, worked the oven and the stove. Iliakov introduced this man as Oleg Chernichev. He would be the one she would have to deal with once their boss departed in the helicopter, she assumed. If she decided to allow them to stay.

There was something she didn't like about the look of these men. They looked like all the men she had encountered in this frigid wasteland, she supposed: rough and weather-worn. Like nervy, nocturnal animals unused to the light of day, accustomed to creeping from their dens in the dark and scavenging along the forest floor for what they could find each night.

She didn't like the way they stared at her so boldly. Especially the red-haired one. Chernichev. In that way they were different from the others, from the ones who had been here for weeks. Perhaps she just hadn't broken them in, yet. That would come, with time.

She had to recognize, however, that her mouth was watering, even as she became increasingly annoyed at this unnecessary distraction. This meant the loss of an afternoon for her and Anatoly and probably the loss of a morning for the workmen tomorrow. They were all out at the fence now, but Iliakov had brought enough steak for the five workmen as well, which meant that this would turn into an especially boisterous night. The lobster and the wine, however, were for the three of them, Iliakov, Miko and Anatoly. Herb-roasted potatoes and creamed spinach rounded out the meal. When she asked about the other three men, Abrek, Zenit, and Chernichev, Iliakov said that they would eat with the workmen. For now they had to stow their gear and prepare their bunks.

"Besides," he said with a wink, "their table manners and conversation leave something to be desired. These aren't the sort of men who are accustomed to polite company."

The wine, she had to admit, was delicious. How had he obtained such a bottle, here, in Primorsky Krai? He had his ways, he said, with his grin.

They discussed the plans for the larger enclosure, for the warmer weather, while they ate. Iliakov told them stories about wildlife he had encountered in Angola, in Afghanistan. He did not talk about the wars themselves.

"We're in a similar line of work, you and I," he said to Miko. "Or at least, I was in a similar line of work, before moving to the private sector." He put air quotes around these last two words, as though pronouncing this new capitalist jargon brought a funny taste to his mouth.

"How so?"

"I specialized in recruiting and training soldiers," he said. "My job was to find and bring forth the animal within, you could say, and then teach the soldier how to channel this savagery in a professional, dispassionate way. Clearly you know a thing or two about training wild creatures as well. There is much I could learn from you, I'm sure."

He's trying to flatter me, she realized. He was... interested in her. She could tell from the way he sat straight, chest out, as though displaying a row of medals. In the way he focused his conversation on her, practically ignoring Anatoly —who was perfectly content to devote himself to his food, leaving her to fend for herself in the conversation.

"Our goal here is to be as hands-off as possible," she said. "We cannot allow the cubs to become reliant on us. If they become domesticated, they will not learn the skills to survive in the wild. For now, we must feed them and take care of them, control when they are in the den and when not. We can't let them out in this coming storm, for example. But as soon as the workmen are finished with the fence of the larger enclosure, they will be much more on their own."

"You'll still have to feed them."

"Of course. But we will go to great lengths to make sure that they are not aware of us feeding them."

Anatoly nodded while he chewed.

"Which means no helicopter visits," she stressed.

Iliakov raised his hands in mock surrender.

"I need these workmen out of here," she said. "As soon as possible."

Iliakov nodded. "I'll speak to the foreman before I depart."

"You'll do no such thing," she said. "I've already spoken to him plenty."

"A simple word from me might—"

"Would undermine my authority when you aren't here," she said, as she snapped apart one of the lobster claws, exposing the delicate flesh hidden within. "I have established the hierarchy, I don't need you to mess with it."

His eyebrows lifted. "As you wish."

From the crate in the kitchen the Major produced a cheesecake, topped with strawberries in a thick, clingy syrup. Miko's mouth watered at the sight of it. She hadn't had cheesecake in ages. He cut two large portions, served them to her and Anatoly. He said he preferred a post-dinner cigar to sweets, asked if they minded.

"It's not necessary," he said. "I know they smell atrocious."

"I don't mind the smell," she said. "They remind me of my father."

"Your father smoked?" He clipped his squat, dark cigar, warmed it with his gunmetal lighter. "Forgive my provinciality, but that doesn't seem very Japanese, somehow."

She laughed. "He tried to like them. He would bring them back from his trips abroad, sit in his study smoking and listening to his records. But my mother hated them. So he never really acquired the habit."

"Cuban cigars," he said. He puffed the cigar to life. "One of the few luxuries we Soviets had over the Americans."

The cheesecake was delicious. One bite, and she involuntarily groaned in appreciation, in delight. She covered her mouth, embarrassed. Iliakov grinned, shaped his mouth into an "O," and puffed a series of smoke circles toward the ceiling.

"I'd like to know more about this rogue male," he said.

Anatoly began reporting the details. His weight, his estimated size. The territory a mature male might be expected to command. The injury that probably kept him from ranging quite that far.

Their visitor looked at his wristwatch, stabbed his cigar out on a mound of fat and gristle. High time to get back to the real world, he announced, back to his mundane cares and concerns. He stood up from the table. Miko and Anatoly pushed their chairs back as well. He thanked her elaborately for her hospitality and enjoyable conversation.

As he worked his way into his greatcoat he paused. "Do you play chess, Dr. Katanabe?"

She'd grown up playing Go, against her father. Janpur had taught her chess, however. They had spent many sultry nights sitting opposite each other under the mosquito netting, silently pondering the board between them.

"She's very good," Anatoly said. "I can't touch her, at least."

Despite the compliment, Miko glared at him. She didn't want to give their guest any openings for a return. Despite his delicious gifts.

"When I come to collect my men," he said, his teeth slightly reddened by the pinot, "I'll be sure to bring my board."

THIRTY-ONE

The helicopter lifted off from the frozen snow, swung into the air and rapidly shrank into the gray sky until it vanished behind the treeline. Miko and Anatoly retreated back to the warmth and delicious smells of the kitchen.

Both a little buzzed from the wine, they stared at each other, unsure what to say, what to make of these new developments. The new arrivals.

"That lobster was spectacular," Anatoly finally said.

"I feel like I've just accepted a bribe," Miko said.

He nodded slowly, wiped the buttery slickness from his hands on a dish towel.

"I'm going to see where they're staying," he said. He winked at Miko. "Make sure our guests are comfortable."

He stalked down the main corridor, past the darkened dining hall, past the formal sitting room, long since emptied of furniture and wall sconces and chandeliers. Even the marble fireplace fittings had been stripped away, leaving only the sooty black maw of its hearth. This was where the workmen slept, on sturdy cots. Across the hall, the double doors that led to the trophy room had been closed. He could hear muffled voices behind the doors. He leaned in closer.

"—right there," he heard a man saying. "Unguarded. We could be done with it already. Why muck around?"

He thought he recognized the voice of the man with the large ears. Abrek, that was his nickname. At least Anatoly hoped it was his nickname—hoped his parents hadn't actually named the poor sod after the first monkey launched into space by the cosmonaut program.

"First and foremost, the Monk is out there." This voice was a higher pitch, almost a nasal whine. It carried clearly. *He must be facing the doors*, Anatoly thought. "He may be watching us right now, for all we know."

Anatoly pictured the redheaded man, Chernichev, standing with his back to the gutted fireplace, the stuffed heads of deer and bears spread out around him on the floor, ghostly impressions on the wallpaper where the mounts used to hang. He heard a rustling. Heavy curtains being drawn over windows. Followed by a sneeze.

Abrek said something else, softly, that Anatoly couldn't make out. He leaned in closer, brought his ear against the thin gap between the doors.

"He won't be expecting us," Chernichev said.

The higher and lower voices blended together in an unintelligible jumble of words. Chernichev's voice cut in again: "We don't eliminate him first, then nothing else matters. You could collect all the money in the world and it still won't be enough to save your life. Because he will hunt you down, and kill you. I promise you that."

A few more muted protests, less strident now.

A hand clapped Anatoly on the shoulder. He jumped and yelled. Looked up at the one they called Zenit in the confines of the darkened corridor, his heart suddenly beating triple-time, his neck and cheeks and ears suddenly flushed with burning heat, a quick clamminess in his palms and armpits.

A smile spread over the man's face. Tattoos crept out from under the collar of his turtleneck, spiraled up like ivy toward his stubbly jawline, toward his ears.

"Just came to make sure you men were settling in okay," Anatoly managed. *Not bad*, he thought.

"We're comfortable, friend," Zenit said, as he opened the

door and pushed his way into the room. His arm wrapped around Anatoly's shoulders and guided him in alongside. "But let's see what the lads have to say."

Once across the threshold, Chernichev and Abrek stared at Anatoly. Chernichev stood with his back to the vacant fireplace, just as he had imagined. Abrek sat on an old, moth-eaten couch, leaning over a map spread out on the floor in front of him. The curtains had been drawn, and this room had also been stripped of its light fixtures, but the men had produced two large battery-powered camp lanterns, presumably from among their gear. One lamp sat on the couch next to Abrek, the other on the floor near the map. Abrek also held a small flashlight in his hand. He aimed it into Anatoly's face, causing him to raise his hand and squint. The man lowered the light.

"You men finding everything you need?" he stammered.

Chernichev hooked his foot around one of the black duffels, partly unzipped, and shoved it under a nearby wing chair. The bag moved with a clank and clatter of metal on metal.

"Indeed," he said. "Kind of you to ask. I'm sure if we need anything the foreman will be able to direct us, once he returns. You needn't concern yourself with us. We can fend for ourselves."

Anatoly nodded, cleared his throat. "If anything does come up, you can let me know."

Chernichev pressed his lips together in what seemed to be smile. His hands were clasped behind his back.

Zenit dropped his arm from around Anatoly's shoulders, and he took that as a sign that he was free to leave. He bid the men good evening and left the room. What was this about a monk? Were they Meyerhaeusen employees or not? The fastest way to find out would be to call Samuel at the Polygon. He would know, one way or the other.

But first, he needed to find Miko, and tell her. He was sure he would find her in Control.

THIRTY-TWO

No longer a young tiger, with boundless energy and curiosity, his bones ached, his body ached.

Khagan was hungry. He was always hungry. Hunting required work. Required patience. With each winter he became less and less patient. More and more confident in his ability to kill what he wanted, when he wanted. He knew how to evade the two-legs when the interloper invaded his territory. And he knew how to be clever when he chose to invade the two-legs' farms, and take one of his kept animals. He had learned to suspect his snares, to avoid his traps.

He crossed the empty field, entered the trees, moved noiselessly among the pines until he came near the large old house. Men had come to occupy this place as well. Though they arrived only a short time before the other, solitary one, they did not associate with him. Did not even seem to be aware of his existence, while he definitely kept clear of them. Was he afraid of them? He seemed more familiar with the ways of the woods than they. Perhaps his independence proved him to be the stronger one—Khagan knew that the two-legs were typically gregarious animals. They kept in groups, two at a minimum, for safety. Not like tigers. Not like Khagan.

A few windows at one end of the lower floor glowed

brightly, spilled their light out onto the fresh snow. Khagan kept well back from the light, in the trees, hidden. Scenting the wood smoke, the smell of flesh burning, according to their disgusting custom. The steady murmur of their ceaseless communication—another characteristic of the two-legs—punctuated by the occasional boisterous guffaw. More snow fell, and Khagan did not shake it from his fur, let it accumulate, let it hide him even further.

A door swung open, banged shut. Two men emerged. They babbled and blathered, talking over each other, laughing, back-slapping. They magically sparked the small fire in their hands, but Khagan knew he did not need to fear this fire. They blew a sweetly scented smoke out into the night air, then tossed the fragrant remains into the snow. One went back inside, the other staggered through the snow toward the tree line. He stopped at a tree and began to make his water. He leaned forward, into the tree, propped himself up with his forearm, sighed heavily and rested his forehead on his arm while his water splashed about his boots.

The man shivered. He was not wearing his heavy coat. Khagan slid from cover. Began to circle around to the side, careful to keep out of his line of sight, and away from the splashes of light in the snow.

His tail twitched. His whiskers quivered.

It had been a while since he had brought down live game. The boars were no longer plentiful in his territory. The deer were too nimble, too frightened of him. He did not crave the taste of this creature's flesh in the same way that he craved boar or deer. Much too fatty, too stringy, too sickly. But he was tired of chasing away buzzards and minks and crows for nothing more than a share of days-old picked-over carrion. He wanted a kill of his own. This man would keep him well-fed for several nights.

The ember glowed hot, cautioned him. Reminded him of what the two-legs were capable of. They would seek him out. They would search for him, to retaliate. The ember warned him. Warmed him. But the pangs of hunger burned brighter. Goaded him. Demanded action.

The man's sighing had turned to a mindless rhyming sing-song. His stream began to falter. Still he leaned against the tree.

Unaware. Unwary.

The tiger worked his rear paws deep into the snow. His haunches coiled, tensed. His tail lifted into the air, poised, a counterbalance to the explosive push that would bring his entire weight, his entire being, down onto this hairless, helpless, pitiable creature.

The door opened, cast more yellow light out into the snow. A silhouette filled the doorframe, bellowed. The man squeezed out a last few drops, straightened, hitched his pants closed, turned and stumbled back toward the building.

The tiger had already melted back into the trees, into the darkness, into the snow.

The fortunate man brushed past the silhouette, who remained filling the frame for a moment. This man peered out into the night, perhaps wondering if his eyes were playing tricks on him, wondering if maybe it wasn't time to call it a night.

THIRTY-THREE

January 6, 2001—Cubs five weeks old

Anatoly still hadn't returned with the snowcat, and Miko was worried. Outside the broad windows of Control, snowflakes were beginning to fall, thick fluffy parachutes, drifting down unhurriedly, fully aware that they had plenty of time to bury everything in white. Her reflection was beginning to replace the outside view, as the solitary desk lamp within grew brighter than the dwindling, cloud-shrouded twilight. She turned off the lamp, so she wouldn't have to see the concern on her face reflected back to her. The room fell into darkness, then the dancing lights of the computer monitor's screen saver picked her out in the window. Still worried.

She tried again to raise him on the snowcat's two-way radio for the umpteenth time. No luck. Of course he wouldn't hear her if he was out of the cab, mounting cameras.

She shouldn't have asked him to go. He had told her that it wasn't strictly necessary, that there would be time to place the cameras once the workmen were finished. After the snowfall. But Sergei, the foreman, had assured her that they would be done in two, maybe three more days.

She'd heard that claim before, however.

Perhaps the cloud cover was screwing with the signals.

She checked the bank of CCTV monitors. All but five were dark, as Anatoly had disconnected the perimeter power supply before going out. A couple of cameras mounted on the lodge and the barn showed the empty paddock from several different angles, dim in the evening gloom. These would remain in place; if anything happened they would be easy enough to access. The green screens of the light-amplification cameras showed her the cubs, safe in their den. Vida paced anxiously; Kamal lay stretched out, his twitching, swiveling ears belying the fact that he, too, was awake.

She went downstairs. Checked the garage. Both snowcats still gone. The workmen hadn't returned from the perimeter yet either. Perhaps Anatoly had made his way around the fence until he reached the workmen. Yes, maybe he was coming back with them, or had recruited one of them to help him bring in the last of the cameras.

She hailed the other snowcat. Sergei answered. Informed her that they were on their way back, ETA twenty minutes.

"Have you seen Dr. Stasevich?" she asked. "Out at the perimeter?"

"No sign, *mèm*."

When he left, she had seen the snowcat through the windows, heading out counterclockwise around the fence. Had even glimpsed, through the small side door window, Anatoly driving. Something must've happened to his snowcat.

"How are you returning?" she asked. "Along the east side or west?"

"West."

"You need to change course," she said. "Keep an eye out for Dr. Stasevich. Or his snowcat."

"It's getting dark, *mèm*."

"I can see that. But Anatoly is still out there. His vehicle may be disabled."

The radio went silent. She was sure that the workmen had heard her order, and were complaining. So their dinner and vodka ration would be delayed another fifteen, twenty minutes.

"Did you hear me?" she asked. "Over."

"Message received," the foreman finally said. "Changing course." She thought she could hear the collective groan in the background. "Over."

"Go slowly," she said. "If he's on foot, he'll be walking along the fence."

"Right. Over and out."

She dressed for the outdoors. What was she going to do? Snow was falling. Night was practically here, visibility was limited and would be gone soon. She crossed to the lodge.

The new guys. She could ask them to help. They could set off along the fence, calling out for Anatoly. You didn't need visibility if you stuck to the fence.

The kitchen was empty. The lodge was dark. Felt deserted. She moved down the corridor, past the empty dining room, normally the bustling hub of activity, either eating or playing improvised table tennis once the remains of dinner had been cleared away. Past the empty sitting room, where the men slept on their cots. The double doors of the trophy room were closed. Light leaked out from the gap between the doors and the floorboards. This must be where the new men were staying. Maybe Anatoly had returned, left the snowcat outside for some reason. Maybe the doors would open and she would find him sitting with them, getting to know them, sharing a drink and a laugh. Maybe everything would have a perfectly logical, plausible explanation, and she would feel foolish.

She knocked on the door. The sound elicited a brief, muffled exchange of words on the other side, followed by some rustling, and then the sound of floorboards creaking. The door opened. The one with the large ears stood in the frame. Tufts of dark hair sprouted from every fold in his ears. What was his name? She couldn't recall now.

"Have you seen Dr. Stasevich?"

"A few hours ago," he said. "He asked if we needed anything."

"That's right," a voice called from within. She peered around the man—Abrek, that was his name—to see one of the others, the large one, Zenit, lounging on an old couch. Smoking. The room was full of smoke and the smell of cigarettes. It both repelled her and made her want to ask for one.

"Where is the other one?" she asked.

Abrek cleared his throat, glanced over his shoulder toward Zenit.

A hand on her shoulder caused her to jump. Chernichev.

"Just visiting the jakes," he said, with a smile. He shook his hand, produced a pack of cigarettes with two standing proud. He took one, extended the other toward her.

"Smoke?" he asked. He placed the cigarette in the corner of his mouth.

She sighed. "If you must smoke, keep it in this room. Not outdoors."

"Have a seat." Chernichev motioned for her to enter the room, while Abrek stepped back. "Join us," Chernichev continued. "I'd like to hear more about your project."

He extended the pack toward her again, like a radio handset with a white antenna. Reminding her of her mission.

"I'm looking for Dr. Stasevich," she said. "Have you seen him?"

"Sorry." Chernichev shook his head. Moved past her into the room.

Abrek nudged him. "Not since he came by, right?"

Chernichev turned back toward her. "Oh, well—that was hours ago," he said. "After breakfast."

Miko tried not to let her face show any concern.

"He hasn't come back," she said. "I'm going out to search for him."

Chernichev retreated to an old overstuffed wing chair, near the hearth, where a fire was crackling. He tucked the cigarette behind his ear. Abrek remained standing by the door, staring at her. Zenit lay back on the sofa, eyes on the ceiling.

"Outside?" Chernichev asked. "It's nearly dark. More snow is coming."

"I know," she said. Concerned as she was about Anatoly,

she now found that she couldn't bring herself to ask these men for help.

Chernichev looked from one man to the other. Neither of the others moved, or betrayed any desire, whether to help or to stay where it was warm and comfortable. They were waiting for orders.

"Not really in our purview," he said. "Apologies." He shifted the cigarette from his ear back to his mouth.

She had already turned to leave. She didn't want any of these men accompanying her, anywhere, indoors or out, daytime or night. Especially not Chernichev. There was something about him that told her he was lying. He knew what had become of Anatoly. She had no way to prove it, but she was sure of it.

THIRTY-FOUR

January 6, 2001—Cubs five weeks old

The next day Yuri chopped wood and built a pyre for the tiger carcass. While he worked, she flayed the pelt from the carcass, hung it to dry over a rack. Not all of the creature would be burned. There were parts she would make good use of.

It was nearing the end of day when they finally lit the fire. It blazed high, flames greedily devouring the wood and then the flesh and organs they had placed on the bier. Yuri added more wood as the pyre shifted, and sank. Sparks lifted up into the darkness, racing up to join the millions of stars that stood out in sky. In the morning only bones would be left.

They went into the hut, to eat and to sleep. He needed to get back to his dacha. He needed to prepare. Chernichev would want revenge. Not for his comrade so much as for the payday he'd been denied. The fresh snow might keep him away for a day or two. But the Ferret wouldn't wait very long.

Tomorrow he would leave. Tomorrow morning, first thing.

After dinner, after checking on the dwindling funeral

pyre, Utiuki warmed a bucket of water on the stone stove. She dunked a cloth into the steaming water, wrung it out.

"Bath time," she said.

Before he could protest, she wagged her finger at him. "No complaining. So filthy."

She slowly daubed and scrubbed at the wounds on his cheek. Then she cleaned the rest of his face, his neck, his ears, and with a scoop poured some of the water into his hair. He let her work. She was right, he had needed a bath.

One of his earliest memories was of his mother, washing him in the wooden tub, which they also filled from water warmed on the stove. While she washed, she sang to him in the language of her people, the Evenki. In the language his father didn't want her to teach them. A song about the antlers of the reindeer, how they grew from tiny stumps to full, strong racks that spread across the sky, that pierced the clouds, that held up the stars at night. One of his earliest memories, and one of his only memories of her. Utiuki, too, hummed as she worked.

She helped him out of his sweater and his undershirt, washed his torso, his armpits, the livid bite marks on his forearm.

"What is she like?" Utiuki asked while she washed his back.

"Who?"

"Her." She waved her hand vaguely over her shoulder. Perhaps in the direction of the Project. "That woman with our tigers."

He shrugged. "I only met her briefly."

"And?"

"We barely spoke."

"Why did she get the cubs? Why not you?"

"She's the expert."

"Why don't you like her?"

I don't dislike her, he almost said. "She's very possessive about the cubs," he said, finally. "Like they're hers. Like a mother."

"That's not a bad thing," Utiuki said. "Tell me something bad."

Yuri laughed. "You don't want to like her?"

"One bad thing."

"She might not be tough enough," he said. "For Primorsky Krai."

"Survived this long." Utiuki said. "She must have some tough parts."

"I suppose."

"Is she pretty?"

He thought for a moment. Then nodded.

"See? Easy enough."

"Being pretty is bad?"

"To an ugly old woman pretty always bad."

"But you're not ugly," Yuri said. "And you're not old."

She gave him a sly smile. "Not stupid, either."

She removed his boots, and wrapped the warm, wet cloth around each foot—toes, sole, heel, ankle—and worked through the cloth with her thumbs, scrubbing at the ground-in dirt. One at a time she separated each toe from its neighbors, dug the cloth into the tender webbing. Pulled on each toe with the cloth, cleaning the sides, the knuckles, straightening the toes. Her motions brusque, efficient, repetitive. Making sure no grime hid in the creases, or held fast in the knotty calluses.

Warmth seeped up through his legs, into his body. It felt good to be clean, and warm. Tomorrow morning, at first light, he would return to the sanitarium, to watching over the Project. But for now, he wasn't going anywhere.

He was asleep before she had finished with his feet.

THIRTY-FIVE

January 7, 2001—Cubs six weeks old

She couldn't believe Anatoly was gone. She'd called Samuel, of course, though the snowstorm had played havoc with the satellite phone's reception, and it took her a full eight hours to get the message across ungarbled.

The workmen had not finished with the fence. They had spent the day in the steadily falling snow searching around the perimeter, patrolling in the remaining snowcat, staying within sight of the one landmark they could count on, the black iron fence, calling out for Anatoly, probing the deep snow nearby with metal fence supports. She had stayed close to the radio and the walkie talkies, monitoring, calling, listening. By noon they had found the second snowcat and brought it in. No sign of Anatoly, however.

The cubs were picking at each other, tussling more often than usual, the heavy snow keeping them from going out into the paddock and exercising. Their spats turned into hissing, clawing fights. Should she intervene? No, she knew she could not separate them. Unless one began to seriously hurt the other, she had to let them work out their own issues. Still, she prepared a fresh set of tranquilizer darts, a mix of cyclohexamine and benzodiazepene sedative carefully calibrated to each tiger's mass—one tray of two darts for Kamal, a separate tray with a slightly weaker formula for Vida.

She also formulated two for a much larger, mature tiger. For the rogue male. Just in case. She set these in between the two trays.

Normally, she would keep the gun and the darts downstairs, in the lab. But after charging the darts, she brought them all and the rifle up to Control with her. For a human, the most powerful darts would deliver a lethal dose.

Again—just in case.

She was acutely aware of her own restlessness as well. Anatoly was gone. There was nothing she could do to bring him back. Perhaps he had found shelter in the sanitarium compound. It wasn't that far away. It was a faint hope, and she clung to it.

She had eaten lunch with the men—the old hands and the new men—in the dining room. The mood had been silent, somber. Tense. Accusatory, almost. His disappearance, after all, coincided with the new men's arrival. Once daylight had returned, they had helped with the search, despite the heavy snowfall, she couldn't deny that. They were all doing all that they could, though the conditions were prohibitive. But still.

She took her evening meal back to Control. She'd been sleeping on the couch, as she often had in the past, and she fully intended on doing the same that night as well. When the storm lifted and they dug themselves out, she was going to call Samuel and ask him to contact Meyerhaeusen, tell them to send the new men home. They were not helping. They worried her more than any rogue male who might be prowling about.

Awake, she watched the cubs on the green screens from the sofa, munching absently on rice wafers, when she thought she heard a sound from the staircase. She froze her jaws, listened. Then another. Yes, somebody was coming up the steps.

I locked the door, she told herself. Then, *Didn't I?*

Whoever it was, they were trying to be stealthy. She

quickly slid from the couch, stuffed pillows under the blankets to make it look like a body sleeping there, unaware. Crouching, she moved to the table under the large windows, where a sliver of new moon, finally free of storm clouds, glinted off the chrome-plated barrel of the tranquilizer rifle. She grabbed a yellow-feathered dart from in between the two trays, picked up the gun in her other hand, and stepped softly to the far corner of the room, away from the windows, away from the monitors, which emitted a ghostly green glow. She sat on the floor, pressed her shoulders into the place where the walls came together.

She removed the rubber stopper from the dart with her teeth, loaded the projectile into the chamber, slowly slid the bolt home. Checked to see that the safety was still on. Waited, scarcely daring to breathe.

She heard the door handle turning, then catching short. A second attempt. Relief flooded through her. She had locked the door. It was a new door, too, with a heavy bolt.

A key slid into the lock, and the handle turned all the way this time. None of the workmen had a key, not even the foreman. Which was why she felt completely safe here. The only other person to have a key—the only man to have a key—was Anatoly.

Only Anatoly.

The door opened, and a slim figure, dressed all in black, stole inside. Paused. Slid the door closed. Paused again. Too skinny to be Anatoly. The head swiveled, scanning the room. Waiting, allowing eyes to adjust to the dim. She hoped the chrome barrel of the rifle would not catch the faint silver beams that slanted through the windows. She closed her eyelids to the barest of slits to keep the light from reflecting off her pupils.

The man—the intruder—crept on tiptoes to the couch. Leaned over it. Slowly pulled the blankets back. The back stiffened as he realized the deception. Straightened, turned, surveyed the room more carefully now.

"There you are," he said, voice soft. Chernichev. The white strands of his goatee stood out in the moonlight.

"Here I am," she said. She lowered the barrel, aimed it at her visitor. Switched the safety off with an audible click.

"What's that you've got there?" he asked.

"Tranq gun," she said.

"So you were expecting me."

"What are you doing in my room?" she asked. *All things considered,* she thought, *her voice sounded steady. Controlled.*

"So that thing would knock me out?" he asked. "If you were to shoot me?"

"It would knock out a three-hundred-kilo tiger. But you're no tiger."

"You should try me," he said. He patted the back of the couch.

"First the benzodiazepine would render you unconscious," she said. "But then, at this dose, the cyclohexamine would produce violent seizures. They would last for a few minutes. Finally your heart would give up and stop beating. That is, unless you weigh about two hundred kilos more than you appear to."

She could just see the corner of his mouth turning up in a smile.

"Sounds nasty."

"It's much worse than it sounds," she said. "Believe me."

"I bet you've done that many times before," he said, with an exaggerated sigh. "You may have stopped my heart already."

She ignored this. "Where is Dr. Stasevich?"

His shoulders lifted. "He said he was going out to collect the cameras. Maybe he got lost."

Something in his smarmy tone told her he was lying—and simultaneously told her that he didn't care if she knew it. But she had no way of proving it.

"Take it easy," he said. "I'm unarmed. I'm going to sit down."

Before she could say anything, he dropped down to the floor, leaned into the back of the sofa. She no longer had a stark silhouette to aim at. She kept the gun leveled between them, though. He would have to cross three meters of open floor to reach her, and in that time would come into the light. The dart was designed to penetrate thick animal hides, and would have no problem passing through his clothes. Of course, the sedative would take some time to kick in, depending on where the dart landed. She had no idea what the exact time would be on a human. Twenty, thirty seconds, she guessed.

A lot could happen in thirty seconds. An awful lot.

THIRTY-SIX

A spark turned to a flame, then to a glowing red ember. A cloud of smoke lifted into the field of light above the sofa. A pack of cigarettes slid across the floor, bounced off the wall to her right and came to rest beside her.

"I don't smoke," she said.

"Sure," he said. "But do you want a cigarette?"

Of course she did. The familiar smell caused her mouth to salivate, and she hated herself for the unconscious reaction. But she fought down the impulse to remove even just one hand from the gun. She knew that was what he wanted. A distraction.

"Why are you here?" she asked. These men were here to hunt the tiger, supposedly.

"I go where they send me," he said. "And then I try to make the best of a bad situation."

He took a drag from his cigarette. Smoked for a while in silence. Her initial surge of fear and adrenaline was wearing off. She blinked away the tiredness that begged to return to her bones, to her brain. Willed herself to stay focused.

"We've been hearing a lot of talk about a killer lurking around," Chernichev asked. His tone was playful, but there was an undercurrent of something else. *He's trying too hard*, she thought. *Trying too hard to appear nonchalant.* "Maybe keeping watch over you and these cubs. Sounds like tiger lady has a boyfriend."

"That's why you're here, right?" she asked. "To hunt him?"

"He took something of mine," he said. "And I want it back."

Now he seemed to be referring to an actual person, not a tiger. She decided to play along. See what she could learn.

"Whatever it is," she said, "I don't think he's going to give it to you."

"Doesn't look like it. But I'd be willing to listen to a counteroffer, in exchange. From the pretty tiger lady."

"What do I have that you might want?"

A cloud of smoke filled the air between them. "I think we both know the answer to that question."

"Well, you can forget about that, too," she said.

A low chuckle came from the shadows. "We'll see," he said.

She felt like they were speaking in a series of double entendres, but that there was a third layer underneath the talk about sex. *Not sex—rape*, she reminded herself. This man didn't care if she was willing or not. She lifted the barrel, aimed it at his chest. That was when it occurred to her. These men were soldiers. That park ranger—he was a soldier. He had warned them about men that were coming for the cubs.

He knew these men, she realized. And they knew him.

"You served with him, didn't you?" she asked. "With my boyfriend, I mean."

The man lit another cigarette from the nearly consumed butt of his current one. *He's nervous*, she realized. *No—he's scared. He's scared of the park ranger. What was his name again?*

"Chechnya," he said. "He's using you as bait, you know. How does that make you feel, to know that he's leaving you here all alone, on purpose?"

"What did you two do—in the war?"

"Do?" he scoffed. "What did we *do?* We killed Chechen

motherfuckers, that's what we did. Sorry—separatists. Dirty towel-headed Cossack terrorists."

He leaned forward. Pointed with his cigarette toward the windows. Toward the outside. "In fact, the Monk—that was his nickname—killed his best friend because he went over to the Chechens. Not with a gun, by the way. With a knife. Up close. So he could see his face when he stuck him. So he could watch the life bleed out of him."

He leaned back into the sofa. The ember flared red, then was obscured by a cloud of dense smoke. She kept the barrel pointed just below that dim ember, but she felt her hands shaking. She wasn't sure why. But she sensed that Chernichev had just told her a truth about Yuri.

That's his name—Yuri. Yuri the park ranger. Who wasn't a park ranger. Who was a killer, just like this man sitting across from her. This man who would kill her without giving it a second thought. Had she been asleep, she might be dead already.

"Not very nice company you're keeping," he said. "I bet your parents wouldn't be too pleased if you brought him home for supper."

Leave my parents out of this, she thought. But she knew better than to give him any personal ammunition. She was learning how he was fishing for information that he might use later. *Razvedka*, that was what they called it.

He stabbed his cigarette out on the wooden floorboards. The space heater clicked on with a grumble that smoothed into a purr. Light was beginning to fill the room. His vague shadowy outline was becoming more concrete. Color began to emerge from the monochromatic gloom, slowly filling in the dark forms.

"It's time for me to go." He checked his wristwatch, raised his arms above his head in a stretch. "Care to return my smokes?"

She glanced down at them. It wasn't her brand. And she didn't need the temptation. Then again, she might want one later. And she knew better than to remove one of her hands from the gun, or even to lift the barrel so she could shove the pack across with the wooden stock.

"It's a non-smoking facility," she said.

"I'll be back for them later," he said, with a wolfish grin. "After I deal with your boyfriend."

"You better hope you don't find him," she said. She had sensed his fear. Could sense it even now, behind all the tough talk. He had come here to make himself feel better. To make himself feel like a man, like he believed a man should feel. To dominate a woman one last time—just in case. She had learned something about him. Something that made him less of a man. Much less. "Because I have a feeling he's going to kill you."

"You better hope he does," Chernichev said. "Because if he doesn't—and in case you haven't noticed, tiger lady, it's three against one—then I'm going to come back here, and we'll see whether you're capable of pulling that trigger or not."

"I wish you would try me," she said.

He smiled, and stood up, keeping his hands open in front of him. He glanced quickly over his shoulder toward the brightening windows. Clearly uncomfortable at the possibility of being visible from outside.

"Now's your chance," he said. He moved toward the door, and she tracked him with the barrel of the gun. "In a few short hours, I'm going to make you wish that you had taken it."

She watched him leave the room, watched the door close behind him, listened to his footfalls as he tromped down the stairs, taking no care to muffle the sound now. The bang of the door as he left the lab. Slowly she straightened her stiff legs, pushed her back up the wall until she was standing. She went to the door and locked it. She retrieved the cigarettes from the floor. Went to stand by the window, surveying the world outside, covered in a heavy blanket of white, trees sagging under the weight of snow. Under the staggering density of pure whiteness. She pulled a cigarette from the pack and held it absently to her lips, lit it automatically, barely even inhaled the smoke, certainly didn't taste it.

She still stood there, a cigarette butt between her fingers, the tobacco long since burned away, when three men emerged from the kitchen door in pale gray parkas and matching boots and woolen caps. Camouflage for the snowy conditions. They all bore long-barreled rifles over their shoulders. They dropped cross-country skis into the snow and kicked into them. Fitted tinted goggles over their faces and pushed off, heading clockwise along the fence, out toward the perimeter.

A red sun crested over the treeline far to the east. She winced at the lance of red light that pierced to the back of her brain. They were headed toward the sanitarium, she supposed. The sanitarium must be where he—where Yuri, their target—was living. Yet another rogue male. She ought to be annoyed that he had followed them here. After all, wasn't he the reason why these men were here, threatening her, now? Wasn't he, ultimately, the reason why Anatoly had disappeared? But she was simply too exhausted. Too... *spent*.

Soon the workmen would wake and begin to make breakfast. Maybe today they would finish the fence. Maybe today.

Though maybe after today it wouldn't matter anymore.

THIRTY-SEVEN

January 7, 2001—Cubs six weeks old

Yuri dreamed of Khagan chasing him, the tiger's eyes burning redly, shooting jets of flame like flares. Just as the tiger closed the distance, he woke up.

A visit from Amba, his first thought, as the brightly colored rugs came into focus. That's what Utiuki would say. What was Amba trying to tell him?

They're coming. They'll be here soon. Today is the day.

He scoffed at himself. Was he getting superstitious? Was he finding religion, after all this time?

And yet, he knew it to be true. Something had changed, in the air. The morning sun shone bright, poured slanting light into the hut through the solitary window. He'd slept too long.

Utiuki sat on the other side of the stove. She held his parka in her lap. With a needle and thread she seemed to be sewing a patch onto it. She hummed softly while she worked, but ceased when he sat up, awake.

"Is my coat torn?" he asked.

She shook her head. "Amba likes to play tricks on us," she said, "but this is how we play a trick on Amba." She resumed her tuneless humming.

After a few more stitches, satisfied with her handiwork, she held up the hood, the fur-lined opening toward her, the hood's back facing him. Two big white eyes stared at him, a small dark circle in the center of each.

"Amba won't attack if he thinks you can see him," she said. "Good to have eyes in the back of your head!"

She clearly thought this was quite the joke.

"Does it work?" He knew that this was why tigers themselves had white spots on the backs of their black ears, to discourage rivals or other predators from sneaking up behind them.

"If you keep all your eyes open it does!" she said, with a giggle. "But we don't always keep all our eyes open, do we?"

She handed his coat back to him.

"Thank you," he said. "For this. For everything. I owe you."

He'd stayed too long. He had to get back to his dacha. He knew that Chernichev would eventually find him. And not long after that, the Project. He didn't need Khagan to appear in his dreams to tell him this.

"You worry," she said. "About the *biryuk*." About the wolf.

She was right. He was worried. Not so much that they would come for him, but that in doing so they might find the tiger cubs. Might find Miko all alone. Might also trace his tracks in the fresh snow to Utiuki. If they suspected she knew anything about his whereabouts, they would extract that knowledge from her, ruthlessly. *Razvedka*. The snowfall might keep them away for another day or two. But he didn't expect them to wait for long.

"Where there are no tigers," she said, "the wolves come. And the wolves eat everything. *Biryuk* eats and eats until there is nothing left."

"I need to get back," he said.

"First, you eat."

She handed him a wooden bowl full of the stew that had been simmering on the stove since he had woken up. The aches in his muscles and joints seemed to melt away as the thick, fatty broth warmed his entire body.

He pulled on his coat, drew the newly decorated hood down over his head. She pointed him in the right direction. The sun stood as high in the sky as it would on a winter's day, shining brightly. He just had to follow the sun, and he would reach the sanitarium.

"Come back," she said. "Utiuki always here."

He waved, thanked her again for her help. He left with a genuine hope that one day he would return. Her stew was delicious. It was also nice to have a neighbor, in this abandoned, frigid world swirling with ghosts and spirits.

THIRTY-EIGHT

Yuri heard the concussion not long after leaving Utiuki's hut. He smelled the smoke as he pushed his way through the last of the scrub pines at the eastern edge of the athletic fields. He slowed his pace, brought his Mosin-Nagant down from his shoulder. Staying low, he crept forward until he could see thin trails of pallid smoke drifting skyward.

The fire was not large. His dacha had been destroyed with an explosive charge, rather than torched. The brick-and-iron stove and chimney still stood, and a row of cupboards clung yet to the wall that once separated the kitchen from the living room. Three of the four cabinet doors were gone, however, and the fourth hung at an angle, supported by only one hinge. The exterior walls and the raised wooden flooring had been obliterated; the woolen blankets that he and Evgeny had tacked up for insulation lay scattered through the snow, tattered, writhing in the light breeze that pushed the tendrils of smoke to and fro.

All of his remaining gear, his food, his firewood, his clothing—vanished.

He remained hidden in the trees, surveying the scene through his rifle's telescopic sight. His assailants would have inspected the ruins for signs of his corpse, for proof of his death. To take back to the Major, he supposed. They would know that they had missed him, of course. He assumed that they would have left at least one man waiting for his return, keeping vigil at a safe distance, half a kilometer or so, in a snow-covered blind, taking advantage of the heavy snowfall, most likely with a spotter. That's how he would do it. That's how the Major had trained him, trained Chernichev. Trained all of them.

He was angry, and the anger made him want to find the man or men left behind in ambush, to turn the tables, to have some measure of revenge, and to eliminate at least one of his enemies at the earliest opportunity. But he also knew that this was an emotional response. There was nothing left, nothing to salvage, that much was clear.

If anything, he should be glad. He'd been lucky. They hadn't found him vulnerable in the dacha, at a time when they otherwise might have—he hadn't anticipated that they would strike so soon after the storm. Had it been luck, though? They had only missed him because Khagan had driven him into the forest, away from the sanitarium, where he had found Utiuki's hut and she had welcomed him in. He shook his head. Was all this talk of *amba* the last two days making him religious? Superstitious?

A man wrapped in winter gear left the cover of one of the nearby dachas, and slowly approached the smoldering ruins. Yuri lowered his head even further, burying his face in the snow. The man cast glances over his shoulder at the dachas and the dormitories beyond, and then he peered through tinted goggles toward the trees where Yuri hid. He stepped over what was left of the walls, stooped to examine something, turned it over in his hands, then straightened and continued his search.

Perhaps this was one of the men left behind, tired of waiting for their target to appear. Yuri removed his gloves, lifted the rifle barrel ever so slightly, sighted the crosshairs on the earflap of the man's *ushanka*. Let his body settle in the snow. Switched off the safety.

Something kept him from pulling the trigger. He recognized this man. It was Evgeny.

He couldn't see his friend's reddened nose or his bushy black beard due to the scarf and goggles that he wore, but Yuri knew it was him from the rounded slope of his shoulders, the way he carried himself. The big man always hunched slightly, as though he felt it rude to tower over people.

Yuri whistled at him. A low owl-like whistle that they had used to signal each other in the past. He saw the man's shoulders stiffen, his back straighten. He stood and looked around, and Yuri repeated the call. He had to assume that he wasn't the only one with eyes on Evgeny at the moment, and he didn't want to give away his own position to any distant observers. But he needed to get his friend's attention, and pull him away from the destroyed dacha. Whoever was watching Evgeny was sure to have a bead on him as well, but knew enough to know that this wasn't the man they were after. They would be on full alert, though, hoping that Yuri would see his friend and show himself.

Yuri made the call one last time. Evgeny peered in his direction, and then moved off among the dachas that remained standing. Yuri slowly worked his way backward through the snow, back into the dark safety of the scrub pines. Confident that Evgeny knew it was him, knew where he was, but would take a circuitous route to reach him.

A few minutes later, they met in the trees. Evgeny lifted his goggles and pulled down his scarf, a smile of relief spread across his face.

"You're alive!" he said.

He spread his arms wide, but Yuri still held the rifle. Not raised to his shoulder, but at his hip, with his finger resting lightly on the trigger, the safety still switched off.

With the fresh snow, and his absence, there would not have been a trail for his attackers to follow. There was only one way Chernichev had known where to find him.

His friend halted. His eyes darkened, his arms lowered.

"There was nothing I could do," Evgeny said, his voice quiet. "They threatened my wife. My daughters."

"I know," Yuri said. He knew just how persuasive Iliakov and Chernichev could be when conducting *razvedka*.

"They said they would kill them. Actually, they said they would rape them first, while they made me watch, and then they would kill them."

Yuri nodded. Lowered the rifle, thumbed on the safety.

"I'm sorry," Evgeny said. Yuri waved his hand as though chasing away a pesky fly.

"It's okay," Yuri said. "I don't blame you for anything."

"I want to make it up to you," Evgeny said. "I mean it."

"Tell me why you're here."

"I wanted to warn you," Evgeny said. "Or—to see if you needed help."

"Better be careful," Yuri said, "or Vassily will suspend you, too."

"You haven't heard," Evgeny said with a frown. "Of course you haven't."

Yuri stared at him, waited for him to continue.

"The Brigade has been disbanded."

"What?" Iliakov's prediction had come true. Much sooner than Yuri would ever have imagined.

Slowly, somberly, Evgeny nodded. "We're both out of work. Not that you care."

Yuri wasn't the only one who had found a home in the Brigade. Evgeny had been there for nearly fifteen years. The second-longest tenure, behind only Vassily. He'd begun talking lately about how he was going to run things once that "miserly old bastard" finally retired. Once he became the senior officer, he would implement some of the changes that he and Yuri often discussed on their long, winding drives through the taiga.

Evgeny had his wife to consider, his two daughters. A family that counted on his income.

"I'm sorry, my friend," Yuri said.

He reached up to lay his hand on Evgeny's shoulder. It wasn't just an expression of empathy. He couldn't help feeling personally responsible. If he hadn't cut those cubs from their mother—would any of this happened? It was as though he had triggered some sort of irrevocable curse.

The natural order of things, reasserting itself. With a keen sense of irony. And a healthy portion of vengeance.

"The Amba Patrol," Yuri said, his voice little more than a whisper.

"Gone," Evgeny said.

Those words pained Yuri. In his mind, he had continued doing the work of the Brigade. He had simply refused to follow the misguided orders of its incompetent—or corrupt—commanding officer. But now it was hitting home. If the Brigade was disbanded, then he would truly be on his own. He had thought of this as a temporary measure. Maybe until the snow melted. At most another year or so, when the cubs were grown and released back into the wild. The finality of an ending began to sink in.

The big man searched through his coat pockets until he found what he was looking for, tossed a metallic disc in Yuri's direction. He caught it out of the air. His Brigade badge. The nickel-plated pressed tin, bearing the embossed head and shoulders of a tiger, surrounded by Cyrillic letters painted black: **СИХОТЭ-АЛИНСКИЙ ЗАПОВЕДНИК** —*Sikhote-Alinsky Zapovednik*.

"Nicked it off the old bastard's desk," Evgeny said.

"Not much good now, is it?"

"Let's face it," Evgeny said with a wry chuckle. "It never was much good."

THIRTY-NINE

They had destroyed his shelter, but had failed to find Yuri. Still they were out there, somewhere. Waiting. Watching. Possibly patrolling, searching for him, but more likely lying in wait, waiting for him to appear to spring the ambush.

Evgeny insisted that the Major had only asked him where to find Yuri, and hadn't asked why Yuri had decided to live in an abandoned sanitarium in the middle of winter. Yuri assumed that they hadn't asked because they hadn't needed to ask. They already knew about Miko and her Project.

Arriving late to the scene had saved his life, but now he was a step behind, and trying to play catch up. And where would his enemies expect him to turn now? Where would they expect him to go? Where would they set up their ambush? Even so, he had to get to the lodge. He had to alert Miko. Make sure she and the tiger cubs were okay.

He urged Evgeny to match his pace, and they moved as quickly as they could through the trees and the deep, fresh snow. Though the way would have been much shorter to cross the broad expanse of the athletic fields, that would put them right out in the open, make them easy targets. They kept to the forest. They walked in silence, the only sound Evgeny's labored breathing behind him, the regular scrunch of snow under their boots.

Evgeny had told him that he'd gotten word about the Brigade a little more than a week ago. Maybe a week after he'd returned from helping Yuri carry supplies to the sanitarium.

"Vassily, of course, tried to blame it on us," Evgeny had said. "On you. For bringing so much attention to the Brigade. I told him he could go fuck himself. Rescuing tiger cubs is exactly the sort of thing we *should* be known for."

"It was the Major," Yuri said.

"A Major wouldn't have that kind of pull," Evgeny said.

"You don't know him like I do."

Yuri retrieved his badge from his parka pocket. The appearance of the Major, followed so soon by the elimination of the Brigade, did not strike Yuri as coincidence. He didn't mention the "for profit," ex-*spetsnaz* Anti-Poaching Brigade that the Major had proposed when he'd seen him at the Polygon, when the cubs were only days old. Maybe Evgeny was right. Perhaps Vassily was telling the truth. But Yuri knew that the Major didn't leave things to coincidence, to random chance. To luck.

"You were *spetsnaz*?" Evgeny broke in on his thoughts. "How did I not know this?"

"You knew I was in the Army."

Ahead, buzzards circled lazily against the ominous dark clouds. Crows had begun scolding them from the upper boughs of the taller Korean pines they had begun moving through.

"Christ, who hasn't been in the Army?" Evgeny said, oblivious. "But Special Forces? Why didn't you say anything?"

Yuri slowed his pace. Raised his hand for Evgeny to be quiet. To be cautious.

"It didn't seem relevant," Yuri whispered as his partner came closer.

He lifted the gun stock to his shoulder, sighted through the scope. Among the straight and tall Korean pines, with their naked boles, visibility was improved. Every animal in the forest knew what the buzzards circling meant. A dead animal would bring many more animals, to wait their turn at the trough that the natural order of things provided.

They proceeded slowly, heading toward the commotion, stopping frequently to look and listen. Through his scope he watched a juvenile boar tugging at a carcass of some sort. On any other day, he would have eagerly taken the shot—the boar would have given him several days' supply of meat. But there was no time for that now, they had to reach the lodge. He was about to straighten and adjust their course to skirt the commotion, when something drew his attention, clinging to the carcass: scraps of bright red fabric.

He moved forward more quickly now, not worried about making sounds. Hoping to scatter the boars and whatever else might be picking at the carrion. He and Evgeny reached a clearing, and several buzzards skipped back away from them, large wings lifted like capes, though they refused to fly from their prey.

It wasn't a carcass. It was a corpse.

He knelt by what was left of the body. It hadn't taken long for the buzzards, the boars, the stoats to discover the corpse, and begin stripping the flesh from the bones. The poor man's eyes and ears and cheeks were gone, his face obliterated by a series of small bites. What remained of his parka and layers of clothing were shredded rags. He'd been eviscerated, his organs mostly removed, presumably devoured. His genitals and thighs were largely gone, some scraps of frozen meat still clung to the bones.

Behind him, Evgeny cursed, then staggered away to retch among the trees.

Yuri searched through the remaining parka pockets. Nothing. Searched through the snow nearby. Found a wallet. With identification that confirmed his suspicion.

The body he was looking at had once belonged to Dr. Anatoly Stasevich. What was he doing this far from the lodge? By himself? What had killed him?

Among the shallow pecks in the torso and legs there were several deeper gouges, marked by a flow of blood that had quickly frozen. These could have been made by claws. Tigers were not above eating carrion, especially in the colder months. This didn't look like a man who had been mauled to death, however.

With the barrel of the gun he prodded the man's chin. There, in the triangle of the jawbone, a single slim puncture, a trickle of frozen blood. The fatal blow. Delivered by a *spetsnaz*-trained killer. Left here to look like a man who had died from exposure, or possibly from a tiger attack. Left here for the creatures of the taiga to dispose of.

He wanted an explanation. His thoughts turned to Miko, to the Project.

Evgeny returned to his side. Yuri handed him the wallet.

"Christ," Evgeny breathed.

"See how they unzipped his coat?" Yuri said. "To make it easier for the buzzards."

"Poor son of a bitch," Evgeny said. "What do we do?"

"We have to get to the lodge," Yuri said. "Miko is on her own."

"Should we bring..." Evgeny waved his hand toward the mangled corpse.

They would want Anatoly's body. But that would have to wait. Trying to carry or drag the body with them would only slow them down. There was nothing they could do for Anatoly now—nothing that he would be able to appreciate, at any rate.

Yuri stood up. "Can you manage it?"

"By myself? Where are you going?"

"I have to get to the lodge."

He set off at a jog through the snow.

"Hey! Wait for me!" Evgeny called after him. But Yuri couldn't afford to wait. Couldn't afford to let anything or anybody slow him down any longer.

FORTY

Khagan glided through the trees, skirted around the solitary pool of yellow light cast by the lamp that hung over the door to the barn where the two-legs were keeping the tiger cubs. He kept coming back to the problem of the cubs. He knew that the two-legs kept animals. Dogs, cats, chickens, goats. Sheep, pigs, cattle. Some kept horses. He stayed away from the smell of horses, as they were too skittish, too quick to sound the alarm and let their owners know that a tiger was nearby. For the same reason he avoided those places with dogs, too. Unless he was hungry. Some dogs were foolish enough to run at Khagan, thinking that their ability to terrify the chickens or to herd the sheep or keep the pigs in line made them lord of all creatures. A lesson several had learned the hard way over the years.

There was only one lord of all creatures.

Until two-legs came, with his buildings and his lightning stick.

And now two-legs had taken to keeping tigers. In all his years, he had never seen two-legs keep tigers. Such strange behavior from the two-legs lately. Khagan saw this for what it was: an attempt to claim their status as lord of all creatures.

But there could be only one Khagan. Only one King of Kings.

And to the lord of the forest, young tigers were potential rivals to be driven from his territory, or killed and devoured, subsumed into his flesh, into his being. There was no dishonor in being eaten by Khagan. It was the ultimate sacrifice, the ultimate glory.

He hadn't figured out how to get at them, with impunity. Of course, if he really desired, he could get over the wall that separated him from them. It was not terribly tall. He could get over it, yes, but once he fed, he might not be able to return to freedom, to safety. The ember might slow him. Two-legs with a stick might call down the lightning to strike him. That was when the tiger was most vulnerable, when he committed to the attack, when he struck at the easy, passive animals that man kept for his own ends. The two-legs always guarded his animals as a treasure. The wall and the fence told him these animals would be guarded as well.

New arrivals. Two-legs in his forest, building fires, cutting down trees. Keeping tigers as though they were pets, or livestock. No good could come of this. Fire brought death. Two-legs brought death, with his lighting stick. Death, however, brought food. Easy food. Food that didn't have to be hunted.

He smelled the tiger on the other side of the wall before he heard his padding paws skittering over the icy crust. A little one. Growing bigger. Still not worth a meal. Though, why not? He didn't need to eat as much now as he used to. The hunger was not driving him to take a risk, the way it sometimes did. Sometimes the hunger burned brighter than the ember. But now the ember glowed, not hot, but warm. It warned him to keep his distance.

The little tiger put his paws against the wall, reared back on his hind legs. Khagan smelled the female now, though she kept her distance. The male attempted a roar. A challenge. Little more than a coughing bark. Khagan scoffed. A reply was not even necessary. He batted the flimsy wall where he knew the cub's forepaws pressed, knocked him tumbling back into the snow, hindquarters over head. The metal reverberated in the night air, as did the little one's noisy squall.

With a twitch of his tail, and a shot of his spoor to mark this place, too, as his territory—to issue a challenge to the two-legs snug and safe within their walls—Khagan turned from the paddock and vanished into the pre-dawn gloom.

FORTY-ONE

January 7, 2001—Cubs six weeks old

Not long after watching Chernichev and his comrades set out toward the sanitarium, the cough and rumble of the snowcat firing up in the garage below Control startled Miko awake. She didn't even remember sitting down, or lifting her feet from the floor, swinging them up onto the couch.

The red numerals on the digital clock told her it was 0820. The workmen were heading out toward the perimeter. Were they going to work on the fence? Or continue searching for Anatoly? She hadn't meant to fall asleep. She'd been waiting for them to make an appearance so she could tell Sergei that he needed to take her and the cubs—and himself and the workmen, too—far from the lodge. Back to civilization.

If the Project was to continue, it needed to be somewhere else. Not here. Not with these sinister men lurking around, threatening her, threatening her cubs. Chernichev had crossed a line. She was ready to get the hell out of there. They needed to bring more men to search the woods until they found Anatoly.

She stepped quickly to the table where she had thrown

her parka. Sounded like the snowcat was about to leave the garage.

At the window, a glimpse of orange against white, brought her to a halt. She stepped around the table, peered down into the paddock.

Vida. She was outside.

How?

She hadn't opened the gate to the den, hadn't let them out into the freshly fallen snow.

What the hell was going on?

Vida sat at the far end of the paddock, facing the wall, her back to Miko. The white "eyes" on the backs of the cub's still-rounded black ears stared up at Miko. The cub rose to her feet, placed one of her forepaws on the wall, then the other, lifted herself to standing on her hindquarters. Her nose almost reached the top of the wall. Had the tiger grown half a meter? Had the wall sunk into the earth?

No, of course not. The floor had lifted. The heavy snows had filled the paddock, bringing Vida that much closer to the top. The cub pushed away and sat back down, still facing the wall.

If she wanted to, she could probably jump over it. But *she* never wanted to—

Oh, no—Kamal.

Miko pressed her forehead against the window as she leaned forward to take in the entire paddock. One of Vida's ears half-turned in her direction. Her tail lifted, switched sides, curled around her haunch, settled back down into the snow. Miko turned toward the CCTV monitors, scanned the green screens. Empty.

Back to the window. On the far side of the paddock wall, near Vida, a trail of broken snow stretched away, traced a gentle arc, then began to switch directions, back and forth, aimlessly. Then finally broke in a straight line for the far horizon, vanishing behind a stand of trees.

No—this isn't possible, she thought. *This can't be happening.*

The entire Project—ruined.

The sound of the snowcat ratcheting into gear and roaring away from the garage brought her back to herself. She grabbed her parka, reached for the tranq gun on the coffee table.

Two yellow-feathered tranq darts with thick black rubber stoppers covering the needles sat in a tray labeled "Kamal," two more in a tray labeled "Vida."

She removed the high-dosage dart from the rifle and set it on the table. She replaced it in the chamber with one of the darts calibrated for Kamal's mass, slid the bolt home. Put the second one in her parka's right pocket.

A syringe containing a fast-acting antidote lay between the two trays. She tucked this into her left pocket.

She ran down the steps to the lab. The snowcat's engine began to fade.

She'd forgotten about the cubs. How could she?

She stepped to the two-way radio that would connect her with the snowcat. She picked up the transmitter, and it popped free in her hand, untethered. The cord had been cut. The walkie-talkie cradles were empty. The satellite phone was gone. Communications had been cut off. Sabotaged by Chernichev. Had he also opened the den door?

She ran back up the steps and grabbed the high-dosage dart, put that in her left pocket with the antidote. Just in case she saw Chernichev again. Something told her he was serious about the promises he'd made.

Back down in the lab, she stopped at the door to the outside, about to run after the snowcat shouting and waving her arms madly, in the hopes that one of the men riding in the back might see her.

Stop for a moment, she scolded herself. *Stop and think.*

Vida was out in the paddock, and if Kamal could get over the wall, she might eventually follow her brother. Before Miko went anywhere she needed to summon Vida back into the den. She got some thawed meat out of the refrigerator, pushed it through the feeding slot. Ran back up to Control to monitor the cub. She seemed aware of the food, but for the moment maintained her vigil at the fence.

They had to get out of there. She was not safe. The cubs were not safe. But she couldn't leave Vida out in the open like this.

She retrieved some more meat from the refrigerator, folded tranquilizer pills into the ground meat, and parceled these packets into one of the wooden food toys with sliding doors. Against protocol, she ran out of the lab and tossed the toy over the wall. The accumulation of snow allowed her, too, to reach the top of the wall and peer over, into the paddock. She watched as Vida cautiously approached the toy, sniffed at it.

"Come on," she murmured. Ducked as the tiger began to lift her head. Keeping low, she scurried back to the lab, then ran up to Control, watched Vida work the puzzle from the tinted windows. She grabbed her binoculars from the table, scanned the horizon for any sign of Kamal. She was losing precious time. She shifted her view to the left, to the north. Toward the break in the fence, where the men would soon light their bonfire and set about their work. And beyond, the sanitarium. Where Chernichev, Abrek and Zenit were likely also setting about their work. Had they found the man they were looking for?

They aren't "looking" for him, she reminded herself. *They're hunting him.*

Were they already on their way back to the lodge?

She was sweating in her parka. She didn't want to take it off, only to have to put it back on. Again she reminded herself to slow down. To think things through. To anticipate worst case scenarios. She might have to chase Kamal some way through the snow. The enclosure was enormous. He would be easy enough to track, in the fresh snow. But he would spook very quickly. She would have to pursue on foot—if she followed him on a snowmobile, he would keep running. Even on foot, he might not allow her to get within range of the tranq rifle.

Below her, Vida had solved the puzzle, eaten the food.

She had to hope that she hadn't spat out the pills. She would know in fifteen minutes.

The snow would be deep, and would make for hard going. She might be out there for hours. She needed several layers underneath her parka, just in case.

She would have to make a run to her room in the lodge.

FORTY-TWO

After adding an underlayer in her room, then carrying a dazed Vida into the den and placing her inside the gate, Miko grabbed the binoculars and the tranq rifle and set out after Kamal. She plowed through the knee-deep snow, following the trail the tiger had blazed. For a while she ran to the side of his prints, hoping that she would come back at some point and make similar measurements to those she had gathered from the rogue male. The paddock was too small for Kamal to really open up his stride the way he had now, running free, without artificial constriction. A trove of data to collect here. But now she followed directly in the trail the cat had broken through the snow, grateful he had made her way that much easier. Her boots sank much deeper into the snow than the lighter cat's snowshoe-like paws.

Kamal had reached the southern bend of the iron fence, a tiny silhouette on the horizon. She watched him jump at the bars several times, but soon the cub turned and began trotting to the left, toward the tree-covered slope. The length of a large dog, but lower to the ground, and with a much larger tail that swished to and fro behind him, balancing the smooth rolling of his shoulders and hips.

She turned with Kamal, left his trail and angled toward

the trees. She wasn't going to cut him off, he was too far ahead for that, but she could make up some precious ground.

She needed him to tire, to slow down, to rest. Cutting across the fresh snow made movement that much more of a slog, however. She was the one tiring. She would jog for a few paces, then slow to a high-knees, boot-lifting walk, then attempt to run a few more paces. She could hear it in her heaving gasps, could feel it in her burning chest, her aching thighs. Snow had worked its way into her boots, and her feet were cold and wet.

She hadn't taken the time to put on her gear properly. As she'd dressed in her room, every creak and groan that echoed through the empty lodge had convinced her that Chernichev and his two friends had returned.

Finally she reached the corner of the enclosure where the treeline met the fence. The tiger's trail continued up the slope, hugging the fence.

"Great," she said to herself. "Uphill."

She put her feet in the trail the tiger had plowed through the thick snow, and began to stride in his wake. The same route she had followed before when she visited the workers, or just to stretch her legs and fill her lungs, except on the inside of the fence rather than then outside. Outside, the snowcat's treads had packed down the snow. Outside, the path would've been easy.

Should've been doing this hike every day.

How far ahead was he? His trail kept on, up through the hills, past the little humps in the snow that marked recently cut tree stumps.

At least he was easy to follow. She stopped, rested her hands on her knees. The rifle swung down from her shoulder, the stock banged into her knee. Shit. She opened the bolt, checked the dart, closed it again. Her hands were cold, despite her thick gloves. Which she would need to remove if it came time to take the shot, to fit her finger through the trigger guard.

Not if, she chided herself. *When.*

She glanced down the slope behind her. No sign of

anyone else in the enclosure. She pressed on, her legs aching, her nose running. The fire in her lungs had subsided, but soon they began to burn again.

This can't be happening, her mind screamed with each step, and with each following step she screamed back, *yes, it is happening, but you'll make it right. You'll make it right or you'll die trying.*

She willed herself on. Finally the angle of ascent eased, the ground leveled. She had reached the high meadow.

And there, at the far end of the flat, open, snow-covered space, he sat. His back to her, his attention forward. His black ears, each with its white dot in the center, designed by evolution to look like eyes watching her approach. His left ear cocked back in her direction as she slowed, placed her hands on her knees, and drew gulps of oxygen into her lungs. Ahead of the tiger, a thick column of black smoke rose into the sky.

The workmen. They hadn't seen Kamal. He was screened by snow-covered bushes. Otherwise there would be more commotion, more nervousness. Nor had they seen her.

But Kamal had. A brief backward glance. His lips pulled back, tongue out—the flehmen response. He did not like the smoke, the smell of fire. He turned back toward the men. His left ear remained cocked in her direction, to keep track of her movements.

She raised the rifle to her shoulder, but before she had even sighted along the barrel she knew he was too far away. Out of range. She needed to get closer. She left his trail, worked her way slowly around the fringe of the meadow, among the trees. If she could creep close enough, she could get the shot. From the back would be ideal. But close enough for her to feel confident about taking the shot would almost certainly be close enough to alarm him. Which might cause him to bolt, in any direction. Toward the unsuspecting men, toward the fire, toward the unfinished fence. Or maybe back the way he'd come.

Or toward her. Each step she took crunched through the crust that had formed over the snow. She flexed and squeezed her hands into fists as she walked, trying to will warm blood into her fingers. Now that she had stopped running—now that her breathing had slowed—the sweat that had gathered in her layers was cooling, freezing. She shivered.

Another step, and Kamal again turned his head toward her. She was close enough to see his pink nylon collar, looped through a small beige plastic box—his radio transmitter. He did not stick out his tongue this time. He shifted his body weight. Partially turned toward her. His tail twitched.

"No," she whispered. "Please." She had come as close as he would allow. "Stay. Please stay."

She lowered herself to one knee. Once he turned his head back toward the workmen, she removed her right glove, and brought the rifle up. Her fingers were numb with cold as soon as she took off the glove, she could barely feel the safety switch, struggled to push it to the off position.

She rested the stock on her upraised knee, as Janpur had taught her. She nestled the butt against her shoulder. Lowered her cheek to the stock. Her commingled sweat and snot had congealed into a sort of crust. She wiped at this with her sleeve, aimed down the barrel.

She could not stop shivering. The barrel trembled. So much that the gun was rattling. Or was that her teeth? She could not keep the iron sight centered on the cat's shoulder.

She was going to miss. Janpur's steady voice cooed in her ears: *If you expect to miss, you will miss.* His steady, smug voice.

"Fuck you," she said. Her teeth chattered, and she clamped her jaw. She swiped at the tears that had begun to blur her vision. "Goddammit, Miko—"

She felt a presence next to her. Lifted her eye from the sights, her cheek from the cold stock.

A figure crouched next to her. On one knee, mirroring her. A man.

Janpur? How—

A gloved hand reached out, gripped the place where the chrome barrel protruded from the wooden stock.

He wore goggles and a fur-lined hat with ear flaps, and a scarf that hid his face. But she knew who it was. It wasn't Janpur.

Calmly, but firmly, the hand lowered the gun from her knee.

"Let me," he said.

FORTY-THREE

"Yuri?" she said. The head nodded.

She did not relinquish the gun. "Let go."

"You're shivering," he said, hand on the barrel.

The surge of adrenaline that coursed through her at the sudden appearance of a stranger—she had been too cold to react strongly, too focused on Kamal to startle—had warmed her extremities, flushed her face and even the tip of her nose and her ear lobes felt warm again. She didn't need to ask him how he had come to be there at that moment because she knew the answer. He'd been watching them. Against her wishes. Against all of her repeated requests.

"I'm taking the shot," she said. She tugged the gun back toward her knee, but the hand on the barrel would not let go.

"It's what I do," he said.

Now he wanted to step in and save the day. Save the Project. Save her. To prove that his presence was necessary. To prove that the Project needed a guardian. To show her that he'd been right back at the Polygon. So now he wanted to grab the gun from her and take the shot and with that one act, prove her wrong.

"My responsibility," she said.

"I was trained for this," he said.

"It's my responsibility." Her voice an urgent whisper.

She wrenched at the gun with both hands, leaned back and pulled it toward her chest. His elbow straightened, but his hand remained wrapped firmly around the barrel.

"Miko," he said. "He's going to escape—"

"Give me the—"

Bang.

Though the rifle fired a dart, the gun still used an explosive charge. A yellow flash arced into the sky, far above Kamal's head, sailed over the fence. They stared, briefly, at each other, then turned toward Kamal. Toward where the tiger cub had been sitting.

Kamal burst at full speed toward the workmen. They had also heard the gunshot, turned to investigate, only to see a burly blur of black and orange stripes bearing down on them, flying through the snow, his forepaws splayed wide like snowshoes.

She and Yuri both stood up in the knee-deep snow, began to run toward the men. After Kamal.

Two of the workmen ran back toward the bonfire. One man grabbed a burning branch from the fire and waved it at Kamal as he backpedaled. The tiger cut left, away from the branch's sweep, then back to the right, snow flying.

One of the men carried a long-barreled shotgun. He raised it partway to his shoulder.

"No!" Miko yelled. She waved her arms as she ran, trying to sprint through the snow. "Don't shoot! No shooting!"

The foreman looked toward the trees, searching for the origin of the voice. A voice he undoubtedly recognized. The man with the gun hesitated, even as Kamal veered toward him. He raised the gun across his body as a defensive shield as he staggered back, only to see the tiger lunge away at the last moment. The man fell back heavily, vanished into a drift.

"Don't hurt him!" Miko cried.

She ran toward the men, after Kamal, but the deep, wet snow clung to her boots like quicksand.

Yuri galloped along next to her. "Are there any more darts?"

"One more," she said. She fished it out of her parka pocket. Made sure she pulled from her right-hand pocket.

"Only one?"

"I can make more—"

This was bad, of course, Kamal shouldn't be seeing all these men, but if they could just wrestle him to the ground, pin him down, they could tranq him with the second dart. They could still salvage the Project. He was still young enough to forget about this.

Kamal raced past Sergei, who pointed at the tiger cub and yelled at his men. Two stepped in front of the tiger, waving their arms, bellowing, but even these heavyset men fell back before the cat's furious charge, head low, fangs bared, tail high for balance. Kamal swerved between them, and broke for the space that was not blocked by a bonfire or by men wielding burning branches or by a tall black iron fence.

Kamal was through the men. He shot through the gap in the fence that the workmen were there to fix.

"No—" Miko whispered. Her legs stopped working, her knees and hips lost their ability to articulate.

The tiger bounded across the broad swath of white. He churned through the pristine snow, leaping, coiling, leaping. He plunged toward the trees. He was free.

All she could do was watch. Watch the Project disappear. Watch her career crumble. Her plans, destroyed. Her decision to leave her previous life, to leave Janpur, to make a name for herself on her own, all foolish vanity. All her silly hopes vanished along with Kamal's steadily receding figure.

The tranq gun fell from her hands, disappeared into the snow without a sound. She sank to her knees. In the time it took for her to remember to breathe, for her heart to start beating again, Kamal was gone. The taiga swallowed him.

One by one the workmen's grim faces turned toward her. A jury ready to impart their guilty verdict.

"What have I done?" she asked the low-hanging clouds.

The Project was gone. Samuel had entrusted the Project to her, had believed in her, and she had betrayed that trust.

Worse, she had betrayed Kamal, who was now out beyond the fence, in the middle of winter, alone, in mortal danger. He would starve. Or poachers would find him. Or another tiger.

She looked toward Yuri—toward the judge, who would hand down his harsh sentence, but he refused to look at her. The foreman and three of the workmen jogged toward them. One of them carried the shotgun, in his right hand, the barrel bouncing casually on his shoulder.

She got to her feet and raced toward Yuri, caught up to him from behind. Grabbed his arm to spin him around.

"You should've let me take the shot!" she yelled.

He did not turn toward her as she expected, however. He shrugged off her hand.

"You should've given me the gun," he said.

By then Sergei the foreman and the three workmen had reached them. They looked nervously from her to Yuri and back again. Four burly, bearded men stared down at her, lips tight beneath their mustaches, eyes pinched.

Yuri brushed past them. The man with the gun looked at the foreman, then reached out after Yuri, grabbed his elbow. Lifted the gun toward him with his other hand.

"Where—" he began to say, but Yuri dropped and spun, shoved his hip into the man's groin, hurled the man into a high somersault over his shoulders. The worker landed on his back in the deep snow with the cold steel of the shotgun barrel resting on his forehead, Yuri towering above him, peering expressionless down its length, the stock wedged against his shoulder, his finger on the trigger. The foreman took one step toward them and Yuri released his left hand from the grip and raised it in the foreman's direction, finger extended. He did not move his attention from his prey at his feet, did not lift his finger from the trigger.

"Yuri!" Miko yelled.

He straightened and tossed the shotgun away. Did not look at her, did not acknowledge her presence. He retrieved the tranq gun from the snow where she had dropped it, brushed white powder from the chrome. He turned away from her and the foreman and stalked off toward the bonfire and the remaining men gathered around it.

Where the hell was he going now?

"Asshole," the man's voice quavered from deep within the snow.

A shout from behind turned Miko back toward the place she'd come from. A larger, heavyset man, bundled in winter gear, staggered up the slope toward them, waving his arms and calling out.

Anatoly! You're alive! At least there's some good news today.

She ran toward her partner. The man slowed, stopped, placed his hands on his knees.

"Anatoly!" she shouted as she ran. When she came close, the man straightened to his full height, and she realized that while she recognized him, it wasn't Anatoly. It was Samuel's friend. Yuri's partner, a fellow park ranger. She'd met him back at the Polygon.

The man gasped for breath. "Dr. Stasevich," he panted.

"Yes?"

"He's dead."

She had known, and yet she hadn't allowed herself to admit it. She put her face in her gloved hands. Shook her head. It was too much. First Chernichev. Then Kamal. Now this.

"I'm sorry," the man said. "We found his body in the woods. Yuri thinks he was killed."

They both looked back toward the other men milling about, toward the bonfire. Toward Yuri, who was rummaging through the snowcat's flatbed trailer.

"Where's he going now?" the man asked.

That's what I want to know, she thought. She walked briskly back up the hill toward the men. As she came level with the sheepish workmen, the foreman approached her.

"How did that thing"—Sergei pointed out beyond the fence—"get all the way up here?"

"He jumped the paddock wall," she said. She locked eyes with him. "Like I've been telling you he would."

FORTY-FOUR

He was furious. He should have disarmed her, overpowered her, and made the shot. The tiger would be down, and they wouldn't be in this place.

He glanced at the sky. High, thin clouds spread from ridge to ridge. It was late morning, nearly noon. Another five, maybe six hours of daylight left. He wore his backpack, but it did not contain much: his entrenching tool, his map and compass, dried venison, pine nuts, an insulated canteen of water, half full now. His sheathed Yakut knife hung from his belt on a loop of leather.

At the workmen's snowcat he found some useful items: a folded-up tarp of heavy green plastic, a spool of cord, matches. Three flares. He pushed these things into his backpack, pulled the straps over his shoulders.

"What do you think you're doing?" Evgeny stood beside him, observing. Still breathing heavily.

Yuri glanced at his partner.

"I'm going after him." If luck was on his side, the tiger cub would tire, and Yuri, following his trail in the snow, would be able to get a clean shot with the tranq gun.

He leaned into his partner, lowered his voice. "Take her back to the lodge. Get her and these men on a snowcat and get them the hell out of here."

Evgeny began to protest, but Yuri cut him off. "Wait for me at the lodge. But keep an eye out for the Ferret."

"What do you mean you're going after him?" Miko had come to stand behind them. She swiped at her reddened cheeks with her gloves. "How are you going to catch him?"

"You said you have another dart?"

"Yes, but—"

"Give it over." He held out his hand.

She produced the second, and final dart. He removed the stopper with his teeth and loaded the fresh dart into the tranq gun. He slid the bolt home with a *snick*.

"We should get the telemetry gear," Miko said.

Yuri turned to go. Kamal already had a head start. He would be able to track the tiger through the snow. One shot ought to be plenty.

"His trail is clear, now," Yuri said over his shoulder. "You two go for the radio gear." He hoped this would get her on the snowcat with Evgeny and the workmen.

"I'm coming with you," she said. Evgeny placed his hand on her elbow, pleaded with her in a low voice.

"Out of the question," Yuri said over his shoulder.

"Hey!" She pulled away from Evgeny and ran in front of Yuri, planted herself in his path. "He's my tiger, dammit! He's my responsibility!"

"I don't care whose tiger he is," he said. "I just want to bring him back. You'll only slow me down."

"I won't," she said. "I promise."

"I work alone."

"I have the antidote," she said. She held up a metal cylinder, with a similar rubber stopper over the tip but with a plunger instead of yellow feathers. "If the dose is too strong, his heart could stop beating. He could stop breathing."

He snatched the syringe from her hand before she could pull it away. Tucked the cylinder into his parka pocket.

"Yuri!" she said. "You don't know how to administer it! You don't know the signs. I must be there."

He shook his head. "No."

He was done arguing, done accommodating. He turned

away and set off at a trot toward the trees, following the trail of broken snow Kamal had left behind.

The tiger's pugmarks were easy to follow in the fresh, shin-deep snow. The trees Yuri followed him through were Korean pines: tall, straight, evenly spaced, with crowns far above. A few solitary branches, no longer bearing needles or cones, stuck out stiff from lower down on the trunks, snapping as he brushed against them. But he wasn't concerned about maintaining silence. His only concern was moving as quickly as possible to catch up to Kamal.

The tiger, of course, was eminently suited for movement in this terrain. The splayed pads of his feet acted as snowshoes. His immature weight benefitted him as well—his paws didn't sink nearly as deeply into the snow as Yuri's boots, following along in his tracks. He could only hope that the tiger's youthful energy would soon deplete, and he would tire, slow, and stop.

He knew she was following him. She wasn't calling out, she wasn't being loud. But he was aware of her presence. Over his shoulder he glimpsed her bright orange parka through the bare tree trunks every now and again. She was determined. A pain in the ass, is what she was.

He could only hope that she wouldn't lose his track and get lost in the trees. Bad enough he had to chase a young tiger through the deep snow. Now she was making him responsible for her welfare also.

She reminded him of Sveta. Little Sveta, who when she was five and he was ten, began following Yuri and Ruka into the woods when they would go on their long walks, hunting or simply exploring. At first he was quite annoyed, and he beat her and told her to go home. But Ruka ran after her, barking and nipping at her coat, and he herded her back to Yuri. That, and the look of devotion in her watery blue eyes— the only one in the family to inherit her father's Russian eyes —told him that she was part of the pack now.

"Keep up," he would tell his sister. Of course she struggled to maintain her older brother's pace. He would have to wait for her, or Ruka would get agitated and start barking.

Besides, the reason he went into the woods was to escape his father when he was on the drink, and this way he could protect Sveta from his sullen moods also. It was better that way.

Yuri stopped, listened. Watched back over the trail he had left through the trees. She'd fallen far behind. He needed a break, too. His quads and calves were burning. He dug the jerked venison and the canteen of tea out of his backpack, began to chew on a hunk of the salty, leathery meat while he waited.

Finally, her orange parka bobbed and weaved through the tree trunks. She carried the shotgun slung over her back, the strap diagonal across her chest. As she approached, he held out a piece of jerky, but she did not stop, she pressed forward, following the tracks. Taking the lead.

"Don't you—" he began, the leathery flap of venison sticking out from his glove.

"Not hungry," she said.

"What about—"

"Not thirsty, either."

He took a swallow of water, then put the piece of venison that he had offered her into his mouth and began to chew.

"He's still moving at a run through here," Miko said over her shoulder.

He slung the backpack over his shoulders and followed after her. They walked single-file, Miko in the lead, Yuri close behind. He didn't mind—she could follow the trail as easily as he could. A child could follow this trail.

The ground sloped down, as the trees shortened and crowded even closer. Suddenly they pushed through yet another set of branches and the trees stopped, as though they had reached a demarcation line of some sorts that was hidden by the snow but that the trees' roots recognized as their limit. Kamal's tracks led into this basin.

They glanced at each other, then followed. The snow had drifted quite deep in places here, in others it was thin and tightly packed. They were walking across a frozen river bed. To either side broken gray trunks of long-dead trees rose up, twisted and stunted.

Yuri recognized this place. He had chased Chernichev here, then turned back.

Rocks and boulders grew from the river bed. They had to pick their way more tentatively now, even though the snow gave the appearance of a smooth path. A few tendrils of fog began to congeal into incorporeal banks, and patches. Still Kamal's tracks were easy to follow. But now there were other tracks as well.

"Wait." Yuri held his hands up. He didn't want their tracks confusing the issue. "Wait here."

He ventured forward, scanning the snow. The elegant pinpoint prints of small sika deer. The closer, dense shuffle of boar hooves. Kamal's tracks marred these, showing that he had come after. They all led to a dark break in the snow, a burbling sound, the source of the foggy clouds: a watering hole.

He motioned Miko forward. "Careful," he said. "The ice may be thin."

The break in the ice was not very large. The water swirled and hissed darkly. Steam rose from it as though it were boiling.

Many animals had come here for water. Kamal's prints led right up to the edge. They did not follow them, as they didn't want to break through the ice.

There was another set of prints near the water. Yuri moved forward cautiously. Drifting snow had partially filled them in, indicating that they were at least a day or two old.

These prints were larger. The species immediately recognizable.

"Are those boots?" Miko asked.

Yuri felt exposed, out in the open, no cover nearby. Instinctively he crouched, surveyed the sparse, broken trees around them, the mounds of snow that indicated boulders. Looking for movement. For other signs of man.

"Men made this hole," he said. "It's a lure."

She was surveying the treeline on the far bank.

The bubbling hiss of the water was all he heard. No signs of movement. Then again, there wouldn't be. Nothing even an animal with keener eyes than his, and a more perceptive nose than his, would be able to detect. That was how man hunted. Waiting in ambush, hidden by his carefully constructed blind. He searched again.

There. A slight rise in elevation, covered by trees with low branches. That would be where he would build his blind. That place would give a sniper the best vantage.

"Wait here," he said to Miko, and he set off running.

The snow beneath the trees had been matted down by boots, but partially filled in by drifts. There were several sizes of prints. And in the center of one of the smaller ones, in the gap between the semi-circular heel and the ovoid front of the foot, a smaller rectangle. With four distinct letters in the Western alphabet.

Chernichev left a telltale track. Yuri had been so busy securing his firewood and food supplies and keeping watch over the compound and the enclosure that he had nearly abandoned patrolling the woods around him. This place ought to have been easy for him to find. Chernichev had even led him here before, whether consciously or not. Perhaps the Ferret had been running for this blind. The track led deeper into the trees, further up the slope.

He made some calculations. They'd been tracking Kamal for nearly two hours now. There could not be much more than three hours of daylight left. He glanced up at the thick clouds. They were not going to benefit from any sort of post-sunset glow in the sky to light their way, nor any moonlight or starlight. The setting of the sun would bring complete and total darkness.

He glanced back toward Miko, a wispy outline in the fog. Should he tell her this? Perhaps she already knew, but refused to think about it. To acknowledge it would be to acknowledge that they needed to turn back. Now.

A little further. Another kilometer, maybe, and then...

And then maybe they catch a glimpse. Maybe he manages a clean shot. They wrap him up quickly, and double-time it back. They could at least make it to the edge of the forest. Then they light a flare, the workmen see it, and they come get them on snowmobiles.

How long would the tranquilizer last? An hour? Longer? He realized that he had no idea. They could use the cord to bind the cub's jaw closed and his paws together, wrap him in the tarp—but if he woke up as they were heading for home? What then?

He left Chernichev's track and returned to Miko. He picked up Kamal's trail from the tangle of prints that clustered around the flowing water. Life-giving water, perhaps also death-dealing.

"We're going to find him," he said to her.

He could see that she wanted to believe him, though he could see the slight waver behind her eyes. He wanted to banish that doubt, for good.

A squalling howl broke the silence. Her eyes brightened, she gripped his arm. "That's him!"

It repeated: a piteous yowl, that ended in a plaintive squawk.

She took off running. "Come on!"

He ran after her.

FORTY-FIVE

They moved toward the sound, following the tracks but scanning the horizon as well. The trail led from the river bed into a stand of bare birch trees—a loose assortment, some thin saplings, some grand old towers, a number fallen or leaning into neighbors. The snow covered treacherous footing, a mix of rocks and branches and moldering black leaves that slipped and stank when their boots pulled them free.

The tracks led to a small mound of snow, a pile of bracken that looked like a misplaced beaver dam. Miko fell to her knees, swept snow away, peered in through the branches.

"He's in here!" she called. Yuri switched off the safety. Knelt beside her. He could see a tuft of orange and black fur. The cub had found himself a den, but it looked none too cozy. Perhaps he was stuck. He was certainly aware of the strange creatures staring at him, blocking his exit. He let loose an angry hiss that lowered into his throat, verged into a growl.

"Don't shoot from here," she said. "You're too close. The velocity will be too high."

"I don't have a shot anyway." The cub was wedged back in too far.

He sat back on his heels. What to do?

"I'll wrap my coat around my arm," he said. "I'll reach in there and grab him, pull him out."

She stood up, pulled the shotgun strap up over her head, propped the gun against the mound. "Stay there, keep an eye on him," she said. "Don't let him out."

She went searching through the nearby trees. Found a low, bare branch that met her requirements. The branch ran relatively straight, then forked into two. She snapped the branches off shortly after the fork, leaving her with a two-pronged pitchfork. She tossed this toward Yuri. Went back for another. Found one that was similar, though maybe a little rotten at one end.

"They'll often grab onto a stick that's poking them," she said. "When I pull him free, you pin him down with the fork around his neck, okay? Whoever's free backs up and takes the shot."

"Risky," Yuri said. "The one holding him could get hit."

"Time to take a risk."

"Right."

She held one of the branches by the forked end, and stuck it into the cave of bracken. The low growl rose in pitch. The stick jumped and shook. She used the fork tines as handles, one in each hand, and began to walk backward on her knees. The stick pulled free. She jammed it back in, and again began to pull. Yuri could see now that the cub had it in his claws, and in his teeth.

Snow was falling. When had that started? Light was failing. They needed this to work.

"You got him," he said. "Keep pulling. Nice and steady."

She shoved herself backward through the snow, Kamal still growling and hissing, even with the branch clamped firmly in his jaw. Again the branch pulled free, and again she prodded him, bullied him, antagonized him until he lashed out and latched on.

Yuri got to his feet. Made sure the safety was off, rested the rifle against the mound of bracken, barrel in the air. He poised his stick, fork facing down, over the entrance.

"Let me get him free first," she said.

He grunted. If he pinned him too soon, too much of his body would remain hidden. But too late, and he might bolt.

Kamal's large head came into view, the branch flayed by his teeth down to stringy strips. His ears were pinned flat back against his head, his lips curled back from his fangs. The yellowed teeth were short, but Yuri's forearm vibrated at the sight of them. He knew what sort of damage they could do, despite the cub's youth. He had nearly chewed through a solid, frozen branch with a radius greater than Yuri's ulna, probably about as thick as his femur. The cub splayed his forepaws and dug them through the snow and into the ground, pushing back against Miko trying to drag him free. His rear paws scrabbled furiously for purchase, shot black leaves and loose pebbles out of the little cave.

He was nearly free. Yuri could scarcely believe that this was the same creature that he had pulled from his mother, what—five weeks ago? Six? He was nearly the size of Ruka, only with shorter legs and a broader head. He had seen Kamal in that time, had watched him grow, but largely through the scope of his Mosin-Nagant. He seemed enormous now that he was so close, a striped bundle of tightly coiled muscle and fury.

"Now!"

Yuri stabbed downward, pinned the fork around the cub's neck, drove his face down into the snow. Kamal's hindquarters scrabbled among the slippery dead leaves, and his forequarters were trapped against his body and the snow, unable to push his body up or attack the stick.

Miko dropped her stick and stood up. A keening whine emerged from the cat.

"Am I hurting him?"

She shook her head, moved to stand on the other side of Kamal, facing Yuri. She reached for the branch in between them.

"I got him," Yuri said. "Get the gun. Shoot him from over there." He indicated with his chin.

"You get the gun." She placed her hands lower on the branch. "You take the shot."

The high-pitched keening continued.

"I'm letting go."

She nodded, eyes on Kamal, jaw clenched.

He released, stepped back. Grabbed the gun.

The yowling stopped, and Kamal lurched, flexed his spine impossibly to the side, got his feet under him enough to flip over onto his back, his neck still trapped, his chin pressed awkwardly now against the place where the branch forked. Fortunately this kept him from getting at it with his teeth.

Yuri reached to help keep the branch in place. Miko stepped away from Kamal, leaned down on the branch with more of her weight.

"The gun! Yuri!"

He stepped backward and grabbed the rifle, checked the safety. Took another two steps back. Kamal was now wriggling violently, all four limbs and his tail free and flailing. His forepaws attacked the branch, shook it violently. His tail swung from side to side, and his rear paws bounced off the mound of branches and snow. All claws extended, feet splayed, fangs bared.

"How far back do you want me?"

She glanced up at him. She was struggling to keep the quivering branch rooted in place. He shouldn't have relinquished it.

"A few—"

A swipe of his forepaw hit her boot. Startled at the contact, she pulled her foot back, but this movement stretched the cub's foreleg awkwardly straight.

"Are you okay?"

"His claw is caught!"

He paused, unsure whether to continue moving into position for the shot or to rush in to free her foot.

She moved her foot toward Kamal to flex his foreleg, removed one hand from the branch and bent down to work the claw free. With a violent lurch, Kamal's hindquarters swung to that side, flailing for purchase. One of his rear paws struck Miko's lowering hand, the other her left shin right above her boot. She cried out. Yuri ran forward.

"No!" she said. "Get back! Take the shot!"

The tiger had taken full advantage of the lessened weight bearing down on him, the surprise, and wrenched the rear paws up into the branch where her other hand was struggling to hold it in place. He kicked the branch, and his head popped free.

"Wait!" She was talking to Kamal now. "Your claw!"

She leaned over and grabbed his paw with her right while she pulled her left glove off with her teeth. Kamal on his feet now. Tail swinging side to side, the black stripe along his back fully erect, ears back, fangs bared, hissing and spitting at Miko, he pulled back from her, forepaw still tangled in her boot laces. Yuri raised the gun to his shoulder, sighted along the barrel. The tiger's puckered asshole swung side to side as his rear paws scrabbled and slipped through the snow and dead leaves. Miko stood directly behind him.

She knelt down, took Kamal's snared paw in both her hands. The gloved hand pinched the pad while she hooked the index finger of her naked hand under his claw to pull it free. If Yuri missed his lurching target, the dart would hit her smack in the face.

Kamal lunged forward, batted at the naked hand with what looked like a playful swat, but a second later ragged streaks of bright red emerged from her pale skin. Yuri lifted his head from the stock. Still she worked to free the claw.

He quickly sidestepped left, to get her out from behind his target, out of harm's way. A tree blocked his path, jarred his aim. She released the cub's paw, and Kamal was free.

"Shoot!"

Yuri expected Kamal to turn and run away from Miko, and he was already tracking with the barrel in that direction.

Instead the cub bared his fangs and leaped toward her. She shrieked and lifted her arms, crossed them in front of her like a shield, bare hand exposed. Kamal bulled into her, batting at her with his paws. She instinctively curled down into a ball, her forearms protecting her head, her shins and knees guarding her vital organs.

There was no way he could take the shot. He stood up, ran toward the tiger, yelling.

And as soon as the attack had started, Kamal bounded off her, sprang away into the snow. Yuri lifted the rifle again, even as Miko struggled to her feet. Her body came in between Yuri and his target.

"He's getting away!"

"Duck down!"

She glanced back, realized her position, and threw herself down to the ground.

Yuri found the target—the cub rapidly vanishing. As Kamal ran he lurched drunkenly side to side, unsure which course to take, certain only that he wanted to move as quickly as possible away from his assailants. Yuri tensed his finger on the trigger.

But then released. He lowered the rifle. This was their last dart. With the distance and the erratic movement a hit would have been pure luck.

Luck, as Iliakov had taught him, would always abandon you when you needed her most.

She stood up. They both watched Kamal as he flickered among the birch trees, into view, then out, back in. Then gone. He pushed the safety back on. If he was only going to get one shot, he was going to make it a good one.

They continued staring at the trees, at the falling snow. Snow that, if it kept falling, would soon obliterate the cub's tracks. She put her face in her hands, one gloved, one bleeding, three parallel gashes from her wrist to her knuckles, trailing haphazard trickles and droplets. She stepped toward Yuri, pushed her face into his chest. He lowered the gunstock into the snow, wrapped his arms around her shaking shoulders.

He'd promised her they would get him. The moment had come, and he'd failed.

"I got in the way," she sobbed. "I said I wouldn't, and then I did. I literally did."

They stood there for a moment. Then another. He knew they couldn't delay much longer. Night was coming on.

Snow was falling. Her hand needed attention. Still he held her.

She took a deep, shuddering breath, and stepped back. She lifted her face from her hands. She looked up into his.

"What do we do now?"

FORTY-SIX

From the concern etched into the wrinkles around his eyes, deepening the creases on his brow, she knew they were in trouble. She'd known all along, of course, as they went deeper and deeper into the woods, as the minutes stretched into hours, as the kilometers mounted, as the cold really began to take hold of her, she recognized that they were courting disaster. They were risking their lives.

But all along she had clung to the mantra: *if we can just catch Kamal*.

If we can just catch Kamal, then we'll find a way to get him home. If we can just catch Kamal, all the rest will sort itself out. If we can just catch Kamal, then everything will be all right. A fantasy. A delusion. They'd come close. Achingly, heartbreakingly close.

And still, that voice inside, more of a murmur now rather than a high-pitched shrill, nevertheless insisting: *If we can just catch Kamal*.

But now they needed to survive. While it seemed like the end of the Project meant the end of the world, the shivering in her jaw, deep in her bones, told her that she didn't actually want her life to come to an end in the frigid depths of the Russian taiga, in the dark of night. With this silent man she barely knew. How had her life boiled down to this moment? How had her life distilled so suddenly to this barren place?

At least he'd taken action. He'd given her hope. He, too, was risking his life. Perhaps had already sacrificed his life, alongside her, and they just didn't know it yet.

He surveyed the birch trees around them, the gently falling snow. Seemed to come to a decision. He was the more experienced of the two in these conditions, of course, but she wished he would confide in her the options he was weighing.

"Let's wrap your hand," he said. He rummaged through his backpack, then opened his coat and removed his knife. He lifted his sweater, cut away a strip of fleece-lined flannel from his shirt. Took her hand in his and wrapped the cloth twice around it.

"Thank you," she said, as he cinched a knot directly, painfully, over the back of her hand. "For... giving me hope. We almost—" She couldn't bring herself to finish the sentence.

"We're going to catch him," he said. "But right now we need to shelter for the night. Grab the two branches we were using. We need five or six more straight ones like that."

They moved among the birches, staying within sight of each other, snapping off branches as they came to them. Her knee burned, and she realized that Kamal's claws had torn through her snow pants there as well, leaving her with a couple of deep scratches that had also drawn blood. It wasn't bleeding as profusely as her hand, however. That could receive attention later.

"I have three," he called out.

She also had found three sturdy, relatively straight branches as long as her leg. They met back at the clearing, the matted snow strewn with black leaves. And three bright dots of red. He slung the tranquilizer rifle over his shoulder, took her birch branches and added them to his, along with the forked branch that Kamal hadn't torn into. She grabbed the shotgun and pulled the strap over her head and shoulder.

"Now we need scrub pines," he said. "This way."

He led them back toward the frozen riverbed. He'd seen

a stand of pines on the other side, he told her. She hurried to match his pace, though her knee was starting to burn now, possibly as much from the cold entering the tear in her protective clothing as from the wound itself.

Why did she continually feel a need to prove herself to this man? To prove that she could hold her own, that she wouldn't be a burden, that she wouldn't complain or make a fuss or shed a tear? Too late for all of that now, but still she felt compelled. She'd felt that way around Janpur as well. She'd met Janpur in a similarly hostile environment, only the jungles of Sumatra had been hot and steamy and chaotically loud, teeming with bugs and birds and reptiles and parasites —the diametric opposite of this place, so cold and quiet and empty. So dead. So lonely.

Why did she keep finding herself stuck with men in environmental extremes? Something to take up with her shrink, she supposed. Should she ever have the luxury of time and energy that a psychologist would require. If she made it through this night.

They crossed the frozen riverbed, entered the stand of pine trees.

"What can I do?" She had to contribute. She had to help them survive. She knew it would be tough. And she knew she had to trust him. She just wished she had some idea of the plan.

"Your job is to gather branches," he said. "Cut them from the trees, about shoulder height, maybe a little higher. We want them to have plenty of needles and smaller branches, but not too big, and we want them to lie flat."

He reached into a snow-covered tree, shook and brushed the snow from its branches and cut a bough as an example. From the principal branch the needles bifurcated and spread out into a flat frond, a couple of hands' widths wide. He tossed it on the snowy ground. Handed her the knife.

"Stack them here," he said. "Keep cutting, keep stacking."

He moved off into the trees. Large, clumpy flakes continued to drift around her. Soon she heard the crack-scrape, crack-scrape of him shoveling snow with his spade. She worked as quickly as she could—the short knife cut through the smaller branches with surprising ease—until she had a bushy, dark green pile up to her knees.

Light was failing. They would need kindling and firewood, so she set about looking for downed, dried branches in the last of the remaining light. He would appreciate her foresight. Her competency. Would appreciate that he didn't need to tell her every last thing that needed to be done in order to survive. Clearly a fire was necessary. She was warming now that she was working, moving, but her breath was steaming, and she knew that once they stopped moving the cold would quickly surround them, penetrate them, threaten to overwhelm them.

"What are you doing?" he asked.

She was hauling a very large branch into the clearing where she had finished stacking boughs.

"Gathering firewood," she said. She smiled.

He did not. "If we needed firewood," he said, with a shake of his head, "I would've told you to gather it."

They were nearly out of light now. She couldn't make out his expression in the gloom, but could tell from the tone of his voice that he was dissatisfied. Annoyed, even.

How do we not need firewood?

"Look away," he said. He turned his back to her and struck a flare, then turned around, jabbed it toward her. "Hold this. High, so I can see while I work. I need the knife back."

"I'm sorry," she said as she handed him the knife in exchange for the flare. "I just assumed that we—"

"Don't worry about it." Gruff. Rude, even.

He started cutting more branches from a nearby tree. Began to build a new pile of boughs in the snow. He worked fast, wasn't as careful as she had been to make sure that they matched the size and shape that he had specified earlier. She could've worked faster, too, if she'd known she could take more liberties. But he hadn't really explained what he wanted, or what the purpose was.

After about ten minutes he stopped, looked at the flare. Took it from her, walked through the trees to the place where he had been working, returned without the flare, the red light sputtering behind him, where he had propped it in the snow.

He grabbed the bottom bough of one of the piles and began to drag it toward the flare. She didn't move, unsure whether he wanted the other one moved, or not.

"Bring the other one," he said. Again, sounding annoyed. Was she supposed to read his mind? "If you can."

She followed him, butt first, dragging the other pile between two trees and into a small clearing. The flare cast a demonic glow over a shallow trench that he had dug into the snow. With his entrenching tool, his spade, he had dug snow down to the bare frozen earth, and used that snow to build up waist-high walls on the two long sides and a third, shorter side. He began to lay the boughs down on the ground, all fanning in the same direction, overlapping the boughs as he went, and lining the snowy walls with them as well. Steam poured from his mouth as he worked, red in the fading flare light, and red wisps also rose from his head, and from his shoulders, as his sweat evaporated into the night.

He removed his fur-lined coat, laid it out fur facing up on the bed of pine needles. She began to understand what was going to be required.

"No fire," he said, as though he could sense her discomfort at the dawning realization. "Body heat. It's the only way we'll make it, given what we have."

He now took the sturdy and straight birch branches that they had brought, and laid those across the width of the trench, driving them down into the snow until they were just above knee height.

The flare sputtered and hissed and finally died, but he was prepared with another one. Struck it, and red light chased away the darkness that had engulfed them momentarily.

"Last one," he said, as he stuck it next to the burnt-out casing. The sulfurous reek filled the air around them.

He removed the tarp from his pack and unfurled it, then

folded it in half lengthways. He handed her the folded end, and they stretched the double-layered plastic over the branches, anchored it in place with rocks he must have collected from the riverbed, or while shoveling through the snow. With the spade he began throwing snow onto the tarp.

"Pack it down," he said. "Without putting too much weight on it." He continued chucking snow, while she knelt behind the stones anchoring the tarp and leaned forward, doing her best to pack the powdery stuff firm. They continued to add snow, and pack it down until the tarp was hidden from sight.

"The rest of the boughs," he said, and they threw pine boughs over the small mound. He packed these into the snow with his spade, then hurled even more snow on top of the boughs, until there were no more boughs, no more snow. All that was left was a small burial mound with a dark opening at one end.

"All it needs is a headstone," she said.

"Let's hope not," he said.

FORTY-SEVEN

He pushed the tranq rifle and the shotgun into the hole, laid them along the side, out of the way. Then their packs, almost empty now.

"Okay," he said, clearly uncomfortable. "You need to take your coat off. And as many layers as you can spare. We're going to use these layers as blankets and to stop up the opening. My coat is the mattress pad, and your coat will be the top blanket. Sharing our body heat is what's going to get us through this. Okay?"

She nodded, removed her coat. The frigid air tightened her skin, even though she still wore several layers: a wool sweater, a fleece sweater, an undershirt, a base layer.

"Get inside," he said, "and take the rest of it off as best you can. Down to your thermals. And then put your boots back on. Okay?"

"Head first?" she asked.

He nodded. She wriggled her way inside, careful to keep his coat from bunching up as she went. There was barely room for her to get her arms over her head to remove her sweaters. Her insulated snow pants unzipped to go down over her boots. Once she worked them down to her shins she had to kick her way out of them. She was cold.

This better work, she thought. *This better be right.*

"Ready?"

Before she could answer, his head was in the opening, and he was wriggling up alongside her. He had shucked his outerwear outside, and he pushed it in ahead of him. Now there truly was no room to maneuver. No room to turn. She faced away from him, faced a dark wall. Pine needles scraped her face, forced her back, closer to him.

A faint glow from the dying flare, which he had moved near the opening, cast strange red light and dark shadows into their little cave. He dumped the candy bars and venison strips out above their heads—"dinner is served," he said—set the canteen there as well, then arranged the empty backpack and the bag down at the opening as a sort of plug, along with one of their sweaters.

He was facing her back. She could feel his breath on her neck. He reached his arm over her. She felt herself recoil at his touch. Her shivering was uncontrollable now, shaking her whole body.

"I'm cold," he said. "You're cold. We're going to have to spoon."

"Okay," she whispered, teeth chattering.

This better be right.

He pressed his body against hers. Began to run his cold hands vigorously up and down her arms, her thighs, her calves. As he did his hands warmed, became tolerable, if a little rough and scratchy against her skin. He stretched a sweater over their legs, his kneecaps pressed into the backs of her knees. Then pulled her coat overtop the two of them.

"You can come closer," she said. Her shivering was slowing. He pressed his belly against her butt. One of the branches had worked its way through his coat, and poked into the back of her thigh, or perhaps it was the handle of his knife. She reached behind to push it away, and he recoiled at her touch. She snatched her hand back as she realized the source of the poking had retreated along with him.

"How can you have that now, here?" she asked. "It's freezing."

She recalled Janpur, and how long it always took for him

to get an erection, how much work they typically had to put into getting him hard. She closed her eyes and shook her head. Why was she even thinking about this? In a life-or-death situation?

"This is a pretty typical first date here in Primorsky Krai," he said.

She laughed. "Well I don't put out on the first date. I'm not that kind of girl."

"No," he said. His teeth were chattering less now too. "I didn't think you were."

"Rub my arms again," she said. "I'm still cold."

He did. Then he wrapped his legs around her legs, and moved them up and down as well, shaking her entire body.

"A little too vigorous," she said. He stopped. "But thanks. I'm warmer now."

He was right. Their warmth remained trapped in the small space.

"We need to eat something," he said. He struck a match, lighting up their confined space. She hadn't felt claustrophobic until that moment.

She rolled over to face him, instantly felt the increased cold from the lack of contact. She scooted forward, pressed her thighs into his, her belly into his. Did her best to ignore the erection between them and his stammered apologies.

"What do we have?" she asked. They sorted out what they wanted, and then the match winked out, leaving a puff of acrid smoke. They were both hungry, but they knew they might need to ration as well. They each ate a candy bar, some jerked venison, and drank from the canteen. Their ripe smells from a day of physical exertion and nervous tension filled the small space as well. It wasn't entirely unpleasant, however. There was something about the cold that seemed to eliminate all smells, an effect that seemed to make them somehow less human. Here, that precious scrap of humanity returned.

"We're on a slight upslope," he said, "with our feet at the lowest point. The heat we generate should stay inside. I hope the tilt doesn't make sleeping difficult."

"When did you learn how to do this?" she asked.

"My friend Evgeny told me about it," he said.

"You've never done this before?"

She could feel him shaking his head. Also sensed him smiling, somehow.

"This better work," she said.

"It's working."

"For you, apparently."

"Shh," he said. "Turn around. We need to sleep."

They lay together for a while in silence, too energized from the cold and the quick sugar rush of the candy bars to fall asleep yet, shifting here and there to tamp down little drafts and cold spots revealed by the other's slight movements. The coats, while large and heavy and fur-lined, did not cover them quite completely. A pair of sleeping bags properly zipped together, or even sharing a single one, would've been perfect.

"Why did you name them Kamal and Vida?" she asked.

"They were friends of mine," he said. "In Afghanistan."

"During the war?"

His body shook slightly as he nodded. "Yes."

"They were Afghanis?"

"She was. He was from Chechnya. He was in my unit."

"Must've been a good friend," she said. "For you to name a tiger after him."

She felt him breathing. Inhale, hold... exhale, hold. As though the act required his conscious thought. His full concentration.

"He was."

He pulled his hand away, fumbled in the dark for the canteen. She could hear him unscrew the lid, take a swallow. He tapped her shoulder with it, and she took a swallow from it as well.

"Was he a headstrong pain in the ass, like his namesake?"

She felt a rush of air from his nose. A hint of a laugh.

"He was a Muslim," Yuri said. "He taught me enough of the language and the customs so I could pass for one as well. Since neither of us really looked Russian, they would send the two of us behind enemy lines to conduct *razvedka*."

He rolled away from her, almost onto his back, pulling the coat along with him. As though he were staring up at a starry night sky, rather than the underside of a chilly coffin lid.

"We would pretend to be jihadis from Kazakhstan so we could recon troop dispositions, supply lines, and so on. But every now and then we would get pulled into firefights against Soviet regulars. At first we fought alongside the jihadis to get more entrenched with the local mujahideen leadership, to get them to accept us as one of them. But as the days went on, it really didn't matter anymore. We fought to survive. Same as anybody else."

"What about this man Chernichev? Was he with you?"

He didn't answer. A chill passed between them as he pulled his body back from hers. She scooted back into him, though, followed his body with hers, refused to give up his warmth. She told him how Iliakov had brought Chernichev and the others, supposedly to hunt the rogue male whose tracks they had seen. She told him about her early morning conversation with Chernichev, though she left out the threats he had made before leaving.

"He joined after Afghanistan," Yuri finally said. "When we were fighting in Chechnya."

She had also left out what Chernichev had said to her about Yuri killing his friend.

"I can't imagine," she said. "Being in a war."

"No," he said, simply.

She reached back to grab his hand, and pulled his arm back around her ribs, pulled his body close to hers, for the warmth. She continued holding his hand. It was a rough hand, with large knobby knuckles, and thick callouses like gnarled roots where the fingers grew from the palm.

"We should sleep now," he said.

He put his other arm under her head, for a pillow. Soon she was asleep.

FORTY-EIGHT

Sleep arrived slowly, and with a light touch. The exhaustion that made his body feel so heavy also stretched his mind taut. If the snow continued to fall overnight, there would be no trail for them to follow. Whether they decided to go after Kamal, or return to the enclosure, the way would not be marked for them. He was confident that he could return them to the enclosure using the map and compass, and when sleep finally came for him, he was leaning in that direction, though he knew that Miko wouldn't like it.

You need to get her back to safety. They didn't have the food or the stamina to last another night in these conditions. Properly equipped, he could come back out to continue the search.

Losing two days, though—one to return Miko, one to resupply and get back to this position and try to find the cub's trail again—would make the search nearly impossible. Would mean that even if he were to find Kamal, the poor cub would likely be starved and frozen.

So perhaps he was leaning toward staying and continuing the search, when sleep came at last. *Let's first see if we can find a trace of the cub.* His mind shifted back and forth repeatedly. He could not come to a decision, and that prevented him from finding sleep. *Sleep on it*, he urged himself, *decide in the morning*.

At least she seemed to be sleeping, her breathing steady. Occasionally she snorted, stirred, seemed to startle. Only to remember where she was, and who was in this cramped cave with her, and why, and return to sleep with a sigh.

His left side ached from lying on it for the hours they'd spent in the little cave, but he did not want to move, did not want to disturb Miko or the patchwork arrangement of coats and sweaters that barely managed to cover them.

He was holding Miko, only she was facing him, and they were completely naked, and warm, and her naked body pressed into his. The warm scent of her hair, of her scalp, a mingling of lavender soap and sweat and wool, filled his nostrils and infused him with an emotion he had not felt in some time. Her scent, a perfume of happiness so bright that it scalded his nose as he inhaled. He smiled, and felt that both of his cheeks were whole and unblemished.

In this dream the shelter was brightly lit, and spacious. They lay on a feather bed rather than a crunchy, lumpy mat of pine needle. She lifted her face to his, and in her eyes he could see no doubt, only confidence. Trust.

"You're letting me slip away," she said.

Her words changed the happiness to irrevocable sadness in an instant. And she did begin to pull away from him, he felt her moving in his arms.

"Why must you go?"

"I don't know," she said. Then, "Yuri."

"I'm here."

"Yuri!"

With a violent lurch, she was gone, torn from him, and he was back in the dark coffin, surrounded by a freezing chill, and emptiness. Her shout echoed in his ears.

"YURI!"

Her hands grabbed his waist, his thighs. She was being dragged from him. He reached for her hands, for her armpits, to haul her back to him.

He felt the low thrum more than he heard it, a *basso profundo* rumble that caused the shelter to tremble.

Fully awake, he recognized that growl. Khagan.

Suddenly her hands were at his knees. She screamed. He reached down, grabbed her flailing arms, held them tight, rolled onto his back and braced his feet against the walls of snow on either side of the shelter's entrance. He leaned forward as far as he could, jammed his forehead into the tarp ceiling, bent his knees into the ceiling as well. He straightened his knees, straightened his back, threw his tightly clenched fists back over his head with every ounce of strength. He hauled her on top of him, and her face bumped into his. He let go of her wrists and wrapped his arms around her waist.

"What's happening?" she yelled.

Another yank, more powerful this time, pulled her down his body again, but he had braced for such a pull and did not let her slide far, even though he feared breaking her ribs. He adjusted his grip, locked his hands together beneath her buttocks, and with another push of his legs and a thrust of his hips he heaved her back up, on top of him.

A deafening growl filled the small shelter, followed by a sharp bark.

"It has my boot!"

"Pull your foot free!"

"I can't!"

Another yank. He held her tightly, hands locked behind her thighs, fists jammed in her buttocks, against her coccyx, and they both slid down toward the narrow opening. A glimmer of light appeared down there, only to be blotted out by an immense dark shadow. He braced his feet against the collapsing snow, and hauled them back away from the opening. His coat, which they'd been sleeping on top of, was now bundled down by the opening, and the prickly pine needles dug into his back, into his neck, into his thighs. Their scent filled the air as cold flooded into that small space.

"Get it free!"

"Oh my god I can't!" she cried. "I can't get free!"

He dug his feet into the walls again, braced himself for another pull, even though he was sure that all of his kicking into the walls would topple them down onto them, bury them in snow. No matter what, he couldn't let Khagan drag her from him. He pulled her further up onto him, quickly separated his hands, then reached his left down between them, even though his forearm ached with the effort, his left hand found his right in the gap between her legs, he locked his hands together in a vise grip.

"I got you," he said. Another sudden jerk flexed his wrists, his fingers, ground his knuckles together, drove his fists into the soft place directly between her legs, slammed her pubis into his wrist. She cried out in pain, but his grip held. Another pull, then another, but he refused to surrender his grip, no matter how painful, no matter how awkward. He held Miko's life in that grip.

And then the pressure relented. She buried her face into his neck, sobbed into his ear.

"Is your foot free?" he asked. She nodded.

"He took my boot."

"Good."

He tried to scoot them further away from the opening, but his head was already pressed against the further wall, candy bar wrappers and pine boughs tickled his ears. He lifted his head and peered down over her shoulder toward the opening. A very faint pre-dawn glimmer, perhaps, a deep indigo one or two shades paler than midnight black. A few vague shadows darkened the snow: a sweater, perhaps, maybe her boot.

They both panted, pulling in air in that small space in great heaving gulps.

"Is he gone?" she whispered.

He reached in the dark space, placed his hand over her mouth. On the other side of the flimsy barrier of snow, pine boughs, and a millimeter or two of plastic sheeting, a tiger's nostrils snuffled, searching for scents. Searching for them. For another way in.

FORTY-NINE

The snuffling came from above now, from the side of the trench, then near their heads, as the great tiger sniffed at the precarious layer of snow and pine boughs above them. Branches fell free from where they had been stuck into the walls. He fumbled for the matches among the candy bars. His hand closed around a fold of paper, felt the hole that punctured the image of his friend's body. Then he found the matches, struck a light. The green plastic fabric of the tarp sagged down past the branches that supported the low ceiling. More pine boughs fell inward from the walls. Snow began to shower down over the candy bars, as the tiger dug under the tarp.

The paw appeared, claws extended, and a blast of air through the tiger's nostrils blew more snow into the shelter and snuffed out the tremulous match. Miko clamped her hand over her mouth to stifle her scream. They scooted down away from the tiger, exposed pine boughs scraping their skin and snagging on their base layers, knowing all the while that this would bring them back within reach of the opening, within easy reach of the tiger's enormous paws.

For a moment all was quiet.

A loud snap was followed by a sudden rush of collapsing snow as the tarp began to pull down around their heads, then another crack directly overhead, as three hundred and fifty kilos—or more—of tiger stepped onto the mound of snow and pushed through. A roar erupted from above.

"Get back!" he yelled.

He rolled on top of her as best he could, shielding her from the heavy weights that landed on his shoulder, drove his head down into the ground, tried to shield her from the paws that punched his ribs through the tarp.

The tiger's weight and movement was dragging the tarp out of position, raining frozen chunks of snow and bristly boughs down on top of them. Another crack boomed as the third ceiling support gave way. He was collapsing the ceiling, bringing it down on top of them. Only the flimsy branches and two thin layers of plastic fabric kept the claws from ripping into him as the tiger's paws scrabbled madly for purchase, as the snowshoe-like footpads pinned him to the ground.

Miko cried out, "can't—breathe!" and he realized that he too was struggling for air as the space collapsed down around them, as the plastic stretched, as the weight of the tiger and the falling snow made movement near impossible.

He tried to reach his left hand toward the far wall of the collapsing trench, but it was pinned beneath him as a weight landed square on his back, crushing the wind from his body. The weight ground him directly into the frozen earth—he could not breathe—but then suddenly he could, and the weight was between them, Khagan stood between them, bellowing, digging at the snow, pulling the tarp back, tearing through it.

Yuri's arm was now free, and he forced his hand under the tarp, into the numbing snow, fumbling blindly, reaching into the cold.

His fingers found what he sought, curled around cold metal. He pulled the trigger.

His ears rang from the explosion, his head rang from the kick of the gun, the barrel drove his forearm into his nose, the barrel knocked into his forehead.

The weight remained, a wall of snow and tarp between

him and Miko, but the searching, probing movement vanished, the roaring and snuffling had ceased.

With his elbows Yuri pushed himself back toward the opening. The tarp had been pulled free, the snow and boughs had mostly fallen down into the opening. He lifted his shoulders, bumped against one of the remaining birch branches, pushed it out of the way. His backside and head clear, he pulled the shotgun free of the snow, pivoted on his knees as best he could, searching through the dark for movement. Nothing. He raised the barrel high, and fired again. The second shot he felt more than he heard, ears ringing still from the first shot in the enclosed space.

Miko. He dropped the shotgun, reached into the snow at his knees, found an ankle, found a boot. He stood up and dragged her back through the trench. As she moved, she came alive, began to resist, her arms scrabbled for a grip on what was left of the walls. As he pulled her free, she sat up, covered in snow and pine needles, gasping for air, and began to punch him, clearly thinking she was being dragged once again by Khagan. He stopped her blows by hugging her tightly to him.

"It's me," he said. "He's gone. It's over now. It's okay. It's just me."

"Oh my god," she said.

They were alive.

The trench was obliterated, a shallow crater of snow and pine boughs, dark plastic peeking through in places. A solitary birch branch remained in place. Varying shades of dark and shadow lay scattered about the snow. The sky above glowed faintly in the pre-dawn.

They both shivered. They were practically naked in sub-zero cold, showered in snow, exposed. Yuri dug through the wreckage until he found a coat, his coat. He pulled it free, put it around her shoulders, helped her get her arms through the sleeves.

"Can you stand?" he asked.

She nodded. He helped her to her feet. He retrieved her

boot, helped her into it. Part of the tough leather had been shredded.

"We've got to move," he said.

"Where?" That one word sounded like it had required a supreme effort to pronounce.

"Just, moving."

He tugged the tarp free as well, shook the snow from it, wrapped this around her shoulders, tugged it over her head like a hood. He clambered through the wreckage of the trench searching with his hands in the snow for the matches. He needed to get a fire going. He was shivering uncontrollably now, his fingers numb, despite the adrenaline still coursing through his body, despite his movements.

He stalked to the other clearing, to the firewood and bits of kindling that Miko had gathered. Before too long he had a fire going. He chopped the large branch she had dragged there into usable pieces with his spade, added them to the growing blaze. He stood her close to the fire and shuffled off through the snow, gathering their clothes in the wan red light. They shook the snow free and dressed themselves as best they could. Yuri cleared a space as close to the fire as he dared, and they sat on the tarp, pulled it up around them, huddled under it, as he tossed more branches and pine boughs onto the smoky, hungry fire.

They sat in stunned silence. Shivering, though not so much from the cold anymore. From the shock of the encounter with Khagan. Yuri kept the shotgun close at hand. His ears still rang from the blast.

"Good thing you gathered firewood," he said, as he tossed another of her branches into the flames.

She turned sharply toward him, peered at him to see if he was teasing her. He smiled as best he could, fighting against the wire-like tension in his jaw, the pain in his battered, bleeding cheek.

She laughed, though her laugh came out as strained and choked as his smile.

He wanted to put his arm around her shoulders, around her back, wanted to pull her closer to him again, as close as they had been in the shelter, for warmth. But the fire was going brightly now, and the tarp was collecting the blaze's heat and reflecting it back at them. There was no longer a need to hold her tightly.

The sky began to brighten. A few stars stood out above as the cloudbank receded. The snow had stopped sometime during the night.

"The good news is," she said, "if that tiger was after us, that means he wasn't after Kamal. Mature tigers aren't above killing and eating juveniles. Especially a younger male."

"I've heard that an encounter with Amba is a sign of good things to come," Yuri said. "Even one as horrible as that was."

"Amba?"

He explained the meaning of the Udege word. He didn't explain who had told him that a meeting with Amba might be a good omen—Utiuki was harmless, no matter how close she lived to the enclosure. Besides, she'd been there long before Miko, or him, or the Project, and she would probably be there long after they were all gone.

Miko stared at the flames in silence. She leaned into him.

"Don't let us turn back," she said. "Okay? Don't let us stop looking. He must be so scared."

He was about to reach his arm around her, to pull her closer to him, when she yawned and straightened, separated from him.

He could do that. If he had to sling her over his shoulders and carry her, he would keep them going. He tried to smile, though his raw face felt like it had been stretched taut by the waves of heat coming from the fire. He tossed another branch onto the blaze. Soon there would be enough light in the sky for them to move.

He cleared his throat. "I'm sorry I had to... for the way I, you know... grabbed you. Back there."

She glanced sideways at him, flashed the hint of a smile. Nudged him in the ribs with her elbow.

"Hell of a first date," she said.

FIFTY

January 8, 2001—Cubs six weeks old

As soon as there was enough light, they set out across the riverbed. The clouds melted away, the sky above brightened, though they walked in shadowy gloom. He carried the tranq gun over one shoulder, the shotgun over the other. She wore the backpack, which contained the tattered tarp, rolled up and secured with the length of cord, the spade, the last two candy bars, the battered matchbox, and the canteen. In one coat pocket he carried the compass and the map; in the other his Yakut knife. They were out of flares. They still had one dart.

The trail he followed now was little more than a scattering of dimples in the snow, sometimes nothing more than a faint crease in the smooth blanket of white. He scanned for low boughs that had been brushed bare while nearby branches still held snow. Reading the white book as best he could.

They'd been following the faint trail for nearly an hour when he turned back to talk to Miko. He consulted the map while he waited for her to catch up. She was limping. Trying not to show it, but definitely favoring her right foot, the foot that Khagan had in his grasp, the boot that he had mangled. A sprained ankle. According to the map, Kamal was leading them east by northeast. Into the Core of the *zapovednik*.

He'd told her that he wouldn't let them turn back. That he wouldn't let them stop looking. But they had to be clear-eyed here. They had to be honest with each other, and with themselves. They were in no shape to survive another night in the cold. Not without proper gear, not without proper food. She had to know that by now. Had to know how close they'd brushed up against death the night before.

She hadn't said a word all morning. Possibly in shock. Sleep-deprived. Probably dehydrated as well. Hungry and cold, he was both of those things, too, despite a morning candy bar and steady movement. Their parkas and snow pants and sweaters were tattered, like the tarp, the tough fabric torn and rent like wet paper. Conditions were far from ideal for clear thought. At a time when clear thought was necessary.

Ten more minutes, he thought. *A little further, and then we'll talk.*

Suddenly Kamal's pug marks stood out stark in the snow, the rounded shape of his four toes clearly visible. Yuri waited for Miko, pointed out the shallow impression the cub had left under a nearby tree, indicating where he'd slept, or at least rested. They'd gained some ground. She looked at him, but blankly. No hope in her eyes, just exhaustion.

Don't let me turn back.

Kamal had changed course. Instead of continuing along the valley floor, the trail now veered left, due north, began to climb into low hills, tall pines. He consulted the map. If they continued in that direction, they would intersect the power line access road that he had used to reach the sanitarium with Evgeny. Which would lead them back to the enclosure. They still had a long day's hike ahead of them, but it should be an easier route than trying to follow their tangled trail back through the forest.

The time had come. He needed to get her to safety. They wouldn't stop searching. But they needed to resupply.

Perhaps recruit additional assistance. Time to tell Samuel what had happened. Time to admit defeat.

For now, their path and Kamal's coincided. They would have to see how long that lasted.

They trudged along without speaking, the steady crunching of their boots in the fresh snow and their labored breathing the only sounds, the only language left in the world. Exhaustion and the basic need to survive drove away all thoughts, all other desires. He appreciated life when it was reduced to this elemental level. When all trivial cares and concerns were stripped away. Priorities painfully, frighteningly clear.

They followed Kamal's track through tall Korean pines, up one modest slope and down the other side, into a shallow basin.

Yuri stopped. A dark line of churned snow approached Kamal's trail from the side. The two trails joined. He ran forward to the place where they intersected.

Snowshoes. A man had found Kamal's trail, and began following it up the rise. This slope steepened as it climbed into the trees, casting them in shadow, the morning sun still hidden behind the ridge.

Then an engine, coughing to life. Faint, nearly imperceptible. He pulled his hood back, removed his cap, cupped his hands to his ears.

Voices. From the other side of that ridge.

He turned toward Miko. She plodded along, head down, focused on placing one foot after the other, her limp more pronounced.

He jammed the tranq gun stock into the snow at the intersection. It would draw her attention. He brought the shotgun down off his shoulder, checked the shell in the chamber, removed the safety.

Ahead the trees stood starkly silhouetted on the ridge line, the low winter sun made them glow with an angelic halo. He began to run through the snow.

When he reached the summit, he could hear the engine more clearly, but knew it was receding. He reached a clearing, charged over a chaotically churned surface of prints and dug-up snow and uprooted chunks of black earth. Multiple parallel prints led him through a tight maze of short trees, brought him to the access trail. An enormous metal power line support post towered over him.

He ran into the cleared path, stood among the tire tracks and snowmobile treads. Far away, down the hill, beneath the thick black power cables, a black SUV moved slowly through the snow. He raised the shotgun, sighted at the vehicle. But he knew he didn't have a shot. Even with a Dragunov it would be well out of range, so distant that it looked like a child's toy.

He lowered the gun, turned back to the silent trees. A scrap of pink material caught his eye in the snow. He stooped for it. A nylon collar, looped through a small beige plastic box, severed with a knife. Kamal's radio tracker.

Their tiger cub was gone. He'd been taken. They had no way of following him. He raised the gun above his head with both hands, slammed it down into the road.

The trees trembled slightly in a sudden stirring of wind, as though amused by his pitiful complaint.

FIFTY-ONE

The hill was steep, the snow slippery. She had to lower herself to all fours, using her hands for stability and her feet for propulsion, angling her toes outward—her right foot painfully so—to keep from sliding. She used the tranq gun as a walking stick, driving the butt down into the snow.

Finally she reached the crest, the ground leveled to a plateau where a tangled wall of short birches and gnarled larches rose up in front of her. Yuri was nowhere to be seen.

She continued to follow the mixed trail: Kamal's pug marks, Yuri's bootprints, and the other man's snowshoes. She knew why he had run ahead. She also felt the fear of the unknown: who was this other man following their cub? What did he want? Was he merely curious? Were his intentions sinister? Could it be Chernichev?

The tracks led into a small clearing where the snow exploded into a chaos of prints and impressions, animal and man. A flash of yellow caught her eye, and she stepped from the clearing, forced her way a meter or two into the trees. She crouched down, picked up a yellow-feathered steel dart that had been tossed to the side. The plunger had been depressed, whatever drugs it had contained had been expelled. A narrow path of prints trampled the snow leading from the far side of the clearing.

She followed these tracks until she came to another opening, a broader space, where she had to shield her eyes against the sun that reflected blindingly off the snow. Here she found Yuri on his knees in the shadow of a rusted iron giant: two immense cylindrical legs led up to a narrow torso and then stopped, as though the giant's arms and head had been knocked free, leaving the legs rooted. The ancient power line tower still supported thick black cables, which swooped from the top of the torso, trailed off downhill to the right, rose up a steep slope to the left. A bright ribbon of white snow, cleared of trees, also stretched away from those rusted legs, following beneath the cables. Far below, down at the bottom of the hill, another iron giant gathered in the cables and passed them further along into the trees.

She stood next to Yuri. Shallow prints of snowshoes and the deeper impressions of boots clustered here, joined with even deeper tire tracks and snowmobile treads that followed the access trail down to the right. The forest hushed around them. On the far side of the road grew a darker, denser stand of squat pine trees. The midday sun peeked over these trees, fell on their faces, but did not provide warmth, only blinding light that made them wince and squint. Their exhalations congealed into golden clouds of vapor, then vanished.

He stood up and seemed surprised to see her, as though he hadn't heard her approaching.

He pointed down the hill. "They took him."

She stared, thought she could see a tiny vehicle moving beneath the power lines.

"Then we follow them," she said.

"They have too much of a head start," he said. "They have a vehicle. And you're hurt."

"So that's it? We quit?"

He lifted his gloved hand. It held Kamal's pink radio collar, the plastic transponder still attached.

"He's gone." He shook his head. "We can't bring him back."

She held up the yellow-feathered tranq dart. He frowned as he took it into his gloved hand, turned it over. He handed her the dart and the collar in exchange for the tranq gun. He opened the chamber and removed the dart, compared it to the one she had found. Identical.

"Where'd you find this?"

"Back there," she said. "In the clearing."

He rechambered the dart, handed her the gun.

"That means he's still alive," she said. "Doesn't it?"

He grunted. "Poachers don't take animals alive. They kill them, they cut them up, and they transport their parts. Get it through your head. Kamal is gone."

"There has to be something," she said. "Something we can do."

He straightened. "We have to get back," he said.

"What is it?" she asked.

"Just trust me," he said. "We have to—"

"Vida," she whispered.

Yuri nodded. "Nobody's there to protect her."

"Chernichev," she said. She remembered his cold, close-set, calculating eyes, his tobacco-stained teeth under his red mustache.

"I warned you this would happen," Yuri said. "Samuel did too."

Beneath her snood her cheeks flushed hot. She pulled the scarf down over her chin, but despite having freed her mouth, she found that her lips and her tongue could not form words. And not because of the cold.

"Is that not accurate?" he asked.

"You were there," she finally managed. She pointed her finger, and jabbed his chest with it. "And you didn't stop them."

He turned away, stooped to pick up the shotgun. He brushed snow from the barrel and began stalking up the hill.

"You know I'm right," she called after him.

"I know where we are," he said, without turning, without slowing. "If we hurry we can make it back by nightfall."

Every step on her twisted ankle caused her to wince. But she would not hold them up. She would not slow them down. Vida was in danger—she sensed it now, too. Kamal would have to wait. They would find him later. Right now, she had to secure the other half of the Project.

She had become entirely too fixated on Kamal. She'd forgotten all about his sister.

She swallowed her pain and hiked up the hill in his tracks. They followed the black cables suspended above them toward another rusted giant gleaming bronze in the distance.

FIFTY-TWO

The access road brought them to Red Stag Lodge as the sun was setting. The way was substantially easier, as the snow on the road had been matted down and packed firm by snowmobile and tire treads. Miko had done her best to keep up, despite her limp, but in the end relented and allowed him to carry her piggyback for the final hour, with her wearing the backpack and Yuri carrying both the tranq gun and shotgun across his chest as a counterbalance to her weight.

As they came in view of the Lodge, she smacked his arm, told him to set her down. She could walk the rest of the way. He understood. She didn't want anyone to see her in a weakened state.

Against protocol, lights blazed in the kitchen windows and in the lab. He handed her the tranq gun, leveled the shotgun, and entered through the unlocked kitchen door.

Evgeny and Sergei rose from the kitchen table, quickly gathered around Miko and Yuri.

"They took Vida," Sergei said, with a glance at Evgeny. "We couldn't stop them."

"We hid in the woods," Evgeny said glumly, eyes downcast. "They had guns."

"It's fine," Yuri said.

"They would've killed us without thinking twice," Evgeny said.

"There was nothing else for you to do," Yuri said.

The workmen had taken one snowcat back to civilization. Chernichev and his cronies had taken the other one. Yuri quickly verified that the building was indeed deserted. No trace remained of the recent arrivals in the trophy room. In the barn, they found no one in the lab. Both snowcats had been taken, but the two snowmobiles remained parked in the garage.

Upstairs, Control was also empty. Miko scanned the green CCTV monitors, as though hoping for a glimpse of Vida hidden away in a corner of the den. But she was gone.

"We can try to follow their tracks in the morning," Yuri said, as they returned to the kitchen. Sergei had heated up leftovers from a previous meal, and the smells made Yuri's stomach growl and his mouth water. A heaviness settled down over his bones, pulled him toward the table. He slumped into the nearest chair. They chewed their food in silence. Evgeny had poured out glasses of vodka, but neither of them drank it.

She dug through the backpack. She removed Kamal's radio collar, set it on the formica. Then the yellow-feathered tranq dart.

"There is no evidence that either of them are dead," she said.

"Poachers don't keep—" Yuri began.

"Live tigers," Miko finished. "I know, I know. Too inconvenient, too problematic. But what if there is a monetary premium placed on a live tiger? Especially a cub. A reward of some sort. A bounty. Then it makes sense for them to make the extra effort."

Yuri pursed his lips, leaned back in his chair. "It's just not—"

She raised her finger.

"I know how easy it is to domesticate a tiger. Especially when they're as young as Kamal and Vida. I've spent much of my career doing just that. They are remarkably intelligent creatures. I mean, our Project was trying to avoid that, but someone with the right background and a small facility could easily domesticate them. For whatever reason. Maybe somebody wants them as pets. And if they're willing to pay a premium..."

"I hate to say it," Evgeny said, "but they'd be more likely to sell them to one of those tiger farms, in China, in Korea. Where they breed tigers so they can meet the demand for parts for traditional medicines and libido enhancers."

Miko stared at Yuri. He shrugged. "Wild tigers are prized, of course, but..."

She nodded. Slowly. Reluctantly. She'd heard of such places, of course. Horrible, inhumane conditions, especially for a creature accustomed to roaming as far as tigers must. Rampant in-breeding, with all the attendant health and developmental problems. She hadn't wanted to acknowledge the possibility.

Yuri watched her as his friend spoke, but she didn't flinch. If that was the ultimate destination of either Kamal or Vida—or both—it would be a horrible irony, for him to have "rescued" these cubs, only for them to be confined for life in an abusive breeding kennel.

"Okay," she said, nodding slowly, digesting this new information. "Well, that's a possible reason for them to keep the cubs alive, I mean."

Yuri shook his head. "I know you want to believe—" he said.

"All we have to do is find whoever has them," she said. "And make a higher bid than the offer they have in hand. Tiger cubs are as resilient as they are intelligent. Look at Kamal. He survived in circumstances that nearly killed the two of us."

Yuri glanced at her, recalled the deep scratches Khagan's claw had left on her knee and shin, the ankle that she still favored. Those wounds needed attention. She did not acknowledge his stare, however.

"If they are alive, and there is even a remote chance to retrieve them," she said, "the Project could still forge ahead."

"But listen to yourself," he said, his voice calm. "*If* they are alive. *If* we can find them."

She lowered her eyes to the radio transponder on the nylon collar she held in her hand. He was sure she was taking his words as patronizing.

"We would have to track down Chernichev and his comrades—but remember, these men are dangerous. They don't want to be found. Where would we even begin to look?"

Her face brightened with an idea: "What if you called Iliakov?"

He met her gaze. "As soon we have enough daylight," he said. "We'll get to a farmhouse. Find a phone."

He had considered calling the Major as well. But he didn't want to beg his former C.O. for any favors. Besides, the Major had brought Chernichev and the other two to the lodge. He was in on the plan. Almost certainly the one behind the plan. He could attempt to make a counteroffer, as Miko suggested—it wasn't the worst idea—but he was almost certain it would lead them into a trap.

No—he would find Chernichev on his own. The cubs were beyond rescue. Justice would come faster that way.

"These cubs need us," she said. She stood up, pushed her chair under the table. "We can't just—"

"There is nothing more we can do right now," Yuri said, "except clean our wounds and sleep."

He picked up one of the vodka glasses.

"Let's have a drink." He tried to contort his remaining cheek into an imitation of a smile. Evgeny raised his glass.

"That's it?" she said. "That's your solution?"

He raised the glass to his lips, quaffed a large sip. The alcohol flushed warmth to his face. Though perhaps it wasn't solely the alcohol, but also her stern gaze, her compressed lips. Her hands gripping tightly the back of the chair she stood behind.

"Why not?" he said.

She left the kitchen, climbed the back steps rapidly toward her room.

He knew exactly how she felt—like a failure. He felt the same way. Any attempt to comfort her would only underscore that sinking, widening pit in her gut. No matter how kind the words, she would hear them as a reprimand; no matter how calm the demeanor, she would find his mere presence a reproach.

He held up the glass, but in the end, decided he didn't actually want to drink the rest of it. He pushed back from the table, dumped it into the sink. In all the exertions his wounds had begun to bleed again. He needed to clean himself up and apply fresh bandages.

When he turned back to the table, Evgeny and Sergei were staring at Yuri expectantly. As though it was his duty to follow her, to check on her. To soothe her. He shrugged.

"She'll be back," he said. "When she's hungry."

FIFTY-THREE

Miko had disappeared upstairs. Sergei provided him with towels and some clothes left behind by one of the workmen that were his size. In the lavatory he turned on the shower, let the water warm while he stripped out of his filthy, tattered outerwear, then out of his sweat-stained base layer. He entered and stood naked under the steaming jets.

He'd been living in a fantasy world. What did he think, that he was going to save Kamal for Miko? That he would save the day, save her Project, and return the conquering hero? That she would look up to him with admiration in her eyes? That she would fall in love with him? What were they going to do, then, after—get married and live at the Lodge? Raise Kamal and Vida as their children?

Stupid. Foolish. Sentimental. Soft. But mostly stupid. He could hear Major Iliakov laughing at him. How old was he again? Had he not learned anything about the way life works?

No trust. No fear. No surrender.

This motto had gotten him through Afghanistan. Through Chechnya. Through his goddamn life to this point. What made him think that he no longer had any use for it? What ever gave him the idea that he was somehow superior now? That he could walk a different path?

He toweled himself dry and pulled on a clean base layer and socks. She was waiting for him in the kitchen. She had cleared everything from the kitchen table, except for a small pile of gauze and bandages, a bottle of hydrogen peroxide, a scissors.

She stepped toward him. She lifted her hand, slowly reached for his cheek.

"Let me clean this properly," she said. "And bandage it."

"It's okay," he said. "I'll take care of it in the lab."

She touched his elbow, steered him to the table. "It's the least I can do."

Steam began to rise from the kettle spout, and she turned off the gas. He was overdue for a bandage change. The wound had started bleeding again, and it often leaked a sticky mess of pus and discharge. He could clean it himself, using the mirror, but it would be nice to have a professional debride the wound properly.

With his knife he cut loose the bandage on his forearm as well. She took his wrist in her hand and lifted his arm, turned it, examined the puncture wounds. He pulled his arm free so he could cut strips of gauze. Then he sat on the table, reclined, lay flat on his back. She leaned over him with the water, gauze and bandages at her side. She began to work, briskly, efficiently.

The hydrogen peroxide bubbled and hissed, dripped down into his ear, to the back of his neck. Her scrubbing became more pointed, going deeper.

"There's some slough here," she said. "This is going to hurt."

"Do what you have to do," he said. "I haven't been taking care of it as well as I should."

The pain intensified. He grabbed the edge of the formica table with his right hand.

"I'm going as quickly as possible," she said.

"Thorough better than quick," he said.

Finally she was done. She dunked the cloth in the water, warm now rather than hot, and dabbed at his sweaty brow. Then repeated the motion on her own forehead.

"I'll apply the bandage after it's dried," she said. She stepped over him, came to sit at his other side. "Let's have a look at your forearm."

Again she lifted his arm, examined the puncture wounds.

"I can't believe a tiger had you in her mouth," she said. "That must have been terrifying."

"It was... uncomfortable."

She cleaned the wounds on his forearm, rubbed the cloth down his arm, then back up. As his sweat cooled, the hair on the back of his neck stood on end.

She released his arm and stood, stretched, rolled her shoulders. She fished a pack of cigarettes from her parka and fidgeted with it. Pulling a cigarette free, putting it back. Finally she put it to her lips, and lit it with a red plastic lighter. Exhaled a cloud of smoke.

"I never took you for a smoker," he said.

"I'm not," she said. "Your friend left them behind."

He held out his hand, and she placed the cigarette in his fingers. He touched the butt to his lips and inhaled. He immediately hacked a gout of smoke toward the ceiling. The cigarette fell down beside his head, and she reached for it, rescued it.

"You're clearly not a smoker," she said.

He shook his head.

She took the cigarette back from him, held it pinched in between her thumb and forefinger. She lowered the cigarette to his lips.

"Take in a little," she said. "But not all the way into your lungs. Hold it in your mouth."

He obeyed as best he could.

"You have some in there?"

He nodded.

"Now breathe in normally. Through the mouth."

He opened his mouth and filled his lungs.

"Exhale."

A stream of smoke raced toward the ceiling.

"See?" she said. "Not so hard."

"Nice," he said.

"Not really." She returned the cigarette to her own lips, took another drag. Exhaled. "It's a disgusting habit."

He placed his hand over his eyes, pressed his thumb and forefinger into his eyes until he saw stars. Everything he'd done since he had arrived at the sanitarium had gone wrong. He couldn't have fucked up worse if he had tried.

"This hasn't exactly gone as planned," he said.

It all began with the cubs, with Tatiana. He'd tried to change the natural order of things, and now the natural order was putting him firmly in his place. If he'd listened to Evgeny on that morning six weeks ago, none of this would have happened. He and his partner would still be patrolling the Sikhote-Alin. The war would have continued to fade from his mind, a more distant memory with each passing day.

She stood up and tossed the cigarette into the sink. She picked up the bandages and began applying them to his face.

"You chose to come here." She stretched tape over the bandages, pressed them down against his skin. "You don't get to feel sorry for yourself now."

She was right.

"Your turn." He rolled to his side, hopped down from the table, patted the smooth formica, warm where his body had been.

She lifted the leg of her sweatpants, showed him the clean bandages wrapped around her shin and calf, the heavier tape that immobilized her ankle.

"And your hand?"

She showed him the back of her left hand, where Kamal had raked her with his claws. Also wrapped in gauze, with a hint of three dark stripes showing through.

"It's been a hell of a day," he said. He yawned. "I'm going to sleep."

"Anatoly's room is upstairs," she said. "Across the hall from mine."

"I'll sleep down here." He pointed down the corridor toward the workmen's bunks. "If anybody returns, I want to be the first to know. I'm going to lock up."

"Okay," she said. "Good night, then."

"Good night," he said. He watched her go up the stairs, heard her door close and lock.

He roamed through the empty, freezing lodge, securing doors and windows. Finally he returned to the bunk room. He bundled up the clothes he would wear tomorrow, and threw his parka on over his shoulders for the brief but frigid crossing from the Lodge to the lab. He would sleep in Control. That way he would have access to the snowmobiles. That would allow him to leave first thing in the morning—before dawn even. Before she or Evgeny would even know he was gone. Before they might try to follow him. He would call Dr. Carrington from the road. She was Samuel's problem, as far as he was concerned. He was the one who had called her in. He was the one who had put her in charge. Evgeny and Sergei would make sure she got to the Polygon.

He trudged through the cold night air to the lab, where he kicked off the boots, hung his parka on the back of the chair that sat in front of the computer. He quietly climbed the steps to Control. He did not turn on the lights. There was no moon in the cloudless sky yet, but a few of the screens in the bank of CCTV monitors still glowed, giving off enough light for him to see the sofa, his destination. He set the backpack on the floor, turned on the space heater, and pulled the glowing grille close to the sofa.

He stood for a moment at the large window, looking down over the paddock, dimly lit by the light he had left on in the kitchen, the light protocol no longer important now that the cubs were gone. Beyond, in the black expanse of darkness, spread the larger enclosure. Cold emanated from the glass.

He'd invited disaster when he ripped those cubs from their mother's womb. And now even they were gone, vanished. Almost certainly cold carcasses stretched in the back of a poacher's van.

There was only one thing left: vengeance. Bloodshed. Death. Destruction. Those things, at least, he knew he could do right.

His forehead bumped against the thick pane, and he

pulled himself back, stood straight, hands clasped behind his back.

He was going Ferret hunting. Of that much, he was sure. Oleg Chernichev had ruined everything, and so he had a new mission. He would find Chernichev, and ruin him in return.

But first he needed to sleep for a few hours. And then he would leave, before she realized his intentions. He didn't want her to slow him down, or get in his way. Revenge, Iliakov always said, demanded a one-way mindset. Of course, he had said this to discourage the emotional reaction that would lead to thoughts of revenge. But now Yuri took it as guidance.

He unfurled the woolen blankets and draped them over himself as he stretched out on the sofa. He pulled a flat cushion under his head. The smell of her hair entered his nostrils, almost as pervasively as it had in the dugout shelter. He knew she slept on this couch many nights while keeping an eye on the cubs. He buried his nose in the fabric and breathed the scent in deeply once again, then turned the pillow over. The scent was not as strong on this side. He exhaled, closed his eyes, and sought sleep.

FIFTY-FOUR

A noise from the lab below stirred him awake. A faint click. He wasn't sure if he had even fallen asleep, and he took that disorientation as a sign that he had drifted off. The heater's grille no longer glowed. The moon had risen, and now hung low and full and bright in the second window from right, a distant, baleful eye that glared at him. Had the sound, so sharp in the moment, but fading fast, been part of a dream?

Another sound from below, a muffled thud, told him no, he had not been dreaming.

Chernichev? Returning to the scene of the crime?

A faint creak from the steps leading up to Control. Chernichev had to know that Yuri would come after him. And he had to know that Yuri would first return to the lodge to resupply, refuel, recuperate. Had to know that Yuri's guard would be down, and that he would be tired—exhausted even. If he were the Ferret, now would be the time to make a preemptive strike.

Someone was on the stairs, he was sure of it. The treads ascending slowly. Stealthily. He reached into his pack, found the burled wooden handle of his Yakut knife, slid the blade free from the sheath.

The door opened into the room, and a dark figure stepped through it, eased the door closed behind. Stepped into the silvery moonlight. A fur-lined hood covered the face, a heavy parka hid the body. Through slitted eyelids, not wanting to reveal that he was awake, he watched the figure cross the room toward him, the knife clutched tight in his right, left foot on the floor, right knee under him. Coiled to spring.

Bare hands, pale in the light, pulled back the hood. A moon-bright face under a tiara of black hair pulled up into a knot. Miko.

She shrugged out of the parka, let it fall to the floor. She wore a flannel nightshirt that extended below her knees.

He cleared his throat, to warn her that she was not alone, expecting her to startle, to panic even.

Instead she pulled the nightshirt up, up past a dark triangle of pubic hair, over her taut breasts, her small dark nipples erect in the chill, continued over her shoulders, over her head. She dropped the long shirt onto the parka, a soft rustle of fabric on fur. She must not have heard him clear his throat.

"I'm here," he said, his voice barely more than a whisper, still afraid that he would startle her, that she would scream and grasp at her clothes and flee in a panic.

"I know," she said, as she loosened the knot that held her hair. Dark strands swept down over her face and shoulders. She grabbed the blankets and lifted them, sat naked on the sofa, her skin alabaster in the moonlight, and then backed in under the covers, pushed her shoulders into his chest, pushed her butt into his lap as she pulled the blankets back down. Her hair filled his nostrils with the reek of her lavender shampoo.

"I can't get warm," she said. She reached behind her and grabbed his left wrist, pulled his arm around her. His hand recoiled at the clammy chill of her skin, as cold as though she had been standing out in the snow for hours, staring into the dark forest, searching for answers. He began to rub her body as he had in the shelter, vigorously stroking her arms, her thighs, her belly, her shoulders.

The space heater also kicked on, as though her mere

entrance had lowered the room's temperature by a degree or two, enough to trigger the thermostat. The metal grille began to glow orange.

"That's better," she said, after a while. He left his arms wrapped around her. He pressed his nose against her scalp, against the nape of her neck, inhaled the scent of her skin, the smell of her beneath the soap's perfume, sought the pure smell of her that he remembered from the dugout.

Together they stared at the moon for a while. It stared back. The strange, twisted smile seemed both sympathetic and mocking. She snuggled her body back into his as she tilted her head up, glanced back over her shoulder in his direction. Her lips were dark in the moonlight, and full.

"They're still alive," she said.

"Shh," he said. "You need to sleep. We both do."

"How can you sleep," she asked, "when they're out there, somewhere? They must be so scared."

"There's nothing we can do," he said again.

"There's something we can do."

She ground her butt into his lap. Into his already-stiff prick.

"Miko," he said.

She reached back, tugged at the hem of his silk thermals, pulled them down over his hips. They snagged on his cock, pulled it down and perpendicular to his body, forced it against hers. He pulled it free of the underwear, shoved the thermals down to his knees. She closed her ass cheeks around him, reached between her legs and pulled him forward between her legs. Pushed him up and into her warmth, into her wetness, into her being.

"Miko," he said. Much softer this time. Like a caress.

She shoved back into him, pushed down around his stiffness, drove his back into the sofa cushions, forced him into her. She gasped, panted. He pushed back, pushed his hips into the yielding roundness of her buttocks, drove his prick straight toward her center. Again, then again. Slowly. He wrapped his arms in front of her, gripped her shoulders with his hands, pulled her down and into him with each thrust, penetrating further inside her with each grinding movement, each thrust opening her more fully to him. He jammed his left knee between her knees and levered her legs apart, lifted her left knee, opened her more. The blankets fell away, exposing them to the chill but also to the warming orange glow of the purring space heater.

Now she moaned with each thrust, as he moved more fully into her, as he claimed her, as he made her more fully his. He nuzzled the nape of her neck, inhaled her scent, the smell of the sweat that began to plaster the fine strands of hair there to the soft skin. He dug his teeth into her flesh, into her scalp.

"Oh," she said. "Oh, Yuri."

Her entire body tensed and then released, and he felt her clenching against him deep within her, and he stayed there, in as far as he could go, touching her center, as she pulsed around him, her body trembling, her breathing quick and shallow. And then they lay there, still, pressed together. Sweat slick between their hips, between his belly and the small of her back.

Now he was thinking about the cubs as well, about whether they were alive, as she said. His thoughts turned to the sunrise that would separate them, and to the hunt that awaited him. The moon had nearly lifted free of the window, shrouding them in darkness. The heater clicked and went silent, the orange glow began to fade from the element.

"It's okay," he said. "I don't need—"

She continued to move against him. He pulled himself free. She whirled to face him, worked her body in under his, forced her left leg under his, pulled him onto her. She placed her hands gently on his cheeks, her palm a warm presence against his left cheek, but not on his bandaged, unfeeling right. She wrapped her legs around his, her calves against the backs of his knees, against his hamstrings.

"Yuri," she whispered, and she held his eyes in hers. She opened herself to him completely, and he slid easily inside. "Fuck me."

They continued to stare at each other as they moved

together. She opened further and further to him, her heels grinding into his buttocks and he pushed deeper and deeper inside. As they moved her knees lifted under his shoulders, her ankles clamped against his hips. Sweat and her wetness slicked the skin of her upraised buttocks and his hips, pooled between their bellies. All the while she kept her hands on his face, forced him to maintain eye contact with her, and he lost himself in the bottomless dark wells of her eyes. Sadness there along with the joy, pain along with the pleasure, receiving and giving, giving and receiving.

He felt that knot tightening deep in the base of his root, and instinctively he closed his eyes, squeezed them tight. She smacked his wounded cheek hard, rattling his head, snapping his eyes back open as arcs of pain flared through his vision.

"Look at me," she said.

He did, and he held his eyes open, on her, staring at her staring at him. He watched as she bit and chewed her thick lower lip in concentration, as she tightened herself against him, tried to expel him and shut him out even as he continually forced his way back in. She fought to keep her own eyes open, until she couldn't any longer, and she arched her back and threw her arms over her head in surrender and cried out, a guttural howl, as deep within her she clenched and released against his stiffness, over and over again, pulsing. She writhed beneath him, and he lifted his shoulders and drove himself deeper into her than he thought possible as he came along with her. Their bodies arced apart, then collapsed back together around that hot, slippery knot that was both inside each of them and tightening between them. Shuddering. Shattered. Shaking.

He opened his eyes again and sought for hers, but they were closed to him now, her face turned toward the cushions, and tears leaked from them, tears that he desperately kissed away, tasting their salty sweetness.

"Miko," he said. "Don't cry."

"I'm not." As he wiped at her cheeks with the backs of his fingers she caught the knuckle of his index finger in her mouth and bit down, held it there, tasted the salty wetness with her tongue. "I'm not."

As she sucked on his finger he felt himself stirring again. The space heater clicked, began to purr and glow orange. Tired as he was, he did not want to sleep. There would be time for that later.

FIFTY-FIVE

January 9, 2001—Cubs six weeks old

When he opened his eyes, he had to close them again immediately to shut out the blinding light that poured in through the windows opposite. His shoulders were pressed into the sofa back, and the pillow and blankets smelled of her, but his left hand swept across an empty expanse of sofa cushion.

He opened his eyes again, wincing, allowed them to adjust to the brightness. He could tell from the quality of the blue sky, despite the darkly tinted windows, that the sun had long since cleared the horizon. He had meant to be gone by now. Before anybody was aware. Dispensing with goodbyes and promises.

But that was before last night. He closed his eyes again. Had last night happened? An ache deep inside him, below his belly, and a tender soreness in his prick told him that yes, she had come to him. As did the twinge of regret when his hand did not find her at his side.

A very faint clicking, erratic, like someone tapping out a message in morse, caused him to open his eyes again.

She hadn't gone far. She sat at the computer, back straight, leaning forward, using the keyboard and mouse to scan through what seemed to be grainy video footage. The streaming sunlight from the windows washed over her, rendered her nearly in silhouette, made it impossible for him to make out any details of what she was staring at so intently on the computer screen.

He had put on his silk base layer before sleeping. His shirt and sweater and snow pants and parka were scattered on the floor. The door to the lab below would be within her peripheral vision. How was he going to get out of there without alerting her? It was a mistake to sleep so late. He must have been exhausted.

She ejected a disc from the drive, returned it to a paper sleeve, removed another disc and slotted it into the drive, and began fast forwarding through more black-and-white footage. She was searching through archived video from the CCTV cameras set up to monitor the cubs, looking for clues, perhaps for a sight of the perpetrators. Searching for answers.

He had to admire her determination. Misguided though it was.

He sat up, quietly reached for his snow pants. Began to pull them on slowly, silently.

"You're awake," she said.

She glanced over her shoulder, returned her gaze to the flickering images. He realized that he could see her face reflected in the screen—which meant that she could see the sofa over her shoulder, allowing her to monitor both the video and him as he slept.

He needed to be gone. If farewells needed to be said, then they needed to be said. Better to rip the bandage off, rather than trying to peel it slowly. Don't drag out the pain, meet it head on. Push through it.

Chernichev would not have overslept. The Ferret would be on the move.

He stood up, pulled the snow pants' suspenders over his shoulders, donned his shirt, and crossed the room to stand behind her. On the monitor, the view was from a camera perched high on the barn, looking down on the paddock with a wide-angle lens that also caught a triangular portion of the snowy gap between farmhouse and barn. In the lower left a clock raced up through the digits: the seconds a blur, the minutes ticking steadily, the hour changing every couple of minutes.

A flicker caused her to pause, rewind, move more slowly.

"There," she said.

A brief flash of a man, in winter camouflage fatigues, white with a pattern of grays and charcoals, followed by another, dressed similarly. They both wore black ski masks. She slowed the speed down further, zoomed in.

The first man, when he turned back to motion toward the man following him. A flash of a short beard tufted out from under the mask. A goatee. No color, but not black, not dark. Which meant blond. Or red.

"It's him, isn't it?" She turned toward Yuri.

He stood up. "Chernichev."

"Now we have proof," she said. She returned to the video, played it back again.

"I'm going after him," he said.

"And I'm coming with you."

"No," he said, simply.

This was not open for discussion. He couldn't have her tagging along again. Forcing him to be more concerned about her welfare than his new mission.

She swiveled the chair around fully, to face him. "I held my own in the taiga," she said.

He leaned toward her, placed his hands on the chair's armrests. She leaned back, raising her hands slightly, until she couldn't lean back any further, her chin tucked to her chest.

"You did," he said. "And so did your cub. But where I'm going, you can't follow. Not this time."

She put her hands on his chest and pushed against him, but he did not relinquish his grip on the chair, didn't let it scoot back away from him on its casters, didn't allow her to budge him.

"Don't patronize me," she said. "If this is a rescue, then

you need me there to take care of the cubs. And if it's revenge, then I want to be there for that, too."

Behind him, heavy treads began stalking up the stairs to Control. The thud of winter boots on wood.

"Somebody's coming," she said. She shoved his hands from the armrests and he released his hold. She swiveled the chair back toward the computer, scooted it closer to the desk.

He turned toward the sofa and stooped to retrieve his sweater from the floor. As he straightened, Evgeny's bearded face filled the door's window. The man hesitated, rapped softly on the glass. Yuri motioned for him to enter. He slowly surveyed the room, took in Miko's presence, her snow pants on the floor, the balled-up blankets on the sofa, Yuri pulling on his sweater. A sly grin crossed his face.

"Morning, sunshine," Evgeny said. He cast a sidelong glance in Miko's direction, then raised his eyebrows in an unstated query.

Yuri kept his face expressionless. Evgeny's lips pursed as though about to emit a low whistle.

Instead, he said, "Someone here to see you." He stepped into the room, and allowed the diminutive figure who had followed him quietly up the stairs to emerge from behind.

Utiuki.

FIFTY-SIX

"She said she needed to see you," Evgeny said to Yuri. Miko had barely turned in her chair to acknowledge the new arrivals' presence.

Utiuki surveyed the room. Her eyes strayed to the bank of CCTV monitors. Most of them were now dark. Then she moved toward the wall of windows, slowly, as though in a trance. She stared out through the glass.

"So this is the zoo," she said.

Miko's head snapped toward her. She stood up. "Who's this?"

Utiuki pulled her shoulders back and lifted her chin. Said her name, slowly. Proudly.

"My neighbor," Yuri said. "*Our* neighbor. She lives in the woods not far from here."

Miko extended her hand and introduced herself as "Dr. Miko Katanabe." Utiuki folded her arms across her chest and stared at her.

Miko retracted her hand. "It was never a zoo," she said.

Despite his snow pants and his sweater, Yuri shivered. Evgeny and Utiuki had brought the outdoor chill inside with them. The space heater thermostat clicked and the fan began to purr.

The diminutive woman wrinkled her nose. "Stinks in

here." She waved her hand in front of her nose. "Like cigarettes."

"What brings you here?" Yuri asked.

Utiuki turned away from Miko, her small figure now a dark silhouette against the brilliant blue and white backdrop.

"Tiger cubs are still alive!" she said. "Utiuki watched the *biryuk* load one onto a truck."

"Where?" Yuri asked. "Which one?"

"Here." She turned and pointed down toward the paddock. "Yesterday."

"You're sure it was alive?"

"In a cage." She sketched a box in the air using her hands and the floor: waist high, maybe a meter squared. "Like in a zoo."

"See?" Miko said. She turned in the chair so she was facing into the room. "I told you. Their collapsible crates are gone. Both of them."

Utiuki pointed at Yuri. "You must bring them back."

He shook his head. *Am I dreaming?*

She seemed to take his head shake as a refusal. "Then I don't give you this," she said.

She pulled a scrap of cloth from her coat pocket.

"What is that?" Evgeny asked.

"A gift," she said. She beckoned with her other hand for Yuri to come to her. "From Amba."

Yuri remained motionless. Evgeny and Miko stared at him expectantly. Utiuki smiled.

"See what it is, at least," Evgeny said. He came to stand beside Yuri, nudged him. "Go on."

He crossed the floorboards, stopped in front of the strange woman. She hopped up onto the low coffee table, so she could look down on him, barely. He had called her old, but now that he looked at her, he could not be certain of her age. Thin crow's feet creased the corners of her eyes, and the skin stretched taut over her high cheekbones, but her pulled-back hair shimmered jet black, and a light danced at the center of her narrow eyes. She met his gaze, and did not look away. She patted the scars on his cheek.

"Not so much older than you," she said, as though she could read his mind.

At her touch a surge of warmth flooded his good cheek. He lowered his eyes to the folded-up cloth in her palm.

She pulled back the corners. Lifted free a strand of leather cord. A pendant hung from the loop: a hook of yellowed bone, tapering to a fine point. She dangled the claw in the space between herself and Yuri.

She placed the empty cloth in her pocket, then took up one end of the thong in that hand, spread her hands apart. She nodded at Yuri, inviting him to lean forward, to lower his head so that she could wrap the cord around his neck.

He looked over his shoulder at Evgeny. Part of him wanted to laugh. Wanted to snort. To giggle, even, like he hadn't since his earliest days in the Home for Boys, getting stung across the knuckles by Ms. Demidova in math class.

Evgeny did not smile, or even shrug. Yuri turned toward Miko. Her brow, normally smooth and unperturbed, was creased in a frown. He turned back to Utiuki.

"What is this?" he asked. He knew what it was. But wanted to hear from her.

"Tiger claw," she said. "From the poor child you brought to Utiuki. So Amba can watch over you."

"I don't—" he stammered. This was silly. Mystical nonsense. "I can't—"

She shook, once, the hands that held the cord. The claw danced and twirled. Her dark eyes widened with sincerity. With belief. His face flushed hot with embarrassment, for her. Clearly she believed that this lifeless thing was a powerful totem. That it somehow contained that poor tiger's essence. That it would somehow convey a portion of his strength unto him.

She believed it, but could he? Should he? Would he ever be able to?

She shook her hands and the claw danced again. She grunted. A stern command.

He sighed, and lowered his head, leaned toward her. The claw passed beneath his nose, his chin, disappeared from view as she stepped toward him and her hands busied themselves at the nape of his neck.

Leaning forward he felt a resurgence of the exhaustion he had felt the previous evening. He braced his palms on his knees to steady himself while he fought against a swirl of dizziness. He rested there for a moment, face flushed hot. The room, chilly a moment ago, suddenly uncomfortably warm, as though the space heater was being held centimeters away from him.

The cord dug into his neck, the claw pulled his head toward the floor.

Utiuki braced her tiny hands against his shoulders as he lurched into her. She staggered back toward the windows, his weight nearly pushing her from the low table.

"Whoa, there." Evgeny's hands grabbed him at the ribs. "Easy, partner."

The two of them helped him straighten. He inhaled deeply, the blood slowly drained from his face. He could breathe again. He held the claw in his palm. It burned like an ember plucked from a dying fire, but rather than remove his hand he wrapped his fist around that heat, felt the hook dig into the thick flesh at the heel of his palm.

He pulled his sweater and his silk shirt away from his neck, dropped the claw into the gap. Felt the warmth against his breast, over his heart.

Maybe a part of him wanted to believe. Maybe a part of him could believe. Maybe a part of him already did.

He bowed his head, and lifted it. Embarrassed, again, but not for her, not anymore. For himself. For having given up, for having given in to despair. For shrinking from the challenge that life—that the "natural order of things"—had hurled at him.

"Thank you," he said.

She smiled, but there was no mirth in her eyes. Empathy, but no warmth. She had given him more than a gift. She had given him a duty. And she had no illusions about the difficulty of the path that lie ahead.

"Now Amba walks with you," she said. "Wherever you go."

Yes, the war had found him, had caught up to him. But the war had also brought him a mission. A purpose. He'd failed at that mission, yes. But now the doubt was gone. The blame and the guilt were gone. He still had a chance. The cubs were out there, somewhere. Maybe dead, maybe alive. Either way, he was going to bring them back.

For Miko. For himself. And for Amba.

He was steady now, again. Clear-headed. The claw no longer pulled at his neck, no longer burned at his breast. It was weightless. A part of him.

"Remember," she said. A gleam of daylight reflected from outside danced in her dark eyes. "Where there are no tigers, the wolves come."

"And the wolves eat everything," he said.

She nodded. "Everything, and everyone."

FIFTY-SEVEN

Evgeny looked toward Yuri. "Who told us not to patrol in sector D-12? Where we found Tatiana? Where you first saw this Ferret guy?"

"Vassily."

He'd been thinking the same thing. He'd planned to make his first stop in Terney.

"I'm going with you," Miko said.

"You're too badly hurt," Yuri said to her.

"I'm fine," she said.

He frowned at her. "You could barely walk yesterday."

"I'll go," Evgeny said.

Utiuki *tsked* and frowned at Evgeny. "Bears not friends of tigers," she said.

"For starters," Evgeny said. "I'm a man, not a bear."

"Nobody's going with me," Yuri said. "I work alone."

"Secondly," Evgeny continued, as though he hadn't heard Yuri, "bears and tigers are both enemies of wolves."

"Hm." Utiuki paused, as though considering the possibilities. "Maybe."

"Him?" Miko pointed toward Evgeny. "He's no soldier."

"Hey," Evgeny said. "I was in the Army."

"When was that?" she asked. "Twenty years ago?"

"Been a while," he conceded with a shrug.

"You're going to need more than a claw on a string and a bit of hocus pocus," Miko said.

"Tigers need you here." Utiuki stepped down from the table, laid her hand on Miko's forearm. "For when they return. Utiuki has something to show you. A new place for the zoo."

"It's not a—" Miko began.

"Sorry, not a zoo." Utiuki raised her hands apologetically. "Experiment."

"For the Project," Yuri said. "For the cubs. We're going to bring them back. Be ready."

The drive to Terney—east along the southern side of the Core, over a mix of paved and natural roads, some sections plowed, others following ruts left in the snow by previous vehicles—took a little over three hours, in the end. Evgeny pestered him with prurient questions about Miko and the previous night, but instead of answering them, he told his friend about their adventures the night before last. About how they sheltered in the snow, using the strategy that Evgeny had taught him. About their encounter with Khagan, and how they barely survived. After hearing the story, Evgeny became uncharacteristically silent. Yuri assumed it was because his friend was nervous, bracing for an unpleasant confrontation with their boss. Their *former* boss.

They found the Anti-Poaching Brigade offices closed, the windows dark, the doors locked. It was a Tuesday afternoon. Terney, near the coast, tended to be warmer than the Sikhote-Alin, but the light freezing rain that pelted them made it feel colder.

Evgeny knew Vassily's bar of choice, even his seat of choice. He entered the dive with a story about how Major Iliakov might be starting up a new Anti-Poaching Brigade, and that he might want to continue with the present management structure.

He emerged from the bar with Vassily in a matter of minutes. The man moved unsteadily, smoothed his thinning black hair back across his scalp, a nervous gesture Yuri had become very familiar with. The driving pellets of freezing rain caused them to move rapidly, heads lowered, as Evgeny guided Vassily toward the Brigade's headquarters, and Yuri fell in behind them with ease. He caught the front door as it was closing, grabbed Vassily.

The man protested, reached for something in his jacket pocket, but Yuri was expecting that, grabbed his wrist and squeezed, immobilizing his fingers. Yuri pocketed the small revolver as they pushed their boss—their former boss, Yuri reminded himself—through the reception area into the darkened main room. Double rows of steel desks dimly lit by windows on the far wall, an empty space on each where computer monitors once sat.

They halted at the door to Vassily's office, Yuri on his right, Evgeny on his left. The door was locked.

"Bastard," he said to Evgeny. Then, "I don't know what you guys want from me."

His breath reeked of ethanol and syrup. Cherry syrup, Yuri guessed, or elderberry. So crooked, he couldn't even drink his vodka straight.

"We want you to open the door, for starters," Evgeny said.

Vassily fumbled with his large key ring.

"This is all your fault, you know." He turned his head toward Yuri, though he shied away from eye contact.

"Our fault that the Brigade got shut down?" Evgeny asked. "How do you figure?"

"Our hero here makes the news, and a few weeks later we get the call from Moscow. I told you two that area was off-limits. I told you not to go there."

One of the keys finally fit in the lock, turned the knob. They pushed him inside. Evgeny guided him to his desk chair, sat him down. Yuri shut the door. He did not turn on the light. It had been years since he had conducted this sort of *razvedka*. Years since he had "questioned" a civilian.

He had brought the nylon cord along with him. As well as the lighter. He knew from his previous visit that Vassily's desk contained the other items he would need.

He glanced at Evgeny. Also a civilian. He hadn't been

trained in this. But he'd insisted on coming along. He had to know that his partner was willing to follow him into the dark places. With his Yakut knife he cut two lengths of nylon rope.

"Hold his arms," Yuri said. Evgeny held first one arm while Yuri lashed the wrist to the wooden armrest. Then the second.

"What do you want to know?" Vassily asked.

Yuri opened the drawers of Vassily's desk. Extracted a notepad, and a bottle of cheap cologne. He removed a sheet of paper, twisted it into a rope. He dunked one end into the cologne, then the other, pulled the dripping paper free. The smell of musk and verdigris filled the room.

"We call this the bicycle," he said to Vassily.

"Just tell me!" Vassily said, voice rising in treble and volume. "Whatever you want to know, I'll tell you!"

"Sounds so innocent, right?" Yuri said. He smiled with the good half of his face. Iliakov had taught him the power of the smile in these situations. "So carefree."

He lifted the man's index finger, looped the dripping strip of paper underneath, let the finger snap back into place alongside the others. He twisted the two wet ends together so they stuck up into the air.

"Come on—please." Vassily craned his neck, wrenched in the chair to look back at Evgeny, searching for sympathy. "What is it? What do you want to know?"

Yuri picked up the lighter.

"We don't want to know anything," he said, his jaw set. "Not yet anyway."

FIFTY-EIGHT

It didn't take long for Vassily to tell them that Chernichev and his comrades were regulars at a brothel on the highway north of town. Not very far from the sanitarium—not far from the Project. Sector D-12.

The brothel operated out of an old farmhouse along the Kolumbey River, with a barn and several sheds behind it where the Ferret kept his supplies and stored his contraband. Where he would meet with his buyers.

Evgeny said he knew the place. Said he may have been there, "once or twice." In his younger days.

"Tell me how to get there," Yuri said, as they pushed through the doors, into the stinging pellets of frozen rain.

"So you can ditch me, and grab all the glory?" Evgeny shook his head. "Not a chance. I'll take you there."

"Suit yourself."

They climbed into the pickup and headed back the way they had come, recrossing the Sikhote-Alin. Evgeny drove. Occasionally he studied the rear-view mirror to make sure the police weren't in pursuit, alerted by Vassily.

Yuri tried to sleep again, but the road was rough. He straightened, rubbed sleep from his eyes.

"I arrived in the Sikhote-Alin back in '85," Evgeny said. "I'd pulled my tour."

Every man of a certain age and social background in the Soviet Union had served his tour in Afghanistan. Or two. Or three. Yuri had heard his friend's army stories. Most centered on him being drunker than ever before, and spending the night in military jail as a result. But his quiet, gravelly tone told Yuri this was not going to be one of those stories.

"Wanted to get as far away as possible," Evgeny said. "Wound up here."

Yuri waited for his friend to continue. He, too, had wanted to put as much distance as possible between himself and his past. He, too, had seen this remote, frigid, even hostile corner of the world as a sanctuary.

"The Soviet system was hardly paradise," Evgeny continued. "But the tigers flourished. The state treated poachers much more harshly back then. If you were caught, you would get sentenced to a gulag. The good old bad old days. But the government also reimbursed farmers if a tiger took their livestock. So they wouldn't feel any incentive to go after them. The stick and the carrot. All this logging, and mining that you see these now—very strictly limited. Nothing like it is today."

"The *zapovednik* existed then?" Yuri asked.

"The Sikhote-Alin Reserve dates back to the Czars," Evgeny said. "After the Revolution, tigers were widely hunted and almost eradicated. But after the Great Patriotic War, once the Politburo stepped in, once they brought in staff and enforced the laws, the population rebounded. To well above five hundred. Maybe even as high as seven or eight hundred."

He paused as he worked his way around a slower car. The narrow two-lane road still hadn't been cleared of the most recent snowfall.

"The year before I got here," he continued, "a disease had nearly wiped out the boar. That's a tiger's preferred prey. So they switched to ungulates: red deer, sika, roe. They have to work a bit harder to catch them, but still plenty of game. The tigers adapted. And then the winter of '85 hit."

They drove on for a while in silence. Yuri waited for him

to continue. Whatever the story was, Yuri was pretty sure he hadn't heard it. Evgeny had never prefaced a story in this way.

"That winter was something else. The snow kept falling. The drifts buried vehicles, houses, entire trees even. The next winter, '86, was even worse. '87 wasn't quite as bad, but still much worse than anything we've seen since. This snow, out there today? Nothing. Wouldn't have even registered back then.

"Tigers are hardy creatures. They're very well adapted to the cold and the snow. But the ungulate population—not as resilient. They were decimated. So now you have a large tiger population desperate for food. Farmers' goats began to disappear. Then sheep. Calves. Villagers' dogs. Tiger sightings became frequent. They were coming down out of the taiga. Some were spotted as far south as the suburbs of Vladivostok, prowling for food."

"Man-killers?" Yuri asked.

Evgeny shook his head. "Felt like it was coming, though. A matter of time. People were frightened. Everywhere they turned—another tiger. Headlines on the front pages. Photographs, even. Can you imagine? The state decided drastic action was necessary. Those tigers who came down out of the mountains, those who left the forest, those who attacked livestock or pets, were labeled 'conflict tigers.' They were to be shot."

Evgeny cleared his throat.

"So, that was my job, my first years here. I was part of that culling. I'd just arrived. I'd been told my job would be to protect the tigers. And here I was, fighting through snow up to my nuts, trapping these magnificent creatures and exterminating them. I tried to limit the culling to the old and infirm, but I was new, I had no say. Do as you're told. Same as in the army."

An oncoming truck briefly illuminated Evgeny's face. His hands gripped the wheel tightly as he slowed and moved to the side to give the larger vehicle plenty of berth.

"Worse than the army, in some ways," he continued.

"From '86 to '88, we killed forty-eight of these so-called conflict tigers. Forty-eight."

"I don't know how I could bring myself to do that," Yuri said. He knew for sure now that he'd never heard this story before. This confession.

"I lost count of the number I had to pull the trigger on," Evgeny said, voice hoarse. He swallowed. "I didn't want to keep track. I've probably killed more than any poacher out there, though."

"You did what you had to do."

Evgeny shook his head. Mumbled a string of curses. "I did as I was told."

They drove on through the darkness in silence for a while. His friend's face nearly invisible in the darkness.

"There was one I'll never forget," he said, finally, his voice little more than a hoarse whisper. "Eighty-seven, that last serious winter. I got a call to see about a rogue male, caught in some farmer's razor wire. Khagan, they were calling him. That means 'King of Kings,' in Mongolian or some such. The wire was tangled around his neck and his shoulders. He was bleeding, exhausted. Of course they sent me in to get close enough to shoot him—I was the new guy."

"He fought free," Yuri guessed. "Once you came close."

Evgeny shook his head, stroked his left hand down over his beard.

"No, I shot him. I saw the puff of fur at the entry point, right where the ribs meet the shoulder." He lifted his left arm, touched his upper ribcage with his right hand. "In the armpit. I'd killed dozens with that same shot. But he wrenched free, and ran off. We followed him for a couple of kilometers, but he never went down. If he survived, he probably still has the shell in him."

The wounded were the ones more likely to go rogue, to become "conflict tigers." The wounded, the old, the sick. The ones that couldn't hunt for themselves anymore. They were the only ones to risk contact with people and their livestock, their pets. All healthy tigers knew to stay well away from any signs of civilization.

Yuri laid his hand on his friend's shoulder. "A hell of a thing," he said quietly.

Evgeny turned his head and smiled wanly. "I always knew I would face a punishment," he said. "I always knew it was a matter of time."

"What are you talking about?" Yuri asked.

"It's the natural order of things," Evgeny whispered. He stared out the windshield as he drove. "Just like you said."

Yuri had seen that stare in other men, at other times. He wasn't seeing the road, or Yuri, or anything immediately in front of him. He was staring into the past.

FIFTY-NINE

They didn't stop to eat until they reached the outskirts of Melnichnoye, two hours after nightfall. They shopped for supplies and filled the truck's tank, then headed north, back on the road after a half-hour break.

The road here ran along the edge of the Kolumbey River basin, and was relatively flat and cleared to the left, to the west, with the occasional farmhouse set back from the road, a few with a light above the door, others dark. As they drove cars' headlights lit up the sky well ahead of them, or occasionally grew behind them until they overtook the lumbering pickup with its knobby winter tires.

They reached a bridge, crossed over a frozen tributary to the Kolumbey. Evgeny slowed the truck. He knew they were close. This wasn't the sort of place that advertised itself with blinking neon lights.

In the end it wasn't hard to find. Compared to the sleepy farmhouses, beaten down by the endless succession of long winters, one farmhouse off to the right had accumulated an assortment of trucks and vans and SUVs. The farmhouse's windows were dark; they appeared to be shuttered from the inside with heavy paper or plywood. Yuri told him to keep driving, past the entrance. Motioned for him to continue further along the highway. A barn and several smaller, ramshackle buildings stood behind the main house. An expanse of flat snow spread out on all sides.

So this was where the local loggers and miners and truckers came when they could. To drink, to drug, to whore. To spend the money they'd made that week, or that month. He motioned for Evgeny to pull off to the side of the road.

"You've been here before?" he asked his partner.

"Yeah, maybe," Evgeny shrugged. "Once or twice, I guess."

"You guess?"

Another shrug.

"What's it like inside?"

"You know, there's a bar downstairs, a kitchen. Rooms upstairs."

"What about the barn out back, the sheds—you know anything about those?"

Evgeny shook his head. "It's been years," he said. "My younger days."

Yuri opened the door and stepped down, zipped up his parka. He reached behind the seat for the Mosin-Nagant. In addition to the rifle, he'd brought his backpack, with several lengths of cord, two cloth tarps, a roll of duct tape, a freeze-proof canteen of water, some strips of jerked venison and a mix of dried fruit and nuts. Evgeny was right, gunfire would immediately draw everyone out of the brothel, so the Yakut knife would be his weapon of choice, for as long as possible.

"I'll be right back."

"Oh no you don't," Evgeny said. "I'm coming with."

Yuri sighed. "Stay low," he said.

He set off across the field, aiming toward a stand of pines maybe half a kilometer from the farmhouse. He crouched as he walked quickly, lifting his feet to break through the crusty snow. At least here it was solid enough that he only sank in to his ankles. The clouds were low and covered the sky, so they didn't have to worry about their silhouettes being spotted against reflective white snow.

From the pines he sighted in on the farmhouse with the scope. Evgeny raised binoculars.

The windows had been papered over from the inside. Occasionally a thin ray of light leaked through. Based on the number of vehicles, there could be anywhere from twenty to forty people in the place, depending on how many the two vans had brought. Occasionally the sound of music or the chatter of voices would drift to him, then disappear. As a door opened and closed, perhaps.

Perfect cover, Yuri supposed, for Chernichev to keep his supplies and store his contraband, likely in one of the ramshackle outbuildings. A place to meet with his buyers, without attracting undue attention. One of these smaller wooden huts in particular looked like it was about to collapse in on itself, but the door was new, and sported a heavy, shiny padlock. Easy access to the frozen tributary that ran through the fields provided him and his comrades with a highway into the depths of the forest. A day's journey into the Core of the *zapovednik*, if desired.

"Look," Evgeny whispered and pointed. "The barn."

Yuri dragged his sight left. Through the open barn door, resting on the floor, two rectangular boxes, each covered with a heavy crimson cloth.

"Those are their crates," Evgeny whispered. "That's them!"

"We don't know that for sure," Yuri said. He was starting to believe that it was possible.

"Sentry," Evgeny said.

Yuri raised the scope to his eye again.

A man in a heavy jacket and a knit cap walked into view behind the boxes, came to lean against a heavy wooden support beam. He lit a cigarette, exhaled toward the single naked bulb in a fixture above the crates. Large ear lobes protruded from beneath the cap.

Yuri recognized him. Recognized his ears. Now he was certain he was in the right place. He knew this man from Chechnya. Abrek, that was his nickname. The name of the first Soviet monkey to orbit the earth in the early days of the cosmonaut program. A black nylon strap over his shoulder was likely attached to a submachine gun or machine pistol of some sort.

No sign of Chernichev, however. Or Iliakov.

"The crates are right there," Evgeny said, "and the barn door is open. If we can distract the sentries, we could just drive in and load them up."

"Distracting them won't give us enough time," Yuri said. "We're going to have to kill them."

"That gun will bring everybody flooding out of the house in a heartbeat," Evgeny said.

Back at the house, a couple of men sallied out of a rear door, crossed through the parked cars to the barn. One of them hunched at the corner of one of the crates and lifted the shroud. His comrade—Zenit, Yuri had seen him in the woods with Chernichev—gave the same crate a nudge with his boot. The crate shook, and the man fell back on his ass, while Zenit pulled his foot away rapidly. Abrek laughed.

He remembered the Korean. Remembered Zenit shaking his finger at him. *Big mistake*.

"Should we get the police?" Evgeny asked.

The proper move, Yuri thought, *if they were following Anti-Poaching Brigade protocol*.

"If the police come," Yuri said, "they'll confiscate the tigers. And then the Project is over."

"What about Chernichev?"

"He's probably in the brothel staying warm," Yuri said. "If the cubs are in the barn under guard, with the doors open, then his buyer is going to arrive soon. We need to act."

"Right," Evgeny said. "What's the plan?"

"Get to a spot on the highway where you can see into the barn. Not too close—use the binoculars. Wait for my signal."

"What's the signal?"

"You'll know."

Evgeny turned to go. Yuri grabbed his sleeve.

"Hey," he whispered. "Stay sharp. Don't fall asleep."

Evgeny nodded once, somberly. Soberly. Yuri watched his friend return to the pickup, listened for it rumble to life and swing out into a broad U-turn on the highway, headlights off, before he began his approach.

Between the stand of trees and the cluster of buildings there was no other object to provide cover, only an expanse of snow, so he kept low, on his belly. The dingy white of his parka provided camouflage. Painstakingly he worked his way forward through the cold, pausing often to peer out toward the barn from beneath his hood, to listen, to smell. Every sense alert.

Where was the Ferret?

SIXTY

A low burst of a bassline and a drumbeat thrummed out to him as the back door of the farmhouse opened, and he stopped moving, eased himself down into the snow. Two men staggered down three short steps, stooped by the weight of a third they supported between them. This man seemed barely able to stand, let alone walk. A solitary lamp cast a bluish glow over the few remaining vehicles, illuminated strands of vomit caught in the drunk man's beard. Another man, a bouncer Yuri supposed, pulled the door closed behind them, and the music ceased, replaced by the crunch of the men's boots in the snow, and the groans of the slumped man in the middle.

They moved to one of the remaining vehicles in the lot, a dinged-up and dingy white Mitsubishi. They shoved the nearly unconscious man into the back, and then climbed into the front. The doors slammed shut, the engine roared to life, and the SUV sped from the parking lot and swerved out onto the empty highway.

Silence, again.

He needed to act while he had the advantage of surprise and the cover of darkness. He'd been hoping to catch the sentry unaware. But in the time Yuri had been observing, the man hadn't emerged from within the barn.

He rose up to his feet. Yakut knife in his right, he quickly crossed the distance between the shed and the back of the barn.

He peered in through a clouded window. The filthy glass did not allow him to see much other than a glow off to the right, presumably from the naked bulb he had spotted earlier. Where the crates had been, where the sentry had been sitting. He pried the window open with the stout blade. He laid the rifle and the backpack in the snow beneath the window, and swept snow overtop. The backpack would only weigh him down, and the rifle would be difficult to pull through the window without making noise. He pulled himself up and through, came to a silent crouch inside the barn, moved off into the shadows. The smell of cigarette smoke and a faint cough told him Abrek was still there.

Step by cautious step he approached. Abrek leaned against a wooden support column, his back to Yuri. Occasionally he stamped his feet against the cold. He remained facing forward, toward the open door, toward the parking lot and the brothel beyond. Unaware of the possibility of a threat approaching from behind.

He approached the dim circle of light cast by the solitary, naked bulb. Noted a slight warmth emanating from the squat space heater that purred between the two crates. Abrek flicked his cigarette through the open doors into the night and stepped away from the column. Yuri retreated two steps into the shadows and crouched. He would have to wait.

The guard sat on his haunches between the crates, slowly removed his gloves and extended his bare hands toward the grille of the space heater. A bark and a hiss came from the crate on his left, and the man shifted his feet beneath him, moved as far as he could to his right without touching the crate there.

Finally the man stood and returned to the column. He peered into the darkness of the barn, and Yuri wondered if he had fully closed the window. But Abrek didn't linger. He fished in his pocket for a fresh cigarette. The red glow of the lighter lit up the man's acne-scarred face, a sketch of a beard, darting eyes.

A walkie talkie at the man's hip hiccupped, and he removed it, answered the call. He returned the receiver to his hip, threw the cigarette down and ground it into the wooden floorboard. He pulled the AK-74 that he wore slung over his shoulder around to the front, wrapped his right hand around the stock and the trigger, his left along the barrel. Ready position. He'd been alerted. Had Yuri been spotted?

No—sounds of diesel engines approached from the highway. The sentry turned his back to Yuri as headlights swept into the barn, raked along the rear wall. A large van drove into the parking lot, followed by two SUVs, gleaming black.

The buyer had arrived. He was too late. He'd missed his chance. No—he'd had his chance, but he'd squandered it. He'd moved too slowly.

Where was Chernichev? If he could take the sentry's rifle, he might be able to fight his way out of this, or at least do some damage. Surely Chernichev was the one giving the orders here, and if he could eliminate him, perhaps he could scare off the buyer as well. Buy some time for... for who? Who else was there, but him?

Two men spilled from the back of the van as it came to a halt, and two more jumped from the SUVs as they coasted to a halt. These men wore heavy black parkas, armed with submachine guns. They directed their weapons and their attention out toward the perimeter. They spoke rapidly to each other in a language that Yuri did not understand. He recognized it, though: Chinese. Likely Manchu, the dialect spoken in Heilongjiang province, on the other side of the Ussuri River.

Another vehicle turned from the highway into the parking lot. Compared to the SUVs, it seemed to amble and bounce along the rutted lane.

A battered white pickup. Evgeny's truck.

As the pickup rolled slowly, almost reluctantly onward, it passed beneath the solitary lamppost. Evgeny sat behind the wheel, but he was not alone. A shadowy figure rode beside him in the passenger seat. This man held a gun barrel to Evgeny's head as he drove.

His red goatee briefly flashed in the light, then winked out, as the cab plunged back into shadow.

Oleg Chernichev. The Ferret.

SIXTY-ONE

Yuri backed further into the shadows as the pickup lurched to a halt. Evgeny stepped down from the driver's seat. Chernichev followed him out, came to stand behind him, as he tentatively lifted his empty hands into the air. One of the Chinese men approached, but Chernichev waved him away, forced Evgeny to take a few steps forward.

"*Starshina!*" Chernichev called toward the barn. "I know you're here somewhere!"

Abrek whirled toward the back of the barn, then backpedaled through the door, into the snow-covered parking lot.

"Come on out," Chernichev called. "The game is over."

An older Chinese man, wearing a long fur coat and a *ushanka*, stepped out of the rear of one of the SUVs. The buyer. He did not seem pleased at the delay. The words he exchanged with Chernichev did not seem to mollify him.

"Yuri," Evgeny called out, tremulously. "He says that if you don't show yourself, he'll go after Miko."

A blow in the back caused Evgeny to wince and stumble a half-step forward. "After he kills me."

The two shrouded crates sat on the floor of the barn between Yuri and Chernichev. The men in black were now moving slowly toward the open barn doors, aiming their weapons into the dark corners. If they were to start shooting, the cubs would be in the line of fire. The old furniture and farming implements and machinery that he was hiding behind provided concealment, for the moment, but not adequate cover against the AK-74s the men wielded. He could attempt to flee, back through the rear window, but he would almost certainly be seen. He had not left himself an exit. Chernichev had him at his mercy.

Chernichev had placed the cubs within view and lightly guarded as bait, to lure him in. It had worked. He had been cursing himself for being overcautious, but now it seemed he hadn't been wary enough. Would have been more wary if he weren't so focused on trying to make good on his foolish promise to Miko, and to Utiuki. If he hadn't gotten it in his head that he could be a goddamn hero.

Heroes get killed, Iliakov used to tell him, before he set out on a mission. *I've got no use for heroes*.

Chernichev had him where he wanted him. He didn't quite know it yet, or at least he wasn't one hundred percent certain. As soon as the men entered and began to search for him, he would know for sure.

Yuri only had a precious few seconds left before he would be forced to take action. Two men had reached the threshold, crouched low, weapons raised, at the ready, probably set on full automatic.

He'd been playing "hope chess," as Iliakov called it whenever he made an aggressive move hoping that his opponent would respond in the way he hoped he would, rather than forcing his opponent to accept the only move left to him. The Major would be very disappointed in him. Five years away had made him over-confident. Susceptible. Soft.

Yuri shifted his feet under him, changed his grip on his knife from hammer to saber, readied himself to spring.

The buyer shouted a series of commands. The four Chinese men shouldered their weapons, and in teams of two, they lifted and hauled the crates through the open doors. The lamplight turned the crimson shrouds black against the bluish white of the snow.

The buyer swept toward the crates, his long coattails brushing over the snow. As he reached for one of the shrouds, he hesitated. Looked over his shoulder.

Chernichev and the buyer turned toward the farmhouse, lifted their chins toward the roof, toward the brightening horizon. Evgeny also partially turned to glance over his shoulder. The men looked at each other uneasily, moved their weapons from their shoulders back to their hands. And then Yuri heard it, the *thwap-thwap-thwap* of rotors beating against the sky, a growing crescendo that indicated that the helicopter was approaching rapidly, at low altitude. Skimming the treetops.

The men turned and sprinted back toward their vehicles. Doors opened and they piled inside. One of the SUVs swung into reverse, and as it came to a halt to shift into drive, a spotlight picked it out. A hole appeared in the windshield, driver's side. The vehicle continued to drift backward; its momentum carried it into the parked van with a crunch.

The rotor wind caught the cloths covering the crates and whisked them into the air, first one and then the second. Within each crate crouched a tiger, low to the ground. The cubs' heads pressed back into their shoulders, their tails coiled protectively around their bodies. Kamal—Yuri recognized him from their encounter in the forest, the facial markings clear to him now—hissed and bared his fangs.

The black Kasatka swung into view, low over the farmhouse. Major Iliakov leaned through the open side door, sighting down the length of his Dragunov, eye fitted to its scope. Abrek ran back toward Yuri, but stumbled and fell. He did not raise up from the trampled snow. Another man ran across the parking lot, dove into the snow between two vehicles. A series of rounds crashed through the cars' rooftops and doors, punctured tires.

The second SUV swerved through the snow, and the buyer dove into an open rear door, fur coat flapping. The vehicle's rear tires spun, and it lurched and skidded through the parking lot, desperately seeking the highway, the rear door swinging like an unlatched gate in the wind. Yuri expected rounds to crash into the vehicle, but none did. The door closed, and the SUV swerved out onto the highway, began to pick up speed.

The sudden intensity of the rotor wash told Yuri that the helicopter was coming in to land. The searchlight swept through the people streaming out of the rear door of the brothel, some yelling, some grim. Some ran for the highway, some dashed toward their parked vehicles, others fled off into the snow and the darkness.

Yuri emerged from the barn in time to see the black Kasatka land in the snowy field next to the parking lot. As it touched down, Iliakov hopped from the open side door, the cherry stock of his Dragunov braced against his shoulder, sweeping the long barrel from side to side. He moved quickly through the parked cars toward the brothel, searching for any signs of hostility. No one offered any further resistance.

On the far side of the lot, Evgeny stood in the pool of lamplight as though frozen, his hands raised, his eyes closed. The turbulence swirled around him, tugged at his parka and his pant legs, flattened his beard against his chest.

Yuri ran to his partner. Evgeny still stood with his hands up, beneath the sulfurous glare of the solitary lamppost, though his eyes were now open, surveying the scene in disbelief. Yuri grabbed one of his upraised arms, lowered it. At his touch, Evgeny looked at him, seemed to see him for the first time.

One eye had been blackened, the cheekbone beneath bruised.

"I'm not dead," he said.

"Seems that way," Yuri said.

Yuri escorted Evgeny through the parking lot, toward the helicopter. Toward safety.

Chernichev had vanished.

SIXTY-TWO

Miko hopped down from the Kasatka's open side door into the snow. Yuri's hand rose in an acknowledging wave, but she did not look in his direction. Her focus was on the squalling cubs, naked and hunched in their small cages.

Samuel eased himself down after her, shielded his watery gray eyes from the wind. Heads lowered, shoulders hunched, the two of them ran toward the crates. Kamal hissed at Miko, reared back and lunged forward, whacked the grate with his paw.

She stood and turned, surveyed the parking lot. Her eyes met Yuri's for a split second, then continued to search. One of the crate coverings had sailed toward the black SUV and the van that had come to take the cubs away. A dead man all dressed in black sprawled face-down in the dirty snow, partially covered by the cloth, a fluttering, tangled shroud snagged on his legs and torso. The driver slumped over the steering wheel.

Miko moved toward the cloth. Yuri reached it first.

"We need the coverings!" she shouted as the two of them lifted the heavy drape from the man. A red pool of blood had seeped into the snow beneath his head, the entry wound a deceptively small red dot at his temple. The rotor wash was diminishing, but still tugged at the fabric, still drowned out normal speech. "We need to get them home!"

At the crack of a shot Yuri crouched and spun. Major Iliakov stood between two cars. He lowered the rifle stock from his shoulder. A *coup de grace*. Zenit, Yuri presumed. Eliminating the witnesses. Covering his tracks. The Major moved on, toward the barn. He came to a stop at Abrek's prostrate body at the threshold of the barn, where the man had toppled and skidded to a halt. With the toe of his black boot, Iliakov turned him over onto his back. The man's arm flopped lifelessly at his side, his head lolled at an impossible angle, his neck torn through by a bullet.

Evgeny nudged Yuri, passed his end of the heavy cover to Yuri. "I'll help Dr. Carrington grab the other," he said.

Wordlessly, Yuri and Miko walked the cover over to Kamal's crate, pulled it taut between them and lowered it over the cage. Yuri counted to three, and they lifted, then shuffle-walked the hissing, rattling cage over to the Kasatka. She kept her eyes focused on the precious cargo between them.

A woman tottered by in high-heeled boots toward one of the cars, her coat clutched about her, platinum blond strands whipped by the rotor wind.

Too short for Chernichev, he thought. *Too genuinely feminine.*

Miko lifted her end to the deck, and Yuri shoved the crate into the belly of the helicopter. She hopped up next to it and set about securing the shroud, looping nylon straps around the crate. She anchored the straps through metal loops on the bulkhead and cinched them tight, then hopped down next to him.

"I don't know how you found me," he said. The rotors had slowed and quieted enough for him to speak only a little louder than usual. "But I'm glad you did."

"I have my ways," she said.

They both turned toward the chaos of the parking lot. The second covering had flown to the far side, caught on the fender of an old Lada sedan. Evgeny and Samuel struggled to free it. Yuri watched Iliakov disappear into the brothel, Dragunov nestled in the crook of his shoulder.

I should be with him, he thought, *when he finds Chernichev.*

"Will they be okay?" he asked.

"They're terrified, obviously," she said. "But they'll recover. They're resilient creatures."

"And the Project?"

"So long as these babies are in my care," she said, "the Project will proceed."

"Even with all this exposure to people?"

"If we stop now," she said, "they end up in a zoo, or some sort of facility. And we miss our chance to test our theories."

Evgeny and Samuel arrived with Vida, the shroud flapping loudly against the bars. Yuri helped them load the crate into the helicopter. While they secured Vida's crate in place next to her brother's, Yuri turned from the helicopter and jogged toward the brothel. He was about to retrieve the AK-74 from the black-clad corpse when the Major emerged from the rear door.

He met him at the porch. "Chernichev?"

Iliakov shook his head. "No sign."

"You're sure?"

The Major spat into the snow as he brushed past Yuri. "He would never get pinned down here," he said.

Evgeny joined them, and he pointed toward the dark expanse beyond the lamplight. "He ran that way."

The four men crossed the parking lot. They faced east, toward the brightening horizon beyond the Sikhote-Alin mountains. At the far end of their vision, a double column of naked alder trees lined the frozen stream that led from the Kolumbey River back into the foothills.

"There." Iliakov swung the Dragunov up to his shoulder. The barrel pointed toward a dark silhouette crossing the snowy plain, making for the row of trees. Yuri dug in his backpack for the binoculars. The figure trudged through knee-deep snow drifts, lifting each leg high before plunging it forward, an exaggerated clown-like walk, shifting his shoulders and head side-to-side. The man's hands waved empty at his sides, flailing for balance. He did not carry any sort of long-barreled weapon over either shoulder.

"Is it him?" Yuri lowered the binoculars.

"Who else?" Iliakov asked. He held his gun out toward Yuri.

An Izhmash Dragunov Tigr. A thing of beauty. The designated marksman's rifle, first of the Soviet and then the Russian army. Semi-automatic, accurate well beyond a kilometer in the right hands, extremely reliable, not nearly as heavy as rifles designed exclusively for snipers.

This one was custom-fitted with a dark red cherry stock and hand grip. Yuri longed to hold it. To feel its heft. Its perfect lethality.

"Go ahead," Iliakov said. "Take the shot."

Yuri took the barrel in his left hand, pinched the fingertips of his right glove in his teeth and pulled his hand free, poked his thumb through the hole carved into the cherry stock, rested his index finger against the trigger.

He lifted the PSO-1 scope to his eye. He estimated that the Ferret was right at, or just beyond, the outer limit of the Dragunov's effective range. At this distance, easily more than a kilometer, with the swaying of the target, the dimness of the light, and the potential for stiff breezes across the windswept snow, it would be an impossible shot.

He threw himself forward onto his belly, braced his elbows against the snowpack, the barrel just above the surface. He centered the crosshairs on the lurching figure and squeezed off three shots. The silhouette fell. He pulled the trigger twice more, sent two more bullets downrange, emptying the magazine.

Yuri stood up, brushed snow from his parka. Iliakov lifted his eyebrows.

"You're a natural," he said.

Yuri handed the empty rifle back to the Major and raised the binoculars to his eyes, watched as the shadow rose up from the snow, scurried the remaining meters on hands and knees to the alders and larches lining the river's edge.

Evgeny's voice broke the silence. "Did you get him?" He peered into the faint ambient light.

"No," he said. "Can you get me closer with the helicopter?" he asked the Major.

"No way." Miko shook her head and stepped in between Yuri and the Major. "We need to get the cubs back to the lab, stat."

"We could—" the Major began.

Miko pointed out toward the fleeing shadow. "If he has a gun, he could hit the cubs."

"Right." Iliakov clapped his hands. He whirled his hand above his head, and the pilot waved to acknowledge the signal. The rotors slowly began to gather momentum. Miko strode toward the Kasatka. Yuri fell in beside her as she marched.

"Take the cubs somewhere safe," he said. "But don't tell Iliakov where. You can't trust him."

"I know just the place," she said. "Don't worry."

"Don't tell Samuel, either," he said. "Don't tell Evgeny. Don't even tell me."

She stopped when she reached the helicopter door, turned to face him, her black hair swept into her face by the spinning rotors. She pushed it back with her gloved hands.

"You can't trust anyone," he said. *No trust. No fear. No surrender.*

"I know," she said. Then, she took his cheeks—one rough, one smooth—into her hands, pulled his face down to hers, kissed him once, hard. "Tell me you'll see me soon," she said.

"I can't make any promises."

"So lie," she said. "It won't kill you."

"Be seeing you," he said.

She turned and climbed into the helicopter, joining Samuel on a bench, next to the cubs.

Yuri turned back toward the other men. Iliakov strode across the parking lot in his direction. Yuri met him before he could reach the helicopter.

"I picked this place because I knew you would take care of these assholes for me," Iliakov said.

"You're not getting on that bird," he said.

The Major lifted the unloaded Dragunov, but Yuri placed his hand over the barrel, kept it pointing away. He turned toward the pilot. Spun his free hand in the air, the gesture to lift off. The pilot looked over Yuri's shoulder. The Major nodded, reluctantly. The pilot gave the thumbs up.

"Give me the gun," Yuri said. "I'm not letting him escape again."

The helicopter shuddered and lifted from the ground, swung in a lazy arc toward the dark tree-lined horizon, toward the endless hills of the Sikhote-Alin, toward the dawn. The two men clung to the gun that both separated and united them.

Finally the Major relinquished the rifle into Yuri's hands; lifted his hands in mock surrender, palms empty.

Yuri walked around behind the barn to retrieve his backpack. When he returned to the parking lot, Evgeny was there to meet him.

"I want to come with you," he said. "I want to make that bastard pay."

Yuri shook his head. "Not this time, partner. You'll only slow me down."

Evgeny wrapped him in his arms, pressed him against his barrel chest. His beard tickled Yuri's good cheek.

"I'll have a bottle ready," Evgeny said, "when you get back."

Yuri watched him climb into the pickup. As he drove from the parking lot, the light-sensitive lamp switched off. Not for the first time in their careers, Yuri and Iliakov were the only ones left standing amid the wreckage, amid bloodstained snow, mere shadows in the pre-dawn gloom. Iliakov had rolled the corpse of the dead Chinese man onto his back, and he shook his head as he looked down at his unseeing eyes.

"Sloppy," the Major said, as Yuri joined him.

"You changed sides just in time," Yuri said.

"I'm a survivor," Iliakov said.

"Give me another clip," Yuri said. "I know I'm just doing

your dirty work by going after the Ferret now. But I'm going to finish off your wolfpack once and for all. Maybe we'll have words when I get back."

The Major fished a metal box out of his coat pocket, and Yuri replaced his empty mag with the full one.

"I knew I could rehabilitate you." Iliakov smiled. "*Starshina.*"

Yuri turned toward the snowy plain, toward the river. The sun crested the mountains beyond, and touched the thick clouds with rosy fire.

SIXTY-THREE

January 10, 2001—Cubs six weeks old

The Ferret's trail led across the deep drifts that covered the field, to the frozen tributary that led from the Kolumbey into the trees, up into the hills. By the time Yuri reached the stunted trees and snow-hidden boulders lining the riverbanks, he was sweating and hungry.

The sky had brightened. He brushed snow from a large rock and sat down, retrieved some jerked venison and the insulated bottle of water from his backpack.

The river here was about as wide as the two-lane highway that ran in front of the brothel. Chernichev's bootprints created a dark dividing line right up the center, marching steadily upriver, into the foothills. Either he did not expect any pursuit, or he simply did not care to hide his trail. Speed clearly a greater concern than concealment.

As he followed the prints, snow began to fall. Airy parachute flakes at first, but soon these began to clump together and drive down at a slant, through the alders and larches that lined the banks.

The frozen river carved a wintry highway into the taiga. Flatter than any road—and straighter than most in the Sikhote-Alin—the river gave Chernichev easy access to the game he sought. Then he would extract his catch along the same frozen riverbed—ideal for dragging or towing a sled—down out of the taiga to the brothel, to store in one of the sheds while he contacted his buyer, made arrangements, enjoyed a drink and a woman, and waited for the cash to arrive. Simple. Easy.

As he moved further into the hills, the iced-over river began to narrow, from a two-lane width to single lane. The trees to either side crowded closer to the river's edge and leaned over the frozen, snow-covered path. Its course bowed right, then bent left. Visibility worsened as the snow continued to fall, and the turns in the frozen road became more twisted and pronounced.

Occasionally the bootprints would leave the river and strike off into the trees, but Yuri did not follow them, aware that it was in the dense growth where Chernichev would be most likely to set an ambush. He held to the river, followed the bend, noted where the bootprints rejoined his at the far side of the turn. Chernichev was taking shortcuts where he knew he could. He was intimately familiar with this path.

The snow fell faster, drove harder. Filled in Chernichev's bootprints, till Yuri was following little more than a crease in the snow. If he charged ahead too fast, he risked coming too close, warning his prey that he was being hunted. Risked exposing himself to an ambush. If he went too cautiously, he risked losing the track altogether, as it steadily vanished beneath the driving snow.

Finally he reached the power line, the access trail, a small bridge over the river. He'd lost track of time, and the sun was hidden by the thick clouds dropping their wet, clumpy snow. Enough hours had passed that he was dangerously close to being caught out in the taiga at night again—this time in worse conditions, and even less prepared, than when he had been caught out after dark with Miko.

He followed Chernichev's trail under the bridge, into a broad basin, filled with fog. Nearby stood a few tree trunks, but they were all dead, stripped of branches, gray crooked fingers that reached from the earth toward the sky, strangled by the fog.

He knew this place. This dead place. He'd chased Chernichev here before. Surely he was heading for his blind. He would have firewood and a heavy-duty sleeping bag stashed, a way to survive an overnight in the woods. Maybe a rifle as well. Then, after a day or two, he would return to the brothel, perhaps to a car that he had waiting. Or he could make his way along the access road that led to the Project site, where he could steal a vehicle.

Or take his revenge. Yuri doubted that he would bother trying to take the cubs alive again, but he knew Chernichev was capable of killing everyone there and the cubs as well. Just to show that he could not be defeated. To leave his mark.

The trail continued into the bog.

He followed after. Slowly now. Rifle extended, at the ready. He checked the safety, made sure it was off.

He came to the pair of gnarled tree trunks that leaned against each other, forming an 'X.' He knew where he was now. He left Chernichev's prints, and set off to the right, to the east. Toward the river. He didn't have to follow Chernichev. He could loop around, come at him from behind.

A dark wall loomed ahead, and the ground sloped almost imperceptibly upward. He crouched and ran forward, reached a dense stand of pines. Quickly scanned the snow-laden branches for any bare patches, but found no signs of snow having been brushed by a passing man. He pushed into the pines.

Here it was even darker, his visibility even more limited. The low boughs grew tightly together, their branches grabbed at him, needles hissed as he forced his way deeper within.

He was making too much noise. He stopped and crouched, listened. Nothing but the silent hiss of snow falling on snow. The occasional fluff of a clump of snow sloughing off an overburdened branch.

Then he smelled it. A cigarette. Faint, but definite. The Ferret was nearby. He was close.

Yuri lowered himself to the ground. Began to inch forward beneath pine branches on his elbows, gun cradled in his forearms. A smell of moldering pine filled his nose as he plowed his way through shallow snow and brown needles.

A thin wire dug into his nose, and he froze. He eased backward, making sure to keep the gun barrel beneath the trip wire. Once the pressure eased, he turned his head to the right. Strapped to the tree trunk, less than a meter from his head, a rectangular MON-50 claymore-type anti-personnel mine. Had he been walking, he almost certainly would have kicked through the trip wire, triggered the detonator. At this range the blast would have killed him instantly, or at the very least disintegrated his legs, left him a helpless torso bleeding out into the snow.

Could he use this mine against Chernichev, somehow? Change its angle, lure him into its blast radius?

He crawled around to the far side of the trunk. Scanned forward through the trees from his low vantage as best he could. Breathed in slowly through his nose, but the cigarette odor had disappeared. He shivered with cold now that he was lying in the snow and barely moving. He couldn't afford to wait until Chernichev revealed himself. He had to keep moving.

A low thrum disturbed the silence. It echoed through the dead space, grew into the recognizable racket of a snowmobile engine, coming closer in fits and starts. The sound came from the south, from the river.

Yuri turned and crawled under two trees to the edge of the stand, peered through the snow. The headlight produced a cone of light that picked out a flurry of snowflakes drifting down. He couldn't make out the figure driving the snowmobile, but the machine drove toward the bend in the river, toward the watering hole. Right into Chernichev's line of fire.

The snowmobile came to a halt. The engine quieted, though it continued to rattle. The headlight remained lit.

Faintly audible over the din, a voice called.

"Yuri!"

SIXTY-FOUR

Evgeny.

He exhaled a soft curse. So much for surprise. Now Chernichev knew that Yuri was on his trail.

Again, his partner called out his name, barely audible, lost in the swirling wind and snow.

He knew what Chernichev would do. He would wound Evgeny, shoot him in the leg, hoping to draw Yuri into his line of fire.

And he knew what he should do. What his training told him to do, what the Major would expect him to do. He should use his friend as bait as well. Let Chernichev take his shot and betray his position.

But he couldn't do that. He had to warn Evgeny, scare him away, or at least drive him to cover. He had to get Chernichev to reveal himself some other way. Even if that made him an easy target.

He crawled back to the tree with the mine. He shifted the Dragunov to his left hand, reached the barrel back under the trip wire. Hooked the iron sight against the thin sliver of steel and yanked as hard as he could.

The blast concussed his entire body, filled his vision with stars, wadded his eardrums with a low roar and a piercing whine. The rifle vanished, jerked from his hand. His left shoulder ached. His entire body shook, whether from cold or from the blast, he could not tell.

He struggled to get his knees under him and move away before Chernichev arrived to inspect his trap, but a heavy weight pressed him down into the snow, made it hard for him to breathe.

"Got you, motherfucker!" Chernichev chortled.

He'd emerged from his blind. Exposed himself. But something held Yuri down, ground his face into the snow.

It was the tree. The blast had sawed the trunk in half, toppled it over onto Yuri. He was a sitting duck.

"Think you can sneak up on the Ferret?" The voice was closer now, mere meters away. But facing away from Yuri, speaking to the shattered trees within the mine's cone of destruction. The tree that pinned Yuri down also hid him from Chernichev. For the moment.

Yuri dug in with his elbows, his knees, the toes of his boots, forced his way forward. As he worked his head free, he saw the heels of the boots that he had been following all these kilometers. Those boots stepped away from Yuri, into the wreckage of several trees, searching for a body.

As Yuri fought his shoulders and elbows free, Chernichev poked through downed branches with a long-barreled rifle. Bolt action. He would get one shot. Unless Yuri moved swiftly.

"Your ticket got punched, *starshina*," Chernichev said.

Yuri wrenched his hips free from the spiny branches. Pushed his shoulders up, bent his legs underneath him, freed his ankles, anchored his feet beneath him. He pulled his Yakut knife from its sheath and sprang toward Chernichev, even as the other man became aware of the movement behind him and those boots began to turn.

Yuri leaped as Chernichev whirled, as the rifle swung through the air. Yuri parried the barrel with his left forearm. The gun's sharp report a mere clap compared to the mine blast, but still it knocked the wind from Yuri's lungs. Undaunted, he dove forward, drove upward with the knife toward Chernichev's sternum.

Chernichev sidestepped, but Yuri had expected him to rely on the rifle. The short blade punched through Chernichev's parka and penetrated his ribs. The rifle butt slammed down on Yuri's wrist, and while he kept his grip on the handle, the Ferret pulled back, free. The blade had snapped at the hilt. Finally, after all these years. Yuri tossed the handle away and charged, while Chernichev released the rifle and reached for the combat knife on a bandolier at his chest. The cold and the blast made Yuri's movements sluggish, as though he were fighting underwater.

As Chernichev yanked his knife free Yuri stepped his leg between the other man's knees, grabbed his coat, and flung himself down onto his back, let his dead weight and Chernichev's own attacking thrust carry him forward.

With Yuri latched onto his leg, Chernichev lost his balance. As he tried to break his fall, his knife dug into the ground next to Yuri's head. Yuri torqued his hips to the side, slid out from under with the man's left leg clamped firmly between his thighs. His heels pinned Chernichev face-down in the snow.

He locked his upper arms in a bear hug around Chernichev's calf and straightened his legs, arched his back, ground his shoulders into the snow. The man screamed "no" and reached behind him to tap Yuri's leg, a reflex born of sparring to let your partner know that he had you in submission, that the discomfort was becoming intense. He and Chernichev had sparred many times in training, and then in Chechnya, during down time, to stay sharp and relieve the boredom. But they were not sparring now, and Yuri was not seeking to relieve his discomfort, but to twist it into excruciating pain.

Chernichev squirmed, tried to turn with the pressure but Yuri had him pinned against the ground, and he kept straightening with all his strength until he felt the knee—felt it as though it were part of his own body—give way with a *schlop* that left the man screaming in agony, pounding his fist mutely into the snow. Yuri kept the pressure on, continued wrenching. Chernichev flopped among the shattered pine branches, moaning, spittle flying from his lips, snot from his nose. He was crying. Of course he was. His knee was shattered.

Yuri untangled his legs. Stood up in the small space cleared by the explosive. He leaned over, retrieved the other man's rifle.

Chernichev's leg remained at a right angle, but to the side rather than to the rear. He reached his hand back toward his leg, but then retracted it in horror, knowing that simply to touch the knee would bring more pain. The bile surged within Yuri, as though the joint popping free had also unstoppered something inside him. He fought it back.

He'd broken a man's leg once before, in training, in his early days, before deployment. As he was learning how to spar properly. Comrade Captain Iliakov had taken him aside after, told him simply, "That proved he wasn't worthy."

Yuri cleared the chamber, reloaded, slammed the bolt back into position. Chernichev writhed and moaned. He had flopped onto his side now. Yuri stepped his boot onto the man's neck and jaw, leaned forward, pinning the man into place. Yuri touched the barrel against the man's temple, pushed his head into the ground.

"No, no, no—wait," Chernichev said.

"There's a reason you still call me *starshina*," Yuri said.

"Listen," the Ferret said. "It's all a setup, don't—"

He pulled the trigger and the man's head smashed open. The big gun kicked back against his hand, jammed his wrist. He let it fall to the ground.

He removed his boot from Oleg Chernichev's neck, straightened his back. Pine boughs raked his face, scratched at his eyes. He closed them against the needles. He felt numb. Beyond cold. This was the place that war took him to. This was where killing brought him. Numbness. Unthinking. Unfeeling. Only reacting. Surviving.

"Yuri!" The call came from the river. He opened his eyes.

Evgeny.

SIXTY-FIVE

Yuri pushed his way through the pines, headed down the incline. He stumbled in the shin-deep snow, fell to his hands and knees. His left forearm ached, where the rifle barrel had slammed into his puncture wounds. Worse than that, though, was the burning in his side, above his left hip, below his ribs. As he hauled himself to his feet, bright red spots dotted the white powder. Was the blood on his coat his? Or Chernichev's?

"You got him?"

A black beard floated stark through the gray light toward him.

"I told you not to follow me," Yuri said.

"Good to see you, too, partner," Evgeny said.

Yuri took a few more steps, hesitant on the uneven ground. Evgeny materialized in front of him, a ghost suddenly become flesh. He frowned. Looked toward Yuri's left hip. Toward the ragged hole in his parka. The blood smeared darkly there, dripping down the leg of his snow pants.

"You've been shot."

"I'll be okay." Yuri reached into the collar of his parka, pulled the cord around his neck until the tiger claw lifted free. "See?"

"Let's get you to the snowmobile," Evgeny said.

Yuri took one step toward his friend, and faltered. Evgeny caught him, wrapped his arm around his shoulders, held him up, kept him from collapsing down into the snow. Pain lanced through his gut. He placed his left hand over his hip, as though that would help.

They staggered through the drifts, thick flakes swirling and driving into their faces.

"He could've killed you," Yuri said. "You walked right into his line of fire."

He coughed, and winced. Stopped walking. There was a fire in his belly.

"Come on, partner," Evgeny said, pulling him forward, forcing him to move his feet. "Not much further."

"You could've gotten us both killed." Soon he would go into shock. If he hadn't already. He was cold, but shivering hurt too much.

"A few more steps."

They entered the bright, blinding cone of the snowmobile's headlight. The whine of the idling motor drowned out all thought, all sound. Flakes swirled in front of them, glowed bright for an instant, then disappeared. Just a few more steps.

"I'm going to drive," Evgeny said, "but I'll sit behind you, so you don't fall off."

"You shouldn't have come," Yuri said.

Evgeny smiled. "You're glad I did, though."

His smile disappeared. His hand reached for his throat, then his whole body fell away, slumped through that cone of light, sprawled into the fresh snow piling high on the frozen river.

The shot reverberated down from the distant hillsides, from dark trees on distant slopes. Yuri glanced back along the wobbly trail that he and Evgeny had left behind, toward the stand of pines, half expecting to see Chernichev standing there, rifle in hand. Though he knew that was impossible.

He swung back toward his friend. Blood poured from a hole in his neck. Evgeny lifted his hand, but didn't seem to have the strength to cover the wound.

Yuri fell to his knees and placed his right hand over the exit wound, then his left as well. The entry wound was on the other side of his neck, near the spine.

Evgeny opened his mouth as though to speak, but instead coughed, and blood spurted from his mouth, caught in his beard. He reached his hand out toward Yuri. Grabbed the collar of his parka.

"Sorry," Evgeny said. The blood was getting in the way. He tried to spit, but the blood only burbled, escaped his mouth and ran down his cheek, into his beard. "I fucked up."

Yuri stared at his dying friend. He removed his left hand from the wound, put his bloody glove in his teeth and pulled it off, spat it out. He pried Evgeny's hand from his collar, removed his friend's glove, and clasped the man's giant paw in his own. Evgeny's thick-fingered, calloused grip was tight, as though he wished to crush Yuri's hand. As though he wished to drag Yuri along into the next world with him. But the strength was leaving him.

There was nothing Yuri could do, but give him this one last consolation. Flesh pressed against flesh. A friend to sit at his side, while he left the world.

"My wife." He choked, and coughed up more blood.

"I'll tell her," Yuri said.

Evgeny swung his other hand to grasp Yuri's as well, and much as it pained him to uncover his friend's wound, he swung his right hand up to meet Evgeny's.

"It's a hell—" Evgeny's face contorted into a grimace that plainly spoke of the futile fight for breath, the desperate inability to speak last words. Then the struggle ceased.

"A hell of a thing," Yuri said softly.

He sat heavily in the snow, sank against his friend's belly. The knot of their hands unwound.

SIXTY-SIX

Yuri startled awake. This was no time for sleep. His torso ached. His coat had stiffened, all along the left side, where the blood had begun to freeze.

He reached in under his sweaters, felt the wetness of his silk base layer. This wasn't sweat. His frozen hand trembled as he held it up, stained crimson. He'd been shot through the side. Low, not through the lungs. Maybe a kidney, maybe intestines. Hurt like hell, of course. But he could make it.

He spat into the snow. Except he had no spittle.

He searched through his friend's parka pockets for the key to the snowmobile. Then remembered that the machine was idling, which meant the key was in the ignition. Giant, fluffy, silent parachute flakes fell all around him. Had already begun to cover him. How much time had passed? He had to make it to the machine. The machine could carry him back down the river much faster than he had walked. There was a chance. His only chance.

He fumbled in the snow for his gloves. Struggled to pull them on over his stiff, red, numb fingers. He got his knees under him. Inhaled as deeply as he could, though the pain in his side kept his breathing shallow, fluttering. To steel himself for the effort, for the pain that standing would bring, he counted to three.

Raz... dva... tree...

He cried out involuntarily as he stood, still not fully straight, hands on knees, fighting back bile. He lifted his head toward the snowmobile, winced against the searing brightness of the headlight. Behind the light, a shadow, standing. A man, watching him.

Yuri staggered to his left, out of the glare, hands still on knees. The world spun, and he reached out his hands to cushion himself in case he fell, but his feet steadied beneath him. The snowmobile idled near the riverbank, marked by a dark wall of pines that crowded down the slope to the frozen water's edge. The silhouette remained, impassive, unmoving.

A hood obscured his face, but Yuri recognized the squared-off shoulders, the barrel chest, the long barrel of his Dragunov.

"Chernichev is dead?" Iliakov asked.

Yuri nodded.

"He always was a disappointment," Iliakov said. "Compared to you."

He had many questions for the man who had murdered his friend, and who was about to kill him, but there was really only one that mattered.

"Why?" He glanced at his friend's corpse. The open eyes filling with snow. He should've closed them. "Why Evgeny? He bothered nobody."

The barrel lowered, the shadow's shoulders shrugged exaggeratedly.

"He was in the way," Iliakov said. "No witnesses."

Ten meters separated the two men. Twenty meters from the cover of the trees, the protection of a boulder.

"I did my best to rehabilitate you," Iliakov said. "I sincerely hoped to bring you back into the fold."

"I'm not coming back," Yuri said. "I'm done with your wars."

"I know." Iliakov raised his voice to be heard above the wind, above the erratic rattle of the snowmobile. "The world will be a lesser place without you, my friend, but to me and people like me, it will be a safer place."

The barrel lifted. Iliakov fitted the wooden stock against his shoulder, the sight to his cheek.

"I salute you," Major Iliakov said. "You're the last of a dying breed."

Yuri found his right hand clutched at his chest, balled into a fist. He extended his fingers. Cradled in the worn and creased leather palm of his glove, a hook of bone, tapered to a sharp point. He focused on the claw, rather than on his killer. He'd rather this be last thing he would see. It reminded him of Utiuki, of course, but also of Miko, and Tatiana, and her cubs, safe—for the moment, at least.

The natural order of things, he thought. *Reasserting itself one last time.*

Iliakov lowered the barrel a few centimeters. "What is that?"

"A gift," Yuri said.

An explosion of orange and black and white flashed from the trees, and the shadow was gone. Iliakov's scream echoed through the basin.

Khagan.

The tiger overwhelmed the man, covered him, enveloped him. Swatted at his face, batted at his arms. His hind legs pinned the Major's to the ground, the extended claws tore into the flimsy fabric that covered his thighs, into the equally flimsy flesh underneath.

Khagan's head sought an opening, lowered. Opened his jaws wide, the four fangs each as long as a finger. Iliakov curled into a ball, wrapped his forearms over his head, brought his knees to his elbows. With one backhand swipe Khagan battered the man's flailing arms aside, dug the claws of his other paw into Iliakov's shoulder and rolled him over. He swiftly brought his teeth down over Iliakov's shoulder, and squeezed. Cracked.

The Major's screams echoed through the taiga.

Khagan braced his scarred shoulders and shook his head, twisted and swept the Major's body through the snow.

Yuri limped sideways, scrambled over the rocks along the

riverbank, backed toward the trees. Anything to put himself out of range of that two-and-a-half-meter monster.

Khagan released his toothy grip on the Major, whose shrieks of agony turned to incoherent moans.

The great beast swiveled his head toward Yuri. His flanks pulsed from his exertion. The King of Kings bared his red-stained fangs and snarled.

SIXTY-SEVEN

Yuri released the claw, let it fall against his chest. Extended his empty palms. Stopped moving his feet over the hidden rocks of the riverbank.

Khagan lowered his head toward Iliakov, and the Major wrapped himself into a tattered ball. Claws extended, the tiger began to tear and rend at the fabric that wrapped the man's flesh. The Major's moans turned to convulsive sobs as he begged for mercy, begged for Yuri to help him, to save him. Though busy with his prey, the tiger's yellow eyes and the white tufts of his ears continued to track Yuri.

The Dragunov had vanished, buried in the snow where it fell. The tiger crouched between him and the still-idling snowmobile.

If he could make it to the vehicle, the frozen river would lead him back to the brothel. Back to civilization.

Surely police would be there by now, sifting through the wreckage. What would they make of Yuri, staggering in from the taiga, dripping blood?

They would take him to the hospital. He would survive. But what then? What sort of cage would they put him in?

He sidled toward the still-running machine, facing the tiger. Past his friend's lifeless body, already partly covered in snow, only the toes of his boots and his black beard still clearly visible. *I'll come back for you*, he thought.

As he neared the snowmobile, Khagan swung away from the Major, into the glare of the headlight. His eyes narrowed to glowing slits. His head lowered. His *basso profundo* rumble vibrated Yuri's bones, drowned out the tinny rattle of the idling engine.

The tiger refused to allow him on the machine. He backed away. His feet found the boulders that lined the river's edge, the slope uphill. The tiger returned to batting at the Major's motionless back and thighs. Yuri slid in among the pine boughs, brushing snow from them as he went. Finally he turned his back on Khagan. Raised his hood, with the eyes that Utiuki had stitched there, to look behind him, to play a trick on *amba*.

Utiuki. Her hut was not far. Of all the people he knew in this corner of the world, she was the one he trusted. Evgeny had been his friend. Samuel he admired. Iliakov he respected. He hated him, but he respected him. And Miko—he might love Miko. But Utiuki was the one he trusted. The only one. No matter what his old motto said.

He reached for the claw at his chest. The claw had protected him so far. Now he just needed it to carry him to Utiuki. She would know what to do. He'd made it there once before.

It was hard going, this uphill hike, crowded with squat pines whose snow-covered branches reached for him, scraped against him.

He remembered the forest of his youth, how dark and foreboding it had seemed, until he began to explore it with Ruka by his side, armed with his rifle, his father's old Mosin-Nagant 98. Remembered the thrill as he pushed further into the darkness. He was there again, in those woods, Sveta trailing behind. Telling him that she couldn't keep up, he was going too fast.

He slowed his pace. Stopped and waited for his *sestrichka*. A stark flash of black and white in the dim gray swirl of snow behind the trees, at the edge of his peripheral vision. So Ruka *was* following him. Just as when he was a boy.

Impossible, he thought. *You're seeing things.*

The snow swirled around him, though the intensity had lessened. He felt in his pockets for the compass, but all he found was a slip of paper, folded, well-worn. He pulled it free. Blood had stuck the halves together. His blood. He stared at Kamal and Vida, tried to wipe the blood from their faces as snowflakes dotted the paper. It was useless. The photograph was ruined. All that was left of them were the tigers he had named for them. In a year's time, perhaps, with Miko's guidance and good fortune, those cubs would be grown, would be hunting in these very woods.

A glimpse of orange and black, off to the side. When he turned his head, it was gone.

On he trudged, head bowed, hands on his knees. The claw bounced against his parka.

He stumbled and pitched forward into the snow. He lay there, resting. Finding his breath. Gathering his strength.

How much further? he wondered.

Not much, he told himself.

He stood. Ignored the red stain he'd left behind in the snow. Each step required him to extricate his boot, lift his leg, push it forward. He was so thirsty. He was sweating from the exertion, yet clammy and shivering as the sweat instantly froze.

This time the orange and black crossed in front of him. He blinked. The distance made it hard to be sure in the driving snowfall.

The long, low-slung body had been unmistakable. The calm, measured tread. The enormous paws. The wisp of beard.

Yuri's heart thudded loudly in his chest, in his ears, drowning out all thought.

He lowered his head. One foot in front of the other. Mixed with the occasional drop of blood, stark against the clean white.

When he collapsed again, he lay there until a warm

tongue lapped at his face, startling him awake. It was Ruka, waking him from a dream in which he was huddled in the blankets, in the barn, with his dog. Only now Ruka barked at something behind Yuri, just out of sight. The dog was skittish. He leaped away and then darted back to tug at Yuri's sleeve. He whined, pleaded with Yuri to get up, to get back on his feet. To move. To get away.

He rose, and stumbled forward. He followed Ruka, called out to Ruka, but the dog had run on ahead, his sharp barks diminishing with the distance. He would be back. He wouldn't leave Yuri.

Yuri looked over his shoulder. Nothing but snow-covered pines, and swirling snow.

He felt, more than heard, the low rumble. It shook his chilled bones.

Khagan.

SIXTY-EIGHT

The great grizzled beast kept Yuri within range, while staying behind the trees, out of sight. The King of Kings had dealt with man before. He knew of man's many weapons, and his many deceptions. Had suffered his snares, and his traps. Had even survived his most potent weapon, the stick that brought lightning down from the sky.

The white filled Yuri's vision, broken only by the trudging of his feet, and the occasional glimpse of orange and black through the swirling snow. The rumble of the tiger's breathing seemed to come from everywhere now, from all sides, as the tiger circled him.

Suddenly Khagan appeared beside him. On his right this time. The tiger stalked slowly alongside, his long white beard wisped over the snow. His great paws like snowshoes kept the enormous beast from punching through the fresh powder. The scars on his forelegs and neck rippled with each slow step, as his shoulders rolled high, a peak between his lowered head and long swayed back.

It was foolish, he realized, to think that this magnificent monster would ever need a man to defend him. Presumptuous. Here was Amba, the true Spirit of the Forest. Blessing Yuri by granting him this moment of his company.

He reached out his hand, took one step in Khagan's direction, and the tiger exploded away in a flash of snow and orange. The end of the long tail, used to counter the beast's strong push away, brushed Yuri's face, left him speechless.

Khagan growled again, an octave lower. A warning. Yuri's body went numb. He wasn't going to make it. Amba wasn't going to let him. He clutched the claw at his chest in his right hand. The snow swirled blindingly into his eyes.

He blinked. The wind stilled, and the snow cleared. Ahead, in the distance, at the end of a narrow trail through the trees, Khagan crouched. The tail swished side to side.

Here he comes, he thought. Man against beast. Surrounded by nothing but snow and trees and sky. No tricks. No traps. No weapons. Khagan's throaty growl rose ever louder, filled Yuri's ears, shook his body.

He wasn't going to fear. And he wasn't going to surrender. He turned toward the tiger.

Khagan charged through the trees, head low, tail high, yellow eyes blazing. The tiger's roar became his own, his battle cry surged from him, burned his lungs, scorched his throat, as he opened his arms to meet the tiger head on. The tiger leaped, then lurched, mid-stride. Staggered, regained his gallop, stumbled again. He listed as he ran, tilted and swayed to the side. Low branches brushed against him, then snapped as his bulk crashed through them. He stumbled forward, fell to his knees, drove into the snow at Yuri's side and released a heavy snort through his nostrils.

"Yuri!"

Bewildered, he lifted his head. Heard his name called again. A figure broke through the wall of branches. She held a tree-like antenna out in front of her in one hand, the tranquilizer rifle in the other, shimmering like quicksilver.

Miko.

She dropped the antenna and the rifle into the snow and fell to her knees at his side. A plastic box slung over her shoulder bounced at her hip.

"You're hurt!"

A yellow-feathered dart protruded from Khagan's flank, just behind his right shoulder.

"Khagan." He pointed. She turned to the great tiger.

"He's breathing," she said. "He'll be okay. But we don't have long."

"Kamal?" he murmured. "Vida?"

"Come on," she said. "We're almost there."

She stood up, grabbed him under the armpit and dug her feet into the snow. He pulled on her, hauled himself to his feet.

"How?"

She touched the lower edge of his parka, at his right side. He turned the hem inside out, found Kamal's beige transponder there, the collar's pink nylon crudely stitched to the coat's lining.

"You can't escape me," she said, with a smile that could not mask her worry.

She threw his right arm over her shoulders, began to walk, doing her best to hold him upright as they stumbled forward.

"When?"

"You left your coat in the lab."

"Before you came to see me—that night—"

"That's right."

He felt a smile stretch against the mottled skin of his clawed cheek, the numb skin of his healthy one. *No trust.* The most important of the three, Iliakov always said.

He laughed, though it sounded more like a cough. "Two of a kind," he said.

"Just through these trees," she said.

A few more trudging steps, and he lifted his head. Utiuki stood in the doorway of her hut, wrapped in her colorful shawl, blinking against the swirl of snow. She waved them onward. Yuri leaned on Miko and staggered the final few steps with numbed, unfeeling feet.

The older woman opened the door and entered. Within, Kamal and Vida wrestled in one of the crates. In unison the cubs looked up at the sudden gust of cold air, at the newcomer who stood in the doorway.

"But, the Project—" Yuri said.

"They're alive," Miko said. "That's all that matters."

The brightly colored rugs beckoned him. His parched mouth began to salivate at the earthy fragrance of stew simmering.

"Come inside," Utiuki said.

Miko helped him cross the threshold.

IF YOU LIKED THIS, YOU MAY ALSO ENJOY: DEEP BLACK

BY BRENT TOWNS

Trouble is bubbling between two of London's most notorious crime syndicates…

To MI5, the tension between crime lords proves too good an opportunity to clean them out once and for all—start a war and let them kill themselves off one by one.

But someone beats them to it, and before the dust can settle, someone else takes out virtually every head of London's crime family—including Lucky Rance, the man at the head of London's most corrupt ongoings.

No longer content with staying hands-off, MI5 wants answers *fast*. But as the bodies continue piling up, agents start wondering if the crime lords' theatrics are a smokescreen for something bigger… something far more deadly.

Enter Raymond "Knocker" Jensen, a former SAS man who's always —somehow— prepared. When it comes to getting answers, MI5 knows they need Jensen, a man prepared to stop at nothing until he gets the results he desires.

AVAILABLE MARCH 2022

ABOUT THE AUTHOR

Born in Australia, raised a Mennonite in the heart of Amish country, and educated at Harvard University, Andrew Hallman now lives in Philadelphia where he works in the rare book trade. AMBA is his second novel, and the first in a projected series. Please visit andrewhallman.com to be kept apprised of future releases.

Made in the USA
Las Vegas, NV
25 March 2022